Other Books by ISFiC Press

Relativity and Other Stories by Robert J. Sawyer
Every Inch A King by Harry Turtledove
The Cunning Blood by Jeff Duntemann
Worldcon Guest of Honor Speeches edited by Mike Resnick and Joe Siclari
Outbound by Jack McDevitt
Finding Magic by Tanya Huff
When Diplomacy Fails edited by Eric Flint and Mike Resnick
The Shadow on the Doorstep by James Blaylock
Assassin and Other Stories by Steven Barnes
Aurora in Four Voices by Catherine Asaro
Win Some, Lose Some by Mike Resnick
Velveteen vs. The Junior Super Patriots by Seanan McGuire

—VELVETEEN, VOLUME 2—

SEANAN McGUIRE

ISFIC PRESS
Des Plaines, 2013

VELVETEEN VS. THE MULTIVERSE

Copyright © 2013 Seanan McGuire. All Rights Reserved.

Introduction: "An Essential Ten Percent" Copyright © 2013 Tanya Huff
Cover Art Copyright © 2013 Douglas Klauba
Afterword: "McGuire Begins" Copyright © 2013 Paul Cornell

Without limiting the rights under copyright reserved above, no part of this book may be reproduced in any form or by electronic or mechanical means, including information storage and retrieval systems, without written consent from both the authors and copyright holder, except by a reviewer who may want to quote brief passages in review.

Published by ISFiC Press
725 Citadel Court
Des Plaines, Illinois 60016
www.isficpress.com

Editor: Bill Roper

ISFiC Press Logo Design:
Todd Cameron Hamilton

Book Design by Robert T. Garcia / Garcia Publishing Services
919 Tappan Street, Woodstock, Illinois 60098
www.gpsdesign.net

First Edition

10 9 8 7 6 5 4 3 2 1

ISBN: 978-0-9857989-6-3

e-book ISBN: 978-0-9857989-8-7
mobi ISBN: 978-0-9857989-7-0

PRINTED IN THE UNITED STATES OF AMERICA
by Thomson-Shore, 7300 West Joy Road, Dexter, Michigan 48130-9701
www.tshore.com

This book is dedicated to Joe Field,
who helped to nurture my love of comic books,
and to Shawn Connolly and Wesley Crowell,
who help me keep that love alive.

You are my heroes.

TABLE of CONTENTS

An Essential Ten Percent, by Tanya Huff	ix
Velveteen vs. Blacklight vs. Sin-Dee	1
Velveteen vs. The Holiday Special	26
Velveteen vs. The Secret Identity	39
Velveteen vs. Martinez and Martinez v. Velveteen	52
Velveteen vs. The Alternate Timeline	66
Velveteen vs. The Retroactive Continuity	92
Velveteen Presents Victory Anna vs. All These Stupid Parallel Worlds	105
Velveteen vs. The Uncomfortable Conversation	119
Velveteen vs. Bacon	133
Velveteen vs. The Robot Armies of Dr. Walter Creelman, DDS	147
Velveteen vs. The Fright Night Sorority House Massacre Sleepover Camp	161
Velveteen vs. Vegas	175
Velveteen Presents Victory Anna vs. The Difficulties With Pan-Dimensional Courtship	188
Velveteen vs. Legal	202
Velveteen Presents Jackie Frost vs. Four Conversations and a Funeral	217
Velveteen vs. Jolly Roger	232
Velveteen vs. Everyone	246
Velveteen vs. The Epilogue	274
McGuire Begins by Paul Cornell	289
Appendixes	291

An Essential Ten Percent
by Tanya Huff

PEOPLE WHO WORK WITH NUMBERS really dislike the phrase one hundred and ten percent. If one hundred percent is all there is, the whole enchilada, then, obviously, one hundred and ten percent can't exist in the world as they know it.

Obviously, they don't know Seanan McGuire. Or the world as she knows it.

When Seanan loves something, she loves it completely. Absolutely. One hundred and ten percent. As much as anyone else could love it, and then a little more. If you love it too, she'll happily share her joy and if you don't, well, that's a little sad, but, with any luck, you love something else and, hey, that's good too.

In *Velveteen and the Multiverse*, Seanan's pretty clear about what she loves. She even spells it out a few times just in case you don't pick up the subtler references. And trust me, this may be a book where the protagonist fights crime in a pair of rabbit ears, but it's all about the subtle. Because Seanan doesn't love blindly. She knows that roses have thorns, that the past is a patchwork coat you can't ever get rid of, that friendship takes work, that actions have consequences, that holidays can take on a life of their own, and that deserving a happily ever after and getting one are two entirely different things but that everything's possible. No, seriously, *everything*. Multiverse. Look it up. A choice can change the world–sometimes we need to be reminded of that.

You know the phrase, *it's funny because it's true*? Seanan gets that. You know what the truth sometimes isn't? It isn't funny. Seanan gets that too. She knows that clever without substance is an SNL sketch–and Velveteen is very clever in very many ways where that very clever is used to *support* substance. And Seanan never forgets that everything, even funny and clever, throws a shadow.

This is a book where the holidays are real places. And people. And sometimes not very nice people. This is a book where mundane evil, the kind of evil we all deal with every day, is all the more terrifying because it's so well known

One of my favorite bits out of many favorite bits of Velveteen is where Seanan pulls back to a more authorial point of view and essentially discusses with us, the readers, what's going on. Well, not always so much specifically *what's* going on but *why* what's going on is going on. Why is this a hero and that a villain? Why is freedom valued less than security? Why don't we listen when children cry in the night? This is the way this world works, she says, and holds up a mirror. Don't get distracted by the bunny ears or the corsets or the bright lights or the frost patterns, that's our reflection.

(My other favorite bit, is where she doesn't discuss the whats and whys and wherefores at all. She expects you, the reader, to be smart enough to figure it all out for yourself. Or to put it another way, she takes the risk–and it *is* a risk these days, in this market–of trusting her reader's intelligence. But I digress.)

One of the things Seanan loves is myth and, bottom line, it's myth's job to provide us with a way to explain the unexplainable. We know why the sun rises and sets, so we no longer need Apollo or Amaterasu or Lugh or Ra or Uitzilopochtli, but as we still don't know why we, as a culture, make the choices we do, new myths are needed. Velveteen *is* myth, sometimes literally, and *has* myth, and, as with all good stories, provides us with a way to explain, well, us.

Velveteen is about a young woman who fights crime in a pair of rabbit ears in much the same way Buffy was about a girl who killed vampires. That being, not so much.

For those of you who've read Velveteen in her earlier incarnation on the web, welcome back. It's pretty cool having her collected in one place, isn't it? For those new to the Velveteen 'verse, or, strictly speaking, multiverse, I'm a little jealous that you're getting to read this for the first time. Heading in, you may feel like you've skipped the long exposition ride up to the first drop on the roller coaster and you've begun instead with that first swooping, gloriously overwhelming plunge. You're about to rocket around the track, heart pounding, lips pulled back off your teeth, tears in your eyes unsure if you should laugh or cry, and wonder when it's over how it could possibly be over so soon. I suggest you raise your hands in the air and scream because you're going to enjoy the ride. One hundred and ten percent.

VELVETEEN vs. Blacklight vs. Sin-Dee

VELVETEEN CROUCHED ON THE EDGE of the roof and stared fixedly at the bank below her, feeling like some sort of perverse Easter-themed gargoyle. She'd received an anonymous tip informing her that one of the city's less-than-brilliant criminal organizations was planning a heist sometime around midnight. While she wasn't quite dumb enough to trust anonymous tips–Superhero Rulebook, Rule #18: An anonymous tip that sounds too good to be true is probably another way of saying "trap"–it had been a slow night in Portland, and she was bored enough to check it out.

Sometimes being a city-specific hero sucked. She couldn't even go bother her friends, since The Super Patriots, Inc. would have her arrested if she so much as set foot outside of Oregon. The Princess was off on one of her endorsement tours, and it was close enough to the end of summer for Jackie to be distracted by the various chores and pieces of paperwork required to usher in a successful winter season. How Santa kept her on task was a mystery to everyone, Velveteen and the Princess included. Vel was willing to bet that it involved threatening to cut off her credit cards.

Another minute ticked past on the bank's large decorative clock, and Velveteen resisted the urge to go looking for something more interesting, like a jaywalker or a kid out tagging city property. The thought of taggers just reminded her that Tag was out of town on business–with "business" being code for "off fighting crime in Vancouver, yet another city she couldn't visit without being arrested"–which made her even crankier. What was the point of finally acquiring a maybe-possibly-sort-of boyfriend if half the time he was working outside of the area she was legally allowed to operate in? Not that she was absolutely certain of their maybe-possibly-sort-of status. They'd had three dates, all of which ended with a satisfying amount of kissing, but nothing beyond that. She wasn't sure how she was supposed to signal her desire for anything beyond that. It had all been so natural with Aaron. Everything just *happened.* With Tag…

There really wasn't a good dating guide for the super-powered set. Was it rude to sleep with somebody before you knew their secret identity? Maybe that was the missing step. First date, first kiss. Second date, heavy petting. Third date, heavier petting. Fourth date, reveal secret identity, and then you can have wild, crazy sex all over the secret lair of your choosing. Not that she *had* a secret lair, although she could probably make a case for her bedroom, since it hadn't really been seen by anyone but herself, the movers, and the toys, and the toys didn't count.

Something was happening on the street below. Velveteen snapped into the present, thoughts of her potential sex life dismissed as she focused on the bank doors. *Come on come on come on,* she thought, with surprising eagerness. *Don't make me regret sitting up here for the last two hours. If I made my ass numb for nothing, somebody else is getting their ass so kicked—*

Before she could finish the thought, a man in the dark clothes and ski mask that seemed to be the "in" attire of the modern bank robber came flying through the bank window, impacting heavily with the brick wall on the other side of the street. Two more followed after him before Velveteen had a chance to move. They didn't appear to be flying through the air because they wanted to—more because they were somehow being thrown. If it was another hero working in Portland without filing the proper paperwork, they could finish the mop-up together. If it was a villain who'd just decided to rob the same bank, well…there was nothing wrong with getting a little workout. Velveteen launched herself from her crouch, grabbing the side of the nearby fire escape and half-sliding, half-rappelling down to street level.

One of the robbers groaned when he saw her coming and stretched out a hand in what looked less like a fending-off and more like a plea. "Velveteen!" he croaked. "Thank God you're here! She's killin' us!"

Well, that answered the hero question. "She who?" Vel asked, already reaching out to activate her toy soldiers and start moving them into position around the fallen robbers. Inwardly, she ran through a flip-file of her active supervillains—a pathetic list, unless you wanted to count the entire Marketing Department of The Super Patriots, Inc. Definitely no one who could sling a full-sized man across a city street, except for maybe the Claw, and he was, well, distinctly not the sort of person you'd refer to as "she."

"Her!" said one of the robbers, voice dripping with terror as he raised his hand and pointed back toward the bank. Velveteen turned to see a female figure framed in the open—scratch that, *broken*—window, her costume a shade of black so dark that she seemed to actually swallow the light around her.

"Me," she said, and launched herself at Velveteen.

Several studies have been done on the tendency of superpowered individuals to fight the first time they encounter one another. While conflict is not guaranteed, it happens often enough that multiple names have been put forward for the syndrome. "Team-Up Rage" may be the most commonly used, although the more prurient tend to prefer the simpler, more visceral, "Superhero Bitch-Fight." Casual sexism aside, the syndrome is not limited to superheroines, nor is it restricted to those on the "hero" side of the spectrum. Heroes or villains, seasoned heroes or rookies, the facts are clear: when two superhumans meet for the first time, someone is probably getting punched in the face.

Eventually, that initial conflict will die down, replaced by the normal human responses to making a new acquaintance: the only question is how much property damage the combatants will manage to do before they can calm themselves. Why this happens—some animal urge to protect territory, or merely delusions of invincibility brought on by actually *being* effectively invincible—Team-Up Rage is the reason most normal humans choose to spend a few extra dollars on a superhero-inclusive insurance plan.

(Some sociologists have put forth the theory that the very existence of Team-Up Rage would be sufficient justification for the otherwise morally questionable tendency of The Super Patriots, Inc. to form and train child hero teams. After all, when two heroes have their first meeting at the age of eleven, they will generally restrict their lashing out to hair-pulling and name-calling. If those same two heroes meet for the first time at the age of twenty-one, there's a reasonable chance of one or more city blocks being reduced to rubble. It may be important to note that none of the sociologists to subscribe to this theory have children, or come from families with a history of expression of superhuman powers.)

It does seem apparent that the initial burst of Team-Up Rage serves two major purposes: first, it immediately resolves the question of which of the clashing heroes is more powerful. While this may not seem important to the owner of the newsstand the combatants have just flattened, it allows them to establish and maintain a stable hierarchy. Second, in the case of hero/villain encounters, it allows the hero a chance to potentially end a reign of terror before it gets truly underway. The number of supervillains eliminated in the first throes of Team-Up Rage is high enough that this benefit really can't be dismissed.

In the years since the discovery of superpowers, only six individuals have died during or due to injuries received from a fit of Team-Up Rage. Given the number of clashes, and the average power rating of the superhumans involved, it must be assumed that they are, on some subconscious level, pulling their punches to avoid killing each other. Clearly, there is some social benefit to these impromptu battles, one which escapes the eye of the unpowered human. Regardless, when two superhumans meet for the first time, it's a good idea to get the hell out of the way.

The black-clad woman's fists slammed into Velveteen's stomach hard enough to knock the wind out of her. The impact sent her flying backward, on a collision course with what promised to be a very hard brick wall. Summoning as much focus as she could manage when she couldn't breathe and her stomach felt like it was on fire, Velveteen commanded the largest of her stuffed bears to move into position. She wasn't sure it had worked until the point of impact, when instead of brick, she hit a wall of plush. Plush with hard glass eyes that bit into the skin of her back, but that was still better than hitting anything harder, especially at the speed she'd been going.

"That's going to leave a mark," Velveteen muttered, bouncing back to her feet. Teddy bears pattered to the ground behind her, but she couldn't take the time to assess the damage. She'd repair them later, assuming she didn't wind up needing more stitches than they did.

The black-clad woman was advancing on the robbers, hands clenched into fists and surrounded by coronas of solid darkness.

Velveteen's eyes narrowed, while a small part of her brain began cheering and pumping its fists in the air. She'd been waiting to lay the smackdown on a photon-manipulator since before she left The Junior Super Patriots, West Coast Division, and now it looked like she was finally going to get the chance. In her city, no less, where her license allowed for the use of any force she deemed necessary in stopping and subduing a potential supervillain.

This one was clearly going to require the use of a *lot* of force.

Ignoring the ache in her belly, Velveteen raised her hands, calling down a squad of toy helicopters and stealth bombers from the nearby rooftops. They were joined by reinforcements as the summons spread through the city, awakening the caches she had been tucking away here, there, and everywhere. The first wave caught the woman in black by surprise, forcing her onto the defensive. She threw up a screen of solid darkness in front of herself with one hand, the other groping behind her, like she was trying to grab a weapon out of the air.

"Oh, I *so* don't think so," said Velveteen, and dropped her hands hard, amending the summons. A herd of brightly-colored plastic horses came stampeding out of the alley, each carrying one or more toy soldiers on its back. Rainbow manes whipping in the wind, they circled the woman in black, and the soldiers opened fire. She shrieked, less with pain than with anger, and dropped her shield, using both hands to send a ring of spreading darkness across the ground. It scattered the horses and soldiers like the toys that they were, throwing the formation into total disarray. Velveteen's growing smile died as quickly as it had come, replaced by a scowl.

"Hey, bitch!" she shouted. "Didn't anyone ever teach you to play nicely with other people's toys?" The woman in black—God, would she just declare a code name already? No one went this long without monologuing—whipped around, and promptly answered Velveteen's taunt with several flung spheres of solid darkness. No, not darkness; it glittered when it slammed into the walls, although Velveteen was really too busy dodging to appreciate its finer points. This was light, dialed all the way down the color spectrum to blackness. Not as subtle a distinction as you might think.

Racing to keep ahead of the balled-up black light, Velveteen gritted her teeth and focused on sending a new command to her collection of planes and helicopters. They zoomed away, while the plastic soldiers and toy horses resumed their assault on the stranger's ankles. She stopped flinging her spheres at Velveteen in favor of blasting the things that were actually hurting her, and Vel took advantage of that brief respite to call in one last support squad.

The seemingly-innate supervillain fondness for dinosaurs means that every superhuman in the world, good or bad, has heard the hunting cry of the Tyrannosaurus Rex at least once in their lifetime. Velveteen's T-Rex was only two and a half feet tall and made of vividly painted plastic, but he bellowed just like the real thing. He screamed and charged, the rest of the toy dinosaurs following closely on his heels. The woman in black whipped her head toward the sound, clearly startled, and Velveteen slammed her hands together, signaling the planes to finish their maneuver.

All at once, the planes dropped towels, sheets, plastic garbage bags, and anything else they could find over the streetlights and shop windows surrounding the fight. Darkness slammed down like a sudden curtain. Velveteen stopped running, and listened. She could still hear the pop-pop-pop of the toy soldiers firing at the woman in black, but the faint rushing sound of the thrown domes of black light had stopped. You can't manipulate light that isn't there.

"Do you surrender?" she called, before moving a quick few feet to the left. Just in case.

"Ow!" replied the woman in black. "Ow ow—dammit, call off your weird little army! This stings!" Her voice was distorted by the full-face mask she wore, but still understandable; "mask lisp" was so common among the face-hiders that it just wasn't considered polite to remark on it anymore.

Velveteen wasn't feeling particularly polite, but she also wasn't feeling like taking another hit to the stomach. She waved a hand, signaling a cease-fire, and the sound of guns went silent. Only the scuff of pony hooves against the concrete and the sound of bank robbers running for their lives broke the stillness stretching between them, until she said, "That better?"

"Yes," agreed the woman in black, sounding faintly sullen.

"We done fighting?"

"That depends."

"On what?"

"Are you going to turn yourself in?"

For a brief, terrible moment, it felt like a brick of ice had been dropped into Velveteen's stomach. Barely aware that she was summoning toys from all over the town, teddy bears and baby dolls crawling out of their owners' beds and starting to make their way toward her, she took a step backward. "What are you talking about?" she asked, and wished that her voice wasn't shaking.

"Your accomplices let you take the beating and ran. I don't think they're going to come back for you. So if you'll just give yourself up and come quietly, we can avoid any more violence."

Velveteen blinked. All over Portland, teddy bears and baby dolls turned around and began trudging home as Velveteen started to laugh, slumping back against the brick wall in a vain attempt to keep herself from falling over. Laughter just made her stomach hurt more, which made her start laughing even harder.

It was a vicious cycle, and it only got worse when the woman in black demanded, with increasing anger, "What? What's so funny? Why are you laughing at me?"

"You!" Velveteen gasped. "You attacked me! Because! You thought! I was here! To help the bank robbers!" It wasn't a question. Still slumped against the wall, Velveteen put her hands against her knees and shook her head, trying to get her breath back. "Didn't you check the city roster before you came here?"

"I was just passing through," said the woman in black, anger fading in the face of obvious confusion. "Weren't you here to help them? I mean, you showed up, and they immediately started calling for you—"

"Yeah, because I'm this city's licensed hero. They thought I was here to save them." Velveteen straightened up, breathing finally returning to something like normal, and reached up automatically to adjust her rabbit ears. "So you weren't robbing the bank?"

"What? No!" The woman in black shook her head in furious negation. "Absolutely no. I don't rob banks. But I was in the area, and I've been on the road for days, and I thought that beating the holy hell out of some criminal elements would be cathartic."

"I totally share the sentiment. Just check who's local next time, so you'll know who not to hit. I'm going to have some really impressive bruises to show my boyfriend when he gets back from beating the holy hell out of the criminal element in Canada."

"*You're* going to have some bruises?" The woman in black laughed. "Those little plastic bullets sting! I'm going to be a miniskirt no-go zone for *weeks*." She extended her arm toward Velveteen, clearly intending to shake hands. "I'm Blacklight."

"Velveteen." Velveteen took the offered hand and shook, firmly, flashing a smile at the stranger. "You're a photon-manipulator, right? Really dense light?"

"I thought you'd figured that out," said Blacklight wryly, reclaiming her hand. "Most people assume I'm manipulating darkness. They don't think to shut off my light sources, since that would just make me stronger if I were actually doing what they think I'm doing."

Velveteen's smile faltered slightly. She managed to maintain it–early media-management training to the rescue once again–and said, "I used to do a lot of team-up work with a photon-manipulator. You learn to recognize the tells. Dark light is still light, and darkness doesn't glitter."

"True, true," said Blacklight thoughtfully.

There were no visible eyeholes in the mask that covered her face, but Velveteen still thought she could feel the other woman looking her over–that probing, overly-invasive look that came right before a question she didn't want to answer, usually one that started with some variation on "didn't you used to be...?" She braced herself for the inevitable.

"So when did Portland finally get its own superhero?" asked Blacklight. "I must have missed the announcement, or I wouldn't have started poaching baddies on your territory. I swear, it's so hard to keep *up* with things these days. If I don't check Wikipedia six times a week, I can barely remember who my arch-enemies are."

"I qui–" Velveteen caught herself in mid-word as she realized that the question she was starting to answer had never actually been asked. "I, uh. Not that long ago. I'm only licensed within the state, and I don't think the story got covered by any of the major magazines." That was a lie; *Vixens and Villains* had contacted her three times for an interview, and when she turned them down, ran the story anyway, along with a selection of the most embarrassing pictures from her professional career, including her advancing angrily on the camera crews just shy of the Oregon border. Well. *Vixens and Villains* might be big, but it wasn't like it was *serious*.

"Well, good. This place deserves some standing protection. I've always wondered why Portland didn't have a permanent hero." Blacklight's tone was chatty, all traces of her earlier fury gone. That's Team-Up Rage for you. "I might've taken the position myself, if it was ever posted."

"The Governor of Oregon prefers to remain outside the Super Patriots network for personal reasons, and no, those personal reasons aren't connected to her having a side career as a supervillain. She doesn't." Velveteen shrugged. "I showed up, I was clearly persona non grata with the current core team, she hired me to protect Portland. It's been a pretty good gig, so far."

"That's nice," said Blacklight, glancing back toward the busted-out front window of the bank. "The police should be here soon. Do you want to hang around and tell them that the bank robbers got away, or do you want me to do it? I was first at the scene, after all…" She sounded understandably reluctant. Paperwork—especially the paperwork surrounding a failed capture—was the bane of every licensed superhero's existence.

Tempting as it was to run off and let Blacklight take the heat for letting the robbers get away, the fact was, she probably had the situation under control before Velveteen's arrival went and mucked everything up. And it *was* her town. No sense in letting the new girl think Portland's only official hero was some sort of a flake. "How about we both stick around," she offered, amiably. "They'll probably take it better coming from me, and you can help me fill out all the damn forms."

"It's a deal." She had the distinct feeling that Blacklight was smiling at her, even through the mask. "So if we're going to stick around and play team-up for the police, can I ask you another question?"

Here it comes… thought Velveteen. "Sure," she said aloud. "What did you want to know?"

"Don't take offense, but…what is *up* with those rabbit ears? Did you buy your costume at the Halloween Store or what?"

Velveteen's laughter rang through the stillness of the city air.

In the darkness of the bank vault, the shadows stirred. Just a little at first, barely a twitch or a tingle, but the movement spread quickly, thin lines of electric blue glittering through the dark until—at last—it flowed together into the shape of a hand, fingers outlined by that same glittering blue. It darted forward, vanishing into one of the safety deposit boxes, only to emerge clutching several necklaces and a bundle of unmarked bills. This same process was repeated five times, the hand moving through the metal like it wasn't there at all, like there were no barriers. Each time, the spoils of the ransacked box were dropped into the shadows that had birthed the glittering blue lines, disappearing without a sound. At last, the hand snapped its fingers, making a "click" that was softer than leaves rolling across a dry riverbed, and just like that, the blue glitter was gone; the shadows were just shadows, and there was no one there at all.

The thefts wouldn't be discovered until the next day, when bank management performed their standard post-robbery check of all the bank's valuable assets. Even then, review of the security recordings wouldn't show anything conclusive; just the shadows, reaching out to empty the security deposit boxes.

Just the darkness.

An hour and a half later, after the damage report forms had been filed, the "failure to apprehend criminals due to superhuman intervention" papers had been filled out, the proof of superhero insurance had been provided, and the police were finally satisfied, Velveteen and Blacklight stood atop the highest building they could reasonably be troubled to climb, looking out upon the sleeping form of Portland, Oregon. Velveteen's stomach still ached when she breathed in too deeply, or when she laughed, which she'd been doing quite a bit of since Blacklight showed up. It was oddly…nice…to have someone around that she could laugh with. Oh, she could laugh with Jackie and the Princess, but they had magical kingdoms to run, or at least, in Jackie's case, to fail to destroy out of misuse of powers. They weren't around enough to really hang out on rooftops, laughing.

Blacklight's power set proved to include short-range flight—not uncommon among photon-manipulators, but still impressive. She was actually "standing" a few inches above the surface of the rooftop, her toes pointed delicately downward in the standard "if I fall, I am less likely to face-plant" position most aerial heroes had drilled into them by the age of fifteen.

Drilled…Velveteen stopped studying the city in order to cast a sidelong glance toward Blacklight. "Where did you get your training?" she asked.

It was an innocent question, and she'd been expecting an equally innocent answer. What she wasn't expecting was Blacklight's abrupt landing, stumbling slightly, like she hadn't realized she'd been relaxed enough to float, and her hurried reply of, "Oh, gosh, all over the place. Lots of different places. It was a definite ongoing process. Look, it's been really awesome meeting you and all—sorry about that whole 'attacking you' thing, you know how it goes sometimes—but I should get going."

"Oh," said Velveteen, disappointed and confused at the same time. "Are you on your way out of town already? Where are you heading?"

"Um." Blacklight hesitated before saying, "I'll be in town for a few days. Maybe we can team-up properly before I need to go? Go out, bash some baddies, work a little of the aggression out on people that aren't each other…"

Despite the oddity of Blacklight's initial reaction, Velveteen smiled. Hell, she probably would have reacted the same way if someone asked her where she'd trained, given how much she liked to remember her time with The Junior Super Patriots, West Coast Division. It had to be even harder for an independent hero, after all the crap they had to go through to get a license, rather than a mandatory training session with The Super Patriots, Inc. "I'd like that a lot," she said. "We can remind people why super-teams are even scarier than superheroes. Meet you here around eleven?"

"It's a date," said Blacklight, and waved before trotting to the edge of the roof and stepping off into the dark beyond. A few seconds later, she flew back into sight, turned toward the western edge of town, and soared off, leaving a thin trail of glittering darkness in her wake.

Velveteen stood on the edge of the roof, smiling thoughtfully, and watched her go.

"No, it was actually a lot of fun, once we got past the requisite 'beating the living shit' out of each other part." Vel flopped down on the couch, relaxing into the warm comfort of her bathrobe, deliciously dry against her just-showered skin. "It sucks that the robbers got away, but that sort of thing happens. They'll try to hit another bank or a liquor store or something, and we'll take them down."

Tag chuckled, the telephone wires carrying his laugh across the miles and what felt like straight into Vel's nervous system, making the hairs on the back of her neck stand on end. Was this what infatuation felt like? It had been so long, she wasn't sure that she remembered. "Basically, what you're saying is that you've replaced me with a mysterious woman who dresses like there was a clearance sale at the ninja store. I think I'm hurt."

"Oh, so you want me to start grilling you about all those Canadian heroes the tabloids keep taking your picture with? Tell me, is Poutine 'a really good friend,' or is she the next entry on my arch-nemesis list?"

"What are you going to do if I say 'arch-nemesis'?" asked Tag, sounding genuinely interested. "Does it involve breaking through your house arrest and coming to join me in beautiful Vancouver? We have a ring of art thieves. Lots of flash, reasonably little danger. The perfect date night."

"I understand that people without superpowers think something similar, only when they're talking about that particular scenario, they're talking about some sort of caper movie." A teddy bear walked over to the couch, carrying a Diet Pepsi clutched carefully between its paws. Vel took the can, mouthing "thank you" to the bear, and added, "They pay for tickets."

"And we pay for medical insurance," Tag replied promptly. "It's basically the same thing."

"It isn't the same thing at all, and you know it." She cracked open the can of soda, taking a long drink before she asked, "So when will you be coming home? I'd demand to-the-minute, but we haven't reached that stage in our relationship just yet."

"Soon," said Tag, and laughed, sending more of those delicious shivers across her skin. "Like I said, we have art thieves, and there's just the four of us working here in town. As soon as they're tucked safely behind bars, I'm going to be all yours. I promise."

"You promise, huh? Pretty big words for a guy who hasn't even reached the secret identities stage," said Vel lightly. Then she realized what she'd just said, and froze. "Tag, I swear I didn't mean that the way that it sounded."

"I know, but I'm still going to take it that way," said Tag, suddenly serious. "When I get home, I think we need to talk about secret identities. You know. The sides of us that can have a picnic in the park without getting attacked by Mantor and his Army Ants."

"I'd like that," said Vel. Her voice came out very soft, maybe because her throat was so very dry. "I think I'd like that a lot."

"Good. Now, in the meantime, you just be careful around this Blacklight person, okay? I haven't heard of her, and she could be some kind of nutcase. I'll start asking around, see if anybody knows where she came from, or what her track record is like. It's good to team up once in a while, but..."

"–but that doesn't mean letting my guard down, I know. I can be careful when I have to be. Remember, *I'm* the one who actually went off the radar for more than six weeks. I don't think *you* get to tell me about being careful."

"Fair enough," he said. "Just take care of yourself. I miss you."

Vel sighed, closing her eyes. "I miss you, too, Tag. I really miss you, too."

* * *

The woman sometimes known as "Blacklight" sat on the roof of her cheap downtown motel, knees tucked against her chest, wind whipping her thin nightgown hard against her body. She wrapped her arms a bit more tightly around herself, shivering, but made no move toward the open window of her second-floor room. She'd get some sleep eventually. She could sleep all day, if she wanted to. That was one of the nice things about being in Portland; except for Velveteen, no one was going to come looking for her, and Velveteen would never know who she was without the mask. She was, for a little while anyway, completely free.

She liked the way freedom felt. It made a nice change.

No longer really aware that she was shivering, she tilted her head back and counted the stars, naming them silently in her head when she could, sending silent apologies when she couldn't. Eventually, exhaustion won out over the cold and she drifted off to sleep, still sitting on the motel roof, arms still wrapped tight around her body. The sunrise woke her, and she shuffled to her feet with an awkward half-skip, stepped onto the light, and let it carry her into the room. She shut the window behind herself, but just like nothing can really shut out the darkness, closing the window didn't do anything to shut out the light.

Half a city and a world away from one another, Velveteen and Blacklight slept.

Since the life of a superhero involves a lot of late nights and physical activity, most of them keep sleep schedules that wouldn't be unfamiliar to celebrities or graduate students (not that these three groups of people have much else in common). Velma was still sound asleep when eight o'clock in the morning rolled around and the pounding at her door began, hauling her out of a particularly pleasant dream involving herself, Tag, and an all-night pancake restaurant that had mysteriously failed to stock any maple syrup. She sat bolt upright, eyes still closed, and shouted something unintelligible in the direction of the door. The pounding stopped. Satisfied that she had vanquished whatever door-to-door asshole had been trying to get her attention, Velma slumped back into a horizontal position. The pounding resumed.

"Fucked up times *infinity*," snarled Velma, and jerked the covers back, swinging her feet around to the floor. Her fluffy bunny slippers were positioned perfectly to receive her feet, something she intentionally didn't think too hard about. If she was bringing her slippers to life in her sleep, she didn't actually want to know. The world was better off that way.

Just owning bunny slippers felt vaguely like she was selling-out. Today, generic bunny slippers, tomorrow, genuine licensed Velveteen Bunny Slippers (tm), with her superheroic logo somehow worked subtly into the plush. At the same time, so what? At least she wasn't selling out to The Super Patriots, Inc., and at the end of the day, the word for a superhero who didn't have a reliable source of income was "loser." That, or "fast food employee," since fighting crime and staying in shape to fight more crime really didn't leave much time for a non-heroic career path. If there were any unforgivable lies in the press kits The Super Patriots, Inc. liked to whip up, they were in the company's insistence that their heroes led full, fulfilling lives outside the workplace. Like any superhero had the *time* to hold down a high-stakes job, start a family, and still fight crime? Hell, there were days where she felt like she was doing well if she managed to check her email before heading for the rooftops or the gym.

Wrenching the front door open, Velma snarled "What?!" At least, that was the idea. What actually came out of her mouth was an incoherent moan that wouldn't have sounded out of place in a George Romero movie. Clearing her throat, she tried again, managing a semi-comprehensible, "Wha'?"

The men from the governor's office exchanged an uneasy look. They were low enough on the office pecking order to have drawn the unenviable duty of waking up a superhero who probably didn't want to be woken; they really weren't sure what they were supposed to do if the superhero turned out to be undead. "Running and screaming" were probably going to wind up high on the list.

Clearing his throat, the taller of the two ventured, "Ms. Martinez?"

The disheveled apparition in the doorway nodded vaguely, peering with squinted eyes through the curtain of tangled brown hair that was almost completely obscuring its face. "Mmmlgh," it said, still reaching for that rare and obscure thing known only as "coherent speech."

"Ah." He hesitated, unsure of exactly how he was supposed to continue the conversation. On the one hand, he was here on business. On the other hand, he had no real desire to find out how pissed off Portland's only official resident superhero actually was about being woken up before she was ready. Finally, duty took the lead from self-preservation, and he said, "We were sent to inform you in person that your presence is requested in the governor's office as quickly as possible. We're prepared to give you a ride, if necessary."

Velma scrubbed at her face with one hand, croaking something which sounded, to the men from the governor's office, very much like "fucked-up times too damn many" before saying, quite clearly, "Why? My contract doesn't include being awake before noon."

"I take it from your condition that you have not yet seen the morning's papers?" When Velma shook her head in the negative, the men from the governor's office exchanged a look laden and leaden with hidden meaning.

Velma *hated* looks laden and leaden with hidden meaning, and she hated them even more before she'd had a chance to pour half a pot of coffee down her throat. Irritation was enough to wipe away the last of her exhaustion-based speech impediment (why was it she could understand herself just fine, and everyone else acted like she was Yeti Girl?), and she snapped, "What in the hell could possibly have been in today's paper *and* be important enough to justify waking me up at this sort of an hour?"

The shorter of the two men from the governor's office held up the paper, showing her the picture on the cover—herself and Blacklight, very nicely framed against the moon—and the caption "Good Bunny Gone Bad? Portland's Newest Hero Seen Working With Portland's Newest Villain!"

"Oh," said Velma, feeling the color drain from her face. "That would do it."

The applications of law enforcement involving superhumans and their powers has always been a little, well, iffy. How do you try someone who can convince an entire jury to go along with whatever they say just by wiggling their fingers? How do you arrest someone who can summon volcanos from solid ground? Even assuming you can get the superhumans into custody and hence to court, what sort of punishments fit crimes that are genuinely beyond the reach of mortal men? For a while, the idea of trying all crimes involving superhuman abilities as felonies was in vogue. This stopped after an eight-year-old superhuman with the power to move through solid objects was faced with felony sentencing for shoplifting. Since then, tailoring the punishment to fit the crime has been much more popular.

Of course, given the complexities of applying human laws to superhuman individuals, it's only natural that a great many courts and penal systems have taken advantage of the kind offer put forth by The Super Patriots, Inc. As the world's foremost trainers and managers of superhumans, the corporation has expressed their shame over the number who choose to go villain, and are always willing to take a rogue superhuman into custody, keeping them confined away from the human prison population, and offering them the very best in therapy and rehabilitation options. It's true that they have a very high demonstrated success rate; no fewer than eighty percent of the superhumans remanded to their custody emerge as model heroes, gladly joining and fighting alongside the teams they once opposed.

It's true that of the remaining twenty percent, half emerge even more villainous than they were before, while the remaining ten percent are never heard from again. It's also true that fear of being remanded to the custody of The Super Patriots, Inc. has led to many supervillains making suicide stands rather than risk being brought to justice. Still, considering the damage which a rogue superhuman is capable of, a few suicides seem like a very small price to pay for the knowledge that the majority of villains, once The Super Patriots, Inc. has finished with them, will be villains no more. As to their methods, no one outside the corporation has ever inquired very deeply as to exactly what they are. This might be seen as carelessness. It can also be seen as plausible deniability.

Regardless of how a given city, state, or political body handles their "bad seeds," all areas which play host to superhumans must be constantly on-guard for signs that they may be planning to turn villain. After all, when faced with individuals who spit acid and bend steel with their bare hands, what can a normal man or woman really expect to accomplish? It's better by far to trust their care to those who truly understand them, and to simply avoid thinking too much about the ones who go into rehab and never return.

Or the ones who return with smiles on their faces and with screams in their eyes.

Normally, it took Velma the better part of an hour to really get moving in the morning, and roughly as long to get herself into costume when it was time to go out and start working. Thanks to the raw shock of seeing her own picture on the front page of the paper, she was cleaned up, costumed, and out the door in less than ten minutes, joining the men from the governor's office in their company car for the ride to meet with Governor Morgan. She honestly couldn't have said who was more uncomfortable—her, crammed in between them and waiting to be accused of supervillainy in the first degree, or them, forced to ride with a potentially dangerous superhuman. Even if all she did was animate toys.

All eyes turned toward them as they walked through the foyer of City Hall on their way to Governor Morgan. The footsteps of the men who'd been sent to retrieve her clacked crisply against the marble floor, while her own booted and carefully felted feet made no sound at all. "That's me," she muttered, trying to calm her jangling nerves. "The bunny ninja." One of the men shot her a worried look, and she bit back a sigh, forcing a smile instead. "Sorry. Nerves."

He was saved from the need to answer her by their arrival at the door to Governor Morgan's office. It was standing slightly ajar, providing the hall with a sliver-view of the governor's secretary, busy at work filing her nails behind the desk. The taller man knocked once, more out of formality than anything else, while the second man pushed the door open. "Morning, Sandy," he said. "Is the Governor ready for us?"

"Ready, waiting, and pissed," reported Sandy, all without glancing up from her already immaculately-manicured nails. "I hope you've got a good defense, bunny-girl."

Vel had dealt with the governor's secretary before, and each encounter led her to believe a bit more firmly that the woman was some sort of super in her own right. She never seemed to look away from her hands, and yet the office ran without a hitch, and she always knew exactly who was where. "I'm going with the 'what the fuck are you people talking about' defense," she said, winning a glimmer of a smile from Sandy's cinnamon candy-colored lips.

"If you're done screwing around out there, come and explain to me exactly what the hell is going on," shouted Governor Morgan from behind the second door which marked her inner sanctum.

"She wants you to go right on in," added Sandy needlessly.

"I got that, thanks," muttered Vel, and swallowed before walking forward and pushing open the final barrier separating her from the angry governor of Oregon. The men who'd come to collect her didn't follow, thus proving that they retained some sense of self-preservation. Governor Morgan was sitting behind her desk, clearly fuming. Vel took a cautious step forward, and nearly jumped out of her velvet bodysuit when one of the men closed the door behind her. *Great,* she thought. *At least that'll confine the blood splatter to a single room…*

"Well," said Governor Morgan coldly. She made no move to ask Vel if she wanted to have a seat, something which didn't seem like a positive. Lifting a copy of the paper from her desk, she said, "The bank you were photographed fighting in front of was robbed last night. According to the security recordings, the theft could only have been accomplished through the application of super-powers. Do you have an explanation for me?"

Vel hesitated, reviewing her options. She really didn't have any. "No."

"What do you mean, 'no'?"

"I mean no." Vel scowled, finally annoyed out of her wariness. "Nobody was robbing anything while I was there, and did you *see* the costume that she's wearing? Unless Blacklight's powers include access to a dimension of eternal shadow, there's no way she stole anything bigger than a smile."

"So you're telling me you neither witnessed nor participated in a crime of any kind?"

"Uh, yeah. Even if I was a complete and total idiot and wanted to be a supervillain, do you think I'd go back home and wait like a good little misfit toy until you called The Super Patriots to come and get me? No way. I'd be in some secret lair somewhere, cackling evilly and plotting my assault on the local Build-A-Bear."

Much to Vel's surprise–and relief–Governor Morgan nodded. "Good. I didn't think you were that stupid, but I wanted to be sure. Now about your friend…"

"We just met last night."

"Still. She may be involved."

Vel scowled. "I know. And if she is, she's going to be sorry."

Governor Morgan settled back in her desk chair. Satisfaction curled the corners of her lips upward in a cat that ate the canary smile. "I appreciate your diligence."

Vel, who would have appreciated a few more hours of sleep, some coffee, and a day that didn't start with her being dragged out of bed by government goons, just kept scowling.

Things that are not easily found between the hours of sunrise and sunset: visiting superhumans with photon-manipulation power sets based primarily around mimicking the effects of darkness-based power sets. After an hour of searching the rooftops, Vel–who was now firmly into "Velveteen" mode, having finally washed the lingering traces of her civilian identity down with a pot and a half of coffee– decided that her energies would be better devoted to sitting in Denny's, devouring a Moons Over My Hammy and actually reading the damn newspaper. The damn newspaper, whose headline she blamed for the looks the waitresses gave her every time they scurried over to refill her coffee. She glared at them from beneath her domino mask, making them scurry even faster to get back to the dubious safety of the kitchen.

The article itself wasn't all that bad. Mostly, it drew sketchy connections between the bank robbery and the fact that there was a new superhuman in town, while conveniently ignoring the fact that Blacklight had helped with the arrest paperwork, and even more conveniently ignoring the Team-Up Rage that had accompanied their introduction. Team-Up Rage didn't pass when you were fighting a supervillain; it just got worse and worse, until somebody ended up in the hospital. In fact, the more Velveteen thought about it, the more annoyed she actually became. Blacklight wasn't a bank robber. There hadn't been *time*. And there was something about her...

There was something about her that reminded Velveteen of herself. A faint but general aura of "sometime, somehow, somebody did her really, really wrong." That didn't mean she *couldn't* be a supervillain–most villains had somebody, somewhere, who'd done them all sorts of wrong–but it did mean that Velveteen wanted to give her the benefit of the doubt. At least until they'd had a chance to talk.

And then, if it turned out that Blacklight really was the bad guy, Velveteen was going to kick her ass so hard she lit up like a firefly.

Sunset found Velveteen waiting, with questionable patience, on the rooftop where she'd agreed to meet with Blacklight around eleven. She was hours early, but the idea of going out into the city and trying to fight crime really didn't appeal. With the mood she was in, the odds were good that someone was going to get hurt. Besides, unless Blacklight had been asleep all day, Velveteen was willing to bet that she'd seen the paper, and if she'd seen the paper–

"What the hell is going on around here?"

Velveteen yelped. She also managed not to whirl around in a defensive posture, but it was a close thing, since she hadn't been snuck up on by a flyer in over fifteen years. Not since she passed the finals in Environmental Awareness 101. No one who actually manifested self-powered flight had been able to get the drop on her after that…

…but photon-manipulation wasn't really self-powered flight, was it? Velveteen turned slowly, and said, "I'm supposed to be asking you the same thing. Did you rob the bank?"

"What? No! Did you?"

"No. Just checking." Velveteen shook her head. "Somebody's trying to set one or both of us up."

Blacklight, hovering a few feet above the rooftop, eyed her warily. "What makes you so quick to believe me?"

"Simple." Velveteen shrugged. "You're not with The Super Patriots."

"What?" Blacklight dropped a foot lower, expression—as much as it could be determined through her full-face mask—confused.

"If you were with The Super Patriots, or pretending to be, and you came into town saying you didn't know I was here, you'd have to be an idiot. If you were a known supervillain, the paper wouldn't be slinging a little mud, they'd be burying us both in the local landfill. So that means you're smart enough to stay off the grid, *without* getting recruited or winding up on the watch lists. Unless you think I'm a total idiot, you wouldn't try to pull that kind of stunt here."

"And if I *do* think you're a total idiot?"

Velveteen paused, assessing Blacklight's tone. Finally deciding that it was more amused than anything else, she replied, "I guess that would mean My Little Pony gets another shot at kicking your teeth in."

"Fair enough." Blacklight's descent continued, until she was standing firmly on the rooftop. "So were we actually set up, or was it just a case of wrong place, wrong time?"

"Either-or. At the end of the day, it doesn't really matter. I have a reputation to uphold here in Portland, and that means I can't afford to let some petty thief start making me—or my friends—look bad."

"Better your friend than your enemy," Blacklight said. "What's the plan?"

"Drop back down to ground level so I can get a cup of coffee, then we start checking the other local banks for signs of people fucking around. Sound good to you?"

"I can't drink coffee with this mask on."

"I didn't say the coffee was for *you*."

"I see." Velveteen would have happily sworn in a court of law that Blacklight was smirking behind her mask. But all she said was, "Sounds good to me."

As is so often the way of things, especially in a world including multiple superhumans whose power sets focus purely on the manipulation of probability, it was going for coffee that made everything go completely wrong. (Or, alternatively, it was going for coffee that made everything go completely right. That being the issue with coincidence: so often, it can be flipped around without changing the actual events.) Velveteen and Blacklight entered The Bean Scene approximately ten minutes after meeting up on the roof. It says something about the residents of Portland that no one so much as batted an eye when two superhumans in full costume–and recently accused of going villain– entered the cafe and took their places at the end of the line.

Inch by inch, they moved toward the register. They were still about four people from the front when a barista's voice cut across the crowd like a laser cutting through a solid steel bank door: "Double red velvet mocha-latte for Brittany!" Velveteen's head snapped up in a gesture that was disturbingly like a real rabbit's, eyes gone wide behind her mask.

Blacklight looked at her with evident confusion. "What, do you have a problem with people who destroy good coffee by adding too much syrup or something?"

"No," whispered Velveteen. "I know that voice. But that's impossible. That's..."

("Unless Blacklight's powers include access to a dimension of eternal shadow." Wasn't that what she'd said? Why was this such a surprise, anyway? Recurring villains were a fact of the superheroic life.)

"...that is *so* fucked up," Velveteen groaned.

"What?" asked Blacklight, sounding increasingly bewildered. "You *really* hate mocha, don't you?"

"No." Velveteen glanced her way. "I know that voice."

"So?"

"So the last time I heard it, the owner was trying to kill me."

"Oh," said Blacklight. "Well, hell. We're about to have a really massive throw-down, aren't we?"

"Oh, *yeah*," said a perky, chirpy voice from behind them. "I mean, I was wondering how long it was going to take for you to catch on."

Velveteen sighed as she turned around. "Hi, Cyndi."

The former manager of Andy's Coffee Palace had changed quite a lot since the last time Velveteen saw her. Oh, she was still outwardly perky, blonde, and too cheerful to live, although the black and blue tips on her fluffy, feathered hair were new. There was an odd bluish under cast to her skin, like her tan came, not from exposure to the sun, but from spending too much time in the light of a broken nuclear reactor. Her eyes were pools of infinite black, and filled with shadows like reflected screams.

"Friend of yours?" asked Blacklight.

"Former employer," said Velveteen. "Last time I saw her, she was getting pulled into a dimension of eternal shadow. How did that work out for you, anyway? Did you have a nice time?" She did her best to remain outwardly calm as she reached out with her mind, "feeling" her surroundings for things she could call to her own defense. There weren't many, beyond her own assortment of plastic horses and toy soldiers. Somehow, she had the feeling they really weren't going to be sufficient.

"Oh, you know," said Cyndi. "I suffered the eternal torments of the shadow dimensions before undergoing my metamorphosis and becoming more powerful than you could ever dream. It took about a thousand years. But see, the time differential is such that I didn't even miss the announcement of the new team lineup." She giggled. It was like fingernails being dragged across a chalkboard. "Only now I get to take them all down. Won't that be fun?"

"I don't suppose there's any way I could convince you not to do that?" asked Velveteen.

Cyndi smiled, revealing lines of electric blue crackling across her teeth.

Velveteen sighed. "I thought not."

"Call me Sin-Dee," replied the former manager of Andy's Coffee Palace, just before her human facade melted away, leaving what looked like a woman sculpted entirely from shadow standing in her place. Crackling lines of electric blue skittered across her skin and hair, outlining her still-human features. People sensibly started to scream and run for the doors as Sin-Dee raised her hands and sent a bolt of blue-black darkness shooting toward Velveteen and Blacklight.

"Look out!" shouted Blacklight, and slammed Velveteen unceremoniously to the side.

Velveteen didn't so much "hit" the floor of the coffee shop as "perform a full-frontal assault," landing hard on her chest and actually sliding a few feet across the tile before she managed to stop herself. Flipping onto her back, she was treated to the horrifying sight of Blacklight, held easily five feet off the ground by a fist made of blue-rimmed darkness. Sin-Dee was laughing. Somehow, that made it even worse. Maybe that was why villains laughed; because they knew it always, always made things worse.

Reaching into her one of her belt's components, Velveteen withdrew a handful of green plastic army men as she scrambled to her feet. "*Hey, BITCH!*" she shouted, and when Sin-Dee turned, flung the tiny soldiers in the villain's direction. Responding to her silent commands, the army men drew their plastic guns and began to fire. Sin-Dee shrieked, flinging one arm up to cover her face, and the blue-black fist holding Blacklight prisoner dissipated, leaving the other hero free to tumble to the ground.

"Oh, you're going to pay for that," snarled Sin-Dee, lashing out in Vel's direction with a semi-solid wall of darkness. The army men flew into it and disappeared completely from Vel's awareness. The shock of losing contact made her wobble where she stood, eyes going briefly unfocused. Wherever the toys had gone, it was…away. So far away that she couldn't even begin to feel out where they'd gone. "Stupid good-for-nothing wannabe. You were never good enough for The Super Patriots. You should never have even had the *chance*."

"They weren't good enough for *her*," Blacklight snarled. Sin-Dee's attention snapped in that direction, just in time for a wave of steel-hard anti-light to punch her squarely in the face. She went flying backward, taking out the rack of cream and sugars before slamming into the window. Blacklight glanced in Velveteen's direction. "Vel? You okay?"

"Ye-yeah," said Velveteen, shaking off the disorientation and reaching out to call the rest of her toys to her defense. "You?"

"Yeah." Blacklight's tone was grim. "Sadly, I think she is, too."

Sin-Dee's form wavered and turned liquid, slithering across the floor before re-forming between the two heroes. The blue sparks cycled violently over her skin as she snapped out her hands and, before either Velveteen or Blacklight could react, wrapped them both in veils of shadow.

"See, I knew I was going to need to make you pay for what you did to me," she said, almost conversationally, as her shadows slid around Velveteen's throat and pulled tight. "It's not like I resent having superpowers, *finally*, and I guess everybody needs an origin story, but you totally destroyed what we'd been trying to create, and that was, like, a total bummer, you know? So destroying you was, like, totally necessary."

"You robbed the bank," spat Velveteen. "You set us up."

"And you banished me to a dimension of eternal shadow, so I guess we're about equal, huh?" Sin-Dee flicked her fingers. A band of shadow slithered over Velveteen's mouth. "Now hush. This is my first monologue, and I want to enjoy it."

Velveteen's eyes narrowed, her gaze flicking toward Blacklight. The photon-manipulator was glaring in mute fury, the shadows circling her almost invisible against the darkness of her costume. She'd referenced The Super Patriots. She wouldn't say where she was trained. Maybe...

Stretching as much as she could against the bonds holding her, Velveteen flicked her pinky finger twice toward Blacklight. *You able to fight?*

After a moment's hesitation, Blacklight flicked her pinky back, once. *Yes.*

Velveteen bit back a sigh of relief. Now she just had to hope that they hadn't changed the signs between training groups and regions. Something about the way Blacklight fought—something she really didn't want to think about too hard just at the moment—told her that they probably hadn't. Squeezing her eyes tightly shut, she took a gamble, and tapped the first two fingers of her right hand together three times in a scissor-motion. The gesture had a different meaning for every power set. For an elemental, it meant "do your worst." For an elastic hero, it meant "elongate your limbs and escape." For a photon-manipulation, it meant "blind the room."

If Blacklight's powers were really limited to black forms of light, they were screwed. But if, as Velveteen suspected, they weren't...

There was a long pause, long enough for Velveteen to start thinking she'd guessed wrong. Then the room lit up with a brilliant white light, so pure that it was blinding even through her closed eyelids. Sin-Dee screamed. The bonds holding Velveteen off the floor dissolved and she hit the ground, slamming her head into the tile floor hard enough that a different sort of darkness came flowing in. She had time to wonder if Blacklight was all right, and whether any civilians had been injured. After that, unconsciousness claimed her, and she didn't have time to wonder anything more.

* * *

When Velveteen came to twenty minutes later, she was lying on a stretcher in the street outside, being examined by a crew of city EMTs who knew enough about treating superheroes to have left her mask in place. What she could see of the coffee shop from her current position was a disaster zone; broken glass and shattered coffee mugs were strewn everywhere. "Hope the owner had his superhero insurance paid up," she mumbled, and tried to push herself up onto her elbows.

"Stop that," said the nearest EMT. "You need to hold still."

"Blacklight. Is she–?"

"Your friend had to go. She stayed long enough to fill out the incident paperwork. Once we've finished looking you over, you'll be free to go and find her."

"The security cameras captured everything," added a man Velveteen recognized from the governor's office as he wandered over to the little cluster of medical personnel and battered superheroine. "The papers will be running a retraction tomorrow. You did a good job tonight."

"Tell that to my skull," Velveteen muttered, and subsided. Despite the pain, she couldn't stop thinking about what had just happened. Not the fight, specifically–fights were part of the superhero status quo, irritating and painful as they were–but the way it ended. The way Blacklight knew the finger-code, and the way the room had filled with light that wasn't black at all. Settling on the stretcher, she closed her eyes and tried to relax. The EMTs would take it from here, and she really didn't feel like moving. She just wanted to sleep, and think about the light, and what the light might mean.

Nobody noticed when Velveteen drifted off into shallow dreams. Not even Velveteen.

In the wreckage of the coffee shop, the shadows gathered together, slowly, moving with uncertain jerks. For a moment, it looked almost like they lifted off the floor, forming an uneven bulge that might, from the right direction, look like the body of a woman. A few faint blue sparks gathered, dancing over the surface of the darkness. Then the bulge sank down into the floor, the blue sparks fading away as the deepest of the shadows subsided, and the shadows that remained went still.

For the moment, anyway.

VELVETEEN
vs.
The Holiday Special

Twelve years ago...

IT TURNS OUT THAT THERE are good things and bad things that come with being a junior superhero. The good things were a little nebulous; if pressed, Velveteen would probably have had to settle for "I don't have to live with my parents anymore" and "Yelena and I get to share a room," but they were still there. The bad things, on the other hand, were numerous, and easy to spot. More classes, as The Super Patriots, Inc. legally had to educate their underage "wards" to the standards of the state, while also teaching them how to control their powers and not level too many buildings. (Not a huge danger for Velveteen, unless the building was made out of Lego. Still, the theory was sound.) Sessions with Marketing, and with the company therapists who were supposed to keep them all well-adjusted and happy. As if. Still, for the most part, she was reasonably sure that she was happy. Usually. Mostly.

At the moment, "happy" wasn't even in her vocabulary. In fact, at the moment, her desired vocabulary consisted pretty much entirely of words Marketing didn't even know she knew.

They were only fifteen minutes into the filming of the eighth annual *Junior Super Patriots United Christmas Extravaganza*, and Velveteen already felt like screaming. Possibly with a side-order of "raining down fiery destruction from above," if she could convince somebody to lend a girl a little bit of a helping hand. Cosmo-not, maybe; he seemed to be having almost as little fun as she was, what with Marketing continually demanding he summon up another cosmic light show. Or Dotty Gale, who was probably wishing she'd tornadoed herself back to Fairyland the second the summons to TV Town arrived.

Not that the TV Town heroes seemed all that thrilled with the situation. Deus Ex Machina kept complaining about the writing, which was something of a statement on its quality right there, Leading Lady had thrown her makeup mirror at Sparkle Bright for daring to suggest that maybe she could get away with wearing a little less foundation, and as for Master Chef, well…

Velveteen really just hoped that the Claw could stay out of his way, or at least avoid winding up in a room with him, a pot of boiling water, and access to melted butter.

She could hear the heels of the woman from Marketing clacking along the edge of the stage as she conducted her furious search, followed by her shrill, focus-group-approved voice demanding, "Has anyone seen Velveteen? She's due back on the Santa's Workshop set in fifteen minutes, and Makeup needs to approve her hair before she goes on camera."

Because I look SO GOOD in ringlets, Velveteen thought, and shrank further down into the shadows. She'd been able to tolerate the green and white version of her regular costume (still trimmed with her standard Velveteen Rabbit brown, mustn't confuse the kiddies when they're demanding their limited-edition Santa's Helper Velveteen action figures, oh no!). She'd been able to put up with them adding holly clips to her ears, and painting her nails in bright pine green. But everybody had to draw the line somewhere, and she drew the line at looking like the brunette Shirley Temple.

"It's okay," whispered a voice beside her. "She's gone."

Almost a year of part-time superhero training and full-time media spotlight had taught Velveteen that unexpected voices almost never meant anything good, and frequently meant serious pain was about to enter the scene. She whipped around, only wincing a little as her shoulders slammed into the steel girders supporting the stage. Then she blinked.

The girl perched next to her was glowing faintly, in the off-hand sort of way that Velveteen typically associated with Sparkle Bright or Firefly, except that this glow was blue-white, instead of being rainbowed or gently gold. The color of the glow made sense, considering the girl's pastel blue skin and long white hair, assuming that someone being pastel blue could ever be said to make very much sense. The blue skin and natural nightlight look didn't exactly go with her mall rat attire or hot pink jewelry, but clearly Marketing hadn't been able to get their hands on her wardrobe coordinators yet. They would. They always did.

Say something cool, Velveteen thought, before opening her mouth and asking inanely, "Are you a supervillain?"

"I've thought about it, just to make my parents mad, but it seems like too much work," replied the glowing girl, with an equally glowing grin. She offered a hand, displaying a clearly home-done hot pink manicure. "I'm Jackie Frost. My parents are doing some of the special effects."

Parents. Parents parents parents…Velveteen quickly reviewed the list of specialists that had been brought in for the production, and guessed, "Jack Frost and the Snow Queen?"

"Uh-huh." Jackie shrugged. "They said to not get underfoot. They're trying to keep Marketing from noticing me."

Velveteen winced. "That's a good idea. I wish Marketing would stop noticing *me*."

"We could get out of here."

"How?" The idea was appealing. It was just that it also happened to be completely impossible.

"I can use Mom's magic mirror to teleport home. She totally lets me."

Velveteen hesitated, thinking of her friends trapped in holiday-special hell. Sparkle Bright kept getting forced to play fireworks display, the Claw was being stalked by the world's best argument against seafood restaurants, and Action Dude…she didn't even like to *think* about what Marketing was doing to *him*.

"Can we bring my friends?" she asked hopefully.

Jackie grinned.

Convincing the rest of The Junior Super Patriots, West Coast Division to take a trip through a complete stranger's mother's magic mirror was easier than Velveteen expected it to be. It helped that–in addition to the Claw's problems with Master Chef–Firefly had been teasing Sparkle Bright again, to the point that the younger photon-manipulator was obviously fighting back tears, and Action Dude had been the target of all the other Majesty-type heroes-in-training since the filming of the special began. The West Coast Division was currently the youngest team in The Junior Super Patriots franchise, and the "upperclassmen" were more than happy to remind its members of their place in the pecking order. Any chance at an escape was worth the risk.

"Besides, what's she going to do?" muttered the Claw. "Kidnap us to the Smurf dimension?"

Sparkle Bright, whose media education began and ended with what her handlers taught her, wiped her eyes and asked him, blankly, "What's a Smurf?"

The Claw rolled his eyes. "You smeared your mascara," he said, and went stomping off to observe Jackie as she tried to activate her mother's magic mirror.

Things weren't exactly going smoothly in the magic mirror department. Jackie was waving her hands, muttering in a language that sounded like gibberish (but she swore was elvish), and occasionally blowing veils of frost across the glass. This would have seemed more mystic and impressive if the frost hadn't possessed a tendency to form itself into unrelentingly cute images. Her latest was a perfect frost etching of two ice-skating penguins. The penguins were holding hands. Velveteen couldn't decide whether to be impressed or nauseated.

"Maybe you should kick it," suggested Action Dude. "That's what my dad always does when the television doesn't work." He paused, ears reddening. "Did. What he always did."

Velveteen shot him a sympathetic look, wishing she was brave enough to hold his hand. It was always hard when things brought back memories of their parents; of the lives they'd had before The Super Patriots, Inc. stepped in and changed everything. Only the Claw still had any contact with his family, and that was just because it was his dad who mutated him. "Are you sure you know how to work this thing?" she asked.

Jackie glared. "Why don't you try it, bunny-girl?" She stepped back from the mirror, spreading her hands in disgusted invitation. "Be my guest."

The penguin-laced frost was still clinging to the glass. In the distance, Velveteen could hear the shouts of the woman from Marketing as she realized that her newest junior team was completely absent. That, alone, was what gave Velveteen the courage to step forward, touching the glass with gloved fingertips, and ask, "Please, Mr. Magic Mirror? Can you take us anywhere but here?"

The penguins were wiped away by a sudden blaze of brilliant blue-white light. Whooping with delight, Jackie–who didn't seem exactly capable of holding a grudge–grabbed the Claw with one hand and Action Dude with the other. "North Pole, here we come!" she hollered.

"Wait, what?" squawked Velveteen, as Action Dude grabbed her by the wrist and Sparkle Bright grabbed onto the Claw's free, well, claw. Then the light washed everything away, and they were gone.

The woman from Marketing saw the flash of light and walked briskly toward it. By the time she got there, even the mirror had disappeared, leaving nothing but an empty room.

The transit through the mirror was completely smooth, marked only by a taste like peppermint and pine needles on their lips before they were tumbling out into the cotton candy snow. Almost literally cotton candy snow; it was only a little bit cold, and when Velveteen wiped it off her face, it tasted just like spun carnival sugar. "I thought you knew how to steer," she complained, before realizing that no one else was saying anything at all. Frowning a little, she turned in the direction the others were staring. Then she froze, too, joining them in their silent awe.

Jackie, standing off to one side–her high-top sneakers not sinking into the snow so much as a fraction of an inch–smirked. "Like I said, Mom lets me use her mirror," she said. "Welcome to the North Pole."

"Oh, my God, Santa's really and truly real," whispered Sparkle Bright.

"Duh," said Jackie.

The scene in front of them was like something out of a fairy tale or a dream, the sort of dream you have after a day of pressing your nose to store windows and dreaming of things you know you'll never have. The buildings looked like they'd been crafted from gingerbread and icing, with sugar-candy windows and striped peppermint support beams. More of the cotton candy snow covered them in a decorative veil, and Velveteen knew that if she slept in that snow, she'd wake up more rested than she'd ever been in her life. Warm light bled through the windows, casting calliope shadows on the snow banks. The door on the biggest house, the one right in front of them, was standing open.

Her triumph firmly established and her superiority assured, Jackie offered the four a bright smile and said, "Come on this way. You're probably gonna want to meet the Big Guy, and I *know* he's gonna want to meet you."

Sparkle Bright's eyes lit up, and not from her powers. "We get to meet the *real* Santa?"

"Duh," said Jackie again, and turned to head inside.

"Vel Vel Vel we're gonna meet *Santa!*" squealed Sparkle Bright, and seized Velveteen's hand, hauling her across the yard and into the welcoming hallway ahead of them. Action Dude and the Claw followed more slowly, but not by much. Once the last of them had stepped through, the door swung shut of its own accord.

The hallway in Santa's house smelled like gingerbread and cocoa, and it didn't look a thing like the Santa's Workshop set dreamed up by the designers of the *The Junior Super Patriots United Christmas Extravaganza*. For one thing, Candyland-themed sensibilities aside, it wasn't anything near tidy enough. The set had been obviously that: a set, a place you filmed a kid-friendly adventure without allowing things to become too visually confusing. This was just as obviously nothing of the sort. Shelves lined the walls from the floor on up, all of them crammed with knick-knacks, antique toys, and things too weird for Velveteen to quite identify. The few open spots between the shelves were packed with framed pictures, paintings, and even paper-cut cameos showing the outlines of old-fashioned strangers.

One of the paintings showed a little glowing blue girl who could almost have been Jackie herself, if not for the subtle differences in her features. "Your mom?" Velveteen guessed, pointing to the picture.

"My great-grandmother," Jackie replied, and grinned. "There have been Snow Queens in Christmas Village for a long, long time."

"And there will be many more to come, unless you manage to melt us all, you naughty child," boomed a jovial voice from behind them. The sound of it filled Velveteen's head with thoughts of Christmas—good thoughts, the ones that were normally drowned out by memories of empty stockings and boxes of stale generic-brand cereal wrapped in birthday paper and presented like they were all the jewels of India.

"*SANTA!*" Sparkle Bright let go of Velveteen in order to launch herself at the vast, red-and-white-clad figure filling the hallway door. Santa Claus, faced with a self-guided blonde cruise missile riding a blast of rainbow, did the sensible thing: he laughed and plucked her out of the air, swinging her into an embrace that looked as warm and welcoming as a mug of hot chocolate with homemade marshmallows on top. Sparkle Bright laughed in tandem, sending firework sparks dancing all over the room as she flung her arms around his neck and hugged him for all that she was worth. "I *knew* you were real, I just *knew* it, people said you were just a story, but I *knew* it! You had to be real, you just *had* to!"

"Yes, my dear, I'm very real, and I like to breathe," said Santa, laughter turning just a trifle strained.

Blushing electric green, Sparkle Bright let go of his neck. "Sorry, Santa."

"It's all right. You're very welcome here, Yelena." Looking toward the others, he said, "You are all very welcome here. You are very good children, and I'm glad to have the opportunity to meet you."

Action Dude and the Claw mumbled their greetings, both of them looking overwhelmed. Velveteen, however, had encountered holiday archetypes before—had, in fact, been relentlessly tormented by holiday archetypes, in the form of Hailey Ween and Scaredy Cat and all the rest of the insanity in the Autumn Land. She'd been perfectly willing to follow Jackie home if it got them out of the filming of the Christmas special, but the phrase "North Pole" hadn't come into things until they were already committed, and the chance of meeting the representatives of the holiday itself had *never* been mentioned. Glaring at Santa seemed wrong somehow, so Velveteen settled for staring fixedly at her feet, refusing to look up and meet his eyes. She didn't care whether he was jolly as holly and shaking like a big bowl of jelly. He was a holiday, and holidays didn't mean anything good.

Santa greeted each of the others by name—*real* name, not code name—and while neither of the boys was quite as enthusiastic as Yelena (sometimes explosions weren't as enthusiastic as Yelena), they both snapped out of their shyness pretty quickly, answering his questions like they'd known him for their entire lives. In a way, they had. He was Santa, after all. It wasn't until Jackie's voice rejoined the discussion that she realized what he was asking them; whether they'd like to have some gingerbread and cocoa in the kitchen. Before she could get her bearings back, she was alone in the cluttered living room with Santa Claus. She could feel him watching her. She didn't know what to do.

"Hello, Velveteen," said Santa, his voice lowered several notches from his previous jovial boom. Why was he using her code name? She felt unsure of her place in the world, like there was nothing holding her to who she'd been but the memories of too many bad

Christmas mornings, too many missed meals and parent-teacher conferences.

She said nothing.

"I've been hoping I'd get the chance to meet you properly," said Santa, and Velveteen raised her head, ready to face the music at last. Whatever that music might be.

Santa didn't say anything. He just looked at her, expression solemn and compassionate and, yes, very, very kind. She understood why Yelena had loved him at once, and why he'd been able to win the boys over so quickly when nothing really won Aaron over before he'd had a chance to consider every angle. She also understood why he terrified her. With someone who looked that kind, it would be so easy to overlook a little betrayal.

"I don't want to go back," said Velveteen. "Please don't make me."

"Ah," said Santa. "But where is it that you don't want to go back to? I'm not trying to send you anywhere. I'm a little surprised that you think I might be."

"Halloween," said Velveteen immediately. "I don't want to go back to Halloween."

"Why did you think I'd do something like that?"

She looked at him, dark eyes wide and grave, and answered, "You called me 'Velveteen.' Not 'Velma.' You called everybody else by their real names. So why not me?"

"Ah," said Santa, understanding washing over his face. "I think I understand. Come over here, Vel. Sit down with me a little bit." He walked to a large red velvet couch only a few shades darker than his suit—how was it that she hadn't noticed it before? Was the house changing when she wasn't watching it? The idea seemed likely and upsetting, all at the same time—and sat, patting the cushion next to him. Entirely unsure of what else she could do, Velveteen walked over and sat down, still looking gravely up at him. At least he hadn't asked her to sit in his lap. There was that, anyway.

"Now, my dear, there are a few things you should know. The first is that you are always welcome here." Seeing her expression turn to surprise, Santa smiled. "For you, we've just met, but for me, I've known you for your entire life. Velveteen Sofia Martinez, that's who you are, at least for right now. I've been watching you since you were a baby. Worrying about you, sometimes, but watching all the same. Holidays can't touch you unless you're particularly attuned to them, and unless there's a need. Christmas is happy to have you visit. Would even be happy if you wanted to settle here. But we don't need you the way that Halloween did, and so there's no reason for me to attempt to keep you here—nor, I promise, is there reason for me to send you back there."

Still confused, Velveteen said, carefully, "But why am I not Velma anymore?"

Santa's smile faded, replaced by a look of sorrow so deep it verged on anger. "Because your parents never taught you who Velma *was*, and they gave her away without a second thought. Oh, don't worry—you'll be Velma again someday, when you figure out precisely who Velma needs to be. Right now is the time for you to be Velveteen. Enjoy it."

Velveteen eyed him warily. In her experience, when adults said something like that, there was a silent "while it lasts" tacked onto the end. "If you already knew me, and already know all of this, why were you hoping you'd get to meet me 'properly'? Did you send Jackie to the filming just to bring us back here? 'Cause I just thought she was being nice." More quietly, she added, "Guess I should've known better."

"Jackie does what she does entirely on her own, and no one can control her. Not me, and not her parents. She'll be a fantastic Snow Queen when her time comes. Assuming she doesn't manage to slaughter us all by mistake between then and now. No, my dear, this meeting was one of those things that had the potential to occur, but had an equal chance of never happening at all. I'm truly glad that it did. Especially now. This is a wonderful time for you."

"What do you…" Velveteen paused, understanding washing over her. "You're a time-traveler. That's how you do it. That's how you can be everywhere on Christmas. You travel through time."

"Something like that, and nowhere near so dramatically as your hero-types tend to do. I don't zip about solving mysteries and preventing crimes. I simply give gifts to children, and watch them as they grow up."

Velveteen's expression darkened. "So where were *my* Christmas presents?"

Santa chuckled. The sound was like the Northern Lights somehow, all color and wonder and proof that magic lives in even the most modern world. "Oh, child. The world is your Christmas present. You only need to decide the time has come to unwrap it."

* * *

Velveteen was quiet and a little thoughtful-looking when she walked into the kitchen, just a few steps ahead of a smiling Santa Claus. The rest of The Junior Super Patriots, West Coast Division, were seated around a weathered old cherry-wood table, munching their way through a plate of gingerbread cookies. Each of them had an enormous mug of cocoa in front of them, and somehow it made perfect sense, given the sensibilities of the place, that the Claw's mug was actually shaped to fit easily into his massive claws. Jackie was sitting at one end of the table, and a smiling, white-haired woman who looked suspiciously like a "Mrs. Claus"-type was seated at the other. Yelena and Aaron looked around as Velveteen and Santa entered, both of them smiling brightly at the sight of her.

"Vel!" called Aaron, waving a cookie in her direction. "Come on, have some cookies. They're *amazing*."

"The cocoa's better," said Yelena firmly, and stuck her tongue out at him. He stuck his tongue out right back. And Velveteen, unexpectedly, giggled.

"Whoa," said Jackie, after the silence had managed to get a little bit too long for her to tolerate—so once it had been more than a few seconds—"you can actually laugh. I was starting to think you were, like, morally opposed to it or something."

"Vel's just a little shy," said Aaron staunchly. "Don't tease her."

"It's okay," said Velveteen, moving to sit down between him and Yelena. "I don't mind if Jackie wants to tease me. Can I have some cocoa?"

The woman from Marketing had just about run out of patience for the antics of junior heroes who didn't understand how lucky they were to be in the good graces of The Super Patriots, Inc. She turned on one three-inch heel, intending to storm back to the director's office and inform him that the West Coast Division was being cut, and would be punished for their absence. There, standing in front of her, were the four missing heroes—and more, they were finally properly dressed. Velveteen's hair was in perfect Christmas corkscrew curls. Sparkle Bright looked like a literal angel, floating a foot above the floor on a tide of sparkling glitter. Action Dude had donned his fur-trimmed holiday cape (the one he'd been steadfastly refusing to wear all week), and even the Claw had finally embraced the holiday spirit, wearing reindeer antlers in front of his waving antennae. The woman from Marketing stopped dead, staring. Finally, carefully, she said, "Children...?"

"We're sorry we were missing," said Sparkle Bright, with deep and chastised-looking gravity. "I was worried I wouldn't be able to remember my lines, so Vel was helping me with them, and we just sort of lost track of time."

"We went to find the girls," said Action Dude. "Teammates in trouble, be there on the double."

Faced with one of the primary rules of every Super Patriots team, all the woman from Marketing could really do was blink. The four were better groomed and better prepared-looking than she'd ever seen them, and to a certain degree, she was afraid to look a gift horse in the mouth. There was too much of a chance that it might bite. "Well, I should hope you're sorry," she said, almost automatically. "Every minute that you're not on that set costs the company money. I just want you to think about that the next time you complain about needing to pose for new posters."

"We're sorry," chorused the junior heroes, in perfect unison.

Something about that made the woman from Marketing uncomfortable...but there just wasn't time to worry about it. They were already far too late for such piddling concerns. "This way," she said, and led the four back toward the set where filming was about to resume.

Safe in Santa's kitchen, well-plied with cocoa, cookies, and gooey fireplace s'mores, The Junior Super Patriots, West Coast Division, watched through the magic mirror as the four dolls (courtesy of Santa's workshop) obediently followed the woman from Marketing off to be filmed. The toys were certainly believable, if you hadn't spent any real amount of time with the four, who might be well-trained, but were still just kids. "And they're really going to believe this all night?" asked Velveteen.

"They always have before," said Jackie brightly, and grabbed another cookie. Santa shot her a chiding look, and she smiled brilliantly before shoving the cookie into her mouth. "'sides," she said, around a mouthful of crumbs, "toys 'have better."

"She means that my toys behave better," translated Santa. "They don't have actual superpowers, just the illusion of them, but with Jack and the Snow Queen on hand to make sure nothing gets out of control, they'll be fine. They'll play your parts perfectly, and you can go back after they finish with makeup removal."

"This is really nice of you, Santa," said Yelena. She was almost literally starry-eyed, bursts of silver and rainbow glitter appearing around her at random. If she were any happier, she might be in danger of having her head pop right off and go flying around the room under its own power.

Velveteen was a little warier. Santa had been good to them so far, and his toys were wonderful, but… "It seems a little too easy," she said.

Santa looked at her solemnly. "Nothing is ever easy, my dear, but that doesn't mean that everything has to be hard. Be children tonight. Just for one night, be children. You deserve that much out of the holiday, and it's a luxury that you won't encounter very often in this life."

"What do you mean?" asked the Claw, voice going anxious.

"Just that time is short, and childhood passes faster than we ever think it will." Santa leaned over to ruffle the Claw's hair, which was still brown and straight, just like it had been when he was a human boy. "Now run and play, all five of you. I'll make sure the exchange goes smoothly when it's time to send you home."

"Last one to the skating pond is a rotten egg!" shouted Jackie, and took off running. The other four, lacking any better ideas, followed her, and only Velveteen looked back.

In a matter of seconds, Santa and Mrs. Claus were alone in the kitchen. Reaching over to take her husband's hand, Mrs. Claus asked, "Well? What do you see for them?"

"Darkness. So much darkness. It'll take at least one of them, and maybe more, if they're not careful. There's love between them, and that may be the most dangerous thing of them all, because love is what opens the cracks that let the darkness in." Santa stroked his wife's fingers, still looking after The Junior Super Patriots—looking after the children. "They're going to be hurt more than they'd think possible if you asked them, and they've all been hurt before, so damn badly. It's inhuman what some people do to children. It's just inhuman."

"But they'll make it through? They'll make it out the other side?"

Santa pulled his hand away from hers, shaking his head. "I don't know, Anna, I honestly don't. It's murky, like even they haven't figured that out just yet. The future can always change, but for at least one of those four, there isn't much of a future as things stand now."

"You don't mean…"

"I'm afraid I do." Santa sighed heavily. "Maybe we'll be lucky. Maybe the little animus will choose Halloween, and that will be enough to put paid to what's hanging over them. If not…"

"The future will be what it's going to be. Isn't that what you always say?"

"Yes. But that doesn't mean I can't wish that I could change it." Santa took her hand again, and they sat quietly, listening to the distant sound of children's laughter.

After that night was over, none of them would ever quite agree on what the best part had been. Yelena loved the Northern Lights, which she was able to grab and twirl around her like gauzy scarves. Aaron liked playing snowball baseball with the elves, who didn't care if he occasionally blasted into a snow bank or lost control and went tumbling off into the sky. The Claw liked the icy water beneath the frozen ponds, where his lobster's skin kept him from getting cold. He could dance through the water like Yelena danced through the sky, and he didn't feel like a freak at all. Velveteen…

Velma liked the toys in Santa's Workshop. But most of all, she liked watching Yelena dance in the sky and the Claw dance in the water, and she liked the sound of Aaron laughing. She liked knowing that her friends, for once in their lives, were really happy. As she watched Yelena changing for bed, her own pajamas warm and comforting, she tried not to think too hard about what it meant that they had so little laughter in their lives. Maybe that was just part of being a hero. One more thing they didn't put in the brochure.

"Merry Christmas, Vel," said Yelena, sliding into her bed.

Velma smiled as best she could, lying down with her own head on her pillow. "Merry Christmas, Yelena," she said. And to all a good night.

VELVETEEN
vs.
The Secret Identity

V ELVETEEN LOUNGED AGAINST THE WALL of the movie theater, listening with mild disinterest to the screaming, crunching noises coming from inside the lobby. A piercing wail rose briefly above the rest, cutting off as abruptly as it began. Velveteen yawned. More crunching noises followed, along with a high-pitched male voice shrieking "LET GO LET GO DEAR GOD I SWEAR I'LL NEVER DO ANYTHING LIKE THIS AGAIN JUST LET G–" The words dissolved into more incoherent screams.

The flip-phone clipped to Velveteen's belt began ringing.

An observer who wasn't either running for their life or being pummeled by the contents of a Build-A-Bear franchise location would have seen the bunny-eared superheroine smile as she checked the phone's caller ID, straightening her domino mask with one hand and opening the phone with the other. "Tag? Hi! No, I wasn't doing anything important…"

More screams sounded from inside the theater. They were a little weaker than the previous ones, but still loud enough to earn a frown from Velveteen, who put a hand over the phone as she called, toward the door, "Can you finish it up in there? I need to take this call." The screaming from inside stopped abruptly, accompanied by the sound of one final, convulsive "thud." Velveteen smiled. "Thank you!" she chirped, and uncovered her phone. "Tag? You still with me?"

"I am," replied Tag, with cautious enthusiasm. "Am I calling at a bad time?"

"What? No! Why would you think that?"

"I don't know. The screaming? I mean, either you're in the middle of battle, or you're answering your phone while you're at the movies, which is tacky."

"Oh, no, it's really no big deal. Just some of Cinemaniac's thugs trying to rob the movie theater so he could use the projectors to bring an army of unstoppable rubber monsters to life and wreak havoc on downtown Portland." A small procession of stuffed toys began emerging from the lobby, dragging unconscious henchmen along with them. "They picked the wrong movie theater to rob."

"Out of curiosity, where would one find the right movie theater to rob?"

"Someplace that doesn't have a seriously bored local superheroine missing her boyfriend? I mean, just as a thought." Velveteen walked over to the first of the prone thugs, prodding him with the tip of her boot. He groaned, but otherwise didn't respond. "I may have allowed my toys to take my aggressions out on these boys just a teeny-tiny little bit."

"Meaning...?"

"Broken bones, but no coroner."

Tag laughed. Somehow, coming from him, the sound was entirely affectionate. "You're hot when you're violent."

Velveteen's army of toys began tying up the downed thugs, moving with practiced efficiency as they secured hands and tightened knots. Vel stepped back, letting them work. "So to what do I owe the honor of this call? Please tell me you're not calling to say that you're going to be out of town for another week. I'm running out of people it's socially acceptable for me to hit."

"Actually, I was calling to tell you that I'm getting home tonight," said Tag. "Want me to join you on patrol?"

Velveteen paused. While the idea of patrolling with her significant other had its attractions—and was supposed to be the ultimate goal of all good superhero couples, since tandem action shots always played well in the papers—she hadn't exactly worn the nice costume for tonight's outing. Or brushed her hair. Or bothered to put on mascara. Why go to the trouble when she wasn't talking to the press or setting up any intentional photo opportunities? Apparently, because boyfriends were like supervillains and would ambush you when they were least expected.

"How about you meet me at the usual place instead?" she asked, hoping he wouldn't notice her pause. "That'll give me time to do the paperwork on this latest bunch of morons. Maybe we could grab something to eat?"

"I'd like that," Tag said. His tone turned serious as he added, "I haven't forgotten what we talked about before, you know. The picnic, and the…talking."

"Neither have I," said Velveteen, and swallowed hard. She liked Tag. She did. She really, really liked him. But did that mean she was ready to take the next big step in their relationship? And if she wasn't …and if he was…would the relationship survive until the morning?

"I'll see you there," said Tag. "Later, Vel."

"Later," she echoed, and snapped the phone closed. She looked around as she slid it back into her belt, finally spotting one of the larger teddy bears. "Hey, you," she said. "Get over here and help me get these idiots bundled up for delivery. I have a date to make."

The teddy bear trotted obediently over, followed by the rest of her plush minions. Velveteen bent to help them, letting herself focus on her work, and not on the evening ahead of her, which suddenly looked a lot less like a pleasant date, and a lot more like one of those exams she was always afraid of failing. The ones that had Consequences. Velveteen knew way too much about Consequences. For one thing, she knew that she didn't like them.

For another, she knew that she liked avoiding them even less. Whatever else she did tonight, she was going to see her boyfriend, and she was going to see what happened next.

Maybe it wasn't exactly heroic of her, but when one of the men started to wake up again, Velveteen took great delight in bouncing his head off the floor of the lobby. Not hard enough to concuss him (if he wasn't already); just enough to make him stop moving. And then once more for good measure.

And then it was time to go. Whether she was ready or not.

One might expect the romantic lives of superheroes to be fraught with peril; they are, after all, superheroes. Everything else they do is fraught with peril, so why should their personal relationships be any different? Especially considering the well-established tendency of superhumans to become involved with other superhumans, it seems only natural that they would enjoy romances full of danger, disaster, and the occasional battle for the survival of mankind.

All these things are accurate. The average superhero relationship will involve multiple kidnappings, mistaken identities, alien invasions, and supposed deaths before achieving a measure of stability. The trouble is that all these things do not prevent superhumans from also suffering from the slings and arrows of a normal romantic life. "It isn't all spandex and starlets," said Jolly Roger, in an interview given shortly before his well-publicized disappearance. "The hard parts don't get any easier just because you can fly." When pressed to provide details on "the hard parts," he declared the interview to be over, transformed all the water in a six-block radius into rum, and flew away on his spectral pirate ship. Three days later, he was gone. And that, in its own way, tells us everything we need to know about superhuman relationships.

When all else fails, we must turn to statistics. The divorce rate among minor heroes (those ranked below "marketable" levels, who may or may not be on active duty with one of the super teams) is roughly equivalent to the divorce rate among normal humans, if not slightly higher. The divorce rate among supervillains, when it can be tracked at all—something that is not always possible, as their public personas rarely include a spouse or children—is substantially elevated, implying that the strains of the superhuman lifestyle can put substantial stress on a marriage. The major heroes, on the other hand, reveal a frightening duality. Those who are on active duty tend to marry and remain married, their love seemingly enduring everything the world can throw at them. Those who are *not* on active duty, or who are removed from active duty, tend to become single almost immediately.

This raises the question of whether superhuman relationships are any stronger than those of normal humans, or whether they might not be, in some ways, weaker…and whether The Super Patriots, Inc. might be engineering their more well-known and beloved family groups for their own benefit. How many of our role models are trapped in loveless relationships, unable to leave them for fear of being somehow penalized by the corporation which essentially owns them?

Perhaps more chilling…what happens when the day arrives which makes this fear no longer sufficient to keep the heroes of the world in check? How long before our superhumans rise up, not for freedom or justice, but for the right to love freely and without fear?

Velveteen—Velma—oh, she didn't even know anymore, and that was half the problem—looked mournfully at her reflection in the bathroom mirror. One of the stuffed bears was adjusting the tilt of her rabbit-ear headband, the good one that she generally reserved for court dates and casual photo ops. One of her eyes was normal: mascara on the lashes, a little hint of gold eye shadow on the upper lid to make sure her eyes wouldn't vanish into her domino mask if someone happened to snap a picture. The other was somewhere between a train wreck and a disaster: three shades of eye shadow, a jagged line of eyeliner, and a certain smudgy quality that could have looked sexy, but really just looked like she'd been finger-painting with her cosmetics. According to the book propped open in front of her, following their step-by-step directions would result in a "dramatic, feminine allure, sure to win your suitor's heart as soon as the masks come off." After trying five times to get it right, Vel was starting to think that the book had been written by a particularly nasty supervillain.

The mascara wand bounced off the mirror, leaving a black smudge behind, and fell to the floor, where it rolled behind the toilet and disappeared. She glared at her reflection for a moment more before picking up the book and checking the back. "Intended for use by active members of The Super-Patriots, Inc. and their associated chapters; all rights reserved," she read. The book promptly joined the mascara wand on the floor. She might not know much about doing her makeup for civilian occasions, but she'd be damned before she let Marketing tell her how it was done.

The real trouble with doing your heroing out of a box of second-hand hand-me-downs and leftovers from your own teen years was the fact that you couldn't really be picky about your sources. Vel reflected grimly on this harsh truth as she wiped the makeup off her face, scrubbing until only a few streaky mascara-ghosts remained. She was on her own for this.

The bear made one last adjustment to her headband and hopped down from the back of the chair, while a fashion doll with an unfortunate mohawk tapped her high-heeled way along the sink, holding up Vel's basic velvet domino mask in her unyielding hands. She waited there, her fixed plastic smile eternally patient, until Velveteen took the mask from her.

"Thanks," said Velveteen.

The doll inclined her head, painted expression not changing, and turned to tap away.

Vel sighed, turning back to the mirror. No makeup; hair in need of a trim, or a style, or *something* to make it look moderately more fashionable than mud; rabbit-ear headband that had seemed childish on her when she *was* a child, and now looked either cynical or pathetic, depending on your point of view. At least her uniform fit, and was even, thanks to the Princess's mice, reasonably flattering; at least she'd been doing this long enough that she was starting to get some actual muscle definition back. Skin-tight velvet unitards weren't forgiving on anyone.

At least she knew how to conduct a midnight encounter when she was doing it behind a mask. Vel lifted the domino mask to her face, pressing down on the edges until they adhered to her skin. When she lowered her hands, Velveteen looked out of the mirror at her. Velveteen, child hero turned teen dropout turned surprise comeback. Velveteen, who faced down supervillains and Marketing and monsters, and still got out mostly sane.

Velveteen, who was scared out of her mind.

"Fucked-up times five billion," muttered Vel, and turned to leave the bathroom. Like it or not, it was time for her to go. It was time to meet her boyfriend…for the very first time.

One of the teddy bears turned the lights out behind her as she left.

Tag managed to beat Velveteen to "the usual spot"—the roof of the downtown branch of the municipal library, which offered shelter from the elements, lots of interesting things to climb on, and, best of all, access to the rooftop storage shed, allowing them to tuck little things away for later. Little things like picnic baskets, and buckets of ice, and bottles of champagne. There wasn't room in the storage shed for a table, but a few minutes with a Sharpie had been enough to fix that. The table and chairs he'd sketched into existence would only last for a few hours. That should be more than long enough.

A scraping sound to the right brought his head snapping around and his heart surging up into his throat. The pigeon that had just landed on the edge of the roof looked at him blankly, cocking its head first to one side, and then to the other. Tag sighed. The pigeon cooed inquisitively.

"I'm not going to feed you," said Tag. The pigeon continued looking at him. Tag flapped his hands in a vigorous "go away" gesture. "Go on, shoo. Scat. Get out of here. This is a private party. Come back later. Shoo."

The pigeon fluffed its feathers, looking briefly like it was going to settle in exactly where it was. Then it turned, almost lazily, spread its wings, and flew away into the night. Tag sighed again, this time with relief.

"Stupid bird could have ruined the entire mood," he muttered.

"And that's in addition to providing the Princess with a blow-by-blow description of whatever goes on here tonight," said Velveteen from behind him, in a conversational tone. "Not that I think every pigeon in the city is working for her, but well. When one of your best friends can talk to birds, you learn to be a little wary of anything feathered that hasn't already been battered and deep-fried."

"Vel." Tag turned, his smile lighting up his face like the halogen streetlights illuminated the street below. Faced with that much delight, Velveteen couldn't stop a smile of her own from forming. She didn't pull away as he reached for her hands, either. "You came."

"I did," she agreed, still smiling. "I missed you. How was Canada?"

"Cold. How were things here in Portland?"

"Damp. Full of crime."

"I heard about some of that. Thanks for not turning out to be a supervillain while I was out of town, by the way. That would have really put a crimp in our relationship." Tag froze, eyes widening behind his mask as he realized that he had just dropped the "R" word into casual conversation. Which was, to judge by the sudden tension in Velveteen's smile, no longer exactly casual.

"Tag…" she began.

"I brought dinner," he said, cutting her off mid-sentence. He gestured toward his carefully-drawn table. A checkered picnic blanket covered the empty spaces in the tabletop, and mostly obscured the slightly sketchy-looking Sharpie legs. "It's pizza from that place you like downtown. The one that does the chicken and artichoke hearts with extra mushrooms."

Some of the tension eased out of her smile. "You don't like mushrooms."

"Ah, but you see, I am smart. I bought two pizzas."

The sound of Velveteen's laughter was nothing like music, but it was still music to his ears.

They both relaxed a bit as they ate. It helped that they were still wearing their masks, which kept them on familiar ground. Tag told jokes about Canadian superheroes and the impossibility of finding a convenience store in Montreal if you didn't know to look for the winking red owl. Velveteen talked about teaming up with Blacklight, and what a relief it was to finally feel like she had a community of friends that she could really relate to.

Eventually, of course, all the food that could be eaten had been eaten, and all the sodas were gone, and the legs of the table were starting to blur around the edges, signaling its impending disappearance. With a small sigh, Tag stood, starting to pick up the dishes. Velveteen moved to do the same, and he waved her back to her seat.

"I've got it. I just need to get things put away before the table decides to turn two-dimensional again." Tag placed the paper plates inside one of the pizza boxes, stacking it atop the other box before removing them both. "I'm getting better about keeping things animated for extended periods of time, but I'm still not up to more than a few hours."

"That's still impressive," said Vel. "I can keep my toys moving for as long as I'm paying attention, but they de-animate after they hold still for like, twenty minutes. I am not your girl for a stake-out."

"I don't know," said Tag, with a small, lopsided smile. "I think we could have a lovely stake-out together. Just you, and me, and a nice rooftop on a clear night…"

Velveteen smiled back, amused. "Ah, but how much crime would we be fighting?"

"Crime? What crime? I see no crime." The table legs blurred a final time, and then dissolved. Tag grabbed the tablecloth before it could hit the ground, managing–barely–to keep the remaining debris from their dinner from spilling across the rooftop. "Looks like we're eating dessert off our laps."

"Trust me, I've done worse." Vel leaned forward, studying the table sketched on the roof. "Can you do that with anything?"

"Mostly. Watercolors and pastels don't have much cohesion. Chalk works a little bit better, but it doesn't hold up in a strong wind." Tag dropped the tablecloth next to the cooler, bending and rummaging with his back to her for a few moments. When he straightened again, he was holding a bowl of strawberries, a bottle of champagne, and two plastic wine flutes. "I was so disappointed when I realized that. I'd wanted to go dance with the penguins."

"You realize you just admitted to watching Disney movies, which is, by definition, uncool," said Vel. "I say this with love. One of my best friends is basically a walking Disney movie."

"I want to come to one of your karaoke nights sometime. Which, I assume, happen wherever you happen to be, since hanging out with a Disney Princess means never having to say you weren't prepared for a musical number." Tag handed her a wine flute before setting the strawberries on his chair and popping the cork on the champagne. "It's really good to see you, Vel. I missed you."

Suddenly aware that the mood was turning serious, Vel smiled somewhat anxiously up at him. "I missed you, too. It's good to have you back."

"I didn't mean to be gone for so long." Tag filled her glass and sat, putting the strawberries down on the roof between them. He busied himself for a moment more with filling his own glass before clearing his throat and saying, "So…"

"Yeah," Vel agreed. "So. Very 'so.' This is about the most 'so' it's ever been."

Tag took a deep breath. Then he laughed, nervousness mirroring Vel's own. "I've never actually done this part before. The 'let's reveal our secret identities' part."

"Me, neither," Vel admitted. There had been Aaron, sure, but he was just…just *Aaron*, who trained with her, and lived with her, and had never really had a secret identity. Not where she was concerned. Except maybe for the part where he was secretly dating her best friend behind her back. Maybe "cheating bastard" was Action Dude's real secret identity, and she'd never known Aaron Frank at all.

"I guess that means I should go first," said Tag. Reaching up, he touched the painted-on rainbow swirl of his mask with the tips of his fingers. It pulled away from his face for a brief second, a dash of color hanging in the air, and then it was simply gone, fading into the nothingness he called his creations from. "Hi. My name is Tad Sinclair."

"It's nice to meet you," said Vel, automatically, before grinning. "Tad? Really? And you chose the superhero name 'Tag' for *yourself*?"

"Hey, at least it meant I didn't have to learn to duck when I heard it shouted during a fight," said Tad, somewhat defensively. He dropped his hand. "Feeling a little naked here, Vel."

"Sorry." Her grin faded into a timid smile as she reached up and removed her own domino mask. "Velma Martinez. At your service, I guess."

Tad blinked. Then he laughed. "Wait–you're really a Vel? And you laughed at my code name?"

"It was Marketing's idea," she said defensively. "I just got used to it."

"We can get used to anything," said Tad, and leaned forward, holding up his plastic wine flute for a toast. "It's nice to finally meet my girlfriend."

Vel's smile was much less timid as she tapped her glass against his. "My sentiments exactly."

It wasn't safe to sit around in public with their costumes on and their masks off. By mutual agreement—and after a lengthy make-out session, to properly celebrate the sharing of their secret identities—Velveteen and Tag both put their masks back on. Hers was the easier to apply, requiring only a few dabs from the tube of specially formulated adhesive she carried in her utility belt ("No superheroine should leave the lair without it!"). Tag's had to be drawn on the rooftop in marker before it could be lifted off the concrete and slipped into position.

"How come the table didn't last, but the mask will?" asked Vel, watching him.

"I'm just moving the mask from one surface to another," explained Tad. "The table was sitting in three-dimensional space, and that's a lot harder on the art." Almost as an afterthought, he waved his hand across the Sharpie sketch that had been their table. It promptly disappeared. "There. Always clean up after yourself."

"You know, that's about the only Junior Super Patriots lesson I've heard you mention," said Vel. She adjusted her ears with one hand—now definitely Velveteen again—and asked, "What made you leave?"

Tag paused. "I guess that's something I should tell you," he said, finally. "It's not worse than giving you my real identity, right?"

"Right," said Vel, encouragingly.

"Come over here." He sat down on the edge of the roof, motioning for her to join him. Vel walked over, and he pulled her down to sit beside him on the barrier than separated the rooftop from the open air. She obligingly nestled against him, resting her shoulders on his chest. There was something very comforting about that position; something very decidedly *right*. A long, comfortable silence stretched out between them before Tag finally spoke, asking, "Did they make you do those once-a-week sessions with a counselor in the West Coast Division?"

"Ugh." Vel wrinkled her nose. "Yes. They were mandatory, even. I think the only ones I ever missed were when I was kidnapped or missing or off visiting Winter. Why?"

"Visiting…never mind. I'll ask about that later. We had them in the Midwest, too. But I had a serious crush on one of my teammates–Match Girl."

"Isn't she Firecracker now? The one who does all the fire safety spots?"

"That's the one." Tag sighed. "She was, if you'll pardon the pun, seriously hot. And she barely even knew I was alive. I was being classed as a support string hero, and she only wanted to date a front liner." He laughed. "I know how sour grapes that sounds, but seriously. That's what she told me. 'You're nice and everything, but I want to go out with a guy who *matters.*'"

"What a bitch," said Vel.

"We were kids. We were all horrible to each other, just so we'd have something to do. Wasn't the West Coast Division like that?"

Velveteen quieted for a moment, remembering games of tag with Sparkle Bright, flying with Action Dude, and playing endless games of Scrabble with the Claw. "Not until the very end," she finally said, in a very small voice.

"You got lucky. We all pretty much hated each other, and having Match Girl blow me off was the last straw. I decided to spend some time sulking."

"What does all this have to do with counseling?"

"I'm getting there." Tag kissed the top of her head. "See, my new emo image didn't include making time for mandatory therapy. So I started making drawings of myself, pulling them off the paper, and sending them instead."

Velveteen tilted her head back to blink at him. "You can do that?" she asked.

"I can do that. My doubles can do anything I can do, except use my powers—I guess a drawing can't bring a drawing to life. I would make my sketches, send them to counseling, and use the extra time getting my sulk on. Only…" He hesitated, expression going a little vague. "Only it didn't work the way I thought it would. I started sleeping better. I was happier, I had an easier time understanding things, I felt…I felt *awake* for the first time in years. All the way awake, I mean, not just like I was having a sort of slow day. I reacted better."

"What?" Velveteen pulled away, twisting to fully face him. "That's what happened to me after I quit. It was like I'd been dreaming for years—"

"—and all of a sudden you wake up, and half the things that made perfect sense while you were sleeping seem absolutely horrible now." Tag looked at her gravely. "I dodged counseling for almost two months before they caught me and tried to make me go back. Lucky for me, it was the day after my eighteenth birthday. I said no."

"So they fired you?"

"Yeah. For 'inappropriate use of my powers.'" Tag's face twisted like he'd bitten into something sour. "They said it was 'conduct unbecoming of a hero,' and promised that I'd never work with a Super Patriots-sanctioned team again. So far, they've kept their word. Every time there's a big team-up, as soon as The Super Patriots are in, I'm out. But I can't help feeling like it was worth it. I think…I think I got back something I didn't even know they were taking away."

Velveteen bit her lip, worrying it between her teeth. "I think you're right," she said, finally. "And that scares me, because I left friends there when I walked away."

"They're all grown-ups now, Vel." Tag smiled wryly. "You can't make them run if they don't want to."

"I know," she admitted. "But it's hard."

"What isn't?" he asked, and leaned forward, and kissed her.

"But was it a *good* date?" Jackie pressed. She was sculpting a snowman as she talked, with her phone set on speaker and being held up by a helpful penguin. (Penguins, lacking thumbs, were always glad when she found them a job that didn't require fine motor skills.) "Did he make you feel all warm and fuzzy?"

"It was a terrifying date," said Vel, slipping out of her bathrobe and sitting down on her bed. Her house was toasty warm, just the way she wanted it to be after spending a long night on the rooftops of Portland. "But yeah, it was a good date. Sort of a wonderful date, even. He brought champagne."

"And?"

"And what?"

"Did you go all the way?"

Velma paused. "You realize that if I were anyone else in the entire world, I'd think you were asking about my sex life, right?"

"Yeah, but we both know you don't have a sex life, so we're all good. Did you do it with him?"

"Yes, Jackie, you incorrigible snoop, we did it." Velma switched the phone to her other ear, sliding further back on the mattress. "He told me his secret identity, and I told him mine."

"And? Dish, girl! Was it magical? Was it amazing? Did it rock your entire world so hard that you're still a little shaken? I demand details!"

"It was…" Vel hesitated before finally saying, "It was good. I really like him, and I think maybe I can like him even more now that I know who he really is. But it was a little scary, too, and not just because of the whole 'giving up the greatest treasure any superhero has.'"

"And now we're back to the bad sex jokes," said Jackie. She took her phone from the penguin, clicking the button to switch off the speaker before pressing it to her ear. "What else happened that scared you?"

"It was something he said." Velma scooted over until she could get herself under the covers, drawing them up to her chest before she said, "He told me why he left The Super Patriots. I think I know what's going on with them. And it's nothing good."

The two superheroines continued to talk for the better part of an hour. When they were done—when Velma's phone was off, and she was tucked safely beneath her blankets, eyes closed and curtains drawn—a patch of darkness detached itself from the shadows outside her window, retreating until it reached the street. Once there, it resolved itself into Diffuse, a shadow-manipulator who worked for The Super Patriots, Inc. She glanced back over her shoulder several times as she produced a phone from the pocket of her cloak, checking to see if she'd been followed. There was no one there.

Pressing the first button on her speed dial, she raised the phone to her ear and waited for the answer on the other end. She didn't have to wait for long.

"Sir?" she said, hesitantly. "It's Diffuse. I'm one of the agents assigned to the Velveteen situation." There was a pause as she listened, brow furrowing. When she spoke again, she sounded more confident—and more afraid. "Yes, sir. That's why I called."

"I think we have a problem."

VELVETEEN
vs.
Martinez and
Martinez v. Velveteen

IT WAS A BEAUTIFUL AFTERNOON, which, for Portland, meant "it wasn't actually raining at the moment, and the weather forecast indicated that this incredible state of affairs might continue for as much as six more hours." The sun was shining, the birds were singing, and Velveteen–official superheroine of the city of Portland, Oregon, which was arguably even weirder than the weather–was sitting on a brick retaining wall three stories above street level, watching one of the city's other superheroes beat the living crap out of a supervillain dumb enough to interrupt his date. Their date, actually. After six weeks of giggling on fire escapes and unmasking behind locked doors, she and Tag were finally taking their relationship public.

Good things about going public: not needing to pretend that they were "just friends" whenever the media was around (as if the media had ever believed them). Being able to officially list each other as approved for team-ups on the state roster. Jackie no longer threatening to "accidentally" post candid photos of them making out on every superhero discussion forum from here to Anti-Earth. Picnics in the park. The possibility that Action Dude would see a picture of the two of them making out and realize that he'd been wrong to ever let her go but ha-ha, too late now, sucker.

(Vel understood that "My ex is going to be jealous because I'm dating you" probably wasn't the basis for a long and healthy relationship. At the same time, she couldn't quite muster up the capacity to care.)

Bad things about going public: every stupid supervillain in Oregon suddenly thought that if the two of them were out together, they'd be an easy target, since they'd be so busy gazing stupidly into each other's eyes that they wouldn't notice the man sneaking up behind them with a lightning gun.

"Are you almost done?" she called, adjusting her rabbit-eared headband with one hand. They weren't quite to the "secret identities in public" stage. Sure, it meant fewer supervillains at your picnic, but it was considered gauche to bring both sides of your relationship out of the phone booth at the same time. "I don't know how long the potato salad will stay safe to eat."

"Just about there!" Tag grabbed a Sharpie from his belt, ducking away from the madly swinging supervillain long enough to scrawl a quick lasso on the nearest wall. Yanking it free, he swung the lasso overhead before looping it neatly over the villain's shoulders and pulling it tight. Finding his arms suddenly pinned to his sides, the supervillain staggered backward, and the ton of bricks Tag had sketched out a few minutes previously promptly fell on his head.

Covered head to toe in pastel brick dust, Tag turned and grinned at Velveteen. "See? The potato salad is fine."

"Will the potato salad still be fine when we finish filling out the police reports?"

Tag's grin widened. "That's why we eat while we wait."

Convincing the Portland Police Bureau to send officers to the roof was relatively easy; like any city with a healthy superhuman community, they had learned to adjust in little ways, like equipping all patrol cars with ladders and size XXXL handcuffs. The supervillain Tag had detained turned out to go by the uninspiring moniker of "Brick," which just made his brick-based defeat all the more pathetic. Velveteen sat on the retaining wall chewing idly on a cookie, and watched as Tag finished filling out the last of the forms. Her own statement–"Yup, I saw the fight, yup, he initiated super-powered combat without provocation, yup, I'll be happy to come down to the station tomorrow and sign things confirming what I saw"–had taken less than five minutes to complete. Tag, on the other hand…

Sometimes Velveteen suspected that the real downside of living the superhero life wasn't the attacks, ambushes, dimensional rifts, or constant threat of alternate universe doppelgangers trying to take over your life. It was all the damn paperwork.

After what seemed like half the afternoon, Tag handed the arresting officer's clipboard back to him, snapped a quick, joking salute, and turned to walk back to the wall where Vel was waiting. "Sorry that took so long. I hope you weren't too bored over here by yourself?"

"I had cookies," she said solemnly. "No afternoon which involves my boyfriend wearing spandex pants while beating up a supervillain, *and* comes with bonus cookies, can be entirely bad."

Tag laughed. "You know, I would worry about your standards, except that I enjoy being able to live up to them."

"That's me. I'm a cheap date because otherwise, I'd be out of every price range that I have an interest in." Velveteen slid off the wall. "Our picnic seems to be over. Care to walk a girl home?"

"That depends."

Velveteen raised an eyebrow. "On what?"

"On whether you're the girl I get to walk home. I'm sorry if this makes me sound like a slacker, but I don't really feel like escorting any damsels in distress right now." Tag reached over and took her hand, lacing his fingers through hers. "Not that I'd be averse to distressing you—or was that *undressing* you?—if that's what you had in mind for the rest of the afternoon…"

"Get me home and we'll see," said Vel, and winked. Flirting was still a little difficult, full of rules she'd never bothered to learn and pitfalls she'd never figured out how to avoid, but she was getting better. It helped that Tag had almost as little experience as she did, and was always willing to be patient with her. That probably wouldn't last forever. Hopefully, it would last long enough.

As neither of them was actually high-profile enough to have a signature vehicle (and what would hers be, anyway? The Bunny Mobile? Hugh Hefner probably already owned the trademark), and driving civilian cars while in a superheroic identity was a no-no, they actually did walk, on foot, back to the government-owned building that contained Vel's "office." Once there, they changed to their street clothes and walked to the parking garage where she'd stowed her beaten-up car for the duration of their picnic.

"You know, you could probably get a new car at this point," said Tag—Tad, now that he was out of his costume—fastening his belt.

"This one's been with me through a lot," said Vel—still Vel. Sometimes she thought Marketing hadn't even been trying, with her. "I'm going to keep it as long as it can run."

"I can understand that," said Tad.

Vel slanted him a smile. "I sort of thought you might."

When they pulled into her driveway, there was a man in a three-piece suit standing on the porch. Velma stiffened. "Do you know him?" she asked.

"No," said Tad. "He doesn't look like a supervillain…"

"Maybe he's with the homeowners association, and he's here to yell at me about weed abatement."

"Does this neighborhood have a homeowners association?"

"I sure hope so."

Velma stopped the car and got out, walking briskly toward her porch. Tad was close behind her. She heard the small "click" of a Sharpie being uncapped at the same moment that she heard the rustle of green plastic army men moving in the gardenias planted beneath her window. If her unexpected guest was looking to make trouble, he was going to be in for a nasty surprise.

He turned as Velma and Tad came walking across the lawn, his gaze focusing on Velma. "Velma Martinez?" he asked.

She stopped, frowning warily. "Yes?"

"Here." He thrust a large manila envelope toward her. She took it automatically. "You have been served. Have a nice afternoon." Not waiting for her reply, he turned and walked briskly away.

Velma opened the envelope, only dimly aware that her hands were shaking. One look at the papers inside confirmed her darkest fears. She sighed.

"Vel?" said Tad. "What's wrong?"

"My parents." Velma wiped the tears from her cheek with the back of one hand as she looked back toward her boyfriend. "They're suing me for emotional distress and financial support."

"…oh," said Tag.

"Yeah. Oh."

Superhuman law is a complicated thing, and one which has led to more than a few vicious legal battles, all of them fought by men and women who might lack superpowers, but possess law degrees. (While superhuman lawyers exist, they have thus far been required to recuse themselves from cases relating directly to superhuman law, for fear of conflict of interest.) How do you try a child whose superpower manifests on the playground of their daycare? Is breaking a statue which used to be a living human, prior to meeting Medusa, vandalism or manslaughter? The list goes on, and the cases only get stranger.

For the most part, American superhuman law has been shaped by the intervention of the largest superhuman special interest lobby, The Super Patriots, Inc. They have reliably hired lawyers, provided scientific data, and organized focus groups to confirm public opinions relating to the more complicated theoretical issues. The Super Patriots, Inc. have even gone out of their way to seek rulings on specific situations before those situations can arise, demonstrating a level of foresight and consideration which is truly admirable in an organization of their size and standing.

At the same time, some people have suggested that there might be a less altruistic motive behind the involvement of The Super Patriots, Inc. with the creation of superhero law. After all, those voices argue, at the end of the day, The Super Patriots, Inc. retains control of the majority of the world's superhumans. Thanks to their careful intervention, it is not murder when a supervillain is killed in conflict with a registered hero (the estate of Harmageddon v. Sweet Pea), it is neither theft nor willful destruction of property if, during a superhuman conflict, a registered hero makes use of civilian cars, fences, or other objects to prevent further damages (the city of St. Paul v. Dairy Keen), and superhumans cannot be declared legally dead until they have remained both biologically and etherically inactive for a period of no less than seven years. (It should be noted that, during this seven-year period, their merchandising rights and trademarks will remain active and under the custodianship of their estate. In ninety percent of all cases covered by this ruling, the estate is managed by The Super Patriots, Inc.)

At the end of the day, the fact remains that superhuman law is essential: without restrictions and guidelines, the sheer number of superhumans in North America would present a clear and present danger to the unpowered population. Only through agreed-upon legislation can people with the kind of power that they possess be kept under any form of control. Which still begs the question of what will happen on the day when, inevitably, heroes and villains alike reject the laws which have been used, for better or for worse, to reduce them to a more human level.

The lawyers have not yet had a satisfactory response to this issue. The Super Patriots, Inc. has no comment.

"You don't have to do this, you know," commented Jackie, lounging on Vel's bed like it was her personal property. The bright orange bedspread—a bargain-bin special from the Bloomington Coat Factory—clashed jarringly with her pale blue skin. That was almost reassuring, at least as far as Vel was concerned. Seeing Jackie dressed in a three-piece suit, with makeup that didn't look like it had been applied with a paintbrush, was disconcerting enough. Seeing Jackie on top of something that went with her skin tone might have been enough to trigger a panic attack. "All you have to do is come with me to the North Pole. There's no way this lawsuit will hold water there."

"Don't be stupid," said the Princess. She continued working on Vel's hair, trying to get it to layer properly under the band of her formal bunny ears. They were only half the height of her usual accessories, and made of brown velvet that matched her formal uniform, but that didn't make them easy to style around. "She'd never be able to come back. Frivolous or not, it's a lawsuit brought against a superhuman by members of the normal public. She runs, she's guilty, and she's stuck with your frozen blue butt forever."

Velveteen didn't say anything. She just kept staring at her reflection, watching without comment or complaint as the Princess and her team of woodland fashionistas turned her into something that would be appropriate for a court of law. Behind her, Jackie and the Princess continued their good-natured bickering, and only someone who really knew them, or was really listening, would have heard the manic edge beneath their laughter. They'd been Vel's friends since she was still young enough to cry for the parents who'd abandoned her. It didn't matter that those parents had sold her to the highest bidder just as soon as they got the chance; they were her *parents*. Vel's friends remembered listening to her crying through the walls when she thought she was alone.

As ways for her parents to come back into her life went, this one certainly left something to be desired.

Finally, the Princess stepped back, motioning for the squirrels manning the hairspray can to do the same. She looked at Velveteen critically for a long moment. Then she nodded. "All right," she said. "I think you're ready to face the judge."

Velveteen didn't say anything. The Princess sighed.

"Sweetie, unless you want to go hide in a holiday, you're going to have to deal with this, and you're going to have to deal with it today," she said gently, putting a hand on Velveteen's shoulder. "I know it's hard. But it's something you have to do."

Jackie remained uncharacteristically quiet, letting the Princess do the talking for a change. Out of the three of them, she was uncomfortably aware that she was the only one who was still on speaking terms with her parents. Vel's had handed her over to The Super Patriots, Inc. at the first opportunity they got. The Princess had sought emancipation as soon as it became clear that one of the side effects of her fairy tale abilities was the universe's sudden conviction that she should be an orphan. It was cut all ties with her parents or bury them, and she chose the option that left as many people as possible alive. Both of Jackie's parents were superheroes with winter-themed powers. The closest she'd ever come to losing them was the time she got left out in the sun at the Minnesota State Fair, and her mother had been able to fix that with fifteen seconds of deep freeze and a whole lot of frozen hot chocolate.

She didn't get along with her parents most of the time, but at least she still *had* them. That was something she had to admit that she didn't share with her friends. And if she was being completely honest with herself, it was something she hoped she'd never understand.

Several minutes ticked by before Velveteen took a shuddering breath, finally pulling away from the Princess. "Okay," she said, and stood. "Let's go to court."

The case of Harmageddon v. Sweet Pea determined that, when a superhero is charged with a crime that does not equate directly to supervillainy, they cannot be forced to reveal their secret identity without just cause. (The case of Lindsey Thomas v. the State of Nevada further determined that a superhero charged with a crime that does not equate directly to supervillainy in their civilian identity cannot be "outed" by the courts. While many considered Neon Lass a second-rate heroine, she received a first-rate payout when the jury found in her favor.)

Because of these, and other, precedents, it was Velveteen, not Velma Martinez, who stepped out of the Princess's enchanted pumpkin carriage. It was Velveteen, not Velma Martinez, who walked past the inevitable crowd of paparazzi that assembled for every trial involving a known superhero (although she did have to wonder, grimly, who had tipped them off that she'd be arriving at this courthouse, at this time). And it was Velveteen, not Velma Martinez, who stopped at the courthouse door, next to two people in suits that looked very much like hers, minus the bunny ears, domino mask, and pockets full of little green army men.

"I don't know what to call you," said the man, somewhat awkwardly.

"How about 'late with the check'?" suggested the woman, and glared at Velveteen.

Velveteen was too tired to glare back.

Despite the fact that her—that Velma's—parents had been extorting money from her since she walked away from The Super Patriots, Inc., she had managed to see them only twice since the day when she was essentially sold into corporate service. The first time had been the day she graduated from training to the junior team, when Marketing brought them to the compound for "a touching family reunion." At the time, she'd thought they were being stupid, assuming that she would ever want to see her parents again. After a few more years, she'd realized that they were being cruel, but very, very smart. Remind your junior heroes what you took them away from, and they'll be all the more loyal to what you've given them instead. It was clever. It was manipulative. It was exactly the sort of thing she'd come to expect from Marketing…

…and that was why the second time had happened. When she quit the team, they said she could call anyone she wanted to come and pick her up, but that she wasn't going to travel anywhere on the company's dime. Those perks were over. And Velma, back in full civilian clothing for the first time since she was a little girl, asked them to call her parents.

Her parents came—of course they came, when The Super Patriots, Inc. calls, you come—but their reunion had been nothing like Velma could have envisioned. That was why she was able to look at them now and not feel abandoned, or betrayed, or used. All those feelings had died the day her mother's open palm struck her hard across the cheek while her father looked silently on, both of them hating her for not being the meal ticket they'd been promised for so long.

"Velveteen," she said, quietly. "You call me Velveteen. You don't have the right to call me anything but that."

For a moment, it looked like her mother wanted to argue with her; wanted to make some impassioned statement about how, having given Velma life, she had the right to call her whatever she wanted to. The moment passed. And with a final heartbroken look back at the Princess's carriage, Velma "Velveteen" Martinez turned and followed her parents into the Portland City Justice Building, to find out what horrors her future might hold.

* * *

Velveteen sat in the holding room in her uncomfortable court suit, trying to calm her nerves with breathing exercises. She was never going to be serene—not here, not now, not with her parents sitting on the other side of the room glaring daggers in her direction—but she didn't want to risk losing control of her powers while she waited for her case to be called before the judge. A superhero who loses control in court is a superhero who's about to lose everything, even if the case has nothing to do with powers beyond human ken.

"Always remember that the people can love you and fear you in the same breath," that was what the woman from Legal had said, when Marketing brought her in during Vel's second year. "They want to worship you. They also want to see you fall. Never give them an opening, because if you do, they will take you all the way down, and they'll tell themselves that you deserved it. And so you're aware…" Her smile had contained too many teeth, like a shark in a three-piece suit and sensible heels.

It was her closing words that echoed in Velveteen's ears now, making her feel like she really had the super-hearing Marketing had always hinted might be a part of her power set. "If you give them that opening, as far as the company is concerned, you *will* deserve whatever you get. We may bail you out, because you represent a substantial investment. But we will never forget that you failed us."

Then the woman from Legal had turned and walked away, leaving Vel's tiny class of budding superheroes staring after her in stunned, terrified silence. Maybe that had been the goal. Intentional or not, it felt like that silence had never really been broken; it had been waiting all this time, lurking in the back of Velveteen's mind as it waited for the opportunity to pounce.

She had left this opening. She had stopped paying her parents their blackmail money when she left California—and that's what it had been, that's what it had *always* been, blackmail draped in a veil of filial responsibility and parental concern—and since those payments had always been intended to keep them from going to the tabloids with her secret identity, she hadn't even considered resuming the payouts when she became an honest-to-God superhero again. The thing she'd been paying them to avoid had happened. What was the worst that could happen?

"The worst that could happen" was a contract she'd signed when she was twelve years old, granting her parents a percentage of every payment she received for superheroic deeds. Forever. It was all part of the generous package offered by The Super Patriots, Inc. when trying to convince parents to sign their children over to the corporation. "The worst that could happen" was a lawsuit demanding that she make those payments, with interest, as well as the "sleeper" payments that were meant to accrue when events outside the recipient's control rendered their supporting superhero unable to meet the full amount.

Fifteen percent of everything she'd made since arriving in Portland, and fifteen thousand dollars a year for every year when she hadn't been on active duty. Plus interest, of course. Mustn't forget the interest.

"Fucked-up times infinity plus three," she muttered, earning a stern look from her lawyer (chosen for her by Celia Morgan, which meant that the pleasant-faced man in the Brooks Brothers suit could probably eat corporate law for breakfast) and a bewildered look from her father. Her mother didn't look at her at all.

They sat there for another twenty minutes, waiting for their turn to stand in front of the judge while the lawyers explained why she both did (her parent's lawyer) and did not (her own lawyer) owe a great deal of money. Schrodinger's crime had been committed, and until the lawyer brought the gavel down, she was neither innocent nor guilty. It was a difficult place to be. Not for the first time, Vel found herself feeling sorry for both Schrodinger and The Cat, whose heroic exploits were all-too-often disrupted by the question of which, if either of them, was currently the dead one. Death, War, Famine, and Conquest might be the traditional Horsemen of the Apocalypse, but Vel was pretty sure that Uncertainty, Insecurity, Waiting, and Corporate Law were even worse.

Her lawyer glanced over at her, and offered what was probably intended as a comforting smile. It wasn't his fault that he smiled like a robot that was still trying to figure out its human emotion module. (He probably wasn't a robot. Probably. If he was, well, that was fine. She wasn't opposed to mecha-Americans, and they were allowed to practice law. She just hoped that his law modules were more up-to-date than his emotional ones.) "It's going to be all right," he said quietly. "This is a frivolous lawsuit. The judge will see that."

Unless the judge disagreed with that assessment. Or had a supervillain somewhere in the family, tucked quietly away from the public eye. Or *was* a supervillain who hadn't been unmasked yet–it had happened before, it would happen again, and it would be just her luck if it happened to her. Or hated superhumans, regardless of alignment, and wanted to prove the woman from Legal right. Frivolous wouldn't matter if the judge wanted to see her behind bars.

"Would Mr. and Ms. Martinez and, ah, Velveteen please come with me?" asked a bailiff, sounding uncertain. Vel's lawyer gave her another smile, this one slightly more reassuring than the first, and they stood, all five of them, and followed the bailiff to the judge's quarters.

It could have been worse. That was what she kept trying to tell herself as she stood, ramrod-straight, in her formal uniform and waited for the judge to decide her fate. It could have been a question of facts, which would have meant a jury, would have meant more media, and would have meant her face splashed across every super-focused tabloid in the world. Instead, it was a question of the law, and that meant that it was the judge, just the judge, who was going to decide everything.

On second thought, maybe that wasn't the better option.

"Let me see if I understand," said Judge Kuhn, slowly. He was a round-faced man with thinning black hair and equally round glasses perched on the end of his nose. He didn't look unfriendly. That was a plus. He didn't look friendly, either, but Vel was long past the point of wishing for everything she wanted. "You're suing this young woman for back wages on the basis of a contract you signed on her behalf with The Super Patriots when she was twelve years of age."

"Yes, Your Honor," said Ms. Martinez.

"Contracts of this type have been standard within The Super Patriots, Inc. since they first began employing and training child heroes, Your Honor," said the Martinez's lawyer. Velveteen couldn't remember his name, possibly because she didn't want to. "Child labor laws, and simple ethics, made it clear that we would need a way to pay these children for their time."

"This is true. And while I won't challenge the need for contracts to keep our younger protectors being paid, and to reimburse their parents for the pain of separation," the glance Judge Kuhn shot at the Martinezes made it clear that he didn't think they were experiencing any pain over being separated from their only daughter; Vel felt a surge of hope in the pit of her stomach, "I will note that these contracts are intended for *younger* heroes."

"Your Honor, the contract stated that a portion of Velveteen's earnings would be given to her parents for every year in which she exercised her powers."

"That's an extremely broad interpretation of what seems to me to be a very basic and straightforward contract," said Judge Kuhn. "This promises the hero's parents a yearly stipend for the duration of their career with The Super Patriots, Inc."

The lawyer smiled. Like the woman from Legal, he seemed to have more teeth than his head should have been capable of holding. "If you'll look at the language, Your Honor, you'll see that in actuality, she's pledging to pay her percentage for the duration of her superhero career, regardless of whether she remains in the employ of The Super Patriots, Inc."

"So she owes us," said Ms. Martinez, more stridently than she should have. She glared around her husband at Velveteen, who managed, barely, not to cringe away. "She's our daughter, and she's supposed to be supporting us."

"I believe that normally the arrangement goes in the other direction, at least until a child's eighteenth birthday," said Judge Kuhn. "Regardless, this contract hinges on two clear concepts. The first is that an eleven-year-old child can sign a legally binding document and be expected to abide by its terms into adulthood. The second is that 'career with The Super Patriots, Inc.' and 'superhero career' are exactly and unquestionably the same thing."

"I move that both those concepts are provably false," said Velveteen's lawyer.

"You would, wouldn't you?" shot back Ms. Martinez. "Like she'd even need a lawyer if she wasn't trying to cheat her poor parents out of house and home."

For a moment, it looked like Judge Kuhn was about to lose his temper. Then he took a deep breath, and said, "The first is irrelevant in this instance—something I am frankly relieved to say, since I have no real interest in spending the rest of my career fighting off challenges by The Super Patriots, Inc. legal department. In regards to the second, I remind you of the case of Liberty Belle v. The Super Patriots. She was able to resume her heroic career outside the corporation, as it was based entirely on inborn abilities, and not on augmentation by The Super Patriots, Inc. It is the opinion of the court that the individual known commonly as 'Velveteen' did in good faith retire for several years, during which time her contract with The Super Patriots, Inc. expired. She is under no further financial obligation. We're done here."

"But—" began Ms. Martinez.

Mr. Martinez clamped his wife's hand firmly in his. "Thank you, Your Honor," he said.

"You're all dismissed," said Judge Kuhn.

"Thank you," whispered Velveteen, and turned, and bolted, with her lawyer walking close behind.

Jackie and the Princess were waiting for her on the Justice Building steps. Pigeons blanketed everything, including the photographers foolish enough not to run when they saw the way the weather was turning. The gooey, pigeon crap-based weather. "Well?" asked Jackie, when she saw Vel come bounding down the steps. "How did it go?"

"We won," said Velveteen. "I'm in the clear."

"Oh, honey, thank Hans Christian Andersen," said the Princess, and threw her arms around Velveteen's shoulders. "I knew it would work out."

"Vel?"

Slowly, all three heroines turned to see Mr. Martinez standing on the steps behind them, looking anxious. His wife was nowhere to be seen.

Velveteen pulled away from the Princess, asking, "What?"

"I just wanted to…well, I'm sorry that we did this, and I wanted to…" He hesitated before asking, "Are you happy, Vel? Is this what you wanted?"

A superhero's life. The thing she'd been running away from since the day she turned eighteen. The mask she swore she'd never wear again…

Velveteen smiled. "Yeah, Dad. I am."

"Good." With that, he turned and walked away, leaving the three to blink after him.

As always, it was Jackie who spoke first. "What the hell was that?"

"I think it was closure," said Velveteen, slowly.

"Miracles happen," said the Princess. "Now come on, honey. Let's get you home."

The woman from Legal stood in front of the CEO's desk, her eyes fixed straight ahead at the wall. "I told you there were no guarantees," she said. "It was a shaky case, mostly intended to rattle her, and possibly cause her some financial distress. I never promised anything."

"Neither did I," replied the silky voice of the CEO of The Super Patriots, Inc. "For example, right now, I'm not promising you that anyone will hear your screams."

In point of fact, the screams went on for quite some time. No one heard them at all.

VELVETEEN
vs.
The Alternate Timeline

VELVETEEN STUMBLED INTO HER BEDROOM somewhere between midnight and two o'clock in the morning, muscles aching from a long night of chasing would-be evil-doers over rooftops and through the streets of Portland, her left thumb still throbbing a little from where she'd slammed it in the car door, her domino mask still covering her eyes. She managed, barely, to yank off her rabbit-ear headband and remove her uniform boots before collapsing onto the bed, already half-asleep.

The teddy bears and stuffed rabbits who kept her bedroom from devolving into a state of primal chaos slipped off their shelves and crossed to the bed, where they tugged the blankets out from under her limp body and tucked her in. Vel mumbled something in her sleep, one hand sleepily slapping the covers. The various plush toys exchanged what could only be described as a look, despite their lack of functioning optical nerves. The battered plush rabbit who usually directed the bedroom toys when Vel couldn't do it herself paused a moment before pointing to one of the older bears. The bear clapped its paws together with an air of definite delight, then ran and slid itself beneath Vel's questing hand. She made a small, satisfied sound, pulled the bear close, and sank deeper into sleep.

The plush toys continued cleaning the room, dragging the discarded pieces of Velveteen's costume into the closet, using the small hand broom to sweep up the mud she had tracked onto the carpet. Vel slept through it all…until just before five o'clock in the morning, when the toys abruptly stopped moving and fell over, assuming the traditional positions of inanimate things waiting for someone to come along and play with them. In a way, that was exactly what they were.

The last to stop moving was the teddy bear who had been chosen as Vel's companion for the night. It didn't move under its own power, exactly, but as the mattress sprang back into place, it rolled out of the empty bed and onto the floor, where it stopped just under the edge of the blanket, half-hidden from view. Its blank button eyes stared sightlessly up at the ceiling.

The air in the house hung heavy, still, and undisturbed. There was nothing to disturb it. Velveteen was gone.

The existence of alternate timelines was posited long before the existence of superheroes was confirmed, although "alternate reality science" didn't really acquire a strong following in academic circles until the appearance of the first known visitor from another timeline. Alter-Nate (whose powers consisted mostly of crossing dimensional borders when he was trying to cross streets) opened the door to countless research studies, frivolous grants, and serious discussions of whether turning left would lead to a more positive future than turning right. Alter-Nate himself was only present for the first six months or so of the debate before he went out for coffee and vanished back into the ether. He has not been sighted in our dimension, egotistically referred to as "Earth A," since that day. It is generally hoped that he eventually made it back to his home reality, or at least managed to get himself that cup of coffee.

Since that time, several hundred alternate realities have been documented and cataloged, ranging from dimensions of pure fantasy, the seasonal universes, upward of fifty places claiming to be Hell, an equal number of places claiming to be Heaven and, of course, the inevitable variant timelines. Some stem from simple differences, like the classic "what if you turned left instead of right?" (the "which came first, the chicken or the egg" question of alternate reality science). Others are more complicated, worlds where mammals never evolved, or where superpowers never manifested in the human race.

Statistically speaking, every superhuman will encounter at least one parallel dimension, alternate continuity, or externally manipulated reality during the course of their career. This number is naturally influenced by the lifestyles of the superhumans in question: someone like Jackie Frost, who lives in one world and regularly commutes to another, will encounter substantially more variance in her personal reality than someone like Dairy Keen, who has never voluntarily left the state of Minnesota. There is also the fact that alternate worlds apparently call to each other. If a wormhole opens next to someone who has never left their original reality and someone who has left that reality dozens of times, the odds are good that the more seasoned traveler will be the one pulled into a dimension beyond their understanding. This may be because of some residual radiation left by the crossing. It may also be because the universe has a sick sense of humor.

All Earth A superhumans who undergo training with The Super Patriots, Inc. are required to pass Heroing 101, including units on Alternate Reality Survival and Recognizing a Dreamscape in Ten Easy Steps. There has been, as yet, no evidence to support the claim that these units increase the chances of Earth A heroes surviving in another reality. There has also been no evidence to support the claim that these units get Earth A heroes killed. Given the alternative, most heroes try to remember their lessons. It's the only way to be sure.

Velveteen woke slowly, lured back into a doze several times by the optimally-firm mattress and the perfectly-layered nest of blankets that she had built around herself. She was dozing off for the third time when a male arm was draped around her waist, pulling her firmly backward.

Normally, that sort of thing would have been answered by immediate violence, followed a split second later by actually waking up. But something about the situation—the shape of the arm, the smell of the air in the room, even the mattress underneath them—was so impossibly familiar that Vel's sleeping mind insisted this was just another dream, and allowed her to stay almost entirely limp.

"Vel."

"Mmm."

"Vel."

"Mmm-mmm."

"Vel, honey, you have to wake up. Morning call is in a little over an hour." The owner of the arm leaned over to kiss her cheek, and that was familiar too, so familiar that Velma finally opened her eyes, staring into the dimly-lit room. From where she was, she could see a dresser, a laundry hamper, and a metal shelf packed with toys. She couldn't make out any details, but what she could see was enough to make one thing extremely clear: this wasn't her room.

Slowly, feeling like the world was getting ready to shatter around her, Velma rolled over. Action Dude–no, Aaron; he wasn't wearing his mask, and he was always Aaron when they were alone together, it was something they had both insisted on–looked at her, confusion and concern in those big blue eyes of his. He wasn't wearing a shirt. For one guilty moment, Vel allowed her gaze to drift downward. She hadn't seen Aaron like this since they were both seventeen, after all, and well. You can't blame a girl for dreaming…

No, Vel. Bad Vel. Stop it, she thought firmly, wrenching her eyes back up to his face. That didn't help as much as she would have wanted it to. Not with him looking at her like that. "Aaron?"

"Honey, are you okay? Were you having a bad dream or something?" The concern in Aaron's eyes grew stronger. "I can call Medical if you want me to."

"No!" She almost shouted the word, sitting up at the same time. The blankets went with her, revealing Aaron's pajama pants. They were blue, printed with his Action Dude insignia, and a small war broke out in the back of her mind, between the thought *Thank God he's wearing pajamas* and the thought *I wish to hell he wasn't.* "I mean, uh, no. No, I don't need to see Medical. I'm fine. I'm totally fine."

"Wow." Aaron sat up in turn, frowning at her. "The last time you said 'I'm fine' and sounded that fake about it was after your last trip to the Autumn Country." He paused. "Honey, you didn't–I mean, they didn't–last night–"

Oddly, she had no trouble at all guessing what he was trying to say. "No. Halloween didn't kidnap me last night. I haven't heard from the holiday in years." She looked down at herself. She was wearing a burgundy nightie with lace trim, something she recognized as being as close to "costume pajamas" as Marketing could get without infringing on Playboy. Somehow, it wasn't a shock to see the wedding ring on her left hand. She raised her arm, looking at it, and sighed deeply.

That was the real problem with alternate timelines. Sometimes, when you got right down to it, you found out that you really wanted to stay.

"Aaron, I'm not sure just how to say this…"

"You think you've fallen into an alternate timeline, and you're trying to figure out how to tell me without pissing me off," said Aaron amiably. Vel turned to stare at him. He smiled at her, concern still hanging in his eyes. "This is the third time this week, honey. I'm sort of getting used to it."

"What?"

Aaron offered her that little half-smile that always made her heart jump up into her throat, and said, "We were fighting Dr. Darwin ten days ago. He was planning to use some sort of revision ray to change the history of the planet, so that humans never managed to invade some pristine ecosystem or other. I mean, he was in full-on monologue mode, it was kinda hard to follow, you know?"

"Uh-huh," said Vel. Her mouth was completely dry and her head was starting to spin. She wanted to believe what he was saying. She wanted to believe it *so bad.* "What happened?"

"I managed to knock him over, but he grabbed the gun as he was going down. He was going to shoot me. You didn't have any toys big enough to interfere, and so you did it yourself, because you are a crazy, wonderful, mind-shatteringly impulsive woman. You jumped in the way of the beam—"

"Why is it always a beam?" Vel mumbled.

Aaron heard her, because he smiled, and kept talking: "—and got yourself shot. You were out for a day. I was pretty much useless that whole time. Medical actually said they'd have to sedate me if I didn't stop accidentally breaking chairs. Your..." He faltered, smile fading. "You nearly died, Vel. Okay? You nearly left me. And when you woke up, you thought you were from a different reality. It faded after a little while, but it gave me a pretty major scare. Medical thinks Dr. Darwin's ray sort of scrambled your internal clock, made you start living out lives you never lived."

The unit she'd taken on Alternate Reality Survival so damn many years ago told her that every alternate reality was like this; they all wanted to be treated as the real timeline, the real universe. Velma looked into Aaron's eyes, and realized there was one thing the unit hadn't done anything to prepare her for, not really:

She didn't give a damn whether this was the real timeline or not. "I guess it's a good thing that all my lives involve you, huh?" she asked, and got onto her knees so that she could crawl over to his side of the bed. Aaron grinned up at her, relief evident in his expression. And for the first time in so long that it hurt, Vel leaned down and kissed him.

"How's that sense of reality?" asked Action Dude as they walked down to the hall toward the briefing room for morning call. He was wearing his standard field uniform, and this early in the morning, it was almost bright enough to hurt her eyes.

Not that her own costume was all that much better. It was still burgundy and brown—thank God; she didn't know how she would have handled finding out that she was now the kind of heroine who ran around dressed in neon, or worse, pink—but it was a *lot* skimpier than she remembered, with a high-cut leotard over tights replacing her old unitard and an inexplicable oval cutout running down the length of her back. At least her headband and domino mask were the same as always. She wasn't sure what she would have done if they'd changed.

"Shaky, but I can fake it," she said. "I don't want to go to Medical."

"Good. With as much time as you've spent with them since you got shot, I'm not sure my heart could take it." Action Dude gave her hand a squeeze. "We'll go over things once we finish checking in. In the meanwhile, just smile and nod."

More and more, it was starting to feel like she'd never left The Super Patriots, Inc. "I'm good at smiling and nodding," she said.

Aaron smiled. "I know you are," he said, and led her inside.

The rest of The Super Patriots, West Coast Division were already seated, waiting to begin. Uncertainty was looking up at the ceiling, his eyes mostly focused, for values of "focused" that included "clearly looking at something that wasn't in the room." Imagineer was gazing moonily at Mechamation, who was gazing with equal mooniness at the conference phone. Jack O'Lope was cleaning one of his guns, while Firefly played tic-tac-toe with herself in a grid of light that she'd drawn in the air.

"Where's—" Velveteen began, and caught herself before she could finish the sentence, changing it in the middle to, "—Marketing? I thought we were supposed to be getting started." Inwardly, she finished her original question: *Where's Sparkle Bright? She should be here. This is morning call. She's never missed a morning call.* Oh, God. What if her still being part of the team somehow meant that Yelena was dead? Stranger things have happened in the multiverse. Velveteen realized that she was shaking. She tightened her grip on Action Dude's hand.

"I was waiting for you to assemble," said a voice behind her. Action Dude all but dragged her to the table. As they turned to sit she saw the man from Marketing, impeccably groomed (they always were) and looking far too awake for this hour of the morning, standing in the doorway. "Welcome, Super Patriots. What is your goal today?"

"To preserve and protect the American Way," chorused the gathering heroes, even Uncertainty, who was still staring at nothing. Old habits died hard: Velveteen answered with the rest of them.

"How will you do that?"

"By using our powers to their full potential to defend the citizens of the planet Earth against all threats that might rise to harm them." It was actually a little comforting to recite the old mantra with so many other voices. Like coming home.

The call-and-response went on for quite a while. Velveteen couldn't shake the feeling that the man from Marketing was watching her with a special degree of intensity, like he was waiting for her to slip up. She didn't. Not once. Her timeline had used the same series of questions and answers to open their meetings, and there were some things you never forgot, no matter how hard you tried. Some things sank all the way down to the bone.

Once the preliminaries were over, the man from Marketing got straight to business, presenting a rapid-fire list of sales numbers, upcoming events, and suggestions for improvements. Velveteen let herself glaze out after he got started. She smiled and nodded every time he looked at her, and that seemed to do what she wanted it to; he didn't look any less suspicious, but he didn't look any more suspicious, either.

After half an hour, he encouraged them to "Go out and do good!" before calling the meeting over. Pieces of paper with everyone's patrol assignments had discreetly appeared on a small table next to the door. Velveteen grabbed one as she followed Action Dude out of the room, and was pleased to see that they were supposed to go on patrol together. It made sense, since he could fly and she couldn't, but it was still nice. The last thing she wanted at the moment was to go out on the streets alone.

If the Marketing Department was still up to their old tricks, the bedroom was almost certainly bugged. So Velveteen didn't say anything until they were both in their patrol uniforms (Aaron with a slightly shorter cape, her with slightly sturdier high heels on her boots, and didn't *that* say something about the gender of the people doing their costume designs) and on their way to midtown. Action Dude flew with her cradled in his arms like a starlet from a 1950s monster movie, a sort of casual helplessness that could only be achieved through remarkable core strength on the part of the woman being carried.

(That was something else about this timeline. Apparently, never leaving The Super Patriots, West Coast Division meant living a largely carb-free lifestyle. She'd never been exactly heavy, but she remembered carrying a few extra pounds, thanks to lots and lots of fast food and truck stop dinners. Now she felt like she could crush walnuts with her abdominal muscles. It was a bizarre sensation, although it definitely made wearing the spandex a lot easier on her nerves.)

Once they were far enough from the building that they probably weren't being monitored, Velveteen cleared her throat, leaned in close so that Aaron would be able to hear her above the wind, and asked, "Where's Sparks? Why wasn't she there today?"

Action Dude nearly dropped her.

Several minutes later—after a quick recovery and a *lot* of apologizing—the two of them were standing on a nearby rooftop, Velveteen adjusting her headband and staring fixedly at her husband (ex-boyfriend) as she waited for him to answer her question.

Finally, slowly, Action Dude said, "Vel…in the timeline you think that you…in the timeline you remember right now, what happened to Yelena?"

Well, Aaron, after I found out that you'd been cheating on me with her, she kicked my ass in the locker room, and I quit the team. You're currently engaged to her. You're co-leaders of the team. I probably won't be invited to the wedding. Velveteen swallowed her words, instead saying, carefully, "She's still with the team. I'm not."

Oddly enough, Action Dude looked relieved. "So you're not super-close anymore. You don't, like, spend afternoons drinking coffee and talking about combat tactics."

"No. We haven't done that sort of thing in years."

"Good. That makes this a little easier." Action Dude took a deep breath. "Sparkle Bright's a supervillain, Vel. She quit the team right after her eighteenth birthday. We've been trying to track her ever since."

For the moment, Vel chose to ignore the Marketing-endorsed branding of any superhuman who quit the team as a supervillain and focused on the important part: "She's alive?"

"She was as of last year, when she stopped Marketing from bringing home a nine-year-old metamorph. Don't worry," he added, before she could show alarm. "The kid's fine. Said Sparks just wanted to talk to him about his 'options.' The bad guys are recruiting younger and younger these days."

Or maybe Yelena just remembered what it was like to be sold by the people you trusted into a future that you weren't prepared for.

"I'm glad the kid's okay," she said. "Thanks for telling me. I didn't want to ask during morning call."

"That was a good call. Marketing's been nervous since you got zapped." Action Dude glanced over his shoulder, and for the first time, Vel realized that *he* was nervous. "Honey, you gotta try to come back to me, okay? We can call for help if you really think we need it. White Rabbit or somebody, one of the time manipulators. Maybe they'd be able to get you stable."

"Maybe Jackie could help," said Vel, carefully. "She can borrow her mother's magic mirror sometimes. That might let her look into my heart and see if there's something lodged there."

Action Dude hesitated before saying, "That might not be the best idea. We're not on such good terms with Santa's Village right now."

Velveteen blinked. "We're not on good terms with *Santa?*" she said, disbelieving. "But he's…he's *Santa.* Everybody who isn't on the Naughty list is on good terms with Santa. And Jackie's the one who taught us both how to ice skate."

"Well, sure. But Marketing says it sends a bad message if we associate with them."

For a long moment, Velveteen just stared at him. Then, slowly, she said, "Santa refused to take Yelena off the Nice list, didn't he?"

Action Dude nodded.

"Okay." Velveteen shook her head. "Okay. Come on. Let's get back on our patrol."

Expression utterly relieved, Action Dude spread his arms and let Velveteen hop back into then, curling herself against his chest. He launched them both into the air and soared across the city without saying another word, and if he noticed the thoughtful expression on her face, he was smart enough not to say anything about it. She was just living out a timeline that never happened, that was all. She'd get over it soon. She'd come back to him, and everything would be just the way that it was supposed to be.

His Vel always came back to him.

Patrol was reasonably uneventful: they foiled a mugging, helped a little old lady cross the street, and eventually joined up with Jack O'Lope and Imagineer to defeat Cinemaniac, who was trying to bring the stars of a midnight B-movie festival to life. There was something deeply soothing about using Slinky dogs and teddy bears to bring down Godzilla, and Velveteen was almost willing to forget about the absence of Sparkle Bright by the time they made it back to headquarters. No one had been seriously injured, although they'd all been battered enough to make for some exciting pictures. Even without recent Marketing refreshers, Velveteen found it second nature to pose for the photographers who swarmed the aftermath. Some of those shots would probably make the front page of the local paper.

Afterward, she ate a quiet dinner with Aaron, just the two of them in the dining room attached to their quarters. They didn't talk much, and they didn't need to. She hadn't been with Aaron in her real timeline (if that was the real timeline; why was this one any less likely?) in years, and somehow, that didn't matter, because he was the one, he was her first love and her last love and what were a few years in the face of that?

"What's on the deck for tomorrow?" she asked, over dessert (lavender lemon sorbet, low in calories but high enough in flavor to make up for it).

"We're on backup, so it's a training day," said Aaron. "I think you have a meeting with Marketing to discuss seasonal costume options in the afternoon, and then we have the evening free, as long as no cosmic threats try to undermine the fabric of reality or anything."

"So business as usual," Vel said.

Aaron smiled, relief evident. "Exactly. Business as usual."

They left the dishes on the table. The Super Patriots cleaning service would clear them away in the middle of the night, leaving a fresh hot breakfast in their place—one of the many benefits of living where you worked, and working for a corporation powerful enough to buy and sell small countries. Then they went into the bedroom, and rubbed each other's bruises, and yes, did more than that, once their clothes were scattered on the floor like leaves. Any guilt Velma might have felt was soothed by knowing that Aaron wasn't really cheating on anyone; not really, not technically. She put thoughts of Tag firmly aside. He wasn't here. Maybe he'd never been here. Maybe he was a creation of Dr. Darwin's ray. And even if he wasn't...

Even if he wasn't, she'd always known she didn't love him. She loved Aaron, and Aaron was here, in front of her, looking at her the way he looked at her when they were both teenagers and thought that this was going to be their future. Once upon a time, this was the only future she could imagine. If she took a night to enjoy it, who could blame her?

Aaron fell asleep with his arm wrapped loosely around her waist, looking totally at peace with the world. Velma waited until she was sure he wasn't going to wake up, counting the slow rise and fall of his breathing. It was a soothing sound. Part of her just wanted to relax, to follow him into sleep, and admit that this was the better timeline. This was the place where she belonged.

She couldn't do that. Moving slowly, so as not to wake him, Velma slipped out from under Aaron's arm. He didn't stir. "I love you," she whispered, and stood. It only took a moment to grab her night patrol costume out of the closet, and then she slipped out the door, and was gone.

Sneaking out of The Super Patriots, West Coast Division headquarters was easier than Velveteen expected it to be, maybe because no one in their right mind would be sneaking *out*. It would be a lot harder to sneak back in. Hopefully, she could get Aaron to cover for her, the way they all used to cover for each other when they were kids…although it was mostly Yelena doing the covering in those days, wasn't it? Yelena and her endless bolts of light. Sparkle Bright wasn't a supervillain. It just wasn't possible. Something else was going on.

Velveteen hopped rooftop to rooftop until she reached her destination: the roof of Technophilia, a nightclub for technological superhumans of all types. Everyone knew that heroes and villains alike frequented the place, and no one did anything about it, because a supervillain who was too drunk to stand wasn't going to be robbing any banks, and a superhero who wanted to be left alone to play Halo wasn't going to be righting any wrongs. Almost all the major power sets had bars like Technophilia's. There was only one thing Technophilia had that none of the others did.

Secure, entirely unmonitored, entirely untraceable phone lines.

Velveteen showed her ID at the rooftop door, accepting her visitor's pass (no powers, no team-ups, no pictures, half-off technological augmentation consultation on the third floor) and clipping it to the front of her costume. Then she descended into the club.

The quantum pay phones were on the third floor. If Jackie wasn't an ally, she probably wasn't a good one to call, and so Velveteen dialed the next best number she could think of. The first ring was normal. The second ring sounded like birds singing a happy summertime melody. The third ring *was* birds singing a happy summertime melody. And then the phone was answered.

"You've called the Crystal Glitter Unicorn Cloud Castle, you're speaking to the Princess, what magical emergency can I resolve for you today?" The Princess sounded dead bored. That wasn't unusual. After she'd been in her castle for more than three hours, she usually sounded dead bored. It was really a pity that her powers required her to stay there for six hours a day.

"Princess, it's Velveteen."

There was a long pause before the Princess said, sounding bewildered, "Velveteen who?"

"Velveteen from The Super Patriots, West Coast Division." There was a longer pause. Finally realizing that the Princess wasn't going to fill it, Vel added, "I need your help."

"What would you need my help with, sugar?" The Princess's natural Southern accent was suddenly stronger, a sure sign that she was on her guard. "I'm sure that team of yours can take care of anything your little heart desires."

"I'm sure they could, too, if they were actually my team. I'm from an alternate timeline, one where you and Jackie Frost from the North Pole are my best friends. I need to find Sparkle Bright. They're telling me that she's a supervillain, and I don't believe it. I have to talk to her and find out what's going on. If anybody knows where she is, it's you."

"And so what if I did know?" There was a sudden edge to the Princess's voice, although her accent didn't soften. "Why would I believe that this wasn't a trick? Poor girl's been off the edge of their map for years. What makes you want to go looking for her now?"

"I wasn't in this timeline years ago. I woke up here this morning. If this is the real timeline and I'm just messed up in the head right now, you have my word that I won't tell anyone else where to find her. But if this isn't where I'm supposed to be…she's the most glaringly obvious divergence point between here and home. Because in my timeline, she's the co-leader of The Super Patriots, West Coast Division, and I'm the one they called a supervillain for quitting. That's why we're friends. You thought they'd treated me poorly, and so you came to make sure that I was okay. You brought a whole bunch of rabbits that first time, so I'd feel comfortable. They baked me a sour cream cake." Velveteen stopped, and then added, "It tasted like charcoal, but it was the first time anyone had cared enough to try, and so I ate every bite."

"If this is a trick, you people have stooped lower than I ever thought you would," said the Princess, in a hushed tone. "I just want you to know that. I thought better of you than this, and that's saying something."

"Unless I'm being mind-controlled right now, this isn't a trick. And if I am being mind-controlled, Sparks isn't the only one who's going to wind up being called a supervillain."

Maybe it was the "Sparks" that did it. The Princess sighed. "I'm still not sure this is the right thing to do, but I figure you two girls have things to work out no matter what I do. You want to find Sparkle Bright? You're sure about that?"

"Totally sure," said Velveteen.

"...you really are from another timeline," said the Princess. "She hasn't been Sparkle Bright in years."

"What?"

"You're looking for a woman who goes by the name of 'Polychrome.' To find her, hang up the phone, close your eyes, and count to thirty."

"What are you—"

"And remember, you're the one who asked me. I didn't contact you." The Princess hesitated, and then added, "Good luck getting home."

The line went dead.

Velveteen looked at the phone for a moment, blinking. Then she placed it gently in the cradle, closed her eyes, and began to count. Maybe it was crazy, but she was a grown woman wearing a mask and a headband with rabbit ears on the top. Crazy was sort of her lot in life.

She had just reached twenty-eight when the electrical prod was shoved against the side of her neck, and several hundred volts went coursing through her. Velveteen collapsed like a sack of potatoes, and the world went away.

Waking was a long, slow process made more difficult by the fact that all Velveteen's muscles felt like they'd been scooped out and replaced with strips of wet felt. She was lying down, which was only natural after being electrocuted into unconsciousness. She wasn't lying on her face, which meant that someone had probably moved her.

Swell. Less than twenty-four hours in a world where she was a professional superheroine with a long and distinguished career, and she was already getting herself knocked out and abducted from bars that she probably shouldn't have been visiting in the first place. How much did she really *know* about this timeline, anyway? She was married to *Action Dude* here. There was no way she didn't have enemies.

Voices raised in argument approached the place where she lay sprawled. They were blurred together at first, impossible to untangle. Then they separated, the first, unfamiliar voice saying, "She's not dead. And if she were, I could probably fix it. Might take a little time, probably mess her powers around a bit, but I *could* fix her. Nothing's as easy to reanimate as an animus." It was a woman, British, petulant and worried at the same time, like the opinion of her companion mattered more than anything.

That companion sighed, and said, "I don't want you to fix her. I don't want you to kill her. I'm still not sure why you brought her here." The second voice was also female…and it was familiar. Familiar enough, in fact, to startle Velveteen into opening her eyes.

The ceiling was covered with exposed piping in a variety of sizes, from narrow pipes that looked like they would have trouble carrying anything bigger than a molecule to wide-bore pipes that wouldn't have been out of place in a sewer. Velveteen blinked. The ceiling remained the same. She blinked again, and then asked, in as reasonable a tone as she could manage, "Sparks, why am I lying on the floor in a mad science lair? Shouldn't I be on a slab or something?"

There was a long pause before the unfamiliar voice said sullenly, "I told you I ought to have her up on a slab, didn't I? And you said it would make her uncomfortable on account of she'd expect vivisection."

Velveteen closed her eyes. "I have no idea who you are, or why I should expect vivisection from you, so no, I'm not currently worried about that. I'm a little worried about the fact that I can't move my legs, but I'm assuming that's going to get better, since my toes are starting to tingle. Also, hi, Sparks. Did the Princess call you?"

"She did," said Sparkle Bright–Polychrome, here, and Vel had to admit that it was a good name for her; better than "Sparkle Bright" for a grown heroine. A moment later, Vel heard her kneel, and felt the familiar shape of Polychrome's hand pressing itself flat against her cheek. "Now if you could just explain to me in simple words why I'm not flash-blinding you right now, I'd appreciate it."

Velveteen sighed. "Oh, good," she said. "And here I was worried that this was going to be hard."

When asked to imagine alternate worlds, alternate versions of themselves, most people default to one of two extremes: idyllic wish-fulfillment, realities where every good thing they could imagine happened, and absolutely none of the bad; or absolute vilification, worlds where every terrible impulse and twisted urge was fulfilled to its extreme. This "mirror universe" theory would place Earth A at the median of all realities, a place where good and bad are balanced in equal measure, meaning that all other timelines and worlds must be, in some ways, either superior or inferior, but never of exact and equal worth.

As is essentially always the case, the reality of things is somewhat more complicated than theory would propose.

Alternate realities are divided into three primary types: divergent timelines, worlds whose continuity branched off from Earth A at some point ranging from the distant past to fifteen minutes before the timeline was discovered; alternate dimensions, places which present warped and twisted versions of the world we know; and full-bore alternate universes, where up may be down, gravity may be toxic, and life as we know it may be considered the equivalent of a social disease. Alternate universes range in nature from the exceedingly friendly, like the fairy tale wonderland inhabited by the Princess, to the technically neutral, such as the seasonal worlds, to the actively hostile.

One of the largely unconsidered dangers of transit between realities is downward slippage. It is commonly accepted that a superhuman who has once traveled from one reality to another is likely to do so again. What is less well-known is that each layer encompasses the layers below. A superhuman who has only visited alternate timelines may never see another world or universe. A superhuman who has visited alternate universes, on the other hand, is at risk from every opportunistic timeline or world which comes along.

Scientists who study alternate reality science have discovered, much to their dismay, that the mirror universe theory collapses upon exposure to almost any reality. While there are timelines which are markedly better or worse than Earth A, the majority are, in fact, of equal and balanced value. They are simply the result of different choices. Alternate worlds and universes have more divergent values, but are less likely to contain cognates of known individuals, or of the superhumans themselves. The mirror universe theory is most frequently applied to alternate timelines, and it does not hold up to scrutiny.

This, then, is where the true danger for the traveler between timelines makes itself known: in any world where a **superhuman** exists, they will have a past. They will have friends, and they will have enemies, and because our present is made up of all the choices we have made in our lives, they will not have the information they need to tell friend from enemy. It is not a surprise that many of the superhumans who find their way into other timelines fail to return to their original reality. It is more of a surprise that any make it back at all.

"What are you doing here?" demanded Polychrome. "Why are you looking for me? Who sent you?" She kept her hand pressed against Velveteen's cheek, adding a warning to her words. Give me answers I like, said that hand, or suffer the consequences.

"I'm here because your friend hit me with some sort of stun gun while I was standing next to the payphone in Technophilia," said Velveteen carefully. "I'm looking for you because I needed to talk to you. I'm trying to figure out where the point of divergence is, and you and I seem to be the big anomalies. I sent me."

She was gambling that this version of Yelena would be enough like hers to have suffered through the same endless lectures on recognizing an alternate timeline, the ones they spent pretending to be their own out-of-timeline cognates. They goggled at each other and pretended they didn't know what ceilings were, or that no one in their worlds spoke English. Those games could go on for days, and they were always looking for the point of divergence–big words they didn't fully understand until they got older and learned that alternate reality science was no game.

Polychrome hesitated. Then, more slowly, she asked, "What sort of anomaly are you looking for?"

"The sort that results in a timeline where I'm with The Super Patriots, and you're not," said Velveteen. "In the timeline I went to bed in last night, you're the co-leader, and I've been officially a supervillain in Marketing's eyes since my eighteenth birthday."

There was a long pause before Polychrome's hand was withdrawn from Velveteen's cheek. "Get up," she ordered brusquely. "Before I change my mind and decide you're just messing with me."

"If you let me zap her again, she won't be able to get up, and then it won't matter," offered the British woman.

"You're hanging out with a violent crowd these days, huh?" Velveteen found that, by really focusing, she could get her arms to respond to her instructions. She levered herself slowly into an unsteady sitting position, and turned her face toward Polychrome, opening her eyes at the same time. "Hi. Nice to meet you. I'm Velveteen."

The local version of Yelena raised an eyebrow. "Hello," she responded.

"I like the new look," said Velveteen.

Now the faintest trace of a smile crossed the other Yelena's face. "Okay. Now I know you're not my Vel." Sparkle Bright had always worn white skirts and skimpy tops, all accented with rainbows. Polychrome, on the other hand, wore a solid black unitard, with only a rainbow belt to provide a slash of color. Her sunshine-blonde hair was cut short, practical, with a rainbow streak right up at the front, where it would provide the most immediate identification.

The woman next to her was short, curvy, and dressed in what you might get if a Jane Austen fan convention somehow got caught in the crossfire of a fight between the Clockmaker's Union and a group of angry riveters. Her corset looked like it could have been used to deflect machine gun fire, and there were cogs stitched to the sides of her burgundy leather boots. She was glaring daggers at Velveteen, something that was only enhanced by the large ray gun in her hands.

"I don't like her talking to you," she announced.

"I'm getting the impression that my cognate isn't very popular around here," said Vel, and started trying to stand. It was harder than sitting up had been, but eventually, she managed it, and extended a hand toward the buxom British girl. "Hi. I'm Velveteen. I'm not from this timeline, and I didn't do it. Please don't shoot me."

The British woman looked perplexed. "This isn't how this is supposed to go," she complained, flicking her long red braid out of the way as she turned to glower at Polychrome. "Isn't she supposed to be threatening us by now?"

"Maybe not," said Polychrome, slowly. "You're Velveteen from another timeline."

"Right," said Vel. "When I come from, we're on opposite sides of this conversation. I don't know your friend at all."

"Vel, Victory Anna, Torrey, Velveteen," said Polychrome, with a quick motion of her hand. Her eyes didn't leave Velveteen. "Why did you quit The Super Patriots?"

Velveteen knew a test when she saw one, and she knew better than to lie to any timeline's version of Yelena. She could never lie to her Yelena, and she wasn't going to assume that she could lie to this one. "Because you slept with my boyfriend and then beat the holy shit out of me in the locker room," she said, mildly. "I figured I should probably get out of Dodge after that."

Polychrome stared at her. Finally, in a very small voice that sounded heartbreakingly like the voice of the Yelena Vel knew, she whispered, "That's what they told you? That's what…that's why…" And then she burst into tears.

The effect on Victory Anna was immediate. She swung her ray gun around to point at Velveteen, and said, in an entirely reasonable tone, "You made her cry. That means I get to shoot you until you've got more holes in you than Einstein's theory of relativity."

Velveteen, who was unaware that the theory of relativity had *any* holes, blinked. And Polychrome put out a hand, pushing the muzzle of the gun down toward the floor. "No, Torrey," she said, sniffling. "It's not her fault. It's really not."

"But sweetheart—"

Polychrome wiped her tears away with the back of her hand, leaving glittering pink trails in their wake as she looked toward Velveteen, and said, "I never laid a hand on you in this world. I was too heartbroken after what Marketing told me."

"What did they—" Velveteen stopped, eyes widening. "Did I sleep with *your* boyfriend in this timeline? Oh, jeez, alternate me sucks."

Startled, Polychrome laughed. Then she shook her head. "You really never knew, did you? You always told me you didn't, but I thought you were making fun of me."

"Knew what?"

"Jeez, Vel…" Polychrome sighed. "Marketing called me into a meeting. They said they were being blackmailed by one of my teammates, and that they were willing to pay, because I was such a valuable attribute, but that they wanted me to know. They told me it was you, Vel. They told me you were threatening to go to the tabloids with what you'd figured out. I left the next day."

Velveteen stared at her. "Lena…" she said, barely aware that she'd used Polychrome's given name. "You were my best friend. I would never. No matter what I thought I knew, I would *never*. How could you believe that?"

"The same way you could believe I slept with your boyfriend," Polychrome countered. She put an arm around Victory Anna's shoulders, pulling the other woman possessively close. "Even if I'd been that kind of bitch, which I wasn't, there was just no way."

Velveteen blinked. Polychrome nodded. Victory Anna smirked. And finally, Velveteen said: "You have no idea how much sense this makes. Now how the hell are we going to get me home?"

The underground lair shared by Polychrome and Victory Anna turned out to be surprisingly cozy, once they got out of the creepy room o' pipes and into the living quarters, which were open, well-lit, and filled with places to sit and have a cup of tea. "Torrey's very tea-oriented," said Yelena, as she walked Vel toward the kitchen. "She's from an alternate Victorian England that ceased to exist in a freak accident involving a time machine and a blackcurrant trifle. After spending a few years stranded in parallels without other people, she got very focused on the important things in life."

"Like tea," said Vel.

"Tea, and shooting people who bother my girlfriend," said Torrey, walking over with a tray. She had managed to put together a complete tea service without leaving them alone for more than five minutes. Catching Velveteen's bewildered look, she held the tray out toward her, and said, "I have many talents. And I never miss what I aim to hit."

"Noted," said Vel. She looked back to Yelena. "So you're, um…"

"Gay. It's why my parents sold me. I was their perfect little rainbow angel, right up until the day I said I wanted to marry the girl who lived down the street. The Super Patriots, Inc. promised that they could 'fix' me." Yelena scowled briefly. "They failed."

"Oh my God, Lena." Vel stared at her. "I'm so sorry."

"Don't be," said Yelena, eyes going hard. "I'm not broken."

"No!" Vel grabbed Yelena's hands before she thought about it, ignoring the ray gun that Torrey was suddenly holding. "God, *no*, Lena, I would *never* think that you were broken! I'm sorry I was such a lousy friend in *two* timelines that you couldn't tell me. That you'd believe them when they said those things. I was supposed to be your best friend. I was supposed to look out for you. I failed you."

Now it was Yelena's turn to stare. Then, solemnly, she said, "We failed each other. Besides, maybe in your timeline, something different happened. Maybe your Yelena isn't…"

"No." Vel shook her head, remembering the absolute betrayal in Yelena's face that day in the locker room. "It happened the same way both places. All that changed were our reactions."

"Then we both suck," said Yelena, and gathered her into a hug.

Torrey groaned. "Are we going to sit here talking about feelings until The Super Patriots show up looking for their runaway bunny? I ask out of natural curiosity, mind, and because I want to know if I need to turn on the laser traps in the steam tunnels."

"I think we're done," said Yelena, letting Vel go. "We need to get you home. This isn't where you belong."

"Some things about it are nice, but…yeah. I need to get home. My toys will miss me, and I bet your Vel is *not* getting along with my Sparkle Bright."

Yelena groaned. "I'm still using that code name? God, it's a wonder I haven't gone supervillain for real."

Vel laughed. "You'd make a great villain. You could glitter people to death."

"Hey, I'd be subtle." Yelena snapped her fingers, sending a spray of black sparks into the air. "All visible light is my toy."

Vel's eyes widened. Then, before she could think too hard about what she'd just realized, she said, "Aaron told me I'd started hallucinating other timelines after Dr. Darwin zapped me with some kind of crazy time gun. Maybe this world's Vel hasn't been hallucinating. She's been skipping worlds."

"So that's our first stop," said Torrey, sounding pleased to have someplace to *go*. "Let's go talk to Dr. Darwin."

Vel frowned. "But…he's a supervillain."

"Sweetie, you forget," said Yelena, and grinned. "In this reality, so are we."

Victory Anna couldn't fly any more than Velveteen could. Instead, she drove a modified hover-cycle, once standard Super Patriots-issue, now stripped of most of its decorative flourishes and somehow rigged to run on steam. There were apparently useless gears welded all over the outside. Velveteen, who was tucked in the side car, decided it was better not to ask. If this was one of those things that flew because the driver believed it would fly, the last thing she wanted to do was make Victory Anna doubt its aerodynamic properties.

Polychrome flew easily alongside, propelled by a stream of navy blue glitter. She swerved close enough for Vel to hear her above the wind as she called, "It's not that we're *bad*. We're just not considered good guys anymore."

"I know how that goes," Velveteen called back. "What about that metamorph Action Dude told me about?"

"The kid?" Polychrome looked briefly regretful. "We almost got him not to sign…they prey on kids, Vel. No one should go through what we went through. We didn't get a childhood because of them."

Velveteen paused. Then she shrugged and said, "We got each other. I think that might be better than what we would have had without them."

"Yeah. Nothing's easy, is it?" Polychrome straightened. "We're here." She zipped ahead before Vel could say anything, landing lightly on an unlit rooftop. Then she lit up like a beacon, guiding Victory Anna in.

"Not bad for a maiden flight," said Victory Anna smugly, climbing off the motorcycle.

"I'm pretending I didn't hear that," muttered Velveteen. She looked around the rooftop as she got out of the side car. "This is Dr. Darwin's hideout?"

"No," said Polychrome. "This is where we go when we want to get his attention. No one's ever seen his hideout."

"You're sweet and all, maybe a bit daft, maybe a filthy liar, but there's no way we'd take you to his hideout, even if we knew where it was," said Victory Anna.

"Fair," Vel admitted. "Now how do we get his attention?"

"I sent him a text," said Polychrome.

"A…text." The idea of texting villains to arrange for meetings had never occurred to her. Maybe because "come over and let me beat you up" was a little tacky.

Polychrome smiled. "Welcome to the future."

"Our future, maybe, but you, evil-doer, are about to be the PAST!" boomed a dramatic voice, dripping with justice.

Polychrome and Velveteen exchanged a look, before Vel groaned and dropped her head into her hands. "Oh, swell," she muttered. "It's the cavalry."

Victory Anna grinned, pulling a ray gun out of thin air. "I love the smell of carnage in the evening."

Velveteen felt a hand on her arm and looked up, meeting Polychrome's anxious blue eyes. "You have to pick a side, Vel. I'm sorry. I can't let you stand here and not fight."

"You're my best friend," said Vel, feeling only a slight pang at the thought of facing Aaron across a battlefield. "Let's kick their asses and send me home."

Together, three women who might or might not be supervillains turned, and waited for The Super Patriots, West Coast Division, to descend.

Action Dude was the first one to hit the roof, followed closely by Firefly, who was carrying Jack O'Lope by the back of his vest. Firefly and Jack fell into offensive postures. Action Dude held up his hands, showing that they were empty (as if that mattered; as if he couldn't bench-press a tank when the urge took him). "This doesn't have to be like this," he said, in the same sonorous voice that had been booming catch phrases only a minute before. "Vel, honey, you're just confused, that's all. Come on home, and we'll make sure everything gets sorted out. You haven't done anything wrong."

"This isn't my home," she shouted back. "I'm not your Vel. Polychrome and Victory Anna are just helping me get back to my own timeline." She paused, a thought striking her. "How did you find me here? I didn't tell anyone where I was going!"

Action Dude didn't say anything. The quick, guilty glance he took at her ears told her everything that she didn't want to know.

"Oh, Aaron," Velveteen whispered, too softly for anyone but the wind to hear, and who was the wind going to tell? "I thought you loved me more than you loved them." If he'd loved her that much, he wouldn't have activated the tracking device in her headband when he woke to find her gone. He would have let her take care of things. But he didn't, and he hadn't. He'd just followed the party line, the same way he always had. The same way that he always would.

The whine of Victory Anna's ray gun powering up was loud enough to catch everyone's attention, including the just-landing Mechamation. "Ladies and gentlemen," she said brightly. "I invite you all to attend a demonstration of the raw power of steam, science, and torqued-off mad genius whose girlfriend's well-being is being threatened by assholes without the sense Epona gave the French."

"Does she always talk like that?" asked Velveteen, too bemused to wallow in betrayal.

"All the time," said Polychrome fondly. Her hands moved as she spoke, gathering a large ball of glowing green light. She paused, frowning as she looked at Velveteen's belt. "Vel, are you armed?"

"I wasn't planning to get into a superhero fight against this time-line's Super Patriots when I left the house!" said Vel. Casting about with the part of her mind that housed her powers found…absolutely nothing. There were no toys close enough to call. "I think I'm dead weight on this one."

"You always are," shouted Firefly, and stopped when the rest of The Super Patriots turned to glare at her. "What?" she asked. "I was taunting the villain. I'm supposed to taunt the villains."

"Not when the villain is Vel," snapped Action Dude. "She's not bad, she's just confused because of stupid Dr. Darwin. We're here on a rescue mission. You don't taunt the victims."

"I can hear you, you know," said Velveteen.

"So can I!" declared Dr. Darwin, stepping out of a large rectangular doorway that had suddenly opened in the middle of the roof. It closed behind him, leaving the short, pudgy mad scientist standing between the two super teams. "Now you will feel the wrath of DR. DARWIN!"

There was a long pause as every other superhuman on the roof, including the newly-arrived Imagineer and Uncertainty, stared at Dr. Darwin. Dr. Darwin pulled a ray gun from inside his lab coat. Victory Anna scoffed.

"Mine's bigger," she said.

That was, in some strange way, the straw that broke the metaphorical camel's back. Everyone started moving at once, and the fight was on.

Watching the fight was sort of fascinating, in an academic, I'm-going-to-die way. Firefly and Polychrome went head-to-head almost immediately, their photon blasts illuminating the night sky, while Jack O'Lope and Victory Anna shot bolts of gleaming energy at one another. Mechamation and Action Dude went after Dr. Darwin, who shot his own bolts of energy at the pair. Both dodged easily, as Mechamation's army of tiny robots began swarming out of her pockets and toward the evil genius. That left Velveteen and Uncertainty. They exchanged a look.

"This is awkward," said Vel.

"There is an eighty-seven percent chance that you will seize control of Mechamation's toys and use them to defeat me if I initiate hostilities," replied Uncertainty. "There is also a ninety-nine percent chance that you're telling the truth, and aren't actually this reality's version of Velveteen. I'm just glad you're *a* version of Velveteen, since the alternatives are far less pleasant."

Velveteen blinked. A bolt of light went zipping by overhead. "Sometimes talking to you is extremely weird," she said finally.

"I know," said Uncertainty. "It is my purpose."

"Right." Velveteen turned to peer around the increasingly chaotic roof. None of the various rays, beams, or bullets were entering the small area around herself and Uncertainty; that would be Uncertainty's quantum field making sure that they didn't get hurt. "Where's Imagineer?"

"Maintaining the coms back at headquarters, and making sure Marketing doesn't realize that the rest of us are gone." Uncertainty grimaced as another collision of photon blasts turned it momentarily as bright as day. "There is a sixty-four percent chance that they'll notice within the next fifteen minutes."

"Fucked-up times fifty-seven thousand," muttered Velveteen.

To her surprise, Uncertainty smiled. "I thought that might be you," he said. "Earth A."

Velveteen blinked at him. "You can identify my source reality from the way I swear?"

"You'd be surprised at what profanity can tell you about a person."

"I guess." Velveteen ducked to avoid having her ears grazed by one of Dr. Darwin's rays. "Any ideas on how to get me home? This is a nice world and everything, but I don't belong here." More than nice, in some ways; the idea of finally being with Aaron, really and truly, was so tempting that it hurt. But Aaron loved The Super Patriots more than he loved her, and there was her Yelena to think about. If she was going to make things right, she had to go back to her own timeline.

For the first time, Uncertainty looked abashed. "I am unfortunately unable to predict the mechanisms via which an individual might move between timelines," he said. "It is outside my available data set."

Velveteen paused as she puzzled that through. Then she asked, "Is this your home timeline?"

Uncertainty looked at her calmly. "All timelines are my home timeline."

Velveteen stared at him, briefly forgetting that they were standing in the middle of a superheroic battle that might get one or both of them shot at any moment. "That makes…so much sense," she said slowly. "Why did I never think of that before?"

"Because every time the probability of someone realizing my nature rises toward certainty, I adjust it downward," said Uncertainty.

"…oh. So you're telling me now because…?"

"There is a ninety-four percent probability that any solution which you find for returning to your original reality will result in your forgetting some part of this timeline," said Uncertainty. "Six percent is worth the risk."

Velveteen stared at him. If she was going to forget what she'd learned, what was the point in going back? Why not stay here, where she had the life she'd always thought she was going to have? Sure, things weren't perfect, but they were closer than they were when she'd come from...

And Jackie and the Princess and Tag would always wonder where she'd gone, no matter how much they might come to like her replacement, and she'd never have the chance to fix things with her version of Yelena, no matter how much she wanted to. "I guess you're right," she said, slowly. "Six percent is worth the risk." Then she whirled and bolted away from him, running full-speed toward Dr. Darwin.

Uncertainty sighed. "There was a ninety-nine percent chance that you were going to do that," he said mournfully, to the air where Velveteen had been a moment before. "Good luck."

Velveteen seized control of half of Mechamation's robots as she ran, using them to distract the combatants long enough for her to reach the startled-looking Dr. Darwin, who was too confused by having a non-physical hero charging at him to bring his gun to bear. She grabbed his shoulders, giving him a solid shake before he pulled away.

"Send me back!" she shouted. "You're the one with the stupid zappy ray gun of fucking up my entire life, so use it right now, and *send me back!*"

"I–" stammered Dr. Darwin. This was an experience utterly unheralded in his villainous career, and he had absolutely no idea how to respond. He'd never had a superheroine *ask* him to shoot her before. Finally, he settled on the evil option: "No. If that's what you want, then no." He moved his ray gun away from her, aiming it at the sky. "I'll never send you back. Never never nev–"

The blast from Victory Anna's ray gun caught him square in the back, and he collapsed like a broken doll. Velveteen stood there staring at him as Victory Anna strolled over and bent to retrieve his ray gun. "You were the first one she ever loved, you know," said Torrey conversationally, as she adjusted the settings on Dr. Darwin's gun. "You broke her heart. Took me years to fix it. So I'm probably going to enjoy this a bit more than I ought to. But I also know that wasn't you. Your Lena have a girl?"

"No," said Vel.

"Tell her from me, she'll be happier if she gets one. I recommend a scientifically-inclined young lady from London, but what do I know?" Victory Anna took careful aim at Velveteen.

Somewhere across the battlefield, Action Dude shouted her name. Velveteen closed her eyes, doing her best to ignore him. *I am going home,* she thought. *Aaron, I love you, but not this you, and I am going home...*

"Say 'trans-dimensional transit'," said Victory Anna cheerfully, and pulled the trigger.

The blast from Dr. Darwin's gun caught Velveteen square in the chest, flinging her backward. She didn't hit the roof; instead, she fell, and kept falling, down, down, down the rabbit hole between worlds, until she landed, hard, in what felt like a snow bank–except that snow banks were supposed to be cold, and this one was as warm as sheets fresh from the dryer. Velveteen opened her eyes, and blinked slowly at the man standing in front of her.

"Oh," she said, unsurprised. "It's *you.*"

"Yes," Santa Claus agreed. "It's me. Hello, Vel. Welcome back to the North Pole."

VELVETEEN
vs.
The Retroactive Continuity

VELVETEEN LEVERED HERSELF OUT OF the impossibly warm snow bank, eyeing the red-clad figure in front of her with wary suspicion. "What kind of game are you playing here?" she asked. "Was any of that even real?"

"It could have been," replied Santa Claus, an understanding smile on his jolly round face. He always looked jolly, except when he looked furious. It was deceptive, holiday cheer used as a mask for true emotion. "You could have decided to stay there, and then it would absolutely have been real. It's a wonderful life, Vel. You, of all people, should know that."

"You created that timeline to teach me a lesson? Did it work?" Velveteen looked down at herself. She was back to her usual weight, which was something of a relief, since she understood her body's limitations in a world where she allowed it to eat potato chips. Her costume had changed, going from the alternate universe "sexy bunny" design to a bows-and-bells trimmed holiday style, complete with short skirt. It was the grown-up version of the costume she'd worn for the old Super Patriots holiday specials. Somehow, that made it even worse.

"I think you're the only one who can know that, Vel," said Santa. "We've missed you. I kept hoping you would come to visit."

"I decided that it was best if I stayed out of the seasonal lands, since they all kept trying to keep me," Vel countered, and eyed him suspiciously. "Did Jackie put you up to this? Was this whole 'kidnap Velveteen to an alternate timeline and see what she does' routine her idea? Because I *will* kick her ass."

"I would very much like to see that," said Santa gravely. "But no, this wasn't Jackie's idea. It was mine."

"Don't hog the credit," said a familiar female voice. Velveteen turned to see a teenage girl with pale blonde hair streaked in orange and green, wearing a patchwork witch's costume and holding a pumpkin-shaped trick-or-treat bucket in one hand. "I helped."

"Hailey," said Velveteen. The word fell between them like a curse.

Hailey Ween, current Halloween Princess and guardian of the Autumn Land, smiled. "It's good to see you, too, Vel. I'm with Santa. We've missed you in autumn."

"Are all the seasons in on this?" demanded Vel, turning back toward Santa. "Is the Easter Bunny going to spring out at me next?" She paused. "No pun intended."

"Summer wasn't involved, since that's the only season that has no claim on you, but yes, Spring was a part of this. I provided the wonderful life narrative thread. Hailey provided the trick and the treat of getting you into another timeline."

"And Easy was the one who made sure everything was hidden where it needed to be," said Hailey. "He bends time better than any of us. Has to, to hide all those eggs without help."

"God. Why am I the subject of a seasonal conspiracy? Did I not buy enough greeting cards last year or something?"

"Vel," said Santa chidingly. Velveteen stopped, feeling obscurely like she was eight years old and at risk of the Naughty List. That was Santa's power. He rewarded the good little boys and girls of the world, and he made even the worst of the bad little boys and girls crave his approval and fear disappointing him. It would take a hardened supervillain to stand up to Santa's disapproval, and that was something she'd never been, despite Marketing's best efforts at branding her. "The seasons are involved in your life because you need us to be, and because we need you. You're special. You know that."

"I don't want to go live in a season, okay? I'm just starting to get my life back together. If I was going to chicken out on the real world and go running to Halloween or Christmas, I would have done it years ago, when The Super Patriots, Inc. was making sure I couldn't hold a job or keep an apartment."

"But we gave you the real world, the way that you could have had it, if things had just gone a little bit differently," said Hailey. Velveteen glared at her. She shrugged. "You had it all there, Vel. You were co-leader of The Super Patriots, West Coast Division. You were married to your childhood sweetheart. All it cost you was the best friend you'd already given up, and you threw it all away. So why do you think a season would be any worse?"

"I'm a superhero. I'm not a holiday."

Santa smiled, and his smile was kind—his smiles were always kind—before asking her, quietly, "What do you think the rest of us started out as?"

Velveteen didn't have an answer for that.

The question of what creates alternate or parallel timelines is one which can drive even the most fervent devotees of alternate reality science to drink heavily, because even after years of study, experimentation, and tragic lab accidents (some of which resulted in new timelines to observe), no one really knows. Why does one missed bus connection create eight possible worlds, while a political assassination sinks into the multiverse without so much as a ripple? Why do some people live and die without once causing reality to shift, while others throw off new continuities like they were nothing to be concerned about? Theory after theory has been put forth and, thus far, none of them have managed to hold water.

Here is what we do know, more due to trial and error than any more scientific approach: some people attract alternate universes the way that probability manipulators attract luck. These people are not necessarily important, and may seem to have little influence on the worlds in which they live. They eat, sleep, go to work, fall in love, and live their lives never realizing that they have universes shifting all around them. Sometimes this "universal attraction" is a temporary thing, collecting around a series of events which have brought or will bring the person in question into contact with another reality. Sometimes it happens throughout their lives. And sometimes it happens because the worlds are jockeying to see where that person will wind up staying, whether it be their world of origin, or one of the other realities that spin around them like water circling a drain.

Once an individual has slipped between realities once, it becomes easier for them, more likely to happen over and over again, until eventually, they stop moving, or they die. Neither of these outcomes is always desirable, but no known reality seems to care very much for the desires of the people that inhabit it. Realities care even less when they're fighting for ownership of a prize, or a person. We are rarely able to ask the people who have been put into such a position what they think of the situation. It seems likely that most of them would be unimpressed, and would be quite pleased with anyone who could offer them a way to *stop* skipping between worlds.

In the end, we can at least be sure of this much: no matter how much momentum a person may have when they begin the process of moving between worlds, they will eventually run out, and stop. Nothing can keep moving forever, not even in the multiverse, and given time enough, all things find their place.

Whether they like that place or not is entirely beside the point.

Seeing that Velveteen wasn't going to stop glaring without some sort of reason, Santa sighed. "Velveteen, please. We're your friends. We just want to help you be happy."

"*She* isn't my friend," Velveteen shot back hotly, jabbing an accusing finger at Hailey. Hailey rolled her eyes, but didn't protest. "She's kidnapped me to her stupid Halloween world three times. I barely got out the last time. I really thought better of you than this, Santa. I never thought you'd team up with her to go against me."

"And I never thought you would turn your back on your friends and your responsibilities because you were too scared to figure out what was broken," Santa replied. His tone stayed mild. "You knew that the Marketing Department was lying to you. You were hurt and confused, but you knew, on some level, that what they were saying didn't make any sense. You knew for sure after Yelena attacked you in the locker room. But you did nothing to fix it. You did nothing to find out what was really going on. You just. Walked. Away."

"That isn't fair," whispered Velveteen.

But the worst was yet to come. Santa shook his head, and said, "I thought better of you."

Velveteen closed her eyes. Not fast enough; the tears escaped anyway, running hotly down her cheeks. Then Santa's arms were enfolding her, the sweet gingerbread and peppermint scent of him just as much a part of the embrace as the feeling of warm velvet pressed against her cheeks. For a moment, she considered fighting. The moment passed, and Velveteen collapsed against Father Christmas, sobbing in earnest.

"My poor Vel," said Santa, stroking her back with one huge hand. "We've all treated you hard, haven't we? Every single one of us, from the very beginning. I wish I could tell you that it was over, but you're nowhere near your ever after, yet, and not even I can tell you whether it's going to be a happy one. You have a long way to go before you get to hang your stockings by the fire, fill your cup with Christmas cheer, and leave the rest of the world to its own devices."

"Hey," said Hailey, with sudden heat. "Don't you use this to try to influence her toward Christmas, Fat Man. You don't need her like we do, and the deal was that we'd all work together to remind her that she has to stay active, not to shove her into your jolly clutches."

Velveteen pulled away from Santa, sniffling a little as she dragged her hand across her nose. It left a wet trail on her glove. Sticking her hand behind her back, she glared at Hailey. "Stop talking about me like I'm some kind of toy you get to play with," she said. "I'm right here, and there is nothing you can ever, *ever* do to influence me toward Halloween."

"Sorry, sweetie, but a sweet treat like you can't trick a girl like me," said Hailey, and grinned, showing all her teeth. They seemed a little pointier than they were supposed to be. "If there was nothing I could ever, *ever* do to influence you toward Halloween, I wouldn't be here now. But you still glow like a jack-o-lantern at dusk when I look at you, and that means you can still be ours. You just don't want to admit it to yourself."

"I'm back in the field, I'm back behind a mask—what more do you people want from me?" Velveteen turned her glare on Santa. "I've done more in the last six months than I have in the last six years."

"Yes, you have, and I'm very proud of you, Vel. You'll never understand how proud I am. But you have so much more to do, and so much less time than you think."

"What are you—"

"It's time for trick or treat," said Hailey. There was a sharp edge in her voice, a razor in her American-girl caramel apple sweetness. "Our trick, our treat. If you come out the other end without being tempted, we put you back. If you don't, we bargain."

"Santa?" Velveteen's voice came out as a whisper, even though she hadn't intended for it to be.

"Halloween has the right to test and trick you, Vel; I'm here because I wouldn't let you go through it alone." He offered her one massive, red-gloved hand. Instinct made her reach out and take it without thinking about the possible consequences. He was Santa Claus; he was, and had always been, her friend. "You've already passed the first trick."

That first trick had nearly been enough to break her heart.

Velveteen looked uncertainly up at Santa, and asked, "So what comes next?"

It was Hailey who answered, grinning ear to ear all the while. "The Hall of Mirrors, silly rabbit. Let's see if you're so wedded to the real world after *that*."

The Hall of Mirrors, Santa explained as they walked, was a place where the various possible realities reflected on each other, becoming visible from the right angles. "It's where we found the world we sent you into."

"So it was real," said Velveteen, seizing on the idea of a world where Yelena might not be happy, but at least had someone she could genuinely love; a world where Marketing had never managed to interfere with their lives the way they had in this timeline…

"No," said Santa, a sad note in his voice. "It was a potential, not a reality. That's how we were able to insert you without removing someone else."

"Oh," said Velveteen, in a very small voice.

"Look at it this way: the bad stuff wasn't real. Isn't the good stuff a small price to pay for that?" Hailey ran ahead of them, through the ever-warm snow, to the door of the great gingerbread palace that waited, with bakery patience, for them to arrive. She grabbed the handle and tugged. It remained stubbornly closed. "Hey, Santa, I can't get in."

"That's because you have no possible futures left," said Santa, wearily. "Once, it would have opened for you easily. But only one of you became the Halloween Princess, and now every other version of you that might have been is dead and gone and in her grave. The House of Mirrors is not for you."

Hailey turned and pouted at him, petulant as the teenage girl she was always going to be. Velveteen remembered a time when Hailey had seemed grown-up and exciting, so much older and wiser and stranger than anyone else she knew. That time had passed, and now Hailey was just another kid who needed to be told "no" a little more often.

"This place sucks," said Hailey, confirming Velveteen's impression of her even more.

"Not too fond of you, either, witchy-bitchy," said Jackie's sharp, familiar voice. Velveteen turned to see the blue-skinned girl materialize in a swirl of snow, a trick she could only pull off at the North Pole.

The smile she turned Velveteen's way was almost apologetic. "Hi, Vel. Sorry about all this. It wasn't my idea."

"Hey, Jackie," Velveteen replied, raising the hand that wasn't clasped in Santa's in a vague wave. "I know it's not your fault." Jackie's mother was the Snow Queen; her father was Jack Frost. Both of them worked for Santa Claus. Out of the four winter heroes Velveteen knew, Jackie was the one with the most personal freedom outside the North Pole, and the least freedom inside it. As long as her mother was Snow Queen, when she was at home, Jackie did as she was told. "Are you going to let us in?"

"Yeah. You need me or Mom here if you want the mirrors to reflect the right way. Otherwise, you just get lots of dopey-looking images of yourself as you are, not yourself as you might have been." Jackie casually flipped Hailey off as she walked up the steps of the gingerbread palace. They froze under her feet, turning into slabs of blue-white ice. When she put her hand on the door, it froze as well. Bit by bit, the sweet cookie facade fell away, replaced by hard angles and cold, unyielding snow. The door swung open. Jackie turned to face the others, and spread her arms. "Enter, wanderers, and let the cold consume you."

"And you people say Halloween is creepy," complained Hailey, and flounced past Jackie into the snow palace.

Jackie smirked. "Never said it had a monopoly," she said. Her smirk faded, replaced by a look of concern, as Velveteen and Santa mounted the steps. She didn't say anything. She didn't even meet Velveteen's eyes. And somehow that wasn't a surprise at all; somehow, that was just the next logical step in this insane fairy tale merry-go-round of seasons and parallel selves.

Velveteen and Santa walked past her. Jackie stayed outside on the frozen steps until they were safely past the threshold and down the hall. Then she stepped into the Hall of Mirrors, and closed the door behind herself.

Inside the Hall of Mirrors was nothing but darkness. Velveteen felt Santa's hand slip out of hers, and groped for it, but there was nothing there to catch. "I'm sorry," he said, from somewhere that was very close and very far away at the same time. "This may not be the right way. It's the only one."

Then the lights came on, and she was standing by herself in a twisting maze of mirrors, the sort you could find in any carnival fun house. But the reflection directly in front of her wasn't shorter or taller or fatter or thinner or any of the other things a normal mirror would do; it was just her, in street clothes, with her hair worn long and tied in a high ponytail. There was something off about her expression, and it took Velveteen a moment to realize that it was the absence of pain. This was a Velma who had never known regret.

Almost without meaning to, Velveteen reached for the mirror. Her reflection did the same. Their fingertips met, and merged–

–and her name is Velma Martinez, but her friends call her "Vel." They make jokes about her teaming up with some meddling kids and their stupid dog to fight crime, and she just smiles, and fights crime in the way she went to law school for: one case at a time. She never developed superpowers, although the mandatory screening she underwent during her first year of law school showed that she had the potential, if she'd been exposed to the right set of conditions when she was a kid. It's genetic, apparently. She'll have to think about that before she has children of her own–

Velveteen yanked her hand free with a gasp, staggering backward. She didn't notice the next mirror until her back hit it, and she fell, with a lurch, into–

–they called her "Velveteen" when she was with The Junior Super Patriots, made up a bunch of crap about how she animated toys with love, and then when she left, they told the world that she was a supervillain. Fine. If that was how they wanted to play things, fine. It's Roadkill now, and the things she brings to life aren't exactly thrilled about the way that they died. She has a lot of pretty little zombie pets just itching for the chance to bring a world of hurt to the people who snapped their spines and left them on the road. If Marketing wants a bad guy, they're going to get a–

"Whoa, Vel, whoa!" Jackie's hands grabbed Velveteen's arms and yanked her forward, away from the mirror that had her captive. "You gotta be careful in here. You can get lost."

"What…" Velveteen looked over her shoulder at the mirror. This reflection had short-cropped, spiky hair and a costume that was modeled on her original bunny design, but with an undead reinterpretation that she really didn't want to think about too hard. The reflection stuck her tongue out. Velveteen turned away. "What is this place?"

"Potential. People you might have been, people you might be anyway. Some of them never existed, most of them never will. But all of them are you."

Velveteen looked back toward the mirror where Velma Martinez, lawyer, was looking calmly out at her. She was alone. But the

Velveteens to either side of her—one in a white bunny costume with a pink bow on one ear, one in a black leather bustier with a rabbit-shaped necklace—were accompanied by their own glowing blue girls. She raised a shaky hand and pointed at Velma. "She's alone because I would never have met you if I weren't a superhero."

"Exactly." Jackie let her go. "Only touch the ones you're sure of. Most of them won't know you're here, but there are some heads you don't want to look inside, even when they're versions of your own. Maybe especially when they're versions of your own. We're our own worst enemies."

"Have you been through here before?" asked Velveteen.

"The day I became my mother's heir. I had to walk this hall and touch every reflection, and let me tell you, you do *not* want to do that. It was worth it for me. It's not something that you need to do." Jackie began to walk. Velveteen fell in beside her, unsure of what else she was supposed to be doing. "You need to look at your reflections. Find the ones that feel like they could fit, and look inside them."

"But you just told me not to."

"No, I told you to be careful, and not look at all of them. Like, the ones where you're an obvious supervillain? Not necessary to your mental health. There are about eighteen versions of you where you're Roadkill, another ten or so where you're the Puppeteer, and a couple of really nasty ones where you go by Marionette. If you see a reflection of you with strings hanging from her wrists, don't touch them."

"What's wrong with those versions of me?"

"They're dead."

Velveteen didn't have an answer for that.

After an hour of walking through a maze filled with people she might have been, Velveteen was tired, frustrated, and increasingly unsure of exactly what this was supposed to prove. Then they turned a corner, and faced a corridor filled with mirrors that held no reflections at all. "What the…"

"This is part of the maze," Jackie said. "Try a mirror."

Velveteen stepped cautiously toward the first empty mirror. Reaching out her hand, she touched the glass, and–

–it wasn't a good death. No death is a good death, exactly, but some are better than others, and this wasn't a good death. She'd gone up against Marketing one time too many, without anyone to support her, and this time, they'd decided to hit back. The last thing that went through her head before she

crumpled to the pavement was Oh, Aaron, oh, God, not you, too... *and then she was gone, and it didn't matter anymore—*

Velveteen gasped as she jerked herself loose. Wheeling on Jackie, she demanded, "What the fuck? You have to make me live through my own *death*?! I know this wasn't your idea, Jackie, but this is insane!"

"It's a possibility." Jackie gestured with both hands, indicating the full length of the hall. "It's a common possibility. I won't make you live through more than one of those; I'm just going to tell you what they all have in common. In every one of them, you went up against The Super Patriots, and you did it without a team. There's not a single empty mirror where you went up against them with someone to support you. Maybe someday those mirrors will exist. They're not here now."

"So what are you saying? Don't go up against The Super Patriots with nothing but a box of Barbies to support me? I think I got that part."

"I'm saying that if you don't want to team up with people, and team up with them long term, you need to get away from the idea of ever challenging The Super Patriots."

Velveteen frowned at her. "I wasn't thinking about challenging them."

Jackie sighed. "Weren't you? Come on." She turned to head down another corridor. "I'll show you your teams."

There were fewer mirrors in this corridor, maybe because she had fewer people she trusted than she had ways to die at the hands of the Marketing Department. In one mirror, all four members of her junior class stood together in tattered, obviously homemade uniforms, their hands clenched and their jaws set against an enemy she couldn't see, but could easily imagine. In another, she stood next to Tag, the Princess, the Claw, and Dr. Darwin, of all people, the five of them wearing matching matte black costumes and lab coats.

The third mirror showed her standing next to Polychrome, Victory Anna, and Action Dude, all four of them wearing their uniforms from the timeline she had just abandoned. Velveteen stopped there, a lump in her throat, and reached for the glass without allowing her fingers to quite touch it. "He would have joined us," she whispered. "If I'd stayed, he would have joined us."

"That man has always loved you more than he loved America, apple pie, or common sense," said Jackie. "That didn't make staying there the right thing to do. Those weren't your versions of the people you loved. They were close, but close is no cigar."

"He would have joined us," Velveteen whispered. She turned to the next mirror, where she was standing between Tag and a woman she didn't recognize, a woman in a green and brown uniform, with a bi-color domino mask covering her eyes. "Who's that?"

"Her? That's Jory. Her sister's the Governor of Oregon in our timeline. She took the position to keep The Super Patriots out of her state after they got Jory killed. She never forgave them. In a world where Jory didn't die, Celia wouldn't have been in a position to offer you sanctuary. You would have kept running, and eventually stopped in Vancouver. Jory wouldn't have stayed with The Super Patriots after her eighteenth birthday. Her powers made her partially immune to their conditioning, and they hate that."

"Jory," said Velveteen, thoughtfully. "What happened to her?"

"What happens to any of the kids who die on Marketing's watch? She was asked to do too much, too soon, and she didn't dodge fast enough. She was twelve years old when she died. Her real name was Jennifer Morgan."

"So I could be a supervillain or a casualty or a holiday or part of a team, and you had to bring me here to make me understand that?"

"No, silly," said Hailey, from the mirror behind her. Velveteen turned. The Halloween Princess was grinning at her from behind the glass, her arm around an uncomfortable-looking version of Velveteen herself. "We had to bring you here to make you see that you didn't have any good options. Most of them you've already cut yourself off from. You're just treading water, waiting to give up and come to the seasons. We want you to come now, before you're too tired to be much good."

"Subtle, Hailey," snapped Jackie.

"Stuff it, you frigid bitch," replied Hailey.

"I am putting you both on the Naughty List if you don't stop it right now," said Santa. Velveteen looked toward his voice. He was standing in the hall next to her, not crowding a reflection. "Velveteen. We didn't bring you here to make you choose us. I wouldn't have been a party to that."

"Then what?" she asked.

"We brought you here to make you choose *something*." Hailey stepped out of her mirror, sliding out of it as easily as a knife sliding through a pumpkin's skin. "You're moving again, but you're treading water. If we can't have you, we want it to be because you're doing something more important than sustaining the reality of our seasons."

"What can I choose?" asked Vel bitterly. "Stay here, go to Halloween, or go home?"

"You can choose any of the reflections you've seen," Santa said.

Velveteen paused. For a moment, everything was still. Then she asked, carefully, "Can you change the reflection you took me from? You're Santa Claus. You're magic. And you, you're the Spirit of Halloween. If it's a big enough trick…can you do it?"

"There would be a price," said Santa, carefully.

"Yeah, I figured." Velveteen took a deep breath. "Give me what I want, and give me a year to fix things with The Super Patriots. Then I'll give you each a season, and give you my final decision at the end of that time. Willingly. I'll come willingly, and I'll let you show me why your time of the year should win."

"And if you choose none of us?" asked Hailey warily.

"If I choose none of you, and you all agree that I didn't give you a fair chance, you decide what to do with me." Velveteen looked challengingly toward Santa. "Fair?"

"Fair," he agreed, sounding almost reluctant. "What is it you want for Christmas, little girl?"

And Velveteen told them.

"Governor Morgan? Velveteen is here to see you. She says it's urgent."

Governor Celia Morgan of Oregon looked up from the report she'd been reading. "Send her in," she snapped at the intercom.

She had barely started to look down again when the office door opened and Velveteen stepped inside. She was wearing her costume—of course she was, superheroes always wore their costumes when they went out on business—and she wasn't alone. Another woman in spandex followed her, this one wearing a green and brown patterned leotard over brown tights, with green boots and a bicolored mask. Her hair was long and brown and loose, curling madly around her cheeks.

She looked familiar. Celia would have sworn that she'd never seen her before in her life.

"Velveteen." Celia removed her glasses. "And…Velveteen's friend. Hello, and welcome. Are you here to request authorization for a team-up? As long as you're not with The Super Patriots, I'm happy to let our resident superheroine make her own tactical plans."

"Cece..." The stranger reached up and carefully removed her mask, revealing wide hazel eyes. Celia's heart seemed to seize up in her chest. Jennifer Morgan, now an adult, now alive, smiled uncertainly at her sister. "It's me."

"Merry Christmas," said Velveteen, the words lost in the din of two sisters who had been lost—one in a world where a hero died too young, one in a world where a little sister fell victim to a fight that should never have followed a junior heroine home—fell into each other's arms, shouting and crying and demanding answers, all at the same time. It might have been harder for them if they'd lived in a world where this sort of thing didn't happen. Luckily for everyone, they lived in a world where this sort of thing happened all the time.

Once it was clear that she had been well and truly forgotten, Velveteen let herself out.

Velveteen made it all the way home before she broke down crying, collapsing onto her living room couch and clutching her stuffed bunny rabbit, the one she'd picked up in Isley, and sobbing into the plush. Eventually, even the tears dried up, and she had nothing left. That was when she pulled out her phone and dialed the one number she had for the person she most needed to speak to.

There was no answer on the other end. Just a beep as the voicemail picked up, no name, no message. If you needed those things, you didn't need to be calling her.

"Blacklight? It's Velveteen." Vel sniffled, wiping her nose with her hand for the second time in a day. She was so tired. "I need you to come to Portland when you get the chance. I think it's time for us to have another team-up." She hesitated before adding, more quietly, "Please come. I need you." Then she hung up and dropped the phone, sinking deeper into the couch.

She was still there when the sun went down. This time, she remained where she was all through the night, and while she didn't sleep much, at least she slept in the same reality until dawn.

VELVETEEN
Presents
Victory Anna vs. All These Stupid Parallel Worlds

Another London, in another 1884

V{ICTORIA COGSWORTH WALKED DOWN THE} stairs into her father's underground laboratory, stepping carefully to avoid any untoward puddles of unidentified slime that might be waiting to adhere themselves to her boots. Biology was quite the least appealing of the sciences. Its tendency to create undifferentiated mess and muck and then leave it strewn about to trip up a poor girl trying to deliver the tea was *entirely* inappropriate.

"Papa?" she called. "I've brought the tea. Papa, are you down here?" *Where else would he be? He went down the stairs; the stairs connect to the kitchen; I was in the kitchen; he did not come back up the stairs.* As the teleporter was, at present, quite broken, all logic dictated that he was still in the laboratory. "Papa?"

An oddly-shaped pile of dusty rags near the large contraption her father insisted on calling the Eventually Effective Time Machine–on the theory that eventually, his tinkering would lead him to discover the solution, at which point he would promptly travel back in time and tell himself how to make it work more promptly, paradox and potentially unmaking reality be damned–caught her eye. The first chill of uncertainty slithered over her skin. "Papa?" she asked, stepping closer.

It was the tea service, or more specifically, the blackcurrant trifle, which saved her. Held in front of her as it was, it was the first thing to hit the time bubble that her father's careless tinkering had created. As it pierced the soap bubble film of causality that was keeping all reality from being swallowed by the void, it was sucked into a whirling paradox of infinite dessert possibilities. Trifles past, present, and future suddenly filled the lab, consuming and being consumed at an improbable pace. Victoria found herself awash in a sea of deadly deliciousness.

She had been raised a scientist, by a scientist, and for all that she was distraught—her father was almost certainly dead, and the tea was most definitely ruined—Victoria kept her head about her. Her father had always taught her to remain cool in a crisis, and he would have been proud of her that day, had he not already been lost to her. Moving quickly, she flung the tea service at the Eventually Effective Time Machine (now perhaps better referred to as the Unfortunately Effective Time Machine) and drew the light pistol from her belt in almost the same motion. It worked on the same principle of fusion which powered the sun, and fired, not bullets, but blasts of super-heated plasma too bright to look directly upon.

"I'm sorry, Papa," she whispered, and fired, her plasma bolt tearing through tea service, blackcurrant paradox, and time machine all in the same second. Light exploded into the room, coming out of everything, like a supernova objecting to the petty laws of physics.

And as simply as that, the world ended.

Another San Diego, not very long ago at all

The temptation to "accidentally" pull the wrong gun from her belt and blast the bunny-eared bitch into a thin scrim of undifferentiated molecules was higher than Victory Anna wanted to admit, especially where Polychrome might hear her. She struggled to live up to Poly's ideals, and one of those ideals was not shooting people simply because she felt like it. It was funny, really. They were the supervillains in this little pantomime, but it was the heroes of the piece who seemed far less concerned with the fact that innocent people might get hurt.

And Velveteen was the worst of a bad lot. Still. If this woman truly was the Velveteen from another timeline—one where she wasn't such a raging bitch—then she didn't deserve to be reduced to her component atoms, no matter how satisfying the idea might be. And if she wasn't the Velveteen from another timeline, at least Victory Anna would have the rare pleasure of shooting her in the chest with a ray gun.

Velveteen closed her eyes, clearly bracing herself against the blast to come. The sheer determination on her face was enough to finally convince Victory Anna that maybe Poly's instincts were right about this one; maybe this was the good version of the woman she'd come to see as just shy of an arch-nemesis.

Good luck, and may Epona's white horses carry you safe, thought Victory Anna. Aloud, and with her usual manic good cheer, she said, "Say 'trans-dimensional transit'!"

She pulled the trigger. And as simply as that, for the second time in her life, the world ended.

Worlds, it must be said, are in some respects like soap bubbles: a thousand of them pop every second, winking out of existence so abruptly that they might as well never have existed in the first place. And once they're gone, they're gone. Something close might exist–probably exists, in the vastness of the multiverse–but the original world is lost forever. Those few exiles who have somehow survived the destruction of their home realities have been known to say, with a deep and abiding sorrow, that a thousand country songs were right. You can never go home again.

It was bad luck, really, and nothing more than that, which caused the destruction of Victoria "Victory Anna" Cogsworth's world to coincide with the creation of the Wonderful Life scenario intended for the Earth A version of Velma "Velveteen" Martinez. It was more bad luck that any parallel world, naturally occurring or artificially made, will need a past to justify its present. The fake world had stretched itself backward, uncurling like a flower, and the inadvertent time traveler had been brought to a sudden, unplanned stop inside a new reality.

If not for that accident of timing, Victoria's trajectory would have hurled her into Earth A, where things would have gone very differently indeed. But while reality may be malleable, the past is harder to change, and for four long, wonderful years, Victoria believed that she had found herself a replacement home. It was hard, at times. This wasn't her world. Their Victorian Era corresponded roughly with her own, but they followed some silly monotheistic church, not the good old C of E (although they *had* a C of E; it was just the Church of England instead of the Church of Epona). Their wars were different, their scientific accomplishments were different…and at the same time, so much was the same. Like love. Like people looking down on lovers, for loving.

Like lovers not caring if they're looked down on, not once they have each other, not once they understand that love can live through hardship. Like friendship, and people caring for one another.

Having access to the internet, mail-order scientific supply catalogs, and ice cream year-round was really just the icing on the cake that was Yelena. For Lena, Victoria would have endured anything, any indignity, any insanity that the world wanted to throw at her. And then, in an instant, Yelena was gone, and the battlefield was gone, and everything was gone but Victory Anna herself, and she was falling down, down, down, into a blackness that never seemed to end, but that still somehow tasted like blackcurrant trifle. It was over.

...it was over, that was, right until she landed on her ass on the very rooftop she'd just been so rudely yanked away from. It was day. That was wrong. It had been night, deepest night, and there had been a battle raging all around her...

But it was daylight now, and there were no signs that there had ever been a battle here. There were no signs that there had ever been a *person* here, at least not since the building was constructed. Pigeons perched on the roof's edge, watching her with brainless yellow eyes. Gravel and pigeon feces covered everything—including, she was sure, her own behind. Victory Anna clambered to her feet, keeping a firm grip on the ray gun she'd stolen from Dr. Darwin, and attempted to brush the mess off the back of her skirt. It wasn't going easily. Pigeon shit was annoying like that.

"Poly?" she said, more out of reflex than because she actually expected to receive a reply. Dr. Darwin's stupid gun had clearly come with some sort of unexpected recoil, one that knocked her forward a few hours or even days through time. Always a risk, when you were dealing with bloody morons who thought that neutrinos were Nature's way of providing better evil Legos.

As expected, Polychrome didn't answer her. Also as expected, Victory Anna's flying machine was gone, cleared away with the rest of the detritus from the fight. The image of Poly trying to fly the contraption home was almost as amusing as the situation was irritating. Victory Anna sighed, slung the ray gun (she was already beginning to regard it as "hers") over her shoulder, and started for the door that would let her access the stairs. Time to get home, before Poly started to worry about her.

She needn't have been concerned.

"Pol? I'm home." Victory Anna stopped at the doorway to the converted section of steam tunnel that housed their lair, squinting into the gloom. It was like all the lights had been turned off, even the digital read-out on the DVR. That wasn't right. Victory Anna swallowed the first scrambling signs of panic and called, more loudly, "Lena? Stop playing silly buggers. Turn on the lights."

Polychrome—Yelena—didn't answer her.

"Lena, this isn't funny."

There was still no answer.

Keeping the panic at bay was no longer an option. Victory Anna inched slowly forward into the dark, waiting for the ground to change texture as she stepped onto the carpet, or for a couch to block her progress. Neither of these things happened. All she felt underfoot was stone, and the air smelled like heat, stale urine, and the clamminess of the underground. It was like no one had lived here in years, if ever. "Lena?" she whispered.

Her questing hands finally met resistance: a pipe, covered with rust and traceries of moisture. She remembered that pipe. It had been situated right in the middle of their lair, up until the day when she removed it, first working for hours to re-route the water it had been carrying back into the municipal supply. There was no way that pipe could be there. Not unless—unless—

Victory Anna left their lair at a dead run, making her way rapidly back to street level. She didn't even look around for hero patrols when she emerged from the tunnels. She just sprinted down the street toward the nearest coffee shop with a "Free WiFi" sign.

If she'd been paying attention, she might have seen all the other subtle changes in the neighborhood she thought of as her own; all the other things that were warped or out of place. She wasn't paying attention. All her attention was on running.

The barista looked up when Victory Anna came bursting into the room, and blinked. "Whoa," he said. "Is there some sort of comic book convention in town?"

She stared at him. It took several seconds before she finally found her voice and asked, as sweetly as she could muster, "Is there a public-access terminal I can use?"

"Sure," he said. "In the corner. You're in luck, it just freed up."

"Yes," said Victory Anna weakly. "In luck." She walked over to the machine, signed in, and began to type.

Finding what she needed was surprisingly easy; all she had to do was run a search for "San Diego Superheroes." What came up was an endless list of articles about comic books, about everyday people who had managed to rise to meet supposedly impossible odds, about firefighters and policemen and politicians. Not a single superhuman. She tried the websites of the superhumans she knew were online. They all came up missing. There was only one answer that made sense:

Somehow, the recoil from Dr. Darwin's ray gun had been enough to blast her right out of her own reality and into this one. Well. That was a thing she knew how to handle easily enough. "May I use your restroom?" she asked, standing.

"It's in the back," said the barista.

"Thank you for your hospitality," said Victory Anna solemnly, and walked into the back of the coffee shop, where she joined the line of people waiting for the bathroom. As it inched slowly toward her goal, she struggled to slow her heartbeat and calm her breathing. It would reduce the trauma of what she had to do.

When it was finally her turn, she stepped into the small, bleach-scented room and closed the door firmly behind herself. Then she turned to face her reflection, using it as a guide while she carefully lined the ray gun up on her own chest. *Epona guide me,* she thought, and closed her eyes, and pulled the trigger.

Three hours later, when the barista finally got approval from his manager to take the locked door off its hinges, there was no sign that she had ever been there at all.

Victory Anna woke up to the sound of someone knocking vigorously on the bathroom door. She pushed herself, groaning, to her feet. "Just a moment!" she shouted.

"Hurry up!" shouted the knocker, giving the doorknob a good rattle to illustrate his point.

"Oh, my aching head..." Victory Anna looked around the bathroom. It looked exactly the same. That didn't tell her anything. One off-market coffee shop restroom was very much like another. She holstered her ray gun, turned, and opened the door.

The man who'd been knocking glared as he pushed past her, and all but shoved her out of the bathroom in the process of slamming and locking the door. Victory Anna sighed and walked out into the coffee shop, which, like the bathroom, looked exactly the same. Well, almost the same. The barista was gone, replaced by a woman who could have been his sister. She looked at Victory Anna, and blinked.

"Please don't blow up my shop," she said.

Victory Anna grinned. "Oh, good," she said. "You recognize me." Then she turned, humming to herself, and walked out onto the street.

She was halfway back to the hidden entrance to her lair when a voice declared behind her, "Stop, unlicensed gadgeteer, and identify yourself!"

"That's a bit rude, don't you think? I have a name, you know." Victory Anna turned to see which of the various possible superheroes was accosting her...and froze, unsure of what other reaction could possibly be appropriate.

The Super Patriots, West Coast Division, lowered themselves dramatically to the sidewalk in front of the frozen Victory Anna. The blond man at the front of their small formation was wearing a black suit with starburst white designs on the shoulders and boots. He was accompanied by a woman in a red suit that seemed to have been molded to resemble a lobster's carapace, a woman with rabbit ears, antlers, and a sheriff's silver star, and a man in a silver jumpsuit, with a tool belt around his waist.

"Identify yourself," repeated the blond man.

"You're the Super Patriots, aren't you?" asked Victory Anna.

The members of America's premiere super team exchanged a look, clearly baffled. Finally, the woman in the lobster corset said, "Yes. Who are you?"

"You're the bloody Super Patriots," said Victory Anna. She stabbed a finger toward the blond man. "You control light, don't you? What do they call you?"

"Prism," said the man, sounding as confused as the lobster girl. "Who *are* you?"

"In a dimension where you had the good sense to be born with breasts, I'm your girlfriend," said Victory Anna. She pulled the ray gun from her belt. The Super Patriots shouted, beginning to move– but not quickly enough. By the time they started to attack, she had pulled the trigger, and was gone.

This time, the blast deposited her on a sidewalk. It was dark. Victory Anna staggered back to her feet, head spinning, and squinted at the sky. There were no stars. There wasn't even a moon. "What the hell?" she asked, of no one in particular. "Is this the dimension of bloody eternal night or something?" The empty sky gave no answer.

When all else failed, the local coffee shop seemed to be a decent barometer of the changes. Victory Anna started walking back toward it, keeping the ray gun out this time, in case she needed to leave quickly. As she approached, she saw that the lights were on. That was a good sign. If there was any light at all, it was unlikely that the Dark Gods from beyond the Walls of What-Is had managed to break through and eat everyone.

Although she might have preferred that, considering what she saw when she looked through the coffee shop window. The menu was as elaborate as it had ever been, but instead of coffee, tea, and assorted types of cocoa, the beverages on offer consisted of blood, blood, and assorted types of blood. It was remarkable how many sorts of blood there were, once you decided to go exotic. Not that the naked mole rats likely appreciated the steep cost of their plasma. They'd be rather too busy being dead.

When vampires have consumed the world, there's really only one thing to do. Victory Anna backed slowly away from the window, watching to be sure she hadn't been spotted. Then she turned and ran off down the street.

Time to find a payphone.

It turned out to be surprisingly easy to locate a public phone in a world dominated by vampires, possibly because they were harder to lose in a world cast into eternal darkness than your average portable. Victory Anna dialed quickly before wedging herself into the corner behind the phone bank, blocking herself as much as possible from view. The phone rang once, twice...

"Hello?" asked the familiar honey-sweet voice of the Princess.

Victory Anna wanted to relax. She didn't allow herself that luxury. "Princess, hello. I have two questions for you."

"Do you now?" asked the Princess, tone going suddenly suspicious. "Why am I answering them?"

"Because I had the number for your castle, which means I must have good reason for calling you," said Victory Anna. "First question: do you recognize my voice?"

"Can't say as I do, sugar. Am I supposed to?"

"Apparently not. My name is Victory Anna. I'm a science heroine from a parallel dimension. Your cognate is an ally of mine." Dimensional travel just made things so *complicated.* "Which brings me to my second question: are you a vampire?"

There was a long pause. "You really aren't from around here, are you?" asked the Princess, finally. "Honey, we're *all* vampires. Have been since Lord Byron woke up from his undying sleep and decided to remake the world in his glorious image."

"How could he even get to you?" asked Victory Anna. "You live in a castle made of rainbows and unicorn laughter, for Epona's sake! He'd have to—" She paused. "He turned all the little girls in the world, and you simply became a vampire, didn't you?"

"I'm their living nightmare," the Princess confirmed. "Look, whoever you are, whatever world you came from, you need to get out of here, and you need to get out *now*. I may be a vampire who doesn't bite people for fun, but I'm in the minority. Get in your little science machine, and go home."

The line went dead. Victory Anna looked miserably at the receiver. "But that's what I'm trying to do..." she said, to no one in particular. Then she removed the ray gun from her belt. By the time the local equivalent of The Super Patriots showed up, following the scent of fresh blood, she was long gone.

The next world seemed to be entirely populated by mer-people. "Seemed" was the relevant term; Victory Anna only had time to see a few of them swimming toward her before the need for oxygen caused her to blast herself again, sending herself hurtling out of that underwater reality. At least the ray gun was no longer knocking her out. Drowning would have made things awkward.

The world after that? Robots. After that, post-alien invasion, like something out of H.G. Wells. The worst was the world that appeared to have been completely bent to the whims of the Marketing Division of The Super Patriots, Inc. Every hero was iconic, every color was bright, and every eye Victory Anna met was full of screams.

When she finally found herself in a bucolic countryside straight out of a Ray Bradbury story (and no one she encountered was willing to tell her what had happened to San Diego, something she was *not* willing to spend too much time considering), Victory Anna had had quite enough. She found the local train station and begged her way onto the next train up the coast. Portland still appeared on the map, as did San Francisco, even if Seattle had followed San Diego into unexplained oblivion. "Never liked rain, anyway," she said to the confused ticket agent.

"You have a nice trip, miss," he said. If her outlandish attire struck him as odd, well, he didn't say anything; it wouldn't have been polite.

Victory Anna took her ticket and walked down the wooden platform to wait for the train. When it arrived—a long, battered thing with an engine that chugged mournfully along like it had been wounded and was wondering when it would be allowed to lay down and die—she climbed aboard, found her seat, and collapsed. She was asleep before they pulled out of the station, and she remained asleep most of the way up the length of California, as all the exhaustion caught up with her at once. Jumping between worlds is hard on a body, and she'd done it a dozen times in less than eight hours. She was done.

Portland, Oregon: Earth A

Velma Martinez—occasionally known as "Velveteen," official superheroine of the city of Portland, but only when she was wearing the headband with the rabbit ears on it—walked up the path toward her front door, most of her attention focused on digging her keys out of her pocket without dropping the two bags of groceries in her arms. Under the circumstances, she could probably be forgiven for not realizing that there was someone hiding in her geraniums until that someone stepped out of the bushes and shoved the muzzle of a ray gun against the back of her neck. Velma froze.

"I have been through eighty-seven parallel realities to get here, and most of them were *balls*," said Victory Anna wearily. Exhaustion made her accent stronger. "Now I don't know what you did, and I don't know how you did it, but you're going to *un*do it now. If you do, maybe I won't shoot you."

Velma closed her eyes. "Hi, Torrey," she said, quietly. "I'm sorry you're here."

"I bet you are, me having the drop on you and all. Now send me home."

No, thought Velma, *that's not why I'm sorry.* "I can't," she said aloud. "I'm not the reason that you're here. Put down the gun. We need to go inside so I can make a phone call."

"What, calling your allies to come and apprehend me?"

"No. Calling the man who can make you understand what's really going on."

And Victoria Cogsworth—who was really a quite reasonable person once you got to know her, and when you weren't casually erasing her world and all the people she cared about from existence—paused for a moment before finally lowering her ray gun. "Do you have running water?" she asked, in a small voice. "I'd commit acts of blasphemy and possibly homicide for a hot shower."

"I have plumbing," Velma confirmed.

"Oh, thank Epona," said Victory Anna, and followed her inside.

Victory Anna stayed in the bathroom for the better part of an hour, showering, crying, showering again, and finally blow drying and braiding her hair. When she finally emerged, dressed in a borrowed bathrobe that Velveteen had stolen from the Crystal Glitter Unicorn Cloud Castle the last time the Princess had a sleepover, she found Velveteen sitting on the couch, waiting for her. Her erstwhile nemesis was properly dressed in velvet unitard and bunny ears, making it clear that the time for civilian identities was over.

The woman sitting next to Velveteen on the couch was familiar the way that everything in this universe was familiar: so close to normal, and yet so far away at the same time. Her skin was the proper shade of Rankin/Bass holiday special blue, and her hair was appropriately white, with highlights that mimicked the Northern Lights. But it was also cut too short, in an asymmetric bob, and her eye makeup was a blend of silvers and pinks that the Jacqueline Frost Victoria knew had stopped using years ago. Victory Anna stopped at the end of the hall, staring.

Jackie spoke first. That was right, but the words she said were wrong, loaded with a degree of compassion that Victory Anna simply couldn't believe from the daughter of the Snow Queen: "Victoria, I'm so sorry."

Victory Anna's mouth went dry. "What are you talking about? What are you doing here?" She looked to Velveteen. "Why in the world would you call Frostbite to explain the situation to me? She's not going to help us."

Jackie groaned. "Oh, sweet Christmas. Vel, she's been living in a reality where you and I didn't stay friends. Most of those are Frostbite worlds. It turns out that without people to tell me when I'm pushing it, I can get a little, well, bitchy."

"There's a shocker," deadpanned Velveteen. She focused on Victory Anna. "Jackie's here because she's one of my best friends, and she's going to take us to the man I mentioned before."

"Don't worry about getting dressed," said Jackie. "The mirror takes care of everything."

"What are you talking about?" asked Victory Anna. Jackie just smiled and pursed her lips like she was going to whistle. There was no sound; instead, a stream of cartoon snowflakes flowed into the room and covered everything briefly in a veil of white. And when the whiteness lifted…

…they were someplace else, standing in a snow bank that smelled like peppermint, and was as warm as fresh cotton candy. The sky overhead was an oddly cheery shade of navy blue, spangled with silver stars that looked like they'd been cut from tin foil. Victory Anna yelped, hand going automatically to her belt as she reached for a ray gun that wasn't there. Then she yelped again, staring down at the holiday-themed version of her usual uniform which had replaced her borrowed bathrobe. All the gears were the golden shade of Epona's sacred bridle, and her normally brown leather corset was done in white. "What in the bloody…?"

"Dammit, Jackie, I liked that bathrobe," said Velveteen, sounding annoyed. Victory Anna looked away from her own attire. Velveteen's clothes had undergone the same sea-change as her own; she was now wearing a brown velvet mini-dress over burgundy tights, and had a sprig of holly in her hair.

"Sorry. Magic mirror travel isn't an exact science," said Jackie. She reached into the nearest snowdrift, pulling out a large, flat box wrapped in brightly-colored paper. "Do not open until Christmas."

"Which means 'open before going home,' since it's always Christmas here. Thanks for giving back my bathrobe." Velveteen tucked the box under her arm and turned to Victory Anna. "Come on. There's someone you need to talk to."

Jackie and Velveteen started walking down the drift toward a distant glow. Victory Anna followed, and realized that the illumination—which she had initially assumed was the Northern Lights—was coming from a small village nestled just beyond the curvature of the hill. A large man in a blue robe trimmed with gold rope was waiting for them, a wreath of holly crowning his head. Victory Anna stumbled to a stop.

"Snowfather?" she whispered.

"Ho, ho, ho," said the man Velveteen and Jackie knew as Santa Claus. There was no jolly twinkle in his eye. "Hello, Victoria. I'm sorry we had to meet like this."

Victoria Anna took a shaky breath. Then, as so many do when faced with their personal incarnation of Father Christmas, she burst into tears, ran the rest of the way down the hill, and threw herself into his arms. "Snowfather, I'm so glad you're here!" she wailed. "I've been jumping through all these worlds, and it's been a bloody *nightmare*, and I just want to go *home!*"

"Oh, Torrey." Santa put his arm around her and turned her around, so that they were both facing the open door to his cottage. "My poor, poor dear. We have so much to talk about, you and I…" He led her inside and shut the door, leaving Velveteen and Jackie standing in the snow.

Minutes slipped by. Finally, Jackie asked, "Cocoa?"

"Is it spiked?"

"Uh, have you met me?"

"Then yes, cocoa. Please." Velveteen followed Jackie down the village road to another small house. The pair went inside, and all was, if not merry, at least so very, very bright.

"The spare room is yours for as long as you want it," said Velma, opening the door to the second bedroom. She'd been using it for storage since she moved in. A call to the Princess had triggered some emergency home decorating, and her boxes were now stacked neatly in the garage, while the room was clean and equipped with all the standard furnishings: a bed, a dresser, a standing wardrobe. Well, maybe the wardrobe wasn't exactly "standard," but there was only so much normal you could expect from a bunch of woodland creatures with contractor's licenses. "I'll call the governor in the morning, and we can get started on getting you a hero license, just so The Super Patriots don't come sniffing around."

"Lovely," said Victoria dully, and walked into the room. She sat down on the edge of the four-poster bed, a puppet with cut strings, and closed her eyes. "I'd like to be alone now, if you don't mind."

"…okay," said Velma. She closed the door gently as she left the room, and walked down the hall to where Jackie was waiting.

"Well?" asked Jackie.

"I don't think this is going to work," Velma said. "She hates it here. She hates me in specific. Why can't she stay in Winter?"

"Because in her original world, there was no Christmas, and having her in Winter for too long would warp things," said Jackie calmly. "Besides, if she doesn't connect with people, she's probably going to turn into a supervillain."

"Oh, yay," said Velma. "You make her a more appealing roommate all the time."

Jackie sighed. "She has nowhere else to go, Vel. You know what that's like."

"I know. That's why she can stay." Velma glanced back toward the hallway. "I just hope this doesn't go badly."

"Me, too, Vel. Me, too."

The two of them sat in silence after that, and tried to pretend they couldn't hear the distant sound of Victoria Cogsworth, alone in her room, sobbing.

VELVETEEN vs. The Uncomfortable Conversation

It was a beautiful Portland night, which meant that it wasn't raining, although it had been raining an hour earlier, and would probably be raining again in another hour. Velveteen, sitting once again like an Easter-themed gargoyle on the edge of the municipal library roof, wouldn't have minded a downpour. Hell, she wouldn't have minded a *blizzard*, as long as she didn't have to go back to her house. She wasn't a "living with roommates" kind of person. The last roommate she'd been willing to live with voluntarily had been…

Had been…

Had been Yelena, back when they were Velma and Yelena, best friends, not Velveteen and Sparkle Bright, teammates, or Velveteen and Sparkle Bright, mortal enemies. Lena was the only person Vel had ever lived with happily, and even though all that had been years ago, sometimes she still missed waking up and knowing that there was someone else she really, truly trusted in the room with her. Under normal circumstances, she probably would have grown up to fill that role with a boyfriend or a husband, but she'd never had normal circumstances, had she? She'd never had a chance.

What she got instead was superpowers, and an unwanted housemate from a dimension that didn't exist anymore by way of a dimension that never existed in the first place, and a cold rooftop under a starry sky, and waiting for someone who might not decide to show up. In short, what she got was her life, and now that she had it, she was going to have to live with it.

Somewhere in the city below her a horn blared, and somewhere else, someone screamed. Velveteen twitched toward the sounds, but forced herself to stay where she was. Portland had survived before she showed up; it could survive for an hour or so now that she was on the job. Besides, Tag and Jory were both out there on patrol, fighting the good fight against petty crime, parking violations, and the occasional really *stupid* mugger.

(Velveteen understood the attraction of living a life of crime, she honestly did. Make your own hours, be your own boss, and never worry about the office dress code. She just couldn't understand what would drive a person without superpowers to take up a life of crime in a city that had a resident superhero. Especially since the plural of "superhuman" was essentially "squadron." It was extremely rare for anyone with powers to be fighting solo for very long; they attracted each other, like self-illuminating moths with a tropism toward world-ending crisis events.)

Fifteen more minutes. She could wait on the roof for fifteen more minutes before she had to admit that Blacklight wasn't coming, and either she'd been wrong about Blacklight's secret identity, or that secret identity was the reason that Blacklight wasn't coming. It didn't matter which it was. If she was still alone in fifteen minutes, she would leave the roof, return to street level, and dispense justice until she was tired of punching people in the face. Which, judging by the way she currently felt, might be the better part of a year. Fifteen more minutes.

Those fifteen minutes raced by like they had super speed. When the last one was gone, Velveteen closed her eyes and sighed heavily. "Damn," she murmured.

"I'm not sure the situation calls for profanity," said a voice behind her. Velveteen turned to see a familiar female figure, dressed head to toe in form-fitting black spandex, hovering about six inches off the roof. Her toes were pointed demurely downward, the flying ballerina. "Sorry I'm late."

"It's okay," said Velveteen, and stood. Her hands were shaking. She balled them into fists and stuck them behind her back, where hopefully they wouldn't be noticed. *Keep it together, Vel...* she thought. "Thanks for coming. I know I don't usually call you out of the blue like that, but this was sort of important."

"I'm always open to a team-up with you," said Blacklight. The black mask that covered her face shifted slightly, like she was smiling under the fabric. "Your call surprised me, I'll admit. Is everything okay with you? You sounded a little bit stressed out in your message."

No, everything is not *okay with me; everything hasn't been okay in a very long time.* Velveteen took a breath, trying to sort through her thoughts. Then she opened her mouth to say what she'd called the other heroine to Portland to hear. What came out instead was: "Do you want to go beat the holy crap out of some muggers too stupid to find themselves an unprotected city?"

"I thought you'd never ask," said Blacklight. By the tone of her voice, this time she was definitely smiling.

It is a generally accepted truth that superhumans do not make friends easily. Their jobs are naturally isolating; they have trouble forming casual bonds with the people around them, fearing that too much familiarity might lead to murder or mutation. Classes of superhumans can be common, but some specific power combinations are incredibly rare or even unique, leading to enhanced feelings of isolation. A superhuman with an uncommon power set knows, deeply and without question, that no one understands them.

As a consequence of this daily isolation, when a superhuman does manage to form a close emotional bond with another individual, whether superpowered or non, those bonds tend to acquire strength at an accelerated, almost unhealthy rate. Friendships and undying rivalries are born in a matter of hours, all fueled by the desperate, undeniably human need to connect–to know that someone, somewhere, understands them well enough to love them, or hate them. It doesn't seem to matter which emotion wins. It's the connection that matters, the feeling that, for one brief moment, they are not alone in this world.

Superhuman relationships can change forms repeatedly during the lives of the parties involved, going from platonic friendships to romantic entanglements to sworn enemies without visibly affecting the status quo. Superhumans do not, for better or for worse, "move on."

It has been suggested that this tendency is exacerbated by the policies of The Super Patriots, Inc. regarding interpersonal communication and interaction. Rather than offering peer counseling and support, The Super Patriots, Inc. isolates groups of young heroes to "forge teams out of lone wolves and individualists." The official documentation on this policy claims that it is the only way to give superhumans any concept of teamwork, which does not come naturally to people who can juggle cars. The world's few solo heroes say that this is not just bullshit, but *dangerous* bullshit; superhumans are just people, and they will develop their personal stances on teamwork and friendship without having a corporate model thrust upon them. The Super Patriots, Inc. naturally claims that this is exactly what the dangerously unstable elements within the solo hero community would like everyone to believe, since a world without teams would be a world more open to manipulation by those same dangerous elements.

Whatever the truth may be, these things are certain: superhumans don't forge bonds easily...and once those bonds are formed, they rarely, if ever, let go.

Blacklight darted and weaved in the air like a monochromatic lightning bolt, leaving trails of black glitter behind her. They sparkled for only an instant against the night. The light pouring from her hands was equally black, visible because it was so much darker than the darkness around it. Seeing light that black coming from the other heroine's hands made Vel's heart hurt a little. Yelena's powers weren't emotion-based, exactly, but the spectrum of her blasts was affected by her emotional state. Most of her colors didn't match up to any normal color wheel—she blushed blue when she was embarrassed, and she shot out beams of bright yellow when she was angry. But depression and heartbreak and sadness had always been darker than her other colors, trending finally into absolute black. The whip she'd used on Velveteen during their first, and last, real confrontation had been made of black light.

"Velveteen! Check your twenty!" shouted Blacklight. She blasted another mechanical bank robber with a solid bolt of blackness. He went down hard, stuttering and spitting sparks.

Velveteen didn't even turn. She just waved a hand, and Breyer horses swarmed the robot that had been able to slam into her, knocking the thing over and allowing the G.I. Joe dolls—sorry, action figures—that had been riding them to begin the process of hog-tying the struggling automaton. Another robot charged straight at her. This one, Velveteen grabbed by the head and flipped over her shoulder. It landed hard, and stopped moving.

In satisfyingly short order, nothing was moving but the two heroines and Velveteen's army of animated toys. Blacklight turned her head toward the other woman. "Are you hurt?"

"No. You?"

"No." Blacklight landed, prodding a robot with her foot. "New villain?"

"Oh, probably. I was about due for one." Especially now that Tag was in Portland practically full-time, and Jory was still getting accustomed to the idea that her sister was alive, well, and Governor. Adding Victory Anna to the mix had made a resident supervillain practically inevitable. "Looks like whoever it is does the robot thing. I like the robot thing. If they have anything I can call a face, they belong to me."

Blacklight did a double-take. If her face had been visible, she would have been blinking. Then she said, "I always forget how versatile your powers really are."

"That's me. The most versatile support heroine on the West Coast." Velveteen wasn't going to get a better chance than this; she knew it, and she still hesitated, waiting for the sick feeling in her stomach to go away. It didn't go. Finally, she took a breath and forced herself past it, saying, "Look, we don't have to wait around here for the cleanup crew. I can call this in and say that we were in pursuit of another incident. The paperwork can wait until tomorrow."

"What's the other incident?" asked Blacklight.

"There's something I want to show you."

Blacklight went still, apparently considering the statement. Velveteen held her breath, wondering if it was obvious just how nervous she was; wondering if there was anything she could have said or done differently, anything that would have guaranteed the other woman would come with her. She was just starting to believe that she'd failed, this wasn't going to work after all, when Blacklight shrugged.

"Sure," she said. "I don't have anywhere else to be tonight."

Velveteen grinned in relief. "Come on. Follow me."

Like all major cities that wanted to maintain a good relationship with its superhero population, Portland had established regular maintenance on selected rooftops around town, making them safe places for conversation and the occasional stakeout. The superhuman community repaid the city by avoiding those locations when they were planning to have a full-blown battle. Even a supervillain can respect the convenience of a rooftop where you don't step on broken glass every time you forget to look where you're putting your feet. Of course, the media usually kept a close eye on those rooftops, hoping to catch a few candid pictures of a hero–or villain–that could be used as filler. And that was why, when she needed a place to talk privately,

Velveteen steered as far away from those superhero roach motels as she possibly could.

Sadly, Blacklight didn't seem to understand the logic behind Velveteen's choice of locations. "I realize this is your city, and that you're the one with all the local knowledge and everything," she said, slowly, "but why are we hiding behind a giant doughnut the color of Pepto-Bismol? Did I miss something? Is Easybake on the loose again?"

"As far as I know, the Baker still has Easybake under wraps," said Velveteen. Then she paused. "There is something wrong with my life that I can say those words and they make sense and are not a sign that I have hit my head."

"There's something wrong with my life right now," said Blacklight. "What's wrong with my life is that I'm standing in the shadow of a *giant pink doughnut.* Please explain the giant pink doughnut. I'm having a really hard time with it."

"Voodoo Doughnut is a Portland landmark," said Velveteen. "No supervillain will attack the place, because it's where they get their four a.m. bacon maple bars. No superhero will come near the place, because everything contains carbs. It's the perfect spot to have a private conversation."

"Why are we having a private conversation?" asked Blacklight warily.

Velveteen took a deep breath before reaching up and removing her domino mask. It was a small thing, and could never have concealed her identity from someone who knew who she really was; like most heroes, she wore it out of tradition, and to maintain the polite social fiction that she could live a normal life if she wanted one. Taking it off was still one of the hardest things she had ever done. Blacklight stiffened, every line of her body screaming confusion and surprise. Velma lowered the mask.

"Yelena, I'm so sorry," she said.

Blacklight recoiled. "What are you talking about?" she demanded. "Did you hit your head while we were fighting those robots? Did one of the robots hit your head? You're clearly delusional. Put your damn mask back on before somebody sees you."

"I'm not going to put my mask back on," said Velma. "And if I'm delusional for taking it off, you're delusional for thinking that you could fool me like this forever. I *know* you, Lena. I've known you for most of my life. You're the only sister I've ever had. Did you honestly think you could fight beside me and never have me figure out who you were?"

"I don't know what you're talking about," snarled Blacklight. She gave a little skip, ending with her hovering a foot in the air. "You need to seek psychological help."

It would only take a few seconds for Blacklight to launch herself from the roof and disappear, and once that happened, Velma knew that she was never going to get another shot at this apology. She took a deep breath, and blurted, "Marketing lied to you."

Blacklight froze.

Seeing her chance–maybe her only chance–Velma continued: "They told you I was going to go to the tabloids. They said I'd been demanding money in exchange for silence. But I never did, Lena. I never did that. I didn't even know what they told you I was threatening to tell."

"And what is it that they told…Lena…you were threatening to tell?" asked Blacklight, in a low, dangerous voice.

"If you're not her, I can't tell you," said Velma. "It's not my secret now, and it wasn't my secret then. I don't tell other people's secrets. I'm a better friend than that."

"If you're such a good friend, why did you leave?" For the first time since they arrived on the roof, Blacklight didn't sound confused, or angry: she sounded almost hurt. "Shouldn't you have stayed and tried to fix things?"

"I left because Marketing lied to me, too. They told me that you and Aaron had been having a relationship in secret, because you didn't want your parents to find out. They said you'd been using me as a distraction. They even had copies of an interview the two of you had supposedly done together." Velma's mouth twisted in a small, bitter smile. "They wanted me to understand that I was a second string hero at best, and that the two of you, you were going to be stars. Stars shine brightest when they shine together."

Blacklight's heels hit the rooftop with a soft but audible thump. "What?" Her voice was barely above a whisper.

"I was hurt. I was confused. I believed them. I shouldn't have, and I'm sorry, Lena, I'm so, so sorry. I was a terrible friend. I should have trusted you. I should have *talked* to you. But I didn't. I let them drive me away, because…" Velma took a breath. In for a penny, in for a pound. "I was jealous, you know? Everyone knew you were going to be first string, that you were probably going to lead the team one day, and I was always just going to be the girl who brought toys to life. Part of me wanted to believe them, because if you were a bad person, I wasn't being a bad friend by being jealous of you. I'm sorry."

For a long moment, Blacklight said nothing.

"Please say something," said Velma. "Please. Tell me I'm crazy again. Tell me you're not who I think you are. But please say *something*."

"You weren't a bad friend," said Blacklight.

Velma blinked. "What?"

"I said you weren't a bad friend." Blacklight slowly reached up and pulled off the hood that concealed her face. Her hair, freed from its confinement, tumbled down her back. She wasn't wearing any makeup. She looked tired. "I'm the one who kicked the crap out of you in the locker room. If someone's getting the 'bad friend' trophy here, I think it's going to be me."

Even though she'd been sure she was right—well, almost sure; sure enough to confront the other heroine, anyway, and that could have gone really badly—Velma froze, mouth working silently. Finally, she said the first thing that came into her head: "How do you fit all your hair under that mask? You should look like a conehead."

A small smile tugged at the corners of Yelena's mouth. "Imagineer made it for me. It's supposed to be a trans-dimensional shower cap."

"And it covers your face because…?"

"See, the nice thing about Imagineer is that she's so busy thinking about what she's going to do next that she doesn't ask very many questions. I told her I didn't want to smudge my eyeliner, and she bought it without a second thought."

Velma shook her head slowly. "Wow. And she's supposed to be defending truth, justice, and the merchandising revenue?"

"We just keep her away from open flames and things pretty much sort themselves out."

Silence fell after that. Velma and Yelena just looked at each other for a long while, two former friends turned bitter enemies turned…something else. Maybe. If they could find their way across the rooftop, and across all the things it represented.

Finally, Velma spoke. "You're the reason I got to Oregon, aren't you? You zapped me across the state line."

"I don't think of it as zapping, exactly, but…yeah." Yelena shrugged. "I thought you deserved a chance. You never really had one."

"Neither did you, you know."

"You know who I am now," said Yelena. "What did Marketing use to make me hate you?"

Velma took a deep breath. "They told you that I was going to tell the tabloids that you were gay."

Yelena didn't say anything.

There didn't seem to be any good way out of the conversation, and so Velma kept barreling forward, saying, "I never said any such thing. I didn't even know that you liked girls like that until a couple of weeks ago."

"What happened a couple of weeks ago?" asked Yelena suspiciously.

In for a penny, in for a pounding: "Santa Claus and Hailey Ween—you remember her, she's the current Halloween Princess, she kidnapped me when we were kids? Yeah, her—decided I needed to start living up to my responsibilities, whatever *that* means, and they created a whole alternate timeline to show me what could have happened if I hadn't left The Super Patriots. Only it turns out that for me to stay, you had to go, so in that reality, you were the one who walked out when we turned eighteen."

"And somehow, that told you I was…" Yelena stopped, seemingly unable to get the word out.

It was odd. Marketing had been controlling their lives since they were children, and Velma could make a real case for them having practically ruined her life on several occasions. But she had never felt more like setting the entire department on fire than she did when she realized that Yelena couldn't make herself finish that sentence. "No," said Velma, gently. "*You* told me. After you introduced me to your girlfriend. Who hit me with a cattle prod. I guess no matter what world we're in, we were always going to have a falling out."

"What makes you think what's true for her is true for me?" asked Yelena. There was a sudden coldness in her voice, like she was just waiting for the blackmail to begin.

"I know you, Lena," said Velma. "Even if you never speak to me again after this, even if this ruins any chance we had of being friends, I *know* you. I knew it was true as soon as I saw your alternate with Vic—with her girlfriend. That version of you looked at her like she was the whole world. And you've never looked at Aaron that way. Not once."

Velma stopped talking. For a long moment, Yelena didn't say anything. Velma winced, looking down at her feet. She wasn't sure how many long silences one conversation could contain, but this one had to be approaching the limit, if it wasn't there already.

"I knew I was a lesbian by the time I was ten years old," said Yelena. Velma's head snapped up. Yelena kept talking. "My parents found out a year later, and sold me to the corporation, so that Marketing could talk me out of being 'a sexual deviant.' They tried. They're good at talking people out of things, and talking people into things, but they couldn't talk me out of who I was. I guess that's why they decided I needed to be with a boy who'd hold my hand in public and smile for the cameras and not care when I only ever let him kiss me when people were looking. The worst part is, I *wanted* to do it. After what they told me you did…I was terrified of being outed to the press, and I was so mad at you. I hated you for betraying me. It was the best way I could think of to hurt you."

"It worked," said Velma. "I hated you for years."

"Why did you stop?"

"Because I met that other version of you, and realized we'd both been played. We should have been best friends forever, Lena. It should have been you and me against the world. But instead, we wound up on different sides. They put us on different sides. I can't hate you for that. But I can sure as hell hate them."

"I realized there was something wrong when they started telling us that you were a supervillain," said Yelena. "I was willing to believe that you were a back-stabbing little bitch. Marketing worked hard, for a long time, making sure that I thought everybody was out to get the front pages. But I couldn't believe that you were evil. The Vel I knew could be selfish and pushy—"

"Hey," protested Velma.

"—but she wasn't *evil*." Yelena shook her head. "Aaron didn't believe it, either. He helped me get to Oregon in time to get you over the state line. It's easier when we work together. Neither one of us can stand up to Marketing on our own."

"I think they do something to your head when they get you by yourself," said Velma. "I've been dating a guy who used to belong to the Midwest team, and he stopped buying the party line when they stopped getting him to counseling."

"I think you're probably right," admitted Yelena. "The longer I'm away from headquarters, the clearer my head gets. When I'm being Blacklight…I don't know. It's like she really is a different person. A smarter person. I think better, I react faster, and it's not just because

I'm working with you again." She smiled. "Although that helps. It was never the same without you, Vel."

"That's because I'm awesome," said Velma, and laughed—only somehow the laughter translated into crying, and the crying into sobbing, until she was standing on the rooftop with her face in her hands, trying to make the tears stop. She didn't hear Yelena's approach, but then the other woman's arms were around her shoulders, and they were both crying. Velma uncovered her face, put her arms around Yelena, and wept like her heart was breaking, when that wasn't the case at all.

After spending far too many years wounded, her heart was finally starting to heal. And so two heroes held each other in the shadow of a giant pink doughnut, and cried.

When they were finally finished crying—and had the pounding headaches and aching eyes to commemorate the occasion—Yelena and Velma sat down side-by-side on the roof of Voodoo Doughnut, not looking at each other. Velma leaned back on her hands, looking up at the sky. Yelena looked down at her black-gloved hands.

"So," she said, finally. "Now what?"

"I don't know," said Velma. "I just had to apologize for letting Marketing do that to us. I couldn't live with myself if I didn't at least try."

Slowly, Yelena asked, "So you don't care that I'm…that I'm gay?"

"God, no," said Velma, finally looking at the other woman. "Why should I give a damn about that? You were my best friend. You were an awesome roommate. I've missed you. What difference does it make if you're gay or straight?"

"It makes a difference to Marketing," said Yelena bitterly. "They were pretty confident that it would make a difference to everybody else."

"Well it doesn't," said Velma. "At least not to me."

"I've missed you," said Yelena, glancing up. "Everyone there is so fake all the time. Like they're posing for the cameras even when the cameras aren't on."

"I remember," said Velma. "I'm sorry I left you there."

"I'm sorry I tried to kill you with a light whip," said Yelena.

"Don't worry about it; I know you weren't really trying to kill me."

Yelena blinked. "Really? How?"

Velma smiled a little. "If you'd been trying to kill me, I would've been dead."

"You were always more powerful than you thought you were, Vel," said Yelena. "It used to drive me crazy, the way you put yourself down all the time."

"I had people supporting my point of view," said Velma. Marketing had always been more than happy to make sure she understood her place on the team, and that place was *not* on the front lines. "Anyway, that's over now. I'm figuring things out. I'm getting it all under control."

"I know. I've been watching you." Yelena paused, grimacing. "That sounded better in my head, I swear. I'm not stalking you or anything. I just wanted to know that you were doing okay, and then you seemed so happy, and I just wanted to fight with you again. That's why I put on this costume. Because I wanted to fight with you, and know that everything was okay again. Like it should have been from the beginning."

Velma sighed. "And that, right there, is where Marketing fucked up. If they hadn't tried to drive a wedge between us, I would have stayed with The Super Patriots forever. That's where my friends were." They could have kept all her merchandising dollars–and she and Aaron would probably have married by now, maybe even had a kid. Lots of superhero wedding and superhero baby gear for the fans to buy. But they threw that all away because they were worried about their light manipulator not playing properly in Peoria. Bitterly, Velma added, "Idiots."

There was no need for Yelena to ask who she was talking about; she already knew. "So what do we do now?"

"I don't know. I don't want to go back to being enemies–"

"I don't think I could do that if I wanted to."

"That's reassuring. I really don't want you to hit me with another light whip." Velma grinned. After a pause, Yelena grinned back. "But how much of this is Marketing going to figure out?"

"None of it, if we don't let their spies report back to them," Yelena said. Then she turned, and directed a blast of brilliant white light at the shadow beneath the big pink doughnut. There was a shriek, a thud, and a woman's outline was left where the shadow had been. The outline turned solid, and the body of a second-string shadow manipulator who went by the code name "Diffuse" collapsed onto the rooftop.

"What the fu—" Velma caught herself before she finished the word. If she started swearing, she was never going to stop. "That was a spy! Watching us! Me! You! Here!"

"I know." Yelena walked over to Diffuse, prodding the fallen heroine with her toe. Diffuse groaned. Yelena responded by throwing a ball of glittery pink light almost the same shade as the doughnut at Diffuse's head. Diffuse stopped groaning. "Marketing's been monitoring your movements for some time now. I didn't have a way to warn you without blowing my cover, and it's not like they were coming back with anything interesting."

"Says *you*," said Velma. "It's my privacy that they've been violating."

"At least you got to have privacy," Yelena snapped. "I haven't had any since The Super Patriots bought me. She never found out anything too sensitive. If she had, Marketing would have tried to send us after you, and I would have found a way to warn you about what was coming."

Velma took a deep breath. "Wow," she said, finally. "I never really got out of the superhero life, did I? I just put it on hold for a little while."

"No one gets out until they're dead."

"Maybe not even then," said Velma, thinking of Jory. "What do we do with her?"

Yelena looked tired. "I have no idea."

Velma paused. Then she reached for her mask. "I have an idea," she said. "But you're going to need to trust me on this…"

Anyone observing the scene would have seen something which seemed to make no sense at all: a doorway made of twisted black corn stalks rising from the ground at the graveyard's edge. Two figures, one all in black and one dressed like a cross between the Easter Bunny and a modern jazz dancer, supported a third figure between them. She was limp, and her arms and legs seemed to trail off into shadow. Then the doorway lit up, showing a moonlit pumpkin patch where no pumpkin patch was (not unless you were looking through the door, something which was not to be advised), and a blonde teenage girl stepped into view.

Anyone observing the scene would have needed the sense to stay out of hearing range, but they would have seen the discussion punctuated with nods and vigorous gestures, and ending when the woman with the fade-out arms and legs was dumped unceremoniously through the door, which closed behind her. Then the other two turned, shoulders slumped in exhaustion, and made their way into the night.

"Now what?"

"I can't go back. They'll know someone had to tell you about Diffuse."

"It's a little crowded at my place right now. But I bet Jackie will let you come and stay with her, for a little while."

"And what happens after that?"

"After that? We take the bastards on, and we win. There isn't any other option left."

"If you say so," said Yelena.

"I do," said Velma, and took her hand.

Together, they walked on into the Portland night.

VELVETEEN
vs.
Bacon

J ACKIE FROST, PRESUMPTIVE HEIR TO the role of Snow Queen and guardian-in-training to the season of Winter, stood framed in the crystalline glitter of her mother's magic mirror, staring at her friend and sometimes ally, Velma "Velveteen" Martinez. Opening her mouth, the blue-skinned girl uttered four words, each weighted with the strength of prophecy:

"You *cannot* be serious."

"Trust me, I don't believe it either, but yeah, I'm serious," said Vel. "Yelena needs a place to crash for a few days, until we can figure out our next move."

"Okay, just ignoring the part where it's borderline impossible for me to get past you saying 'Yelena needs a place to crash' when you're not talking about *shooting her out of the sky*, why does it need to be the North Pole? We're busy up here! We're doing important things! Secret Christmas things! Do you want to be responsible for getting the entire East Coast accidentally placed on the Naughty List? Well? Do you?"

"She's allergic to pollen, which puts the Princess's place out of the running, she can't go back to the dorms or she'll wind up re-brainwashed before she even finishes getting un-brainwashed, plus there's the whole part where she told me about their spies, I wouldn't send my worst enemy to stay with Hailey, and my place is full of Torrey," said Vel calmly. "You remember Torrey, don't you? Dimensionally-displaced time travel girl who, oh, right, dated a parallel-universe version of Yelena for years and might not take very well to me announcing that she's coming to stay with us? Sorry, Jackie. I don't care how much you hate the idea. Yelena needs a place to stay, Santa said I could always ask the North Pole for help, and I'm asking."

Jackie's lower lip wobbled. "You hate me and want me to be miserable," she said, in an accusing tone.

"If that's what you have to think in order to sleep at night, you go right ahead and think that," said Vel amiably. She turned her back on the mirror, walking to the door at the front of the room and opening it to reveal a tired-looking blonde in an obviously borrowed sweatsuit. The legs were too short and the shirt was too large, making her look like she'd been the victim of a terrible laundry day prank. "Hey, Lena. It's all settled, and you're good to head for the North Pole."

"Really?" Yelena looked past her to the mirror, where Jackie's reflection was standing with arms crossed and nose stuck ostentatiously into the air. "The North Pole doesn't look like it's feeling the love here."

"The North Pole is *totally* feeling the love," said Vel, shutting the door again. "The North Pole is practically turning cartwheels. Jackie, on the other hand, is a stone cold bitch."

"I can hear you, you know," said Jackie.

"This is me, not caring. Do you see my 'I don't care' face?" Vel walked toward the mirror with Yelena close behind her. "Jackie."

Jackie didn't turn.

"*Jackie.*"

"What?"

"She has—"

"I have nowhere else to go," said Yelena, cutting her off. Jackie finally turned, blinking at the pale heroine. Yelena sounded…not defeated, exactly, but worn-down, and vulnerable in a way that she hadn't allowed herself to be since the day when she attacked her own best friend in the locker room. "I can't go back to The Super Patriots. Even if I wanted to, even if I was stupid enough to think that I could somehow play off the whole thing with Diffuse and infiltrate them from within, they'd change my mind."

"She means that literally," said Vel. "You know that. Come on, Jackie. Marketing is basically the definition of the Naughty List. Help us defy naughtiness."

"That's a low blow," grumbled Jackie.

"I learned to fight from The Super Patriots," said Vel. "I only fight fair when somebody's aiming a camera at my face. So will you do it? Please? For me?"

Jackie groaned. "Oh, sweet Claus, I am going to regret this…" Her reflection turned to Yelena, stabbing a finger toward the other girl. "You will not touch *anything* you're not given permission to touch. You will not harass, bother, interact with, or even talk to the elves. You will not go into my room."

"Anything you say," said Yelena.

"Want her to hold her breath the whole time, too?" asked Vel.

Jackie paused, shooting a quick glare at Vel before sighing, looking back to Yelena, and saying, "The North Pole is happy to extend you the hospitality owed to all who come to us with open hearts, honest souls, and a healthy interest in hot chocolate. But so you're aware, if you fuck up, they're never going to find your body."

"I understand," said Yelena. She turned to Vel, hugging the other woman as she whispered, "Thank you."

"Don't thank me; we've got a long way to go before we're anywhere near out of these woods," said Vel, hugging her back. "Now go get some sleep. I'll call you in the morning."

"Sleep," said Yelena, laughing a little unsteadily. "I remember enjoying sleep…"

"No one will mess with your dreams here," said Jackie. "Whatever nightmares you want to have, they'll be your own."

"You have no idea how happy that makes me," said Yelena. She brushed her hair out of her eyes with one hand, leaving a sparkling trail of glitter hanging briefly in the air. Then she stepped forward, and pressed her hand against the mirror. Jackie's fingers slid through the solid glass, lacing with Yelena's.

"You owe me," she mouthed, eyes on Vel. Giving a single sharp yank, she pulled Yelena toward her, and into the mirror. The glass rippled like water, and both of them were gone. The only reflection remaining was Vel's own: a battered, slump-shouldered girl in a burgundy and brown superhero costume, with a slightly askew rabbit-eared headband holding back her hair.

"I owed her more," said Vel, reaching up to adjust her headband. She looked like she'd been put through the wringer, and technically, she had…but there was something new in her expression, something that it took her a moment to recognize.

She looked hopeful.

"I'd better know what I'm doing," she said to her reflection, which didn't respond. Then she turned and left the room, shutting off the light as she went. She needed to go home, and explain the situation to her roommate before some inevitable wacky coincidence took the explanation out of her hands. That was never a good thing, and she couldn't imagine that it would be any better when the person she was trying to explain things to had a ray gun.

Privately, Velveteen was starting to believe that life never actually got any less complicated. The universe just found new ways to mess with you.

According to the official company records, no working adult superhuman has voluntarily left The Super Patriots, Inc. of their own free will without becoming a supervillain inside of the year. Those individuals who do choose to leave are inevitably characterized in psych profiles and human resources files as "unstable," "unpredictable," and "in need of additional therapy before they can be considered fully integrated into the heroic population." It paints a clear picture of people whose powers have damaged their ability to live normal lives, until they are inevitably driven into the arms of evil. The question then becomes clear:

How many of these people were considered "potentially dangerous" or "a high risk individual" before they made the decision to break with the corporation that trained them, sold them to the waiting world, and, in many cases, *created* them? No one has access to those files but the staff of The Super Patriots, Inc., and no one can deny that it would be potentially damaging to the corporate reputation if it were to suddenly come to light that people left not because they were evil, but because they could no longer live under the watchful eye of the Marketing Department.

Are monsters made…or are they marketed? As long as The Super Patriots, Inc. controls the psych evaluations of a world's superhumans, we may never know the answer.

But there are some who have suspicions.

"Torrey? Are you, uh…are you home?" The air in the living room smelled like gun oil and fresh-baked muffins. Velma sniffed the air, adjusting her grip on the duffel bag that held her costume. Fruit-based fresh-baked muffins. That was a good sign. She was pretty sure that gun oil muffins would be a sign that her roommate's grasp on reality, never better than questionable, had started its inevitable downward spiral. "It's Vel. We need to talk."

"Where else would I be, and who else would *you* be?" asked her roommate, emerging from the kitchen with a tray of steaming muffins. "I need you to eat one of these. I think they may be…not evil, precisely, but morally questionable."

"…right," said Vel, and reached for a muffin. Maybe it was unfair to think of Torrey–more properly referred to as Victoria Cogsworth, of the London Cogsworths–as having a questionable grasp on reality. Torrey had an excellent grasp on reality. It just wasn't the reality that she was currently trying to co-exist with.

"Please let me know immediately if you develop a tingling sensation in your extremities," said Torrey.

Vel paused with her hand out-stretched. Then she sighed, shrugged, and took a muffin. "Right."

"Now, then." Torrey put the tray down on the table near the kitchen door. "What did you wish to discuss? I assume you've discovered my augmentations to the hot water heater. I assure you, they're stable. I don't make unstable modifications to my own domicile."

"Uh, no, hadn't discovered that, but thanks for the reassurance, it's a big help." Still holding the muffin, Vel walked to the couch and sat down, gesturing for Torrey to do the same. Looking suspicious, Torrey followed her, and sat. Vel took a deep breath. "Okay. So. It's like this."

"You've initiated a team-up with this universe's version of Yelena and are unsure how I'm going to react to the idea that the only remaining version of the woman I love is not only unavailable to me both physically and emotionally, but will now be hanging about the city with increasing frequency, leading inevitably to a churning maelstrom of hurt feelings and sexual frustration. On my part, not yours, although potentially on hers, as she was, as I've said, quite in love with you in the timeline where she and I first met."

Vel stared. "Uh…"

Torrey snorted. "Really, Velma. Does the phrase 'my name is Victoria Cogsworth, I am a registered genius' not mean anything to you? Oxford doesn't allow just anyone to take the exams, you know. There are *standards*."

Vel continued to stare.

"The entrance requirements alone knock most dilly-dalliers and flim-flammers right out of the running, and when it comes to the defense of your thesis, well." Torrey's voice took on a strangely smug undertone. "You'd best be bringing your asbestos undergarments, and pray that your projectile-deflection array is prepared to be challenged by some of the best minds of the last eight generations!"

"The last *eight* generations?" asked Vel, despite herself.

"They were doing remarkable things in preservation back in my home dimension," said Torrey. Her face fell as she apparently realized that her professors, no matter how well-preserved, weren't there anymore. No more students would face the wrath of the meticulously maintained head of Galileo. "But I suppose that's all water under the bridge now, isn't it? You must have known that I'd see the pictures of the two of you. It's not like I've had much to do beyond sitting about here and looking up your world's superheroes on the internet. 'Blacklight.' As if that would fool *anyone* who knew Yelena."

"Um," said Vel, and took a large bite of muffin.

It tasted like raspberries and seaweed. After a momentary pause to consider her options, she swallowed. She'd eaten worse.

"It was only a matter of time before the two of you resolved your issues if you were already informally teaming up on a regular basis." Torrey shook her head. "I might have preferred that time to be a little more removed from the now. I'm not sure how prepared I am to meet this timeline's version of Yelena."

"She's really nice, except when she's being a bitchy diva controlled by The Super Patriots, Inc.'s Marketing Department," said Vel lamely.

"Funny." A very small smile twisted the corners of Torrey's mouth. "My Yelena used to say the same thing about you."

"Um." Velma cleared her throat and set the muffin carefully aside. "So anyway. Lena's going to be staying at the North Pole for a little bit. Just while we get things settled and figure out how to keep The Super Patriots from trying to take her back." Not for the first time, she found herself wondering just how many of the "brainwashed superheroes" she'd studied as a child had been totally normal people who just wanted to be left alone until The Super Patriots had them dragged back for reconditioning. "But she'll probably be around more. It's up to you how much you want to deal with her."

"I both never want to see her again and want her to fall naked into my bed at the slightest crook of my smallest finger." Torrey sighed. "Being dimensionally displaced does put one into some rather …unique…situations vis-à-vis one's romantic life. Do not worry about me. I will comport myself respectably. But be warned." She raised a finger. "I will not lie to her. If you bring her home, I will be forced to tell her that I am aware of her secret identity. I cannot deceive her."

"Torrey…" Vel paused, looking for the right words, and finally said, "She's not your Yelena."

"When you were in my Yelena's timeline, did it matter that he wasn't your Aaron?"

Velma didn't answer.

Torrey sighed, and stood. "No," she said. "I rather thought not. Now if you'll excuse me, I have muffins to see to."

Velma stayed where she was, and watched the other woman go.

She couldn't think of a single thing to say.

An hour later, Torrey was in her room doing…well, whatever it was that a dimensionally displaced gadgeteer did when she was alone. Frankly, Velma tried not to think about it too hard. She hadn't gone into her spare room since it was ceded to Victory Anna, and she treasured her ignorance. She was just considering whether or not she should treasure her ignorance while taking a nice, distracting bubble bath when the doorbell rang.

"Coming!" Velma turned off the television, slid out of her chair, and trotted over to the door. She paused with her hand on the knob, peering out the peephole. There was "living like a normal person," and there was "living like an idiot." Pretending that she would never have work follow her home fell into the latter category.

The man standing on the porch with a bunch of daisies in one hand was definitely work following her home, but in the good way. Velma opened the door, beaming. He beamed back.

"Hi," said Tad (better known as "Tag" when he wasn't in his secret identity).

"Hi," said Velma.

"These are for you." He held out the flowers. Looking a little puzzled, he added, "Torrey emailed me and said you were having a bad day. How did she get my email address?"

"I'm pretty sure that if you ask her, the answer is 'certified genius,' so let's not ask her." Vel took the flowers. "You wanna come in?"

"As long as I'm not interrupting." Tad smiled a little. "Look at us. Being all normal-people at each other."

Velma raised an eyebrow. "It's after midnight."

"I didn't say we had a good local model for 'normal.'" Tad stepped inside, moving out of the way while she shut the door. "Where's Torrey?"

"In her room. If she emailed you to come over, she's probably giving us space. That, or she's attempting dimensional tunneling again." Velma walked toward the kitchen. Tad followed. "I think there's a vase in here somewhere…"

"So now that we've answered the 'where's Torrey' question, and you're working on the equally vital 'where can I put these flowers' question…what's going on?" Tad leaned up against the counter. "I mean. Not that I'm opposed to having an excuse to visit my incredibly hot, super-powered girlfriend when nothing's actively trying to kill us, but I get a little concerned when people send me emails commanding my presence, with flowers, at the earliest possible opportunity."

The vase was at the back of the cupboard, behind a bunch of chipped coffee mugs that Velma didn't remember buying. They had just shown up in the cupboards, seeming to sprout from the house the way shelf fungus sprouted from trees. "You remember the lineup of my original junior team?"

"Uh, yeah. It was you, that lobster guy—"

"The Claw," supplied Velma, as she filled the vase with water.

"Right, the Claw. Action Dude, and Sparkle Bright, right?"

"Right." Velma put the vase down on the counter and picked up the flowers. "Sparkle Bright was my best friend, right up until the day when she tried to kill me in the locker room. Well. The day I thought she tried to kill me. It turns out she was pulling her punches, but she was so hurt over the things she'd been told I was saying behind her back that she just…lashed out. And I was hurt enough by the things *I'd* been told that *she* was saying behind my back that I never questioned it."

"She was the photon manipulator?"

"Yeah. She still is."

Tad paused, expression shifting to one of slowly dawning comprehension. Finally, sounding like he'd just bitten into a lemon, he asked, "Is Blacklight Sparkle Bright in disguise?"

Velma paused in the act of placing the flowers in the vase. Then she let them go and turned to face him, scowling. "All right, am I just stupid, or am I literally the *only person on the planet* who couldn't recognize my former best friend because she put on some black spandex and stopped trying to murder me?"

"I think it's the 'stopped trying to murder you' part that kept you from figuring it out," said Tad apologetically. "I mean, you didn't have any reason to think that Sparkle Bright would change costumes and try for a team-up. Not unless it came with contact poison or something."

"Still. I feel like a total idiot right now." Velma shook her head, gesturing for Tad to follow her back to the living room. "I mean, it took traveling to an alternate timeline that never actually existed for me to realize that I was having team-ups with my childhood roommate, and you and Torrey both just figured it out on your own. If it weren't for the part where I'm too stressed to beat myself up, I'd be kicking my own ass for stupidity right about now."

"Alternate timeline? What alternate timeline?"

Oh, crap. "Um. You know. The one Torrey is from."

"You told me she was staying with you as a favor to Santa Claus–"

"Which is technically true, he asked if she could use my guest room for a little while."

"–not that you'd actually traveled to *another dimension*. I'd sort of expect that to be the sort of thing you'd lead with when you were explaining the situation to your boyfriend." Tad glowered at her.

Velma sighed. "Look, I took the Alternate Reality Survival module in Heroing 101, and I passed with flying colors." Largely because Halloween had already been abducting her on a regular basis by the time she had to take her finals. "I didn't want to worry you by bringing up something that had already happened, was already over, and wasn't going to happen again."

"How can you be so sure that it's not going to happen again? Dimensional instability is a thing, Vel. A real thing we have to really worry about."

"Because Torrey's here." Velma looked at him gravely. "She's not really from the timeline I got sucked into. Her *original* dimension was destroyed in some sort of freak time travel accident, and then she wound up caught in that other timeline, which was never supposed to exist in the first place. Me leaving…I popped it somehow." Where "somehow" was code for "the holidays created it to teach me a lesson, and after I was finished, they didn't need it anymore." "So Torrey wound up in dimensional free fall. I can't wind up in that timeline again. If I could, then we'd be able to send Torrey home."

"And now you're…what? If Blacklight is really Sparkle Bright, what happens next?"

Velma sat down on the couch. "What happens next is things get complicated."

"Complicated…?"

"She's leaving The Super Patriots. She's at the North Pole right now, since I couldn't exactly keep her *here*. And tomorrow, we'll start figuring out how we're going to handle things."

"Handle—Vel." Tad sat down heavily next to her. "You're talking about helping the current co-leader of the main team walk away from her contract."

"Yes. She's my friend."

"Vel—"

"Would you want me to leave you? If you were the one who hadn't been able to get out, would you have wanted me to leave you just because it was dangerous to help you get out?"

Tad paused. Took a deep breath. And finally asked, "How can I help?"

Velma smiled.

It had been relatively easy to get the couch set up for Tad, who only really needed a pillow, a blanket, and a pack of Sharpies to feel at home. Velma had kissed him goodnight in the hall, warned Torrey that they would have company in the morning (and that there was male company staying the night), and retreated to her own room, feeling very much like she needed to take a cold shower. Or two. Or three. Or just give up the pretense that cold showers were working, and ask Jackie to put her into the deep freeze. It wasn't that she didn't *want* to spend more time with Tad in a…well, carnal sense. It was that their relationship hadn't reached that point before she went and got herself pulled into the alternate timeline, where she had technically cheated on him by sleeping with a parallel version of her ex-boyfriend.

Thinking about that too hard made her head hurt, and it was late. Frustrated and worried about what the next day would bring, Velma went to bed.

The smell of pancakes woke her bright and early, at the crack of…Velma cracked one eye open and squinted at the clock. Eleven. The crack of eleven. Well, it was before noon, and as superheroes tended to be a largely nocturnal lot, that was early enough to be indecent. She sat up, yawned, stretched, and put on her bathrobe (stolen from the Crystal Glitter Unicorn Cloud Castle) before leaving her room.

The smell of pancakes was even stronger in the hall, as was the smell of frying bacon. Velma made her way to the kitchen, where Torrey and Tad were sharing space at the stove. Tad was making pancakes. Torrey was frying a wide assortment of breakfast meats—some only half-recognizable—in one skillet, and what looked like an entire pound of bacon in another. Both of them were fully dressed, although their levels of formality were dramatically different: Tad was wearing the clothes he'd had on the night before, and Torrey was…well, Torrey. She never looked less that perfectly put-together, assuming that the current standard of "put-together" was "heading for an *Alice in Wonderland* vs. *War of the Worlds* costume party."

Tad noticed Velma standing in the doorway first. He looked up, and smiled. "Hey, sleepyhead. Feeling better?"

"There's bacon. Bacon makes everything better," said Velma.

"It does little to conceal your shameful semi-nudity," sniffed Torrey, without looking away from her assorted meats. "There's company en route. If you'd care to greet them not looking like you're available by the hour, you've got just time enough to change your garb."

"This is my house," said Velma, mildly. "I could kick you out."

"But you won't," replied Torrey.

"Sad but true." Velma looked to Tad. "Company? Company who?"

"Jackie and, uh. Sparkle Bright."

Velma paused. Finally, reluctantly, she asked, "Tad, are you sure you should be here right now? Sparkle Bright doesn't know your secret identity."

"Actually, yes, she does," he said, sounding abashed. "Jackie sort of phoned in on the bathroom mirror while I was, ah…"

"Pissing," supplied Torrey.

"Oh, come on!" said Vel. "How come you say I look like a hooker when I come out in my bathrobe, but you have no problem with bodily fluids?"

"I am a scientist," said Torrey primly. "Everyone must expel waste. Your wardrobe, on the other hand, is a personal choice."

"Anyway," said Tad, before the pair could start flinging things at one another. "Since I wasn't wearing a costume, and Jackie knew me already, she said I should just stay in street clothes and be the mundane boyfriend who knows about superhero stuff, and worry about the revealing myself later. I said that didn't feel right, if you were helping Sparkle Bright get out of The Super Patriots. Long story short, I sort of gave up my secret identity to make your ex-best friend more comfortable."

"…whoa." Velma crossed the kitchen in three steps, put her hand on his shoulder, and kissed him soundly. When she pulled away, she said, "You are the *best* boyfriend, and I will make it up to you. Possibly with dinner, unchaperoned by roommates or teammates or any other sort of people who aren't us."

"Um, okay," said Tad, looking stunned. "It's a date."

"Great. Now I'm going to go put some clothes on," she shot a glare at the seemingly oblivious Torrey, "before company gets here. Try not to burn down the kitchen?"

"Doing my best," said Tad, and kissed her again, quickly, before she turned and walked away.

It was going to be a long day. She could already tell.

Ten minutes later, the three of them were settled on the couch, eating breakfast, and waiting for something to happen. The doorbell rang. Velma stood.

"That's our cue," she said, setting her plate aside, and moved to answer. A glance out the peephole confirmed that it was Jackie—whose naturally blue skin couldn't *possibly* clue the neighbors off to this being the local superhero's house—and a weary-looking Yelena standing outside. She undid the locks, opened the door, and stepped to the side. "Come on in, guys. There's bacon."

"Yay, bacon!" said Jackie, and practically bounded inside, dragging Yelena by the arm. "Delicious, high-calorie, fatty *bacon.*"

Yelena looked like she was about to throw up.

Velma sighed. "Jackie. That's not nice."

"What?" Jackie turned wide, calculatedly innocent blue eyes on Velma. "I'm just singing the praises of bacon."

"Yeah, in front of someone who's been living on a diet plan designed to make her look good in skin-tight spandex for her entire adult life. Have a heart." Velma moved to hug Yelena. "Hey, sweetie. How'd you sleep?"

"Like the dead." Yelena's answering hug was a lot more like clinging than a simple embrace. Velma didn't try to push her away. Yelena had earned a little clinging. "I didn't have any dreams about photo ops or stock prices or anything."

"That'll be the corporate brainwashing starting to wear off," said Tad, from the couch. "Whatever they use on us can't get to the holiday lands. Your subconscious is trying to purge."

Yelena pulled away, blinking at Tad. Then she smiled. "Tad, right? I mean, Graffiti Boy?"

"It's 'Tag' these days," said Tad. "It's nice to see you again."

"You, too." Yelena tucked a lock of long blonde hair behind her ear, gaze shifting to Torrey. The gear-draped redhead was staring at her with something that could only be described as unabashed longing, like she knew better, but couldn't help herself. Yelena's smile wavered, but held. "And you are…?"

"Victoria Cogsworth, registered genius," said Torrey, and put her plate aside. "I fight the criminal element as 'Victory Anna.'"

Yelena laughed. "Oh, like 'Victoriana.' Good one."

Torrey's face fell, longing transmuting into something closer to grief. "Yes, I thought so, too, when it was suggested to me." She stood. "I do beg your pardon. This many powered individuals in a room can only end with someone deciding we need to go on patrol, and I need to collect my pistols before I go up against any of the native ruffians." Then she was gone, fleeing down the hall to her room.

"I…" Yelena blinked. "Did I say something wrong?"

"The situation with Torrey is complicated," said Velma, rubbing the back of her neck with one hand. "She's from a world that doesn't exist anymore, and she's been stranded in a timeline that never existed for the last several years, and right now, she's my roommate. So just go easy on her, okay? She's got a sort of super-science power set thing going on. I think you'll like it." *Also she's hopelessly in love with a version of you that's pretty close to the real thing, and I don't know how either of you is going to cope with that, so let's just ignore it for as long as we possibly can, okay?*

It was going to end badly. But for the moment, this was maybe the best way to put that off.

"Um. Okay," said Yelena. Then she paused, putting a hand over her stomach, and gave Velma a hopeful look. "Am I really allowed to eat bacon now?"

Velma grinned.

Meanwhile, on the other side of Portland, strange things were afoot in the covered parking garage of a small residential building which had been converted, for a time, into a private dental practice. It was *still* a private dental practice, and would remain so for another forty-eight hours, at least, until the damned bank came with their closure notices and loan paperwork. As if it was *his* fault that a superhuman dental practice couldn't find traction in this damp, mold-patched excuse for a major metropolitan area. All the precogs he'd consulted had assured him that this spot would be the site of major superhuman activity.

Maybe he should have asked them for a timeline on that.

But no matter! The men from the bank wouldn't be arriving for days yet, and there was still time to put his final plan into effect. A plan which would, through its sheer daring, guarantee that the name of Dr. Walter Creelman, DDS, would not be forgotten!

The good doctor (who was, by any reasonable measure, really well on his way to becoming the *bad* doctor) looked at his neat lines of carefully-designed robots and began to giggle. Then he began to chuckle. Finally, giving in to the inevitable, he placed his hands on his hips and began to cackle outright.

Those fools. Those silly, ignorant fools. Someone had to show them. And he, Walter Creelman, DDS, was exactly the Doctor of Dental Surgery to do it.

VELVETEEN
vs.
The Robot Armies of Dr. Walter Creelman, DDS

Victoria Cogsworth managed not to slam the door to her borrowed bedroom behind her, although it was a near thing; physical expressions of her frustration had always appealed to her. Usually, those expressions took the form of ray guns and flung spanners, but she was a woman of the world now, no longer a sheltered lab assistant, and she had long since learned that sometimes, you had to take your catharsis where you found it. And yet she knew, without question, that this version of Yelena—who looked so damned like her own, and how was that fair? Of all the worlds to be judged real and play the part of her prison, why did it have to be one where Lena would look at her, and smile, and not recognize her own jokes? —would be upset by the banging. So she closed the door with care, and closed her eyes, and wept.

Meanwhile, in the living room, Yelena was sitting on a faded brown easy chair and staring at the plate on her knees like it was somewhere between the promised land and the temptations of Hell. On the plate was a single small pancake, without syrup, and half a strip of bacon.

"Look at it this way," said Tad, who had moved to crouch beside her chair. "Marketing doesn't want you to eat the bacon. Marketing *hates* the bacon, unless you're getting paid by a major sponsor to pretend you love it. Marketing would slap your hand for even thinking about the bacon. If you eat that bacon, you are taking another big step toward reclaiming your life. You get to eat whatever you want now. You're free."

"Free," murmured Yelena, and picked up the crispy piece of fried meat. "It still doesn't seem possible."

"It will be," said Tad. "Eat the bacon."

In the kitchen, Jackie and Velma stood next to the stove, speaking in low voices. "This is a shitty idea, Vel, and you know it," said Jackie, shooting a poisonous look back toward the living room. "She's not going to adjust. She's going to go running right back to The Super Patriots, and after they've had her for a few days, she'll tell them anything they want to know."

"You're wrong," said Velma. "You don't know Yelena like I do."

"Neither do you. You haven't 'known' her since the day she *tried to kill you* with a light whip. Remember? When you decided to leave the team?"

"Jackie…"

"I'm just saying, maybe right after you start getting your life back together isn't the day to decide it's time for you to start hooking back up with all the people who fucked you over in the first place."

Velma sighed, picked up the frying pan, and dropped it into the sink. A cloud of steam rose from the dishwater. Jackie waved her hand, and the steam fell back down as a gentle layer of snow, which dissolved on contact with the still-heated water. "I don't know what I can say to make you understand, Jackie, but this is important to me," said Vel. "This is something I have to do. You're the one who put me through that mirror world and made me understand how wrong everything is. Why are you the only one who doesn't want to help me fix it?"

"Because I'm the only one who had to watch you picking up the pieces." Jackie's answer was so soft that Velma almost didn't hear it. She turned and stared at her friend, who continued, "Even when you stopped coming to the North Pole, even when you stopped talking back to the mirror…Mom yelled at me every time she saw me, and after a while, I had to stop because it hurt so bad. But I still watched you walk away. I watched you crying every night. I watched you…" She paused, taking a breath, before she said, "We all thought 'okay, this is horrible, but maybe this is for the best. Maybe now she'll pick a holiday, she'll pick a season, and then we won't have to fight anymore.' And then all you picked was isolation. You left us alone—you left *me* alone—and it was all because of her. So you'll excuse me if I don't trust her right off the bat. She's fucked you over before. I don't want to see her do it again."

"I thought you believed in second chances."

"I do. I also believe in protecting the people I care about."

They were still glaring at each other mutely when the kitchen phone began to ring. Jackie turned toward the sound, and blinked like she'd just seen a spider.

"What the sweet Claus is that?"

"Secure landline," said Vel. She tossed her dish towel onto the counter and crossed to the phone, snagging the receiver with one hand. "Speak."

There was a long pause as the person on the other end obeyed her command. Vel's face became blanker and blanker as the moment stretched on. Finally, she nodded.

"I understand," she said. "My team and I will be right there." She dropped the phone back into the cradle and started for the living room.

"Wait!" Jackie ran after her. "What was that all about?"

Vel kept walking until she was standing in the middle of the living room. Tad and Yelena both looked toward her. "The Governor's office just called me," she said. "Robots are tearing up downtown, and as Portland's official superhero, I've been asked to stop them. Anyone who wants to help, suit up. Anyone who wants to stay here, please feel free to finish the dishes."

"I'm game," said Tad.

"You have no idea how much I want something to hit," said Jackie.

Yelena didn't say anything. She just put her plate aside and smiled hopefully at Vel. That expression held a thousand team-ups, an infinity of fighting the good fight against the forces of evil…and all of it together. Vel smiled back, relieved.

The sound of an electric rail gun powering up behind her pulled her attention back toward the hall that led to the bedrooms. Torrey–now Victory Anna, really, as she was in full costume, goggles, impractically small top hat, and all–was standing in the doorway, holding a gun so impractically large that it filled her arms completely. It was connected to an elaborate clockwork backpack. The backpack was ticking.

"Well, then, you lazy bludgers, rise up and don your safety equipment, for the hour has need of both safety…and *SCIENCE*!"

The others stared at her. Finally, Vel shrugged.

"All right: you heard the dimensionally-displaced redhead. Get your costumes on, and meet back here in five minutes." Vel pushed past Victory Anna, not bothering to conceal her relief as she headed for her bedroom. If there was one thing she understood, no matter how confusing the rest of her life became, it was putting on rabbit ears and going to fight robots.

For justice.

The first known superheroic team-up occurred when Majesty, Supermodel, and Jolly Roger–each of whom had been battling the forces of evil individually for more than a year–joined forces to fight back an alien invasion of unknown origins. Together, they were able to accomplish what none of them could have prayed to handle alone. They quickly realized that a team of super-powered individuals would inevitably be greater than the sum of its parts, able to compensate for internal weaknesses while also building on each hero's unique strengths. The Super Patriots were born shortly thereafter. The Super Patriots, Inc. was a distant nightmare in those early, discovery-filled days. It was only later, when the cost of heroism became clearer, that the three would choose to incorporate, and The Super Patriots, Inc. that we know today would begin to form.

It is interesting to note that virtually all team-ups consisting of three or more heroes not sanctioned by The Super Patriots, Inc. have either failed or been branded as supervillains in the eyes of the media and the public within seventy-two hours of their formation. It is almost as if, having discovered the winning formula, the original three wanted to guarantee that it would remain under their control. The question thus arises: if a super team were to form outside the bounds of The Super Patriots, Inc., how long would it be allowed to function before drastic action was taken?

And who would have custody of the survivors?

The first issue was getting them all to the scene of the robot rampage. Sparkle Bright could fly. Jackie could generate ice bridges strong enough for her to skate on them, providing she wasn't worried about hitting people's cars with chunks of falling ice (she wasn't worried). Tag had a Volvo.

The five of them stood in the driveway looking at the rust-speckled, powder blue vehicle. Finally, Victory Anna began, "I don't suppose you'd allow me to–"

"No," said Velveteen hurriedly, before her trans-dimensional roommate could say the words "make it fly" or "turn it into a giant slingshot array capable of flinging us across the city." Vel was reasonably sure that Victory Anna's passion for science didn't extend as far as accidentally killing her temporary teammates, but there was no need to *prove* it.

"We'll all fit," said Tag, with forced good cheer. "I'll even let you take shotgun."

"You have a shotgun?" asked Victory Anna dubiously, eyeing his skin-tight costume.

"In the interests of getting to the robot throw down *without* turning this into a Saturday Night Live sketch, I am making an executive decision," said Velveteen. "Everybody get into the car. I'm driving."

With relief (Tag) and grumbling (Victory Anna), the others complied. Velveteen shook her head, adjusted her bunny-eared headband, and turned to Jackie and Sparkle Bright.

"I want you two to go on ahead, scout out the terrain, and wait for us, unless there are civilians in active danger," she said. "If we're going to be a team, we need to start acting like one, and that means fighting a common enemy instead of each other."

"Are we?" asked Jackie.

"Are we what?"

"Going to be a team."

Velveteen paused. Finally, she said, "I'd like it if we were. I think that, as a group, we have a lot of really good reasons to be opposing The Super Patriots, and at this point, even if we were to decide not to fight, they're not going to let us just walk away. We'll be stronger if we stand together. And if you don't freeze Sparkle Bright's lungs when you think I'm not looking."

Sparkle Bright, who had been listening silent up until that point, burst out laughing. Both Jackie and Velveteen turned to stare at the multicolored glitter explosions this caused in the air around Sparkle Bright's head.

"Sorry," she said, still giggling as she wiped her eyes. "I just…you guys have no idea how much I've missed you."

Jackie looked nonplussed. Velveteen smiled. "We've missed you, too," she said. "Now let's go beat the shit out of some robots."

"I love that we're allowed to swear," said Sparkle Bright, and launched herself into the air with a burst of electric purple light.

"I'll do my best not to murder her, but I make no promises," said Jackie. She made a throwing gesture with one hand. An icy rampway materialized in front of her, and she skated away, rapidly following Sparkle Bright into the sky.

"That's good enough for me," said Velveteen, and turned, walking back to the car. She plopped herself into the driver's seat. "Okay, who's ready to fight some crime?"

"This dimension's heroes are like school-age boys: all talking about the good bits, and never actually *doing* them," muttered Victory Anna.

"Am I offended right now?" asked Tag.

Velveteen laughed, started the car, and drove away.

Meanwhile, high above the streets of Portland, a photo manipulator and an elementalist were trying not to kill each other. At least, Sparkle Bright was trying not to kill Jackie; Jackie wasn't exactly sticking to the "thou shalt not kill" part of the program. After the third time her ice ramp had abruptly intersected with Sparkle Bright's trajectory, forcing the other heroine to adjust course or hurt herself, Sparkle Bright stopped flying. She hovered in midair, folding her arms, and glared at Jackie.

"All right, let me have it," she said. "We may as well stop pretending that we can put this off forever, so let's just go ahead and get it over with before they beat us to the scene."

Jackie turned and skated back along her ice ramp to where Sparkle Bright had stopped. She angled her skates as she braked, making sure to direct a spray of ice chips in Sparkle Bright's direction. "Funny, I was going to say something similar to you," she said. "Only I was going to word it more like 'stop faking, you fake faker bitch.' Vel's a nice person. She's just now starting to unfuck her life. The last thing we need is for you to come in here and screw her head up again."

"Oh, and are you sure that's because you give a shit about Vel as a person, and not just because you're still hoping to recruit her to your holiday?"

"You take that back," said Jackie, eyes narrowing and lips thinning into a hard line. Any low-flying aircraft that had come upon the two heroines would have turned around on the spot, seeing the look on Jackie's face. "Vel's my friend, and I've been one hell of a better friend to her than you have. You tried to kill her."

"Are you honestly telling me that Santa Claus had no idea that Marketing was playing us?" The question was mild.

Jackie's reaction was not. Her expression thawed, becoming almost pained. "We're not allowed to discuss the details of the

Naughty List with people who aren't on it. If I could have told her…"

"You wouldn't have done it, because you wanted to keep her all to yourself. Not the same way I did, maybe–and don't worry, that crush died a miserable death a long, long time ago–but that's just details." Sparkle Bright quirked a very small smile. "So while I have you alone, I'd like to propose a truce. And a deal."

"I'm listening," said Jackie warily.

"I'm not leaving her again, Jackie. I let Marketing split us up once, and I hated who I was while I was with them. I *hated* it. I've been guilty and alone for my entire adult life, and I am done with that shit. But you really have been a good friend to her, and what happened to us wasn't your fault. So you don't try to make her give up on me based on what I did in the past, and I won't try to make her give up on you based on what you might do in the future. Deal?"

Jackie took a deep breath before finally nodding. "Deal," she agreed. "You know, I think I liked you better when you were a malleable little kid."

"Funny," said Sparkle Bright. "Marketing used to say the same thing." She turned abruptly in the air and flew onward, leaving Jackie behind her.

The blue girl watched the photon manipulator fly away and sighed. "You're going to be trouble," she said to Sparkle Bright's retreating back. Then she smiled. "I'm good at trouble."

A moment later there was only the rapidly-melting ice ramp left to show that anything had ever been in the sky at all.

If the people of Portland thought it was strange to see a car crammed with superheroes driving through their streets, they didn't say anything about it. There are some things that are better left unremarked upon. Velveteen did her best to obey traffic laws, although her superhero license did render her exempt from speed limits when in active pursuit of a supervillain or hostile incursion. "Robots trashing downtown" definitely counted as "hostile incursion" in her mind. Still, the people around her weren't exempt from speed limits, and the last thing she wanted to do was splatter herself, Tag, and Victory Anna across the backside of a bus.

It didn't help that Tag had, in fact, allowed Victory Anna to take shotgun, which meant that she was riding in the front passenger seat *with* her shotgun, or at least its mad science equivalent. As a weapon, it was large enough to verge on ludicrous. It had a backpack power source, which was pinned between Victory Anna's ankles as she tinkered with something inside the body of the gun, seemingly unconcerned by the fact that she was in a moving vehicle. Every time Velveteen took a corner without slowing down, she was secretly terrified that the entire improbable machine was going to explode.

"We're almost there," said Velveteen, hands clenched whiteknuckled on the wheel. *When this is all over, I'm talking to the Governor about a minivan.*

As if she had read Velveteen's thoughts, Victory Anna, without looking up, said, "If we can get me an old bus or something of the sort, I can build a flying conveyance to make the next situation of this type a trifle easier."

"That'd be swell," said Velveteen, through gritted teeth.

"We're going to die," said Tag conversationally from the back seat. "That's what I'm taking away from this drive. Oh, that, and we got seriously screwed in the super powers department. Why does super strength need to come with flight? And how the hell does manipulating light keep somebody in the air? I think it's pretty clear that who can and can't fly is totally arbitrary, and we shouldn't be stuck down here with a giant unstable gun in the car, surrounded by people who don't know how to drive."

"Oh, stuff it," said Victory Anna, not unkindly. "I've not blown up anything I didn't intend to blow up in years. You all worry far too much about a little harmless science."

"I'm going to be honest here: I don't even know where to start pointing out all the things that are wrong with that sentence."

"Then it's a good thing you don't have to," said Velveteen, stomping her foot down on the brakes. The car squealed to a stop, accompanied by the smoky smell of burning rubber. Maybe they'd been bending the speed limit a *little* more than was strictly safe. "We're here."

"You sure?" asked Tag.

A large chunk of masonry landed on the street in front of their car. Velveteen reached up and adjusted her mask.

"Yeah," she said. "I am."

The real difficulty with leading an unstoppable robot army into battle is that, at a certain point, your input becomes irrelevant. Dr. Walter Creelman, DDS, sat comfortably on the stoop of what had been (still was, dammit) his dental practice and watched as half his robots went about the business of systematically dismantling the neighborhood. He'd asked them to do it with minimal loss of life, and so far they seemed to be listening. It was very considerate of him, really, no matter how much the people who'd been filed under "acceptable losses" might disagree. Why, when he finished his rampage and presented his (quite reasonable) list of demands to the city, he'd be able to point out a death toll that was still solidly in the double digits. Not something most conquerors were concerned about.

"I told them not to laugh at me," he said peacefully, and took a bite of his peanut butter and jelly sandwich.

On the other side of the chaos, Velveteen and the others were climbing out of the car. Sparkle Bright dropped out of the sky like a glitter-powered comet, pulling up just before she made impact with the pavement. "We've got a problem," she said, without preamble.

All three earth-bound heroes looked at her like she'd just said something *remarkably* stupid.

"I hate to side with the Rainbow Ranger, but she's right," said Jackie, spiraling down her artfully-twisted ice ramp and onto the street. "I wouldn't have spotted it without her."

"Spotted what?" demanded Velveteen. "I love the witty banter as much as the next superhero, but people are dying, so speed it the fuck up."

"This is only half the robots," said Sparkle Bright, cutting off Jackie's doubtless caustic reply. "The other half is moving slow, not breaking anything–and heading for City Hall."

Velveteen paused. Then, pulling a handful of little green army men out of her belt, she said, "Tag, go with Sparkle Bright, and stop those robots. Jackie, Victory Anna, you're with me." She flung the army men to the ground, and they rushed the nearest robots, already beginning to fire their tiny plastic bullets into the air.

"On it," said Sparkle Bright, and grabbed Tag around the waist before he could object. The two rocketed away into the sky, Tag's fading yelp trailing behind them like an afterthought.

There was a subsonic whine as Victory Anna powered up her gun. "*Now* can we fight the army of automatons?" she demanded.

"Yes," said Velveteen, "we can. Teddy bears, attack!"

The teddy bears charged. So did Jackie and Victory Anna. The battle was on.

* * *

"Don't drop me don't drop me don't drop me!" chanted Tag,

clinging to Sparkle Bright's hands as she flew him in low over the rooftops. If he looked down, he could see the marching robots. If he looked down, there was a very good chance that he was going to throw up all over the marching robots. He stopped looking down.

"I'm going to set you down on that corner," Sparkle Bright shouted, raising her voice to be heard above the wind that she was generating. "See what you can do to slow them down, and I'll start blasting from the rear! Maybe we can get them to turn around and go back to the others!"

"Oh, right, because more robots is exactly what we need!" Still, they were dropping lower, and he appreciated that. He appreciated that a *lot*. When his feet touched the sidewalk, he grabbed two cans of spray paint from his belt, and stopped being *quite* so eager to kill his girlfriend. He turned back to Sparkle Bright. "Think you can stop them?"

She grinned. "I think it's going to be fun to try!" Then she was launching herself back into the air and flying toward the robots, shooting beams of light from her hands.

Tag shook his head, muttered, "Photon manipulators," and got to work spray painting a solid wall on the air.

Dr. Creelman first realized something was wrong when one of his robots flew backward out of the throng, slamming into the side of a nearby building hard enough to crack its casing. The second sign of trouble was the redhead in the corset and button-up boots who appeared in the opening the flying robot had created and shot it, several times, with what appeared to be the bastard child of a ray gun and a bazooka. Grinning ear to ear, she turned and ran back into the fray while Dr. Creelman still sat, stunned, with a mouthful of peanut butter and jelly sandwich.

There were more blasting sounds. Dr. Creelman remembered himself and staggered to his feet, swallowing his half-chewed mouthful as he pulled the remote control from his pocket. "YOU FOOLS!" he bellowed. "I TRIED TO MAKE THIS EASY ON YOU, BUT YOU COULDN'T ALLOW THAT! NOW SUFFER THE WRATH OF DOCTOR WALTER CREELMAN, D! D! S!" He flipped the switch that would take the robots from destructive to deadly.

There was a pause as the instruction was transmitted to the robot army. Then they straightened, growing taller as their joints and pistons realigned, and descended upon the attacking superheroes. Dr.

Creelman heard screams and shouts of dismay from the depths of the fray. "Good," he muttered, sulkily shoving the remote back into his pocket. How dare they? All he was doing was making a statement about economic unfairness and the difficulties of maintaining a foothold as a small business, and they had to go breaking his toys? Well, fine. He'd break *them*.

Amidst the crush of robotic bodies, Jackie was forming an ice shield to protect Velveteen, who was on her knees and concentrating as hard as she could. The bunny-eared superheroine's toys were still fighting, and had even managed to take down a few robots—although Jackie couldn't really have said *how*; it didn't make any sense on the surface of things—but they were getting damaged at a remarkable rate, and Vel wasn't animating any new ones. "Think you can hurry it up there?"

"No," snarled Velveteen. "They have faces, but they're blurry. I can't get a lock."

"Swell." Jackie blasted two more robots, this time aiming for the joints in their knees. Frozen robots moved more slowly. She was in favor of things moving slowly, especially when the things in question seemed inclined to kill her.

Of the three of them, only Victory Anna seemed to be having any fun. She was shooting robots left and right, occasionally grabbing pieces that had fallen off their bodies. "Salvage!" she shouted, following her cry with the sound of her enormous gun being discharged again.

"Therapy," muttered Jackie, and kept blasting.

At the same time on the other side of the city, Sparkle Bright and Tag were experiencing problems of their own. Sparkle Bright was dazzling and frying robots as fast as she could, and Tag's paint wall was holding, but neither of them could keep it up forever. "Cracks on the left!" shouted Sparkle Bright.

"I'm on it!" Tag ran for the breaking piece of wall, shaking his can of spray paint as he went. They'd gone through this routine ten times in the past three minutes. The bodies of the fallen robots were creating a barrier of their own, slowing their compatriots enough to make it a little easier to keep things standing. As long as Vel and the others took care of their part, it was all going to be fine. It had to be.

He uncapped his paint can, beginning to add long red streaks of unbroken brick to the top of the ones that were already there. He was focused enough on his work that he didn't see the robot closing in.

Sparkle Bright's scream could have woken the dead.

But it didn't wake Tag.

"*Vel!*" This time, Jackie's shout contained an urgency that was impossible to ignore. Velveteen glanced up to see her blue-skinned friend holding back four robots with a massive ice shield. Jackie cast her a frantic look. "Hurry, or it's not going to *matter* if you hurry."

Ice had collected on the faceplates of the robots, settling into the grooves and rivets and making the subtle pattern of their "faces" easier for her to see. Mouth, eyes, a smooth glossy surface broken by a thin rivet line for a nose...Velveteen's eyes widened as it all fell into place. Raising her hands in a summoning gesture, she clapped them together over her head.

And the robots stopped.

The sound of Victory Anna shooting continued for a few seconds more before the gadgeteer realized that the battle was effectively over. She came clambering over a fallen robot, holding her gun in one hand and dragging an entire mechanical arm with the other. "What, is that it?" she demanded. "That's a bit anti-climactic, don't you think? Nothing exploded!"

"I don't know," said Jackie, gesturing toward the furiously shouting man in the white lab coat. "It looks like *he's* about to blow."

The three superheroes picked their way across the battleground to Dr. Creelman, the surviving robots following Velveteen like good little toys. "Were these yours?" she asked the red-faced doctor.

"Are! They *are* mine!" he shouted, and pulled the remote out of his pocket, mashing several buttons before Victory Anna nimbly plucked it from his fingers. He grabbed for it. She stepped back, and Jackie froze his hands together. He howled.

"It's your lot who give innocent gadgeteers a bad name," said Victory Anna reproachfully, and hit him over the back of the head with the remote.

Dr. Creelman fell like a sack of potatoes. Velveteen nudged him with her foot. "You think he just got bored?"

"I think motives are a problem for the police," said Jackie.

There was a clattering sound from behind them. They turned, robots and all, to see Sparkle Bright–blood and grease in her golden hair–standing amongst the wreckage, Tag cradled unmoving in her arms. She looked at them with pure desperation. "A...a robot," she stammered. "He was at the wall, and...oh, God, Vel, I'm so sorry."

"Tag?" whispered Velveteen. She took two stumbling steps

forward, and then she broke into a run, leaving a stunned-looking Jackie and Victory Anna behind her. "Tag?!"

"I flew as fast as I could, but..." Sparkle Bright stopped talking and bowed her head, tears leaving rainbow trails down her cheeks.

Velveteen stopped a few feet away, putting a hand over her mouth. "I don't...he can't...Tag. Tag. You can't be dead, do you hear me? We're supposed to go out. Just us. Remember? You...you can't..." She, too, fell silent, and just sobbed.

Tag opened his eyes.

"Where am I?" he asked, sounding dazed. Sparkle Bright's head snapped up. Tag groaned. "And did someone get the number of that bus? That evil robot army bus?" Then he blinked. "Vel? Why are you crying?"

"*Tag!*" she leapt forward and slung her arms around him, never minding the fact that he was still being held up by Sparkle Bright. The resulting tangle of limbs nearly toppled over backward, but managed to stabilize, thanks to a few quick glitter-blasts by an utterly confused-looking Sparks. Vel kept sobbing, while Tag kept demanding to know what was going on.

Jackie and Victory Anna didn't move. "Okay, that was...intense," muttered Jackie.

"It still is," said Victory Anna.

"Haven't you got eyes?" snarled Dr. Creelman, staggering back to his feet. "The boy was—" A blast of ice from Jackie cut him off mid-sentence.

"Well," she said, clapping her hands together. "Who wants to call the police and tell them that the robot rampage is finished, but needs some major cleanup?"

"You do," said Victory Anna. "*I* am going to scavenge the parts necessary to construct a rocket car. Much of this could have been avoided if we'd been able to arrive here sooner." She turned and scampered off into the wreckage, still dragging the robot arm she had claimed as her own.

"Coward," muttered Jackie, and pulled out her phone.

"You're sure you're okay?"

"Vel, I'm fine. I've never felt better." Tad watched his reflection in the mirror as he spoke into his phone. Everything certainly *looked* normal. "The paramedics said they couldn't find anything wrong with me. I'm cleared for duty, ready for action, and about to go to bed."

Velma sighed with audible relief. "You scared the crap out of me."

"So you've said. Fifteen times. Sixteen, now."

"I believe in clear communication. Speaking of clear communication..." Her tone changed, turning flirtatious. "I believe I promised you a date? Just you, me, and no supervillains or patrol."

"Can you take the time off?"

"That's the nice thing about having a team: they'll cover for us."

Tad smiled as he turned away from the mirror. "You know, this permanent team-up thing is sounding better all the time. As is this 'us' you speak of. Friday night? You, me, dinner, a movie, and inappropriate displays of public affection during the trailers?"

"I'm all yours," said Vel. "I love you."

"I know, Vel." Tad took one last look back at the mirror. "I love you, too."

They talked for a while longer, finally exchanging goodnights and going to their separate beds. Velma slept almost immediately, comforted by thoughts of justice and team-ups that never had to end. Tad took longer to fall asleep. He kept seeing that robot's hand coming down...

And then there was darkness.

VELVETEEN
vs.
The Fright Night Sorority House Massacre Sleepover Camp

"WHAT THE—" LOUD CRASHING SOUNDS from the kitchen obscured whatever the Princess said next, although judging by the movements of her mouth, it wasn't anything G-rated or appropriate for children. Velveteen had to admire the pinpoint timing of the racket, even though she knew it was probably just going to make the Princess angrier. Anger wasn't the problem. They kept running, and the noise stopped as the Princess continued, "—is going on here? This doesn't make any fairy-fucking sense!"

"What doesn't make sense is how the universe bleeps out normal cuss words, but lets you say 'fairy-fucking,'" said Jackie.

"Less snarking, more running!" snapped Velveteen, taking her own advice and shutting up as she high-tailed it for the stairs. The others followed, trusting Velveteen's unerring sense of self-preservation to get them at least moderately out of harm's way while they regrouped and figured out what to do next. Apart from "survive." That, more than anything else, was turning into the goal of the evening…which might have been why that, more than anything else, seemed increasingly impossible.

Three minutes later, the four of them were wedged into the space beneath the stairs, mostly blocked from casual view by a coat rack laden with leather jackets straight out of the 1950s, denim jackets straight out of the 1980s, and blood-stained lab coats that needed no era to define them. The Princess was down on her hands and knees, whispering into a mouse hole, while Victory Anna sat next to her, trying to pry the cover off a Speak-and-Spell. She was cursing softly but steadily under her breath in a mixture of Latin and English, and what little Vel could understand made her glad that she didn't know what any of the Latin actually *meant*.

Jackie, meanwhile, was keeping a wary eye on the thin sliver of hallway that could be seen through the coats. Voice pitched very low, she said, "This is almost as bad as it is stupid. You realize that, right?"

"We're trapped in a supernatural sorority house that's been in the middle of its own private horror movie since the early 1950s at the absolute minimum, our powers aren't reliable, I don't know how we got here or where everyone else is, or even who everyone else is, and the architecture appears to be a collaboration between M.C. Escher and the guy who did the set design for *Labyrinth*," snapped Velveteen. "Yeah, I get that this is bad."

"You left off the part where we're in our unmentionables," said Victory Anna, not looking up from her pilfered toy. "Really, that's the part that cuts most dearly. You're all nice girls, I'm sure—"

Jackie snorted.

"—but I'd rather not display my entire treasury to casual lookie-loos," concluded Victory Anna, ignoring her.

Jackie turned to Velveteen, one white eyebrow raised in silent question.

Velveteen shrugged. "She has a point," she said. "Love you lots, not so sure I needed you to see me in my underwear." She paused. "On the other hand, this isn't *my* underwear, so I guess 'not so sure I needed you to see me in fan service mode' would be more accurate."

"Thank Disney this place ain't wired for broadcast," said the Princess, causing the other three to look around uneasily.

"Great," muttered Vel. "Because I wasn't uncomfortable enough."

Somehow, whatever mechanism had dumped them in their current situation—a mechanism which, Vel was pretty sure, was going to get punched in whatever it had that was most like a face, when or if they finally figured out what it was—had also changed their clothes. Mid-transition costume changes weren't unheard of in the superhero world, but they usually involved a transition between "street clothes" and "costume," generally right before you got dropped into a pan-dimensional gladiatorial tournament of some sort. Sometimes the costume in question would be a new variation on the norm, like Halloween with its tatters and rags, or Christmas with its fur trim and velvet. Going by that logic, and considering that they were all relatively attractive females, their current "costumes" made perfect sense.

But that didn't mean they had to like it.

Jackie, whose normal costume was revealing enough to disqualify her from the Olympics (even if they'd been willing to let her compete, what with the whole "the North Pole isn't a country" thing), was wearing white boy shorts and a white lace bra, both of which were patterned with small silver snowflakes and stood out starkly against the blue of her skin. Privately, Velveteen thought she looked like an ill-conceived modernization of Smurfette. Not that she was feeling suicidal enough to say it, even if Jackie's ice powers had been increasingly erratic since they arrived in the house, lingerie and all. Victory Anna was wearing frilly bloomers, thigh-high striped stockings, and a brown canvas corset with gears embroidered all over it. Both of them were barefoot. Velveteen herself had found her costume replaced by a brown lace teddy that seemed to have been modeled on something from the early Playboy club, including the white cotton rabbit's tail and wire-supported bunny ears. At least she'd managed to ditch the high heels after the third time she nearly twisted her ankle.

"What I don't understand," said Victory Anna, as she finally managed to remove the back of the Speak-and-Spell, "is why she gets to remain decently covered." She gestured toward the Princess.

The Princess, who hadn't actually met Victory Anna before they were all thrust into this horror movie turned endless sight gag, looked away from her mouse hole to frown at the gadgeteer. "You'd rather the little girls of the world pictured me all nice and slutty?"

Victory Anna raised her head and looked at the Princess blankly. "Haven't the little girls of this world nightgowns of their own?"

Sensing an impending throw-down, Velveteen quickly raised her hands and said, "Princess, Torrey originally came from a dimension without Disney, so she hasn't really internalized what it means. Victory Anna, please keep working on that transmitter. If we can't signal for help before midnight, we're going to be in a world of trouble."

Now it was Velveteen's turn to get the blank look from Victory Anna. "Whatever does midnight have to do with anything?"

"…a dimension without Disney or horror movies," muttered Vel. More loudly, she said, "Midnight is when it gets bad."

In the distance, to punctuate her statement, someone screamed.

Superhuman abilities are generally divided, not only into power levels, but into categories, or "classes." Physical powers, such as enhanced strength, enhanced reflexes, or rapid healing, are the most common, with most superhumans possessing one or more at a low level, even if they are a not a part of that individual's primary power set. Transphysical powers—which is scientist for "Damned if we know how they work, but they're tied to the body, so fuck it" —are also common. This class includes flight, metamorphosis both major and minor (from changing the color of your eyes to turning into an elephant), and manipulation of personal mass, a sub-class comprising growth, shrinking, and phasing through solid objects. The lists go on, with each class and sub-class containing a surprising number and variety of powers. Even the less common classes, such as the animus, contain their own sub-categories of powers. Some are unique. Some are theoretical. All, applied correctly, are dangerous.

And of all the classes, from the physical to the transphysical to the psychic to the temporal, the most dangerous are the reality manipulators. The ones who change, not themselves, but the very nature of reality. They are distinct from transmuters and shapeshifters; while a transmuter can turn a turtle into a tree, the tree will once have been a turtle. While a shapeshifter can transform him or herself into another creature, they will once have been themselves. Once a reality manipulator gets involved, that is no longer the case. They can wander the world leaving a trail of puzzled turtles behind them, rewriting the universe to suit their deepest desires...or their most transitory whims.

It is rare for The Super Patriots, Inc. to recommend the depowering of a superhuman, stating that they do not want to establish a precedent via which a hard-working member of the superhuman community can be permanently punished for a temporary lapse of judgment. (As this sort of sentence is requested only in instances where non-superhumans have died due to either negligence or malice on the part of the accused, the general public is much more positively inclined toward depowering, despite the near-universal suicide rate among former superhumans.) This does not hold in the case of the reality manipulators. When someone can bend the fabric of the cosmos to suit their whims, they are too dangerous to be controlled. The only thing that stops them is depowering or, in extremely unusual cases, exile to a reality of their own creation. Generally, being completely at peace with their surroundings will stop the reality manipulators from exercising their powers.

For a time.

Reality manipulators are quite likely responsible for the nature of the world in which we live, where superheroes form corporations and holidays take on physical form. If that alone is not enough to convince you of the danger that they represent, may your inevitable death occur somewhere far, far away from anything we'd like to keep. Including the Earth.

"What in Epona's name is wrong with this place?" Victory Anna scowled at the guts of the Speak-and-Spell as if they had personally betrayed her. That seemed unlikely; they were spread out across her knees like a mechanical shawl, and weren't in a position to go around betraying anyone.

"What, honey, can't you read the future in its entrails?" drawled the Princess, looking up from her mouse hole.

"Of course not," said Victory Anna, transferring her scowl to the other superheroine. "I'd need a pigeon and some gloves if I was going to do that."

"I don't know what to say to that," said Jackie.

"Why the fuck am I always the one riding herd on the carnival of weirdoes?" muttered Velveteen. The hall was still empty. It wasn't likely to stay that way, but still, she had to risk it. Cautiously, she turned. "Victory Anna, why are you cussing at the broken toy?"

"Because it's still bloody broken," said Victory Anna, sounding utterly disgusted. "This thing isn't broadcasting a signal, making me a cup of tea, *or* shooting out flesh-melting lasers."

"That's, ah, an interesting range of possible functions," said the Princess. She was using the careful tone of voice she usually reserved for speaking to small children with questionable bladder control when they approached her at her public appearances.

"Tea is important," said Victory Anna primly.

"Oh, sweet Claus," groaned Jackie. She dropped her head into her hands. A thin scrim of frost had formed on the wall where she'd been leaning. It melted as Velveteen watched, dissolving faster than it should have. Jackie's ice wasn't natural, and once it had condensed, it normally lasted. "We're all going to die here."

"You don't know that," said Velveteen. "Maybe—"

Her words were cut off by the sound of screaming. Every head in the small room rose, but it was Victory Anna who looked the most alarmed. Her eyes went very wide.

With the feeling that she was standing at the edge of a dam that was on the verge of bursting, Velveteen scrambled to her knees, trying to position herself between Victory Anna and the hall. "Okay, I just need you to hang on a second before you run off. We don't have weapons, we don't have reliable powers, and—"

"Get out of my way, you milk-sop gear-grinding horse-beater! That's the woman I love!" She sprang to her feet more quickly than any of them would have thought possible for someone without super speed, barreling past Velveteen and down the hall before the last pieces of the Speak-and-Spell finished hitting the floor.

Everyone blinked. Finally, the Princess said, "Maybe you ought to think about nudging her over to *decaf* tea."

"I think about it every day," said Velveteen, scooting her way back into the open. "Come on. Let's go keep my roommate from getting herself slaughtered."

"We still haven't seen whoever brought us here..." said Jackie.

Velveteen paused, looking at her like she'd just said something unbelievably idiotic. "I'm not worried about whoever brought us here," she said. "Well, I *am*, but that's just become a secondary concern. The woman who just screamed her head off was Sparkle Bright."

"...oh, crap," said Jackie.

"My thoughts exactly."

They got moving.

Victory Anna ran down the hall without hesitation, her hands itching for the guns she didn't have. Damn whoever brought them here, to this Epona-forsaken place, where nothing worked as it ought, and even the technology refused to come to heel as it normally did! Her compatriots had been distressed from the first, but after losing her home dimension—twice—Victory Anna had thought herself more difficult to frighten. And so she was, until those so-familiar screams began to emanate from the bowels of the cursed manse...

Familiar to you, but not to her, came the thought, insidious as arsenic, unforgiving as an academic review. *She only knows you as Velveteen's cross-dimensional roommate, not her own star-crossed lover. What are you thinking? That if you save her, she'll fall into your arms and make everything make sense again? You're a fool, Victoria Cogsworth, and you'll suffer for your foolishness before this night is over...*

She shoved the thought aside and kept running, scanning the walls for doorways, and for things that could be used as a weapon. If science had deserted her, she'd regress to barbarism, if that was what it took. Whether her Pol knew her or not, whether they were ever even to become friends in this strange new world, Victory Anna had been brought up to never leave a loved one in danger. Nothing in her lessons had told her to make exceptions for parallel universe versions of those loved ones. And so she ran.

The sound of footsteps running along behind her was unnerving, but that was no matter: the screaming was in front of her, and that meant she was being chased, if not by allies, then likely by fellow victims. Somewhere up ahead in the dark, Polychrome screamed again. Victory Anna put on another burst of speed, preparing to fling herself around the nearest corner–

–only to be hauled up short as the Princess, who had learned to sprint in high heels and was thus remarkably suited to running without them, grabbed her by the back of her corset. The Princess also had six inches and thirty pounds on her. The effect was not unlike suddenly being lassoed from behind by a solid wall of irritated Southern belle.

"Let me go!" demanded Victory Anna. "Pol needs me!"

"Her name's not Polychrome here, Tory; it's Sparkle Bright," said Velveteen. "And trust me, I want to save her as much as you do. But we're not going to do her any good if we rush in and get ourselves killed. Now please, can you calm the fuck down and let us help you?"

Victory Anna stopped twisting in the Princess's grasp and simply glared at Velveteen. "While you're standing here lecturing me about remaining calm, Po–'Sparkle Bright' is being subjected to horrors unknown and dangers unknowable. We have to move."

"You have to watch your language, or Jim Henson's going to sue you for copyright infringement," said Jackie.

"Says the girl from the Rankin-Bass special," drawled the Princess, and let go of Victory Anna. "I'm sorry about grabbing you, honey, but Vel's right. We gotta take this careful. Horror movies have their own rules, and if we go rushing in like a half-baked television spin-off, we're going to get cancelled like one."

Victory Anna looked at the two girls blankly. Fearing disaster, Velveteen stepped forward and said, "Okay. We have to assume everyone who's been brought here against their will has slightly dysfunctional powers right now. Maybe that's a big assumption, but it helps us plan. Are you with me?" The others nodded. "Good. Now, I haven't seen Tag. He's the only male hero currently in Portland, so he should have been a target. I think he didn't get grabbed."

"Three cheers for sexism," said Jackie dryly.

"Exactly. We're in a creepy horror movie house, and it's not connected to Halloween or you and I would both know it. That means it probably belongs to somebody who wants to be a horror movie villain, and they're almost always male. This is a hunting preserve."

"And you're keeping me from running to Sparkle Bright's aid *why*?" Victory Anna demanded.

"Because you're unarmed, and horror movie rules say if you run in unarmed, you're going to get there just in time to see her die." Velveteen looked around the hall, finally pointing to a door. "That one. Jackie, I need that door open."

"Sure, make the blue girl do all the heavy lifting. I'm pretty sure that's racist," grumbled Jackie, and moved to try the door. It was locked. Jackie made a sour face before reaching around behind herself and calmly removing her bra.

Victory Anna made a small squeaking sound. The Princess rolled her eyes. "Oh, goodie," she said. "Stripping."

"You can kiss my blueberry ass," said Jackie, before using her teeth to rip into the thin mesh on the side of her bra strap. It gave way easily, confirming everyone's impression that they had been dressed for viewer appeal, not actual function. "You think I want everyone here getting a look at my flawless rack? Nope. None of you are normally cleared for my boobies."

"What, does our clearance get upgraded every time you get your hands on a bottle of tequila?" asked the Princess.

Jackie glared at her as she pulled her underwire out through the hole she'd bitten in the side of the bra. Then, still glaring, she bent and started to pick the lock. "Unarmed, my sweet Aunt North Wind," she muttered.

Victory Anna finally found her voice, demanding, "Is no one else here troubled by the presence of a topless glowing woman?"

"You get used to it," said Velveteen.

"Besides, topless girl gets *results*," said Jackie triumphantly, as she twisted the wire and the lock clicked. "Your previously locked room awaits." She pushed the door open. The others crowded inside while she was putting her bra back on. "Uh, you're welcome?"

None of the others said anything. Feeling suddenly exposed—and woefully unprepared for a fight, since a single underwire did not a full arsenal make—Jackie crowded in after them, and suddenly understood their silence.

The room was covered in blood. It was splattered on the walls and ceiling, and had pooled in inch-deep puddles on the floor. There were no bodies. That was really the best thing any of them could think to say…at least until Victory Anna's gleeful squeal of, "I think I see a hacksaw!" She went charging into the room, ignoring the fact that she was walking through blood, and snatched a, yes, blood-covered hacksaw from one of the counters. "Well? What are you waiting for? You can't be squeamish, we've a friend to rescue."

"I never thought I'd say this, but I miss Halloween," said Velveteen, and started into the room with the others close behind.

Very shortly, the four of them were heading down the hall at a jog, moving toward where they'd last heard the sound of screaming. They were all blood-splattered. It showed up most on Jackie, whose white lingerie seemed perfectly designed to display the blood to its best advantage. Besides Victory Anna's prized hacksaw, they had found a butcher knife (Vel), a fireplace poker (Princess), and a crowbar (Jackie). It was nice to be armed. It would have been even nicer to know where they were going.

"I should never have let you stop me," said Victory Anna. "She hasn't screamed since we unlocked that door. Had you noticed? She hasn't screamed."

"Actually, the screams stopped—" began Jackie, and stopped when the Princess shot her a nasty look. "I'm sure she's fine," she said lamely.

"And if she's not? What then?"

"Torrey…" Velveteen's attempt at an answer was cut off by the hockey-masked figure who burst out of a door ahead of them, charging into the hall. He had a meat hook in one hand and a machete in the other…and a blonde woman in rainbow-striped lingerie on his back, her knees anchored on his shoulders and a strip of barbed wire wrapped around his neck. The man in the hockey mask was screaming in pain as he ran. Sparkle Bright was shrieking in fury and triumph—and probably a little pain of her own, since her hands were clearly bleeding.

The masked man didn't seem to register the presence of the additional superheroes, maybe because he was so distracted by the one in the process of throttling him. He kept charging, forcing them to scatter to the sides of the hall. Sparkle Bright looked back as he plowed onward, and snarled, "You guys want to give me a little help here?"

"She's magnificent," breathed Victory Anna.

"She's getting away!" said Velveteen, and charged after the pair, trying to stab the masked man in the back of the leg as he ran. She missed. As she didn't stab either herself or Sparkle Bright in the process, it was classifiable as a win.

"Allow me," said the Princess, running daintily past her and whacking him as hard as she could in the ankle with her poker. The masked man stumbled and howled. Sparkle Bright adjusted her grip and pulled. And Jackie ran up and hit the man in the back of the head with her crowbar. He howled one last time before going over like a felled tree.

Sparkle Bright released her barbed wire garrote, shaking her punctured hands as she climbed off the fallen mountain of a man. "That *sucked*," she declared, and turned a scowl on the other superheroes. "Where the hell have you guys been? I thought I was all alone in here, at least until Chuckles," she kicked the man in the back of the head, "showed up and started trying to machete me to death. Asshole. Slasher movies are *so* sexist."

"We didn't know you were in here with us until we heard you screaming," said Velveteen. She looked back in the direction that Sparkle Bright and the machete man had come from. "Does he have, like, a slaughter room back there?"

"I didn't check," said Sparkle Bright frostily.

"Okay. Well, where there's a masked man with a machete, there's usually a room full of things that make it easier to vivisect nubile young girls. Victory Anna." Vel turned to the gadgeteer, who was trying to stare at Sparkle Bright without looking at her. It was a neat trick, and under normal circumstances, Vel would have enjoyed watching it for a while longer. Considering the situation, it was better to show mercy. "Torrey, Princess, I want you to go see if you can find us something to tie this guy up. Rope or chains or duct tape or something. It's got to be in his torture kit."

"You know more about torture kits than I'm really happy with, sugar," said the Princess.

"I've spent a lot of time in Halloween."

"Come on, hurry hurry, we've got a lot to do," said Victory Anna, speaking so fast that all her words ran together. She grabbed the Princess's hand and hauled her away down the hall, leaving Vel, Sparkle Bright, and Jackie alone with the fallen would-be killer.

"She doesn't like me very much, does she?" asked Sparkle Bright, before kicking the man in the head again. Jackie and Vel both blinked at her. She shrugged. "What? He looked like he was waking up."

The man hadn't so much as stirred. It seemed better not to point that out. "It's not that she doesn't like you, Sparks," said Vel, choosing her words carefully. "It's more a matter of…"

"She likes you too damn much, and when you're standing here dressed in six scraps of cotton candy and a Gay Pride flag, it takes every ounce of Victorian repression the girl has not to throw you up against a wall and kiss you until your head explodes," said Jackie laconically.

"Uh," said Sparkle Bright.

"Jackie, some of us are capable of expressing affection without resorting to sexual assault," said Velveteen.

"Uh," said Sparkle Bright.

"Hand-holding, cold showers, and sappy poetry are probably about your speed, yeah," said Jackie. "I remind you, I'm the one who dates regularly, you're the one currently on…what, your second boyfriend? Ever? So maybe I'm the authority here."

"Victory Anna has a crush on me?" said Sparkle Bright. "But we only just met!"

The other two turned slowly to look at her, Vel's eyes widening, Jackie's cheeks flushing a slightly darker shade of blue. "Yeah, about that…" began Jackie.

The man on the floor groaned. Sparkle Bright kicked him briskly in the side of the head. "What about that?" she asked.

"We found tape!" announced the Princess, coming back down the hall with an armload of duct tape. Victory Anna was close behind, her own arms loaded down with loops of rope.

"We'll tell you later," Velveteen assured her.

Sparkle Bright looked unconvinced.

Fifteen minutes later, the machete-wielding mountain of a man was securely tied to a chair that Victory Anna had produced from one of the side rooms, and the others were standing around, waiting for him to wake up. The Princess had bandaged the wounds on Sparkle Bright's hands with strips torn from her nightgown.

"I could freeze his eyelashes," Jackie offered. "That usually wakes people up, and even when it doesn't, it makes me feel better."

The man groaned. Conversation stopped as the five superheroines turned to see what would happen next. He tried to stand.

The ropes and tape held him in place. He tried again. The ropes and tape still held. He stopped struggling.

Velveteen stepped forward, leaning close enough to see his eyes through the holes in his mask. "Did you bring us here?" she asked. "Because we need you to send us back, right now."

"Or what?" he rumbled, in a voice like a broken trash compactor.

"Oh, honey. Or nothing," said the Princess. "You're going to send us home, because it's the right thing to do. It's the gentlemanly thing to do. Also because the little redhead found a pair of bolt cutters, and she's in a bit of a mood. It's in everyone's best interests, really."

"You wouldn't," said the man, sounding less sure of himself. "You're good guys."

"I'm freelance," said Jackie.

"I was technically a supervillain for a while," said Velveteen.

"I still am," said Victory Anna.

"I just quit The Super Patriots," said Sparkle Bright.

"I am sweetness, light, and compassion incarnate," said the Princess. "That's why I'm going to go clean a few rooms in this hellhole while you and my friends have a nice long talk about what you've done." She turned her back as if she was going to walk away.

"Wait!" yelped the man. The Princess turned to face him. His voice seemed higher now, more like a teenager's than an adult's. "Don't go! If you go…"

"My friends will take you apart. I know. But as long as I'm not here to see it, I don't have to know." The Princess shrugged. "Loopholes."

"I…crud." The man sagged against his bonds. They were looser now, because he was getting smaller, dwindling from an impossible juggernaut to a skinny teenage boy. He didn't fight at all when Sparkle Bright reached out and took his mask away. He just raised his head, looking at her helplessly. "I'm sorry. I wasn't really going to hurt you."

"So what, the machete is your version of a bunch of daisies?" asked Jackie. She crossed her arms. "Uncool, dude. Way uncool."

"You're a reality-manipulator, aren't you?" asked Velveteen. He nodded, looking ashamed. "Got a thing for horror movies?" He nodded again. "And that's why you created an extradimensional space where you could play out a horror movie of your own. Why us? What made you go for a bunch of superheroes?"

"I…I wanted it to be extra fun. Crossovers are always the best."

"Did you stop to think that it wouldn't be much fun for us?" He didn't say anything. Vel sighed. "Yeah, I thought not. Okay. The way I see it, we have two options here. Option one, we kill you, find a mirror, and have Jackie take us home by way of Santa's Workshop."

"I like that option," said Jackie.

"I don't!" the teenager protested.

"Option two, you unblock our powers, send us all home, and you promise never to abduct someone for your sick games again. Because if you do—if you even think about it—I will know, and I will find you." Velveteen's smile seemed to have a few too many teeth. "Deal?"

"You're the one who controls toys," said the teenager. "Why are you the scary one?"

"Practice," Vel said. "Do we have a deal?"

"Deal," he whispered. "Just untie me."

Velveteen stepped back. "Torrey?"

"This is a terrible idea," said Victory Anna, before stepping forward and cutting the boy's bonds with his own machete. They fell away, even the tape, which should have stuck until someone pulled on it. The room froze. The air shimmered.

And the five blood-drenched, lingerie-clad superheroines were suddenly standing in front of Powell's City of Books in downtown Portland. "Hey, ladies!" shouted someone from a passing car. "Nice tits!"

Victory Anna shrieked and attempted to cover herself with her arms. Velveteen groaned, putting a hand over her face. At the same time, Jackie spread her arms and announced, "Yes! Look in awe upon what you will never touch! Genetics have been kind!"

"Stuff it, Sexy Smurf," snapped the Princess. "I'm going to go find us some kind of gourd or melon to turn into a ride." She stomped off.

"So this is the freelance life, huh?" said Sparkle Bright to Velveteen, smiling wanly at a pair of pedestrians who were openly staring. "Fun."

"There's usually a little less gore," said Velveteen, hand still over her face. "I need a shower. And a shirt. A shower, a shirt, and a long, long nap."

"Sounds good. I just had one question, while we wait for the Princess to come back with a pumpkin or whatever."

"What?"

"Don't these things usually have sequels?"

Velveteen lowered her hand and stared at her friend, who shrugged.

"Just saying," said Sparkle Bright.

"I'm sleeping with a baseball bat from now on," said Velveteen. Sparkle Bright laughed, and together, they all waited in the bright sun for their carriage home.

VELVETEEN vs. *Vegas*

"THIS IS A TERRIBLE PLAN," said Sparkle Bright.

"I don't normally make a habit of agreeing with Stripy the Rainbow Clown, but kid's got a point," said Jackie. She crossed her arms, trying to glare Velveteen into submission. "You're not what I'd call one of the world's top ten all-time planners, and even for you, this is a terrible plan. Most people need to work to come up with a plan this bad. Why do you think this is a good idea?"

"We need leverage on The Super Patriots if we want to have a case when they figure out where Sparkle Bright has gone to ground," said Velveteen–aka "Velma Martinez," "The Super Patriots, Inc.'s Most Wanted Deserter," and, when she was feeling particularly snarly, "The Bride of Chucky" –not budging. "Vegas can give us what we need to even the odds."

"Vegas doesn't help anyone but Vegas," said Jackie. "They *invented* 'the house always wins.' If you go to Vegas expecting to come out on top, you're either stupid or delusional, and I honestly couldn't tell you which one it is. Don't do this."

"What would you prefer, Jackie?" Velveteen gestured to Sparkle Bright. "They're going to come for her. Not 'might.' Not 'could.' *Going to.* I already lost her once. I'm not willing to stand by and let it happen again. That means we need leverage, and the only place we're going to get it is in Las Vegas. It's neutral territory."

"You have a responsibility to Portland," said Jackie. "I'm not going to stay here and do your job for you because you feel the need to hare off like an idiot."

"You don't need to stay here," said Sparkle Bright. The other two turned to look at her. She shrugged. "I'm here. Victory Anna is here. Tag and Jory are here. Four superheroes should be able to keep Portland in one piece long enough for Vel to get to Vegas and back with whatever it is she's hoping to find. I still don't think this is a good idea. I also don't think that there's anyone in this world who can talk Vel out of a course of action once she digs her heels in. All we're doing is wasting time trying."

"Finally, someone speaks sense," said Velveteen. She smiled toothily at Jackie. "You head for the North Pole and annoy the elves. I'll call you when I get back."

"You're going to get yourself killed."

"Maybe, but until I do, I'm going to do my damnedest to do the right thing." Velveteen shrugged. "That means I'm heading for Las Vegas. And whatever happens there, it's sure as hell not going to stay there."

Jackie Frost shook her head, and didn't say anything more.

Prior to the appearance of the "Big Three"–Supermodel, Majesty, and Jolly Roger–there were no known superhumans in the United States. Even taking into account the holiday-themed heroes who claim to have existed for as long as mankind has been capable of commemorating seasonal events, the population of North American superhumans has been rising steadily since the Big Three made the scene. Perhaps unsurprisingly, these superhumans have often chosen to settle in large metro areas, where they can enjoy the company of their peers and commit or thwart super-powered crimes on a regular basis. New York, San Francisco, Detroit, and Toronto sport some of the densest superhuman communities on the continent.

And then there is Las Vegas.

Considered "neutral ground" by heroes and villains alike, this is a city where the flashier, more exotic superhumans tend to make their homes. Resident heroes include Vaudeville, with her glitter and flash, as well as Dame Fortuna, with her elegant, impossible probability manipulation. For all their unique glories, the city's superhumans are often ignored in favor of the mundane glories of the Strip, which is, after all unique. Everyone has heroes at home, but how many people can say the same of Caesar's Palace? The superhuman community can relax in Las Vegas, knowing that they will never become the headline attraction. They like it that way.

Interestingly enough, the high density of probability manipulators in Vegas—at least eight at last count, including Dame Fortuna, her daughter, Lady Luck, and Lady Luck's husband, Fortunate Son—has resulted in The Super Patriots, Inc. having serious trouble establishing a true foothold in the area. Oh, nothing has ever been proven, but after losing eight branch offices to freak accidents (including the historically ridiculous Guinea Pig Stampede), they've stopped trying. The heroes of Las Vegas live untroubled by corporate regulations.

That doesn't mean they aren't aware of what's going on elsewhere in the superhuman community, or that they're not willing to get involved. For a price.

The Princess was able to get Velveteen to the city limits and no further, due to some complicated flight pattern registry that required a bunch of certifications for anyone who wanted to pilot a flying carpet within Las Vegas proper. Velveteen found herself dropped quite unceremoniously at the place where natural desert met aggressive landscaping. She sighed, waved after the departing bit of home decor, and began to walk.

She hadn't gone very far before she started doubting the wisdom of this plan, since the sun was high and merciless, and she was far enough from the Strip that no one was investing in public misters. Grumbling, she tensed her shoulders and kept going. This was going to be worth it. It had to be.

Hiding her concern from the others was getting harder every day; she was tired all the time from the stress of it all. Sparkle Bright had been a defector from The Super Patriots for almost a month. There was no way they didn't know where their former team leader was, and there was *absolutely* no way Marketing was going to let the situation stand. They were going to move, and they were going to do it soon. Velveteen needed to be ready when they did.

She realized as she walked that crowds were starting to form around her. Lifting her head, she discovered that she had reached the Strip—and more, that her destination was not that far ahead of her. She picked up the pace, very nearly trotting to the building surrounded by animatronic pirates. Then she stopped, looking at them dubiously. This was where she was supposedly meeting her contact. She just hadn't expected it to be so…Vegas.

The animatronic pirates ignored her judgmental stare as they continued in their sanitized piratical ways, which consisted mainly of hoisting empty tankards and plundering the ships of their fellow buccaneers. "Fucked-up times five thousand," she finally declared, before opening the casino door and stepping inside.

Entering the Jolly Roger Casino was something like stepping into the hybrid offspring of a Renaissance Faire and a strip club, only with more slot machines and less class. Busty barmaids wearing slutty pirate costumes that were probably purchased at a Halloween store clearance sale worked the crowd, distributing complementary cocktails to the high rollers and snubbing the tourists at the nickel slots. Velveteen froze in the doorway, realizing that for once in her life, her formal "work attire" didn't stand out even in what should have been a mundane locale. No one looked at her twice. It was almost as disorienting as the casino's carefully-controlled artificial twilight.

Then a hand was at her elbow, and a redheaded woman with a sunny smile and an outfit that consisted almost entirely of sequins was tugging her gently out of the flow of traffic. "Velveteen?" she asked.

Normally, Velveteen would have responded with something snarky about "how many women in bunny suits do you have around this place?" Under the circumstances, she was slightly worried about the answer she'd receive. "That's me." She pulled her arm free, eyeing the woman. "You are?"

"Showgirl," said the woman, in a tone that made it clear that she was giving her name, not her profession. "I know you were expecting Dame Fortuna, but I was the one sent to watch for you. Will you come with me? Fortunate Son would very much like to have a word with you before you're allowed to meet with his mother."

Velveteen considered asking for the woman's credentials, but dismissed the idea as unnecessary. Given the number of stuffed pirates and cuddly plush pirate ships scattered around the room, she could re-enact the siege of the Spanish Main if she had to. Short of FAO Schwarz, this was the last place on Earth she needed to worry about an ambush.

"I'm always happy to meet new people," she said. "Let's go."

Getting to Fortunate Son's office required a brief tour of the Jolly Roger Casino, which Showgirl delivered with the smoothly practiced ease of a long-time guide. Gift shops, slot machines, and small theatres were pointed out with the same cheerful, seemingly automatic blandness. Velveteen did her best not to pay any attention at all. She was just enjoying being inside, where the blazing desert sun wasn't.

"...and this is the private elevator leading to the quarters of Dame Fortuna and family," said Showgirl blissfully, pulling aside a curtain to reveal a golden cage. "Anyone caught beyond this point without invitation is subject to seven years of abysmally bad luck. No take-backs, no lucky charms. Going up."

"Wait—what?" But it was too late. Velveteen found herself hustled into the elevator, and then immediately back out again. The cage hadn't moved.

The casino had completely changed.

Gone was the floor of beeping slot machines and dead-eyed tourists, replaced by a sleek, modern-looking security room, the walls lined with monitors that showed the casino Velveteen had so abruptly left behind. A pool table sat dead center in the middle of the room.

The man who leaned against it was barely six feet tall, with desert-sand hair and eyes the blue of ten-dollar poker chips. He leaned against the pool table as Showgirl led Velveteen forward, his eyes raking her up and down and making her wish she'd thought to wear the lead-lined underwear. His power profile didn't say anything about X-ray vision, but with the Vegas heroes, you never knew.

"Fortunate Son, I presume?" she said.

"Velveteen," he said, after an uncomfortably long silence. "I expected something fluffier."

Vel bristled. "I expected something taller, so I guess we're even."

Showgirl looked alarmed. To Fortunate Son's credit, he laughed, shaking his head. "Girl, you are a piece of work. You know you're in the temple of fortunes, don't you? Any one of us could trash your world with a snap of our fingers, and you'd never get it back to where it was before you angered us."

"Uh, hello, have we met? The name's Velveteen. You may remember me from the 10 o'clock News. I'm as close as a hero comes to being excommunicated. If The Super Patriots catch me outside Oregon, I'm under arrest, the Governor of Oregon gave me back my heroing license purely to piss them off—and PS, it worked—and my roommate is from an alternate Victorian England that doesn't exist anymore. My parents just sold their life story to the Pow Network for six figures, while I'm counting quarters for a trip to Starbucks. How are you going to trash my world? Give me bad hair?" She folded her arms, glaring at him. "Bring it on. I have conditioner."

"If you're not allowed outside of Oregon, how did you even get here?" asked Showgirl.

"I told the Princess I needed a lift, and she dropped me off at the edge of town." Velveteen didn't have to feign her shudder. "Flying carpet rides from Portland to Las Vegas are so very not fun. But I'll still call her for my ride home. It's better than the alternative." She turned her attention back to Fortunate Son. "I contacted you because I wanted to make a deal. As far as I'm aware, you usually do those remotely. So what was so important about *this* deal that it meant you had to call me out of my home territory, and why do I care?"

"You must care, or you wouldn't have come," he noted reasonably. "As for what's so important...we've got ourselves a leprechaun infestation."

Velveteen snorted. "I've been to the Spring Country. Leprechauns don't exist outside of the seasonal worlds."

"Sorry to contradict you, missy, but they exist. At least if Lucky Charms is back in town."

"Lucky...oh, that fucker." Vel groaned. "I thought he was dead."

"Guess he had one more four-leafed clover to deploy. Anyway, they've infiltrated the casino, and things are going wrong a heck of a lot faster than Mama likes. Leprechauns bend probability just enough to make it hard for us to see them clear. They're about the size of our mascots, so we figure they're playing dolly, and–"

"You want me to call the toys and see what doesn't respond." Velveteen eyed him skeptically. "Why am I going to do you this favor? You haven't even agreed to help me yet."

"Because there weren't three original heroes," said a voice behind her. It was one of those impossible old-style movie star voices, the kind that promised sin and salvation at the same time. Vel turned to see an elegant blonde woman who could have been cloned from Rita Hayworth herself come gliding up to the group. She was wearing a floor-length green satin sheath dress, and a small smile painted her cupid's-bow lips. "There were four, darling, and I'm the one that got left off the books when they decided to go public."

"What?" Velveteen blinked. "That's not possible."

"Oh, it is. If you're lucky enough." Dame Fortuna smiled. "Luck's always been my specialty."

Velveteen's mouth went dry. "You mean you–"

"All the dirt, darling, all the petty little back-room deals and nasty little lies, I've got it all on paper. You want to take down The Super Patriots? I can't say I have any desire to stop you, but there are a few things you'll need."

"Jolly Roger," whispered Velveteen.

Dame Fortuna nodded. "Exactly that, my sweet little poker chip. You want to find Jolly Roger? This is where you start looking. All you need to do is one tiny little service for the heroes of Vegas, and our files are yours."

If she could find Jolly Roger– the last of the Big Three, the only one whose death had never been confirmed–she could give Marketing something to worry about beyond the activities of one middle-grade animator who'd decided she wanted out. Something even bigger than a runaway photon manipulator. The Super Patriots, Inc. would leave them all alone forever if she showed up knowing how to find Jolly Roger.

"Right." Vel sighed. "What do you want me to do?"

There were approximately two thousand, seven hundred, and eight toys of one description or another within the confines of the Jolly Roger Casino, not counting the ones who were attached to specific children. Velveteen couldn't have explained how she knew the attached toys from the ones who would be happy to help her; she just knew, the same way that she knew all the toys would answer her call if it were truly an emergency. She stood in the middle of the main casino floor with her eyes closed and her hands raised in front of her chest, concentrating.

Fortunate Son and Showgirl stood nearby, leaning up against a bank of slot machines that had started to return jackpots slightly more often than was statistically likely, and watched her work. "So that's an animus," said Fortunate Son. "I'm not impressed."

The doors of the casino opened as the animatronic pirates from outside came marching in, still singing their jaunty pirate songs.

Showgirl hid a smile behind her hand. "How about now?" she asked. "Are you impressed now?"

"…I suppose I am," Fortunate Son allowed, his attention swinging from the pirates back to Velveteen.

She was still standing with her hands raised, but she had started to shake, and a fine sheen of sweat had appeared on her forehead and her upper lip. Toys all over the building started to get up of their own accord, running to reach her. The animatronic pirates moved to form a circle around her, their swords at the ready. Fortunate Son didn't remember them looking quite so sharp, or the pirates looking quite so bloodthirsty.

Velveteen lowered her hands. Eyes still closed, she smiled, and spoke the first words to leave her lips since she stepped back onto the casino floor: "Go get 'em."

The leprechauns, who had been enjoying their anonymity, never knew what hit them. Final count and analysis of the security recordings would show that there had been exactly nine hundred and two leprechauns within the confines of the Jolly Roger Casino when Velveteen cried havoc and let slip the dolls of war. The number dwindled quickly after that.

First blood went to an "I Love Las Vegas" teddy bear that had been sharing its owner's purse with a leprechaun for hours. It whirled on the unsuspecting psychic projection, suddenly showing teeth and claws before ripping the little green man's head clean off his little green shoulders. The leprechaun dissolved in a puff of whiskey-scented smoke, and the teddy bear went seeking new prey.

Casino customers screamed and fled in droves, some pursued by toys bent on taking their leprechaun hitchhikers away. Fortunate Son and Showgirl did not move to intervene. Losing a little business was bad. Acquiring a reputation as a casino that couldn't crack down on pickpockets and cheats was worse. Through it all, Velveteen remained frozen at the center of the floor, the sweat beginning to stand out more and visibly on her face. Her cheeks were starting to redden, and the shaking was getting worse.

The toys battled on, until finally, the last leprechaun's head had been sundered from its shoulders. Velveteen wobbled. Velveteen trembled. And finally, without another word spoken, Velveteen fell, landing on a cushion of suddenly inanimate plush pirates, random Beanie Babies, and "I Love Las Vegas" teddy bears.

Everything was silent.

"I think she's dead." The voice was Fortunate Son's. He didn't sound particularly upset about the idea of having a dead woman in a bunny costume lying on his casino floor. Then again, this *was* Las Vegas. Things like that probably happened every day.

"Be nice," said an unfamiliar woman's voice. It had the same syrupy accent as Dame Fortuna, but it was lighter, sweeter, and somehow more capricious, all at once. "She came here because we asked her to, and she did us a big favor. There's no cause to go wishing her death happen any faster than it's already coming."

"You think the best of everyone, sweetheart."

"That's my job, just like it's your job to think the worst of everyone who isn't family." A cool hand stroked Velveteen's cheek. "Poor little thing. She's burning up, and for what? A few files that Mama should have burned years ago? It's not worth it."

"She's the one who decided to play after we told her what the game was." Fortunate Son sounded almost defensive now. Velveteen, who was only just coming to realize that she wasn't dead, decided that she liked the woman who was scolding him. "It's not my fault if she went and pushed herself all the way into burnout."

"That's the thing. She shouldn't have pushed herself into burnout. I remember the betting pools with her in them, back when she was with that awful junior team. She managed situations much larger than this one without any sign of strain."

"Maybe she's out of practice."

"Or maybe something's draining her." This voice was familiar: Dame Fortuna herself. "I know you're awake, little girl, even if you aren't completely sure one way or another. It's time to open your eyes, get off your back, and have a little talk with Mama."

"You're not my mother," said Velveteen, and opened her eyes…

…only to find herself looking up at the most beautiful woman she had ever seen. Her eyes were the color of new felt on the finest card table ever made, and her hair was the gold of top-shelf whiskey poured in a smoky room where old men bet on ponies and young men bet on souls. She was plainly dressed, T-shirt and jeans, but on her, they were finer than any designer gowns or jewels could possibly have been. Velveteen stared.

The woman sighed and snapped her fingers. Something about the sound changed the picture. She was still blonde, yes, still curvy and soft with big green eyes, but she was only a woman, not the embodiment of all feminine desire. "Sorry," she said. "I came straight from work, and as long as you didn't have your eyes open, I didn't have to dial it back."

"My poor put-upon darling," said Fortunate Son, stepping up behind her and putting his arms around her waist.

Velveteen wracked her mind, despite the pounding headache she had somehow acquired, to remember the family connections of the Vegas heroes. "Lady Luck, I presume?" she ventured. She sat up, or tried to, anyway. Her headache got worse. She allowed herself to flop back down.

"Guilty as charged," said the younger blonde. She leaned back against Fortunate Son, clearly comfortable. "You gave us quite a fright when you collapsed in the casino like that. There was nothing in any of your files to indicate that you'd burn out so quickly."

"I've been tired lately," Velveteen admitted. "I think it's stress."

"Best friend finally escapes The Super Patriots, Inc., you wind up with a roommate from another dimension, and three holidays are jockeying for your hand—I can see where that might get stressful," said Dame Fortuna, stepping up next to her daughter. Seen like this, side by side, the family resemblance was more than just unmistakable: it was absolute. Lady Luck looked like Dame Fortuna twenty years younger, before the casinos took a maiden and turned her into a mother. Dame Fortuna smiled at Velveteen's expression. "My Luckygirl doesn't have a father. Just me, the night wind, and a roll of the dice. It's no wonder we look so much like each other."

"No wonder," said Velveteen faintly.

"It'll be different for me," said Lady Luck. "I think it's important for my babies to know their father. Don't you agree, dear?"

"As long as they have your disposition and not mine," said Fortunate Son.

"How are you feeling?" Dame Fortuna stepped away from her daughter and son-in-law, moving to peer into Velveteen's eyes. "You were out for a good long time."

"It's probably sunstroke," said Velveteen. "I walked from the city limits to your casino. That can't be good for me." Part of her knew that answer was too easy. She pushed that part aside. There were some things it was better to let go.

"You *walked*?" Dame Fortuna turned a glare on Fortunate Son, who had the sense to look abashed. "There's no reason you should have needed to do that. We have a shuttle."

"She didn't call," protested Fortunate Son weakly. "If she'd called, I would've sent Showgirl to pick her up."

"The Princess doesn't have flight clearance for her carpet in Vegas," said Velveteen, trying to prevent a full-scale family brawl. "I didn't realize you had a shuttle."

"Fortunate Son, get temporary clearance for the Princess to fly her carpet in here. I won't have anyone saying that we mistreat our guests, especially after they've publically collapsed doing favors for us."

"On it," said Fortunate Son, and disentangled himself from Lady Luck before walking quickly out of the room.

Dame Fortuna nodded, looking satisfied, and turned back to

Velveteen. "Now you, me, and Lady, we're going to have a nice lunch, and we're going to talk about what you need from me. Vegas may stack the odds, but we always, always pay our debts, when we incur them."

"Thank you, ma'am," said Velveteen. She wasn't so sure about anything that involved getting off whatever she was currently lying on—what *was* she lying on? She turned her head just enough to see the green felt underneath her. Ah. The pool table.

"But first, let's get you a little hair of the dog that bit you." Dame Fortuna leaned in and kissed Velveteen's forehead. Her headache popped like a soap bubble, fading almost instantly into nothingness.

Velveteen sat up, eyes wide, and looked into Dame Fortuna's smirking face. "How did you do that?"

"Most gamblers bet a little freer when they're drunk, and not at all when they're hung over," said Dame Fortuna. "It's not my most useful power, but it can come in handy when you want to keep the game going."

"I can do it, too, almost as well as Mama," said Lady Luck.

"Oof. Remind me never to go drinking with the two of you and the Princess," said Velveteen. She swung her legs around, carefully testing their willingness to obey her commands. Everything seemed to be in working order, despite a faint, lingering dizziness. She stood. "Thank you."

"It's no trouble at all, sweetheart," said Dame Fortuna, taking her arm. "Now let's have that lunch."

"Lunch" turned out to be a private table in the casino's five-star restaurant, which they entered by walking past a long line of hopeful diners. No one said anything about their blatant line-jumping. Everyone was too busy staring at Dame Fortuna, and at Lady Luck, who was once more wearing her devastatingly beautiful work persona. Velveteen felt like a grubby favorite doll as she tagged along in their wake. Vegas might be easy on the eyes, but it was hell on the nerves, at least as far as she was concerned.

Once they were seated, with tall glasses of cucumber water and a bowl of steaming fresh bread on the table, Dame Fortuna focused on her again. "Drink your water," she said. "Then drink your refill, and drink the refill that comes after that. If there's any chance you've been sunstruck, you're going to want to hydrate."

"Hydration is a good idea regardless," said Lady Luck. "This is a desert, after all."

The advice felt bizarrely practical coming from a heroine who was generally regarded as the living embodiment of good fortune. Velveteen sipped her cucumber water and tried to figure out how to raise the topic that had brought her to Las Vegas in the first place.

Fortunately—no pun intended—Dame Fortuna did it for her. "So you're going to look for Jolly Roger," she said. "That's a bold decision for a hero as young as you are. I've followed your career since it started up again, and I never expected anything this ambitious. Why the change of heart?"

Velveteen hesitated before deciding that, when dealing with heroes who may or may not be the living embodiments of the world's good fortune, honesty was the best policy. "I finally have something to defend," she said. "I'm going to do my best to defend it."

"Ah. An idealist. I remember when I was an idealist—back when I was Lady Luck, and my lovely daughter wasn't even a glimmer in a croupier's eye." Dame Fortuna broke open a bread roll, freeing the sweet smell of baked yeast. "You should have seen us in those days, my little bunny-eared heroine. We were gods. This world had never seen anything like us, and oh, how they loved us…"

"So why doesn't anyone know that you were part of the original team?" The question was out before Velveteen realized that it might be a dangerous thing to ask.

Thankfully, Dame Fortuna just smiled. "I was never a member of The Super Patriots; my involvement was over by the time Supermodel decided they needed to be a brand. She couldn't stand having another woman in her spotlight, and well…I'm good at seeing which way the wind is blowing. I cashed in my chips and got out while the getting was good. Sometimes I think I made a mistake. That if I'd stayed, Majesty might have lived, and Roger might not have disappeared the way that he did. But the past is another country, or so some people say."

"Judging by my roommate, the past is a whole different world."

Dame Fortuna laughed. "I wouldn't be surprised. Now come. Let's stop talking about this for a little while, and see if we can't put some color back into your cheeks. I promise, no rabbit stew."

"Gee, thanks," said Velveteen, and picked up her menu.

"I don't think this was a good idea," said Fortunate Son, watching as Velveteen tried to balance three file boxes atop each other. "The Super Patriots are going to know where she got this info, and they're not going to be happy about it."

"No, they're not," said Dame Fortuna. This time, her smile was a skeletal grimace, nothing like the friendly face she showed outsiders. "If they want to talk to me about telling my side of the story, they're welcome to come to Vegas for a chat. I think they'll be surprised by how ready we are for them."

"Besides, Sonny, we came out on top." Lady Luck held up a DVD in a bright cartoon package. "The epic battle of the leprechauns vs. the plush denizens of the casino, available now from the gift shop for twenty-five ninety-five. They're selling like hotcakes."

"The house always wins," said Dame Fortuna serenely, and watched Velveteen carry boxes to the roof.

The Princess brought her carpet in for a careful landing on the roof of the Jolly Roger Casino, knocking her tiara askew and frightening off a large flock of pigeons that had been enjoying the remains of a bag of birdseed. Velveteen waved before hoisting the first of the stack of file boxes and carrying it over to load onto the carpet.

"Uh." The Princess eyed Velveteen's burden dubiously. "Do I even want to know what you've got there?"

"Papers. Records. Maybe, if we're really lucky, a treasure map." Velveteen dropped the box before going back for the next. "Everyone was very helpful, except for maybe Fortunate Son, but 'helpful' isn't really his thing."

"I thought you were coming here for information."

"This *is* information." Velveteen picked up another box, stroking it lovingly. "This is what's going to shift things in our favor. The people here are pirates, Princess. So I plundered."

"You plundered what, the admin office?"

"Something like that."

"Well, was it worth it? Did you get what you needed?"

Velveteen paused, remembering the malice that had sparkled in Dame Fortuna's eyes when she talked about The Super Patriots, Inc. "I think it was," she said, finally. "Now let's go home."

"Mind if we stop for pizza on the way?"

"You wouldn't dare."

"You want to bet?"

Velveteen's screams followed them all the way back to Portland.

VELVETEEN
Presents
Victory Anna vs. The Difficulties With Pan-Dimensional Courtship

AFTER TWO MONTHS OF SHARING her home, off and on, with the woman who might as well have been the love of her life—and very likely *would* have been, had the Snowfather refrained from using his powers to teach her a lesson she still did not fully understand—Victoria Cogsworth had had enough. She rose early, before there was any chance this world's version of her beloved would have arrived via magic mirror from the North Pole, and lay in wait for her roommate.

When Velma finally staggered out of her room and into the kitchen, following the alluring smell of fresh-brewed coffee, she was expecting, well. Coffee. She wasn't expecting to find Victoria, already fully dressed and perfectly groomed, holding the coffee pot hostage.

"We need to have a discussion about Yelena," said Victoria.

"Can it wait until I've had caffeine?" asked Velma. How *anyone* could look perky in a corset before noon was beyond her sleep-fogged ability to comprehend. Quite honestly, she probably wouldn't understand any better once she was awake. At least this way, she could pretend she was still dreaming. Although there was a distinct lack of Tad and whipped cream in the kitchen. So dreaming was probably out.

"No."

Velma whimpered.

Sensing that any chance of a rational discussion was dwindling, Victoria relented and held out the coffee pot. "Oh, all right, indulge your vulgar addictions," she said. "But after you have rejoined the ranks of the living, we must discuss Yelena. Agreed?"

"Whatever you want," said Velma, grabbing the pot and heading for the counter, where her coffee mug waited in the dish drainer.

Victoria watched her go, frowning slightly. She hadn't lived with Velma long, as such things were measured, but she would have had to be blind to overlook her housemate's growing reliance on stimulants. Not just coffee, although that was the most obvious: there were also energy drinks, purchased and consumed while on patrol, and herbal supplements, most of which were questionable at best. "Are you feeling all right?"

"Just tired," said Velma, filling her mug. "I had a late night last night."

That wasn't true: Victoria had been awake when Velma came in from her nightly patrol. It had been barely half-past midnight. As patrols went, that was the equivalent of taking a half-day at work.

And yet all that was irrelevant, and did nothing to forward the discussion at hand. "Be that as it may, we have put off this discussion far too long." Victoria took a seat at the kitchen table, folding her hands primly in her lap, and announced, "I have decided to court Yelena, and would very much appreciate your blessing."

Velma choked on her coffee.

Unwilling to let something as petty as her conversational partner's inability to breathe interfere with her planned script, Victoria continued, "I have drawn up a list of one hundred and three reasons why I would make an ideal girlfriend for your dimension's version of Yelena. It's annotated and simple enough that you should be able to read it unassisted, but I am willing to review it with you if you think this would sway you in the direction of assent."

"You used to date her alternate-reality self!" protested Velma, finally getting her breath back.

"Yes, and that is one of the six items listed in the 'negatives' column," said Victoria implacably. "It ranks just above 'inconvenient height differential' and just below 'homosexual union still tacitly frowned upon by state and local laws,' which I believe could make her uncomfortable with the idea of beginning a relationship with me."

"But that's…it's *creepy*, okay? You know her inside and out, and she barely knows you at all."

"Ah, but you see, that is where you are wrong." Victoria leaned forward, eyes burning with an intensity of focus that Velma normally saw from her only when she was about to take the toaster apart. Again. "This woman is not my Pol. I admit that my physical attraction to her is at least partially based on how much they look alike, and on my intimate knowledge of her more private anatomy—"

"Too much information, seriously," said Velma.

"—but if it were only that, I would have begun courting her weeks ago, and your approval, or lack thereof, be damned. This Yelena is different. She's more vulnerable in some ways, and stronger in others. She's lonely, even when she stands among friends. She needs someone." Victoria looked down at her hands. For a moment, Velma wondered who, exactly, she was talking about: herself, or Sparkle Bright. "She needs me."

"Victoria—Torrey—" Velma paused. "I can't make her love you."

"I wouldn't want you to."

"Yeah, I didn't think so. If you want to court her, that's between the two of you. But you should probably tell her the full story about you and that other Yelena. Starting something like this...I think you're right. I think she's lonely. And I don't want you to mess things up by not making sure she understands exactly what's going on."

"You're very protective for someone who didn't speak to her for years."

Velma shrugged. "We grew up together. She was my best friend. She still is. We may have let each other down, but that doesn't mean I ever stopped loving her. It doesn't mean I ever could."

"Well, good then." Victoria stood, thrusting her hand out for Velma to shake. After a puzzled blink, Velma did just that. "Thank you for your candor. I assure you, I will not harm her in any way."

"Good to know," said Velma, and watched as Victoria gathered her skirts and marched out of the kitchen like a tiny redheaded general marching off to war.

Finally, she said, "That girl is really weird," to the empty air, and sat down at the kitchen table to drink her coffee in peace.

Victoria Cogsworth was a survivor. She had survived the total destruction of two worlds, and the uncontrolled passage through dozens of others. She had survived growing up as a lesbian in a culture where women who loved women were second-class at best. She had survived Oxford, for Epona's sake. But as she carefully braided her hair into the appropriate plait for going courting, she wondered whether she could survive what she was about to begin.

What if this world's Yelena rejected her? Saw her as tainted, somehow, by her love for a version of Yelena who no longer existed, and never would again? What if she presented her suit, and was given nothing but scorn in response?

"Epona favors those who seize the reins of destiny and ride it triumphantly into the future," she said sternly to her reflection, and continued braiding her hair, working the plaits around the crown of her head in a tight style that would have made her intentions perfectly clear to someone from her home world. She smiled a little as she worked, allowing herself a pleasant fantasy in which Yelena was the one stranded in *her* world, under the laws of life and love that she had been raised with. Ah, it would have been beautiful.

Tucking the end of the braid under the base, she stood and crossed to her carpet bag. It was worn and tattered, but it was all she had left of the life she'd been living since that beautiful world was destroyed. If not for Santa Claus, she wouldn't even have had that much. She opened the clasp, pulling out the gold and green courting dress that was waiting for her on the top of the carefully folded clothing. Not for the first time, she wondered whose the bag had been before it came to her. At least there was no chance they would be coming to reclaim it: that was one positive consequence of the destruction of her second home world, at least.

"It is a vain soul who thinks only of her appearance," she chided her reflection, as she pinned her green feathered fascinator into place and studied the overall effect of her outfit. She looked…quite good, really. Perhaps appearance alone would be enough to make her suit plain.

If not, there was always the classic combination of poetry, flattery, and flowers. Victoria retrieved the bouquet of clockwork flowers that she had been working on all week and turned to head for the bathroom, where the mirror Jackie Frost used most often for transport to and from the North Pole was waiting.

Dealing with Yelena's daily commutes to and from Santa's Village had eventually necessitated a series of compromises between the residents of the house and the residents of Winter. The mirror, which would normally have responded only to requests by Jackie herself, was now rigged with catchphrases provided by the Princess. One would open a connection through which conversation could occur; the other would unlock the mirror for transit. While they all knew that Jackie could come and go regardless, she had been respecting the arrangement since it was put in place, and shower-related incidents had decreased dramatically.

Victoria positioned herself carefully in front of the mirror, pausing to adjust the angle of her hat before she cleared her throat and said, "Mirror mirror, on the wall, please would you complete my call?"

Frost spread across the inside of the mirror with disturbing quickness, signifying a connection to the Winter, rather than a connection to the Princess's Crystal Glitter Unicorn Cloud Castle. Victoria waited with ill-concealed impatience until the frost cleared, and was replaced by the puzzled, blue-skinned face of Jackie.

"What's up, gear-girl?" she asked.

Victoria, who would have taken those words as a dire insult from virtually anyone else, smiled. She had grown fond of this world's Jackie Frost, in part because of her unflinching honesty, and in part because she was so different from the cold, uncaring Frostbite. "May I have passage?"

Jackie stared for a moment. Then she laughed. "I'm sorry, it sounded like you were saying…"

"I am saying I would like to visit the North Pole, that I might fairly present my suit to Miss Yelena," said Victoria, her back ramrod straight with the effort of retaining her composure.

"Uh…no. You being here messes up Winter something awful, remember? You're all attuned to holidays that died centuries ago, and never existed in this world in the first place." Jackie paused. "You'd think those would be mutually exclusive things, wouldn't you?"

Victoria grimaced. "As you say. Well, then. Is Miss Yelena available?" she asked.

"Sure, Stripy the Rainbow Clown is kicking around underfoot," said Jackie easily. "Why are you asking? Does Vel want her for something?"

"No, I…" Victoria took a deep breath. "I do. May I speak with her, please?"

"Wait." Jackie looked at her, seeming to take in the carefully selected outfit, the hair, and the clockwork roses for the first time. "You said you wanted to 'present your suit.' Are you serious?"

"Exceedingly so."

"You realize she's never actually done this before, right?"

"And I have 'done this' precisely once, with a girl who never was. I believe that while I may have marginally more experience in this arena, it is, for the most part, irrelevant." Victoria took a deep breath. "Please, Jacqueline. If you have ever been a friend to me, be a friend to me now."

Jackie groaned. "Sweet Santa, you people are going to be the death of me…wait here. I'll go get her." She walked out of the frame, leaving Victoria to face an empty room painted in glacier blue and snowflake white. It was quite nice, if a bit chilly-looking.

This is a terrible idea, she thought. *There is no way she will accept my suit. I should run now, while there is still a slim chance of retaining my dignity.* Immediately on the heels of the first thought came a second: *I would be a fool to reject a second chance at the greatest happiness anyone has ever known. I will be open. I will be honest. And she will love me, or not, as Epona wills.*

"Um, Victoria?"

The sound of Yelena's voice snapped her back into the present. Victoria brought her head up, forcing herself to smile as she presented her bouquet of clockwork roses to the glass. "Hello, Miss Yelena. If you do not have other plans this evening, I wondered if you might do me the signature honor of joining me for lunch at one of Portland's fine dining establishments, followed by a rooftop stroll. I am assured that the views are incomparable, and the forecast indicates a seventeen percent chance that it will not, in fact, be raining."

Yelena blinked. She was wearing a Christmassy sweatshirt with a reindeer on the front, and her hair was braided back in a simple three-strand plait. The braid helped, oddly enough. Victoria's first Yelena had never worn her hair long enough to style.

"Are you asking me out on a date?"

No. "Yes, Miss Yelena, I do believe I am," said Victoria. "Contingent, of course, on your being willing to risk such a situation with me, knowing as you do my past with your parallel world counterpart."

Something hardened in Yelena's expression. "You mean the one who was actually happy? Sounds good to me. I'll be there in an hour." She turned and stalked out of the mirror's field of view.

Jackie appeared a moment later. "I don't know whether to applaud you or start writing your obituary," she said, without preamble. "Good luck either way. You're gonna need it." The mirror frosted over, and in a matter of seconds, Victoria was alone with her own reflection.

"Yes," she said, to no one in particular. "I suppose that I am."

One hour later precisely, Yelena—who had always been punctual, and would probably make it a point to be on time to her own execution—stepped out of the bathroom mirror. She was wearing clean jeans and a nice, if bulky, cable-knit sweater. The outfit was as much a matter of practicality as anything else: whatever she wore had to allow her to wear a full-body unitard underneath.

She was still wearing her Blacklight costume to fight crime, even though she didn't feel like a Blacklight. She didn't feel like a Sparkle Bright, either. At the moment, she wasn't sure *what* she felt, except possibly like she was going to be sick.

The mirror had turned back into a mirror behind her. She turned and looked at her reflection. "It's going to be fine," she informed herself. "She wouldn't have asked you out if she didn't want you to go out with her." And Velma was never going to love her that way. It was time she moved on, or at least started the process of trying.

The mirror, which was probably getting used to people using it to talk to themselves, didn't say anything.

Yelena opened the bathroom door, stepped out into the hall, and was promptly greeted by Victoria's bouquet of clockwork flowers.

"Hello Miss Yelena you look lovely today your hair has the scent of fresh snowflakes I made these for you they'll never die and if you wind them every time they close they'll bloom I can show you how later are you still willing to have lunch with me?" Victoria's words came out in an undifferentiated rush, rattled off one after the other.

Yelena blinked. Then, slowly, she smiled. "They're beautiful," she said, taking the flowers from Victoria. "Thank you. No one's ever built me flowers before." No one had ever really given her flowers before either. Oh, Aaron had tried, but they'd only been together because Marketing told them to be, and he knew she didn't really like him that way. They'd both done what they could to do the right thing while trapped in an impossible situation.

These were really her first flowers. And they really were beautiful.

Victoria's cheeks reddened. Then, pulling herself a bit taller, she said, "I thought, given the hour, and the time difference between here and the North Pole, that the lunch menu at the Dash-o'-Danger steakhouse might be sufficient. I have verified that they can meet your dietary needs."

"What about yours?" asked Yelena, only half-jokingly.

"I am happy in any dining establishment which will provide me with a slice of beef, a baked potato, and a pudding afterward," said Victoria.

Yelena hesitated, looking at her. She looked so earnest, and so hopeful, like this was a chance she'd never dared dream she'd have again. Yelena understood what that felt like. "Dash-o'-Danger sounds great," she said.

"Brilliant," said Victoria. "I'll get my coat."

The Dash-o'-Danger steakhouse had been constructed with the superhumans and superhuman groupies of the world in mind. Bored paparazzi and amateur photographers lounged outside the garish entryway, waiting for a potential paycheck to wander by. A few of them raised their cameras as Yelena and Victoria approached, recognizing the gadgeteer, if not the blonde woman who was with her. Yelena cringed, automatically slowing her pace.

"Are you well?" asked Victoria, with a concerned glance at her companion.

"I don't want my picture taken," said Yelena. "We can go somewhere else."

"No. No, I don't think we will. I'll handle this." Victoria sped up, marching forward until she made a prime target for the cameras. The swarm closed in around her, shutters clicking. "Hello, ladies and gentlemen. I must ask that you cease this at once, and destroy any pictures you may have already taken of myself and my companion."

"Or what?" asked a photographer. The shutters continued to click.

"Ah. I take it you do not acquiesce?"

There was no response but a flash going off.

"Very well." Victoria produced a small brass sphere from inside her jacket, pressed a button on the top, and dropped it. Thick smoke began pouring out, blanketing the area in seconds. Moving quickly, she walked back to where she had left Yelena, grabbed her by the elbow, and steered her past the coughing photographers into the steakhouse.

"Barbarians," she muttered, once they were safely inside. "They'll find this day's film and memory cards have been sadly corrupted. A true tragedy, and one hopes, also a lesson in respecting the boundaries of others."

Yelena blinked at her before she laughed, hiding it quickly behind her hand. Victoria smiled smugly.

"Ah, good. A sense of humor is key in maintaining good relations with the world around you. Well, that and a large ray gun. Shall we put ourselves in line for a table?"

"We shall," said Yelena grandly, and kept laughing all the way to the front desk.

* * *

It was early, and the Dash-o'-Danger was primarily famous as a dinner establishment. In no time at all, Yelena and Victoria were seated in a corner booth, and the waiter had gone to fetch their drinks (Diet Coke for Yelena, an assortment of hot teas for Victoria).

"So…" said Yelena awkwardly.

"Yes," said Victoria. "So."

"You're, uh. From Victorian England. How was that?"

"Oh, very much like your world's version of same. Somewhat more scientifically advanced, although more and more, I have come to suspect that my world simply gained superpowers earlier than yours, and forced them all into a form of scientific advancement." Victoria's smile was wry. "Many of my inventions cannot be operated by anyone but me, much less repaired should they happen to malfunction. My father was no doubt a superhuman of a type, and so am I. I shudder to think of the havoc my children would have wreaked, had I any interest in having them."

"Heh." Yelena grinned a little. "Your kids would totally take apart the microwave and use it to build a death ray."

"I take umbrage to that," said Victoria. "Microwaves are cheap, tawdry technology, used to ruin perfectly good food. My children would take apart meaningful things. Like cars."

"Belonging to other people, of course."

"Yes, of course." Victoria sobered a bit. "It was…there is this impression of the past as being a simpler time, like I must constantly be amazed by the wonders of the world. And I *am* constantly amazed by the wonders of the world. But it's not because my world was simple. It's because this world is magnificent. So was mine. So is every other world that is. They are all complex machines on a scale that I could never hope to construct, and I am in awe of their mechanic."

"Oh," said Yelena.

"And what of you? The shock of joining this world, where things are chaotic and undecided, must be quite great after spending so many years in the sheltered confines of The Super Patriots. How do you find it here?"

"It's amazing," said Yelena. "It's…I'm wearing a sweater, because I want to. I'm out to lunch with a pretty girl who gave me flowers, because I want to be. No one had to approve my outfit, or my date, or what I'm going to be doing afterward. I'm free. I can think for the first time in years."

"That must be lovely," said Victoria slowly. "I…Miss Yelena…"

"I know you dated another version of me in another reality," said Yelena. Victoria stopped talking. "Jackie and Vel told me, I think so I wouldn't think you were totally weird. I also know that the two of you were pretty serious."

"We shared a home and a bed for four years," said Victoria.

Yelena's cheeks flamed orange, her powers turning her blush into something exotic. "Okay, well, that was blunt. I'm assuming, since you're a super-genius and all, that you've already worked out that I'm not her, and I'm never going to be her, right?"

"I have."

"So why did you ask me to have lunch with you?"

"Because you are not her, and you will never be her, but I, like everyone else, have a 'type.' I like tall, occasionally tongue-tied blondes who shoot rainbows from their hands." Victoria shrugged. "It may seem terribly specific, but I note that it has worked quite well for me thus far. You are not my lost love. You will never be the woman who kissed me under the moons of Jupiter, or went with me to bargain for the life of Lady Luck in the Arcade of Destiny. But I believe that, given time, you and I could form bonds just as strong. I am lonely. I think that you are, too."

Yelena stared at her, tongue-tied. Victoria picked up her menu.

"I think I will try the sirloin," she said, thoughtfully.

Yelena didn't say anything at all.

Lunch was excellent–the Dash-o'-Danger generally was, as long as no one ordered the radioactive lasagna–and afterward, Yelena and Victoria went back to the house, where Velma was conveniently absent. They sat down on opposite ends of the couch, Victoria with her ankles demurely crossed, Yelena fighting the urge to fidget.

"So," she said.

"Yes, 'so,'" agreed Victoria. "Have you considered my proposal? Will you permit me to press my suit?"

"You mean, will I keep dating you?"

"Or start dating me, as might be a more accurate descriptor, but yes." Victoria looked at her hopefully. "I can be an excellent girlfriend. I have practice."

"I don't."

"That's all right. I'm sure you have a very flexible learning curve."

Yelena raised an eyebrow. "Is this based on knowing the other version of me?"

"No; it's based on the fact that you have been dwelling at the North Pole with Jacqueline Frost for more than a week, and no one has been brutally murdered. If you did not have a flexible learning curve, her body would have long since been discovered in one of the local skating pools."

Yelena blinked. Yelena snickered. And finally, Yelena laughed out loud.

Victoria tilted her head to the side, apparently trying to decide whether or not to be offended. Yelena kept laughing, and Victoria slowly smiled.

"I see I have amused you."

"Oh, yeah, because you have *no idea* how many times I've been tempted. Like, did you know she swears in front of Santa Claus? Like, *Santa Claus*, the guy who keeps the Naughty and Nice lists. And she leaves wet towels on the bathroom floor, which is completely unhygienic, and she keeps trying to trick me into admitting I'm secretly on the payroll of The Super Patriots, so that she can kick me out before I do any damage. Also, is there a reason she needs to remind us that she's blue all the time? I have eyes. I can see. I can be blue if I want to, but you don't see me prancing around claiming to be the new girl in Smurf Village."

"As you were not created by Gargamel, I doubt that would hold much water even if you were to try," said Victoria.

Yelena paused. "You know about Smurfs?"

"Without creepily reminding you that I shared a residence with a version of you for four years, I will note simply that the show about the little blue forest people existed in my last dimension as well. And my world's Yelena was *very* fond of it."

"Smurfs are comforting," said Yelena, wrapping a lock of hair around her finger. Then she paused. "What did you say the Yelena in your world went by?"

"Polychrome. The Rainbow's own daughter." Victoria shook her head. "I was never sure what led her to select that name…"

"Polychrome and the Patchwork Girl of Oz were friends," said Yelena. "I like it."

"I'm sorry?"

"I said, I like it. 'Sparkle Bright' is really a name for a five-year-old, don't you think?" Yelena stopped fiddling with her hair and smiled. "And I like you. We're both a little out of place, and trying to get over women who we can't be with. Who cares if yours looked a whole lot like me? That doesn't mean this isn't worth trying."

Victoria wanted to cheer. She wanted to punch the air and thank Epona for Her mercy. Instead, she nodded. "Very well, then. I will commence courting you properly, and we shall see where the future leads us."

"You know, in all my 'someday I'll get a girlfriend' fantasies, this was never how I imagined things going," said Yelena.

"It never is." Victoria's smile was radiant. "Isn't it wonderful?"

Yelena laughed again, and was opening her mouth to answer when the doorbell rang.

"It's probably a delivery for Velma," said Victoria, standing and smoothing her skirt with the heels of her hands. "She receives shipments of toys on a daily basis. Wait here." Turning, she walked toward the door.

Velveteen and Tag were cleaning up the last of a hive of giant wasps—probably the work of Insecticide, who thought his name meant "I am a cool supervillain who kills people with bugs," and clearly didn't own a dictionary—when her phone began blaring out a klaxon-like ringtone that she'd never heard before. They exchanged an alarmed look before she moved off to the side, letting Tag handle the rest of the wasps himself while she answered the phone.

"Hello?"

"THEY TOOK HER THEY TOOK HER THEY JUST CAME TO THE DOOR AND THEY TOOK HER YOU HAVE TO GET BACK HERE RIGHT AWAY THERE HAS TO BE A WAY THAT YOU CAN FIX THIS THEY TOOK HER YOU HAVE TO *DO SOMETHING!*" Victoria's words were an anguished howl, so loud and unpunctuated by the normal pauses of human speech that it was briefly hard for Velveteen to realize what she was saying.

Then the three words that had been repeated most often lodged themselves in the front of her brain, and all the air went out of the world.

"Victory Anna, calm down," she said, through numb lips. "Who took who? What's going on?"

"THEY TOOK HER YOU HAVE TO–"

"I can't understand you if you shout! Who took who?"

There was a long pause as the science heroine fought to catch her breath. Finally, in a hoarse tone, she said, "I was sitting in the living room with Ye—with Sparkle Bright when the doorbell rang. I assumed it was a package for you. I went to answer."

"And?"

"It wasn't a package. They said they were from The Super Patriots, Inc. legal department. They said that if she went with them willingly and of her own free will, they wouldn't press charges for her unauthorized vacation. I thought she would fight them, but..." Victoria's voice broke. "But then they said that if she resisted, they would be forced to take me into custody, as they had evidence of my being an unregistered superhuman, even though Governor Morgan got me my license. She went with them, Vel. She said 'don't hurt her, I'll come,' and she went with them. Why would she do that? She didn't have to do that!"

"We'll get her back," said Velveteen. "I'll be home as soon as I can." She lowered her phone, turning to stare dully back at Tag, who was subduing the last of the giant wasps.

He hit it on the head with a graffiti hammer before meeting Velveteen's eyes curiously. "Is everything okay?" he asked.

"No." She shook her head. "Everything isn't okay. Everything isn't okay at all." She was tired. Her head was pounding. And now The Super Patriots, Inc. had reclaimed her best friend.

This was officially war.

She was just no longer sure that she was going to survive it.

The men who had been sent to retrieve Sparkle Bright were not, technically, superhumans: to be superhuman, they would have needed to be human in the first place. They were extremely clever automatons, constructed by Mechamation and sent on the retrieval once it was confirmed that Velveteen was not on the premises. They couldn't be blinded. They couldn't be bribed. But they could clamp their tungsten fingers around Sparkle Bright's arms, holding her to the ground until she could be dragged to the waiting van.

"Get her inside," snapped the man from Marketing, opening the door as they approached. The automatons did as they were told. In short order, Sparkle Bright was strapped to a chair, and turned to face the inhabitants of the van.

Mechamation was there. That made sense; she would need to operate her robots. So was Firecracker from the Midwest Team, probably damning Sparkle Bright's recapture. The two men from

Marketing were unfamiliar, but that didn't really matter; they were all interchangeable anyway.

"You don't have any right to do this," she said, as the automatons closed the van doors behind her. The engine started. "Let me go right now and I won't press charges."

"Oh, no, you see, we do have the right to do this," said one of the men from Marketing. "You broke your contract, little hero, and you're going to pay for that."

"You want my money? Take it. I don't need it."

"Your money is ours; we only gave it to you to make it seem like we cared," said the second man. "We want something much more valuable. We want your loyalty. And we're going to have it."

Yelena paled, involuntary yellow and green sparks bursting in the air around her. She looked toward Mechamation. Mechamation looked away.

Eventually, she started shouting for help. But by then, it was long past the point when anyone could possibly have heard her.

VELVETEEN
vs.
Legal

CELIA MORGAN WAS ACCUSTOMED, AS Governor of Oregon, to dealing with people whose concept of "patience" had been left behind somewhere between their homes and her office door. What she wasn't as accustomed to was dealing with those people plus super powers. Even sharing her home with her sister–Jennifer, Jory, whatever you wanted to call her; the fact that she was alive was more than enough for Celia–hadn't prepared her for the strain of sharing her office with not one, not two, but *five* individuals who could easily kill her with their powers.

For the first time, she actually understood some of the motivation behind The Super Patriots, Inc.'s incessant attempts to control the superhumans of the world. These five…no one controlled them, or perhaps they controlled themselves. Celia honestly wasn't sure which possibility frightened her more.

Jennifer was at home, in costume, waiting for her baby sister's call. Celia hoped both that she would never need to make it, and that Jennifer would be able to reach her in time.

"You can't honestly mean that," said Velveteen. There were dark circles under her eyes. She didn't look like she'd slept since the men from The Super Patriots, Inc. had come and carted her wayward friend back to their offices. It had only been two days. The strain was still showing very clearly in the young anima's face. "They have no legal right–"

"They have *every* legal right," said Celia, trying to ignore the glare from the redheaded gadgeteer, and the way the blue girl was making it snow in the corner of the office where she stood, brooding. It shouldn't have been possible for someone who looked so much like she'd escaped from a Rankin-Bass holiday special to brood, but she was accomplishing it. The other animus—Tag, his name was Tag—just stood next Velveteen, arms crossed, looking at the governor.

And then there was the Princess. But the less Celia dwelt on her, the better.

"That's bullshit," said the blue girl.

Contract law was one of the few places where Celia felt absolutely confident, even in the face of a group of angry superhumans. "No, it's not. I've read the standard boilerplate for The Super Patriots, Inc., and based on that, it should be possible to terminate the relationship between a hero and the corporation. I've also read Velveteen's child contract." She nodded toward Velveteen, trying to remind them with that small gesture that they were in her office, in her state, and that she was one of the only allies they had in the battle that was so obviously to come. "Is there any chance that Miss, ah, Sparkle Bright would have requested a new contract following her eighteenth birthday?"

"None," said Velveteen. "They had her brain so fried by that point that she would probably have gone on working for them without a contract if they'd asked her to. They're *manipulating* their heroes."

"Ah, but the contract explicitly allows for that."

The redhead stiffened, eyes blazing and hands clenching white-knuckled on the arms of her chair. "I do beg your pardon?" she said, in a thick London accent.

Calmly, Celia, calmly; these people are your allies. Ah, but it was so easy to think that when they were somewhere else, wasn't it? Or when they came to her one at a time, these people who could control seasons and make things that had never lived come alive to do their bidding? Five of them was enough to be considered a team. That was one word for a group of superhumans. The other word was "danger."

Keeping her voice level, Celia said, "The contract Velveteen, Jory, and presumably Sparkle Bright all signed with The Super Patriots, Inc. allows the corporation to make 'minor and necessary adjustments' to their psyches, with or without their awareness, in order to keep them calm and productive. Mind-control is usually illegal without explicit consent, but The Super Patriots, Inc. was able to get an exception for reasons of national security." Calling it "an exception" was putting it mildly. The Super Patriots, Inc. had the legal right to completely mind-wipe their superhuman employees, and to rebuild their personalities from the ground up.

"We have to get her back," said Velveteen. "Governor Morgan, what legal grounds do we have here?"

"Quite honestly? None. Two of you are unlicensed outside of this state, one of you is entirely unlicensed—"

"I have diplomatic immunity," said the blue girl, and bared her teeth in what a charitable person might have deluded themselves into calling a smile. "Want to see how much damage it lets me do before Santa puts me on the Naughty List for life?"

The Princess didn't say anything. She just sat there silently in her heliotrope and silver ball gown, watching Celia with sad, judgmental eyes. There was a bunny in her lap, and a falcon sat on the back of her chair. Somehow, she was the worst one of them all.

"Victory Anna and Velveteen are technically confined to the state, but I do have the authority to send you both on out-of-state missions as needed. I can get you all to California, but honestly, you don't have a legal leg to stand on in where The Super Patriots, Inc. are concerned. She's still under contract with them."

"Still under contract…" Velveteen frowned. "Governor Morgan, the contracts we all signed were for children. They held until our eighteenth birthdays. By the time they expired, we were all well and truly mind-controlled. I was only able to resist because I was being regularly abducted by the seasonal countries."

"Guilty," said the blue girl. She didn't *sound* guilty.

"If I'd been doing what The Super Patriots, Inc. wanted me to, I would have been completely under their command. Even if they had the legal right to have me mind-controlled, would a contract signed under those circumstances be legally binding?"

Celia blinked. "No," she said slowly. "It wouldn't be."

"Well, then." The Princess's sweet, sugary tones were underwritten with a thin line of poison, like an apple dipped in arsenic. "It looks like we're going to California."

Most regulation aimed at superhumans can be easily read from two different directions. Looked at one way, it is overly restrictive, even cruel, in its efforts to limit and curtail the freedom of an entire class of people. Very few superhumans became that way voluntarily, and even fewer can be "cured" of their powers, but all are covered by a series of laws which, if enforced to their strictest limits, can strip away liberty, independent thought, and even life itself. No other group of American citizens can be presented with the death penalty for the simple crime of existing. The law is not on the side of the superhuman.

Looked at from the other and opposite direction, the laws which regulate superhuman activities within the United States are designed to protect the majority of American citizens from a clear and present danger, one which can arise without warning and which must, at times, be answered with an unfortunate degree of deadly force. There is no other way to stop the child whose body naturally emits fatal levels of radiation, or to control the housewife who suddenly begins transforming everyone who meets her eyes to stone. Perhaps the child could be confined in a lead-lined room, perhaps the housewife could be blinded—but is either of these alternatives any safer? Will either help the greater populace sleep at night?

Superhumans are terrifying. Whether they are your friends, your family, or your lovers, they are more than they were meant to be, and by their very presence, they make other humans feel that they are somehow less. It is only natural that, faced by such an inescapable demonstration of our place in the universe, the human race would strike back in the only way we knew. With rules, with laws, and with violence.

Most of the crueler regulations—the ones making it legal to use mind-control, for example, the ones making it legal to strip someone's powers with or without wrongdoing on their part—were originally proposed and championed by The Super Patriots, Inc.

Make of that what you will.

Velma "Velveteen" Martinez had crossed the border from California into Oregon while semi-conscious, propelled by a blast of charged photons generated by her former and future best friend, code name: Sparkle Bright. Her return, sitting in the first class cabin of the Virgin America Portland/San Diego flight, was thus a bit of a step up in the world.

There were eight seats in the first class cabin. Velveteen and Tag occupied two. Jackie and the Princess sat across from them, and Victory Anna was behind them. The other three seats were unoccupied. Governor Morgan was not a foolish woman. If sharing her office with the five superheroes made *her* uncomfortable, when superpowers ran in her family, what would it do to anyone who had to share a plane with them?

Traveling incognito wasn't an option. For Velveteen to legally leave Oregon, she had to be traveling on official superhuman business, which meant full costume. Jackie was actually incapable of concealing her true nature, and while Victory Anna and Tag could be inconspicuous if they really had to, the Princess was followed by flocks of birds everywhere she went, in addition to occasionally generating spontaneous glitter and musical numbers.

The flight attendant had passed out drinks and their complimentary cheese plates before disappearing into the back of the plane. Velveteen was pretty sure they were supposed to get better service than this, but she didn't feel like pushing the issue. Sharing a plane with five superhumans was stressful under the best of times. When one of them persisted in glowing bright blue, one was building clockwork bats, and one had somehow managed to produce a bunny and two robins after take-off, well…it was really no wonder the flight attendant wanted to be elsewhere.

Leaning her cheek against her fist, Velveteen yawned. Tag touched her shoulder. "Hey," he said. "Are you sure you're up for this? Maybe it would be better if we sent Jackie and the Princess in first. You know. The ones who never broke their contracts with The Super Patriots, Inc."

"I'm just tired," said Velveteen. "I've been tired before. Tired isn't going to keep me from saving my best friend."

"Vel, you're not just tired, okay? You're asleep *all the time*. I'm starting to worry about you."

"Don't." Velveteen removed his hand from her shoulder. "This isn't the time to worry about me. When Sparkle Bright's home, then we can think about what else is going on."

On the other side of the cabin, Jackie and the Princess exchanged a look.

"You have to deal with this," said the Princess softly, trusting the roar of the plane's engines to keep her from being overheard.

"I'm not sure…"

"Yes, you are. If you weren't sure, you wouldn't be looking at her like that. You have to deal with this."

"Why me and not you?"

"Because, honey, this isn't my kind of fairy tale." The Princess sighed deeply, looking down at the bunny sleeping curled in her lap. "My fairy tales have happy endings."

Jackie winced and turned to look across the aisle. Velveteen, for all her protests, was asleep with her head against Tag's shoulder. He was petting her hair, a concerned expression on his face. When he saw Jackie looking, he raised his eyebrows in question. She shook her head, gesturing for him to focus on Vel.

She'd have to talk to him soon. But not now. Not until they had Yelena safely home.

The plane landed on time; they had no luggage. Even Victory Anna was traveling light, carrying only her carpet bag, which she had assured them all would contain everything she needed for the fight to come.

"I still don't see why we couldn't travel via magic mirror," said Jackie, as they descended the escalator toward the level where they could catch a cab.

"Because that could be taken as a sign of aggression and used to justify a massive superhero fight in the air over San Diego," said Velveteen, stepping off the escalator. "Not exactly good for our 'we're just here to talk' image."

"Nothing ever is with you," said a vaguely familiar voice. The five of them turned to see a black-haired young woman in a skin-tight red and orange outfit standing near the luggage carts. She was holding a sign that read "VELVETEEN & PARTY."

"Match Girl?" said Tag, sounding bewildered.

Her lip curled. "It's Firecracker now, okay? I see you finally managed to sink to the level where you belonged."

"At least I got out."

"You were kicked out. Don't try to make it sound like some big heroic choice. Oh, wait. I forgot." Firecracker redirected her sneer at Velveteen. "You found a girlfriend as incompetent as you are. I guess that must make it easier to convince yourself."

"Wait," said Velveteen. "Are you here to give us a ride or something?"

"Oh, wow, she can read."

"That's it," said Jackie. Snow began to fall around her as she balled her hands into fists. "This is me, kicking the little match girl's ass."

"Now that's a fairy tale I can get behind," said the Princess.

"Hang on." Velveteen raised a hand. Jackie and the Princess quieted, although they didn't stop glaring, and the snow around Jackie continued to fall. "We're here to talk to a lawyer specializing in superhuman law, and have a meeting with The Super Patriots, Inc.'s Human Resources department. Why would we be stupid enough to get into a car with you before we even got started?"

"God, bunny-girl, I don't know, okay?" said Firecracker. "I don't want to be here, and I sure as shit don't want to be driving your second-string ass around. I just know that the boss told me that if I wanted to keep my spot on the team, I would get in the car, come down to the airport, and offer you a ride to HQ, where we could all discuss this like grown adults before we went and got the lawyers involved."

"I don't know—" began Velveteen.

"I say we do it," said Victory Anna. The other four turned to look at her. She squared her shoulders and said, "It is best to know one's enemies. By witnessing the tactics they attempt to use against us before facing us fairly over a barrister's desk, we will be able to deduce how much faith they have in the eventual outcome, and adjust our own tactics accordingly."

"You're the new mad science girl, aren't you?" asked Firecracker. "No one knows where you came from. I don't know what these losers have been telling you, but you should take this opportunity to get a private meeting with HR. Get yourself affiliated with a *real* super team."

"I came by Epona's grace from the glorious Empire of Her Majesty the Queen," said Victory Anna, with withering politeness. "We will accompany you. But do not think for one moment that you will sway us from our righteous task."

Firecracker blinked at her for a moment before turning to the others and asking, "Does she always talk like this?"

"Sometimes she sleeps," said Velveteen.

Tag snorted a laugh, covering it with his hand.

Velveteen hesitated. The others would go along with whatever she decided to do. Talking to the lawyer first might be the right thing to do, but if there was any chance at all that they could resolve this without turning it into a three-ring circus…

"All right," she said. "Take us to your leader."

Firecracker smirked.

The mini-van sent by The Super Patriots, Inc. was perfectly balanced between extravagance and practicality. The seats were plush black leather, and a mini-fridge was set into either side, offering an assortment of snacks, energy drinks, and alcoholic beverages. At the same time, the windows were bullet-proof glass, and the ultra-absorbent shocks meant that they could drive over any terrain in the world without feeling a thing. It was perfect for the transport of socialites and the direly wounded, and made no distinctions between them.

"They sure don't believe in being subtle," drawled the Princess, and swatted at the bluebirds that were trying to restyle her hair. Her ball gown had changed at some point since they entered the van, turning pink and gold, with an ocean of ruffles. "Come on now, shoo. I need to look professional, and birdies don't help."

"We don't agree to anything," said Velveteen, cracking the tab on an energy drink. She didn't want to take anything The Super Patriots, Inc. was offering her, but she was so *tired*. She was afraid that if she tried to stand on her principles, she'd wind up falling on her face. "No matter what they say, no matter what they offer, we don't agree."

"Not even if they offer to return her to us?" asked Victory Anna. The aching need in her voice made names unnecessary.

Velveteen nodded grimly. "There will be strings, and those strings will strangle us," she said. "We find out what they're willing to give. We take notes. We learn exactly what they think they're going to get out of this exchange. And then we go to our lawyer, we explain the situation, and we get Sparkle Bright back without cutting our own throats in the process."

"What if we can't?" asked Tag. All four women turned to look at him. "I'm just saying what we're all wondering. She has a contract. Unless we're willing to go to court to prove that The Super Patriots, Inc. has been using mind-control to get their adult heroes to sign–"

"–which they have, and which we are," said Velveteen.

"They won't let that happen," said Jackie. "I know a little something about labor law, okay? All those elves. They unionized a century ago." She rolled her eyes as the others stared at her. "Do you people think I spend *all* my time doing my nails and plotting to ruin your lives? Don't answer that. Anyway, the crux of the matter is this: The Super Patriots, Inc. has a vested interest in keeping those contracts legal. If we go to court, they could all be invalidated, and the laws about using mind-control on superhumans who haven't committed any known acts of villainy could change. They're not going to let things go that far." She turned toward the pane of mirrored glass that separated them from the driver's cabin. "Isn't that right, Match Girl?"

"I told you not to call me that," said Firecracker mildly, as the glass rolled down to reveal the side of her face. "How'd you know I was listening in?"

"Santa Claus is a master of espionage," said Jackie. "He sees you while you're sleeping, remember? Now answer the question."

"I can't. I'm not the one you're going to be discussing your case with." Firecracker turned smoothly onto The Super Patriots, Inc.'s private drive. Screaming fans lined the street on either side, held back by velvet ropes and robot guards. Most of them were teenagers, Velveteen noted queasily. Some were wearing homemade costumes. Many were holding signs that said things like "WELCOME HOME SPARKLE BRITE" and "AD + ME-ME-ME!!! 4-EVA."

"They can't even spell her name right, but I bet they're real good at screaming it," said Firecracker, a note of bitterness creeping into her voice. The gates swung open at their approach, and they drove onward, entering the perfectly manicured grounds. The looming shape of Headquarters was like a corporate brand against the skyline, designed to be iconic from every angle. Velveteen's queasiness turned into flat-out nausea.

"If it's not you, who is it?" asked Jackie.

Firecracker laughed. "I told you. You're meeting with the boss."

They had reached the head of the driveway. Firecracker brought the van to a stop, and the rear doors swung open automatically, revealing the two superhumans who were standing there, patiently waiting for their guests. He wore orange and blue, heroic as always, the golden boy that every mother adored and every father dreamed of raising. She wore white with rainbow accents, virginal and wild at the same time. His smile looked natural. Hers looked like it barely concealed her rage.

"We're so glad you could come," said Action Dude, putting an arm around Sparkle Bright's waist. "Aren't we, dear?"

Sparkle Bright didn't say a word. She just glared.

Sparkle Bright and Action Dude didn't stay to escort them into the building. Tag privately thought that was for the best, since Velveteen looked like she was torn between despondence and fury, while Victory Anna looked like she was going to start killing people. Jackie and the Princess just looked grim. That was probably a good thing. He and Vel both had history with The Super Patriots, Inc., and Victory Anna was dealing with a broken heart. If they didn't have at least a few neutral parties, this was going to get ugly, fast.

Firecracker led them up the stairs to the main doors. Tag allowed himself to rubberneck shamelessly, even going so far as to turn to Velveteen and comment, "I never got to see the West Coast headquarters. The one time my team came out here, we were doing one of those stupid holiday specials. We never even got the public tour."

"Maybe if you hadn't decided to be an idiot, you'd be living here now," said Firecracker smugly. "State-of-the-art everything."

"I'll take my apartment, thanks," said Tag. "At least it doesn't come with a leash and collar."

Firecracker glared, sparks crackling in the air around her. Then she turned her back on him with a huff and opened the doors, leading them into the grand foyer. It was a huge room, large enough to be considered part of a museum. Ten-foot statues of the current members of The Super Patriots, Inc. ringed the room, caught in perfect, heroic poses and preserved eternally in marble. All of them had their unseeing eyes turned toward the triptych of the Big Three that stood in the very center of the foyer, Majesty, Supermodel, and Jolly Roger frozen forever as they were before the final fall.

"Statues with an animus on the property," said Jackie, studying her nails in a careful display of boredom. "Gosh, this is going to be a long and entertaining fight. Oh, wait. That was sarcasm."

"I know what sarcasm is," snapped Firecracker.

"And yet you don't seem to know that your costume is unflattering for your hair color, skin tone, and body type," said Jackie. "So you'll forgive me if I assume you've missed certain other nuances that would be obvious to the rest of us."

"Stop it, Jackie, okay?" Velveteen sounded more than just weary: she sounded beat-down, like there was nothing left for her to give. "We don't need the full tour, Firecracker. I used to live here. Jackie's been here as my guest. Can we just skip to the part where we talk to Human Resources and you let us leave?"

"You *will* be letting us leave," added the Princess, in a sugary drawl. "Believe me, sweetie, you don't want to deal with the lawyers I have on *my* side. We're all properly licensed and allowed to be here, and we've made no aggressive moves of any sort. Sarcasm isn't illegal yet, even when it's coming from the future incarnation of the living Winter. So don't go getting any ideas about trying to keep us here in that pretty little head of yours. You'll just hurt yourself."

"Oh, trust me," said Firecracker. "I don't want to keep you. You guys are poorly designed, even more poorly branded, your team balance makes no sense, you're like, a taco stand—"

"What the fuck's a taco stand?" asked Jackie.

"It's the opposite of a sausage fest, hello. How are you supposed to appeal to the eighteen-and-under demographic if you focus on a single gender? Did you flunk your Superhero Marketing class or something?"

"No," said Velveteen and Tag, in unison.

"I never took one," said Jackie.

"What the bloody fuck are you on about?" asked Victory Anna.

That seemed to conclude the conversation. The Princess just shook her head, looking faintly disappointed. Firecracker rolled her eyes and led them out of the foyer and down a corridor to a much less showy hallway. This was the more corporate part of the building, where primary colors and photo opportunities gave way to spreadsheets and quotas. She walked on until they came to a plain wooden door.

"Here you go," she said. "If I were you, I would have taken the tour."

"If you were me, you would have run for your life years ago," said Velveteen, putting her hand on the doorknob. "Thank you for the escort."

Firecracker hesitated. Then, almost grudgingly, she said, "Good luck," before turning and fleeing back the way they had come.

"I can't believe I used to have a thing for her," said Tag, shaking his head.

"Your taste has improved since then," said Velveteen, and opened the door.

It was no real surprise to any of them when the conference room contained the current lineup of The Super Patriots, West Coast Division, minus Firecracker, who was only a provisional member after all. Sparkle Bright and Action Dude sat at the head of the table, flanked by virtually identical representatives from Legal and Marketing. Mechamation and Imagineer sat on one side of the table; Jack O'Lope and Uncertainty sat on the other.

"Welcome," said one of the interchangeable representatives. He stood, gesturing toward the open chairs. "I'm Jonathan Smith. I'm here to represent The Super Patriots, Inc.'s Legal Department in this discussion. My colleague, Sam Jones, is here to represent the Human Resources Department. We realize this is somewhat irregular, but hope that you can understand that going to court would not be in any of our best interests. We had the sincere hope that by meeting and discussing our differences today, we can bring this unfortunate misunderstanding to a satisfactory conclusion for everyone involved."

"This is stupid," muttered Sparkle Bright, directing a venomous glare across the table at Velveteen. "There's no misunderstanding. I was stressed out from planning the wedding, I had a minor nervous breakdown, okay? I'm not proud of it, but does the bunny-bitch really have to turn into a federal case? I ran away from home. I thought you of all people would understand what that feels like."

"I'm sorry, are you talking to me?" asked Velveteen. "My name isn't 'Bunny Bitch.' Although it's got a nice ring to it."

"While you are doubtless overdue for a rebranding, I believe we should stay on message here," said Sam Jones from Marketing. "Sparkle Bright was understandably overwhelmed by her duties here, as a member of one of the world's premiere super teams, and suffered a temporary lapse of reason. This lapse, while tragic, was completely understandable. Now that she's home with the people who love her, she'll be able to receive the help she needs."

"Uh-huh," drawled the Princess. "All that sounds real good, and you're right, it would be a shame to drag someone who'd suffered that kind of breakdown through a court battle, but I've got just one little question, if you'd be so kind?"

"Yes?" said Mr. Jones.

"If she was just having a little…let's call it a crisis of faith, shall we? It seems like the least accusatory way to keep talking about things. So if she was just having a little crisis of faith, how is it she was able to fool Santa Claus? The big man doesn't look kindly on liars, especially not ones who exploit the affections of the people who care about them." The Princess cocked her head, studying Mr. Jones. "Seems to me he'd have noticed that something was up."

"While the opinions of Mr. Claus may be of great value to small children around the world, they do not have any legal weight in the state of California," said Mr. Smith. "Furthermore, as the only currently active superhuman originating from the North Pole is a member of your little, ah, 'team,' I must object to the idea that he is somehow an unimpeachable authority. It's clear that allowing Sparkle Bright to be exploited would be in the best interests of one Miss Jacqueline Frost, making it even less likely that Mr. Claus would be considered an expert witness in this case."

"We weren't exploiting her," said Velveteen.

"You were parading me around as part of your freak show," snapped Sparkle Bright, lunging halfway out of her chair, face contorted with rage. "You've always been jealous of me, and when you saw the opportunity to bring me down to your level, you just couldn't resist, could you? You little bitch. I should have killed you in that locker room! Do you hear me? I should have killed you!"

"Mind-control is a delicate thing, isn't it?" said Jackie. She sounded almost bored. Only the frost that was slowly spreading over her chair and the floor around her feet betrayed how angry she really was. "There's a reason Santa doesn't *make* all the children in the world nice. You can change a lot of things. But deep down, the essence of what makes you who you are will always hold on, and will always fight. So you get, for example, irrational amounts of anger from someone who escaped their golden cage, only to find themselves hauled back in against their will. I don't like Stripy the Rainbow Clown much. I think she's a pampered show poodle who pretends to be a pit bull. Even poodles can bite. I wouldn't want to be sitting where you are when she finally snaps her lead."

"You little—"

Action Dude's hands clamped down on Sparkle Bright's shoulders before she could launch herself out of her chair at Jackie. Grayscale sparks popped and danced in the air around her. "This isn't getting us anywhere," he said, with a glance at Mr. Smith from Legal. "Can we please get on with this?"

"I think you may have the right idea." Mr. Smith bent to produce a briefcase from under the table. He placed it in front of himself, opened it, and withdrew a stack of manila folders. "The Super Patriots, Inc. is grateful to you for your service in taking care of one of our wayward heroines in her hour of need. We understand your desire for reparations, and so we are prepared to offer you this quite generous settlement, in exchange for walking away, and never contacting Sparkle Bright again." He began passing the folders down the table.

Victory Anna received her folder, opened it, and calmly studied the paper inside. Then, for the first time since entering the conference room, she spoke. "It seems a fair blood price," she said. "Were we giving her over to be sacrificed at the Church of Demeter for the spring mysteries, I would be quite pleased with this as a payment. Given the circumstances, however, I believe you have woefully undervalued one of the brightest stars in the firmament, and should be ashamed of yourselves. You should be ashamed of your parents as well. They clearly did not provide you with the proper guidance."

"I'm with the time-slipped Victorian girl, which is one of those sentences I never thought I was going to have a reason to say," said Jackie. "You want to buy our girl? You're going to need a lot more zeroes and also a huge side order of fuck you, you assholes, we are not for sale."

"Bless your little hearts, you really tried this time, didn't you?" said the Princess sweetly.

"No," said Tag.

All eyes turned toward Velveteen. She stood, tossing the folder back down the table toward the man from Legal. "You people think you can get away with anything, don't you? Steal our childhoods. Steal our thoughts. Steal our futures. Fuck. That. I'm not taking your deal, and I'm not letting you turn us against each other again. I promised Sparkle Bright that I would be her friend forever. I meant every word."

"That's adorable, but friendship carries no legal weight in the state of California." Mr. Smith stood, all genial pleasantries forgotten as he walked around the table toward Velveteen. "You think we brought you here because we're afraid of going to court. You're wrong. We brought you here because we'd rather avoid a scandal, and because we'd rather avoid tightening the legislation again. Do you honestly think any judge is going to find in favor of allowing a group of weapons of mass destruction to run around without oversight? It will be a bloodbath if you face us in court. Five poorly-trained, impulse-driven superhumans against the weight of this corporation? We will crush you. We will destroy everything you have ever loved. And when the dust clears, we will still have what is ours."

Velveteen's eyes widened. "You made them attend this meeting because you wanted them to know that they couldn't run away from you." She looked toward the gathered members of The Super Patriots. "Don't you understand? You're not free. You're slaves."

"Everyone's a slave to something," said Imagineer. "At least we're slaves with medical benefits."

Mr. Smith smirked. "You can't win. All you can do is choose not to play against us."

"This isn't over," said Velveteen.

"I think you'll find that it is." Mr. Smith stepped closer. "Do not test me, little girl. I've read all your files. I know what you're capable of doing. And I am not afraid of you."

"Maybe you should be." Velveteen raised her chin, meeting his eyes. He wasn't afraid of her? Oh, he was going to change that tune. The foyer was full of statues. She reached out, trying to call them to her…

…and found nothing. It was like she had hit a wall. Exhaustion washed over her, and she flinched, her eyes flickering away from Mr. Smith's for just an instant.

He smirked, clearly reading her motion as a break in her resolve. "As I said. We are willing to go to court with you. But you won't like what happens if we do."

"Someone won't like what's coming," said Velveteen, gathering the last of her strength. "Come on, everyone. We're leaving." She turned and stalked for the door. Her team—her friends, her family—rose and followed her. No one stopped them as they left.

Once the door was closed, Mr. Smith turned to Uncertainty, and asked, "Well?"

"There is a ninety-four percent chance that any attempts they make at interfering with the current course of action selected by The Super Patriots, Inc. will fail," said Uncertainty.

Mr. Smith smiled. "Excellent."

"That means there is a six percent chance that they will succeed," continued Uncertainty. He looked up at Mr. Smith, and added calmly, "Sometimes six percent is enough."

Firecracker was waiting in the foyer. "Well?" she asked, as Velveteen and company stepped back into view. "Where to?"

"The airport," said Velveteen. "We're going home."

"I'm glad you saw reason," said Firecracker, smiling.

Tag moved to walk beside Vel as they followed the fire-manipulator back to the van. "Are you all right?" he asked.

"No," she said, in a very small voice. "I think there's something wrong with me. Take me home?"

"Sure, Vel." He put an arm around her waist, surreptitiously keeping her on her feet. "Let's go home. We'll figure this out."

"We have to get her back." Velveteen put her head against his shoulder, allowing him to all but carry her. "If we can't do it in the court, we'll have to find another way, but we have to get her back."

"We will," said Tag. "It's all going to be okay. You'll see."

Behind them, Jackie and the Princess exchanged a look, but said nothing.

They were going home.

VELVETEEN
Presents
Jackie Frost vs. Four Conversations and a Funeral

THE SURFACE OF THE MIRROR was cold enough that Jackie actually felt it, a short, sharp burst of almost painful chill before she emerged into the warm, peppermint-scented snow of the North Pole. It started snowing almost immediately, fat, angry flakes that materialized from nowhere to follow her as she trudged through the drifts toward the village. Shouts of puzzled dismay came from the direction of the skating pond and the Christmas Tree Forest as the elves, who were surprisingly wimpy about a little cold weather, reacted to the snow. Santa's snow was many things, but it was never *cold*.

Jackie, for all that she tried to be good, tried to stay on the Nice List, was not one of Santa's creatures. She was the daughter of Jack Frost and the Snow Queen, and she belonged to the cold. In moments like this one, when everything inside her felt frozen, there was just too much cold to be contained. She walked quickly, trying to make it home before she caused a full-on blizzard.

She almost made it.

"Mom?" Jackie stepped cautiously onto the icy floor of the library, relieved to find that it was willing to support her weight. Her mother was a creature of ice and snow; she could walk on the thinnest ribbon of frost and never worry about falling. Her father was a heavier creature, flesh and blood and bone, and Jackie took after him. But Jack Frost could fly. Jackie just had to hope that gravity would be kind.

Sometimes she wondered what would happen when she finally stepped up and took over for one of her parents. Would her bones turn hollow, filling with ice and mist? Or would her feet leave the ground, gravity falling away from her forever? Privately, Jackie was in no hurry to find out which way her powers would twist. She liked herself exactly as she was. She'd learned how important that was when she took her tour through the Hall of Mirrors, officially becoming her mother's heir.

"Mom?" she called again. "I really need to talk to you. I need to go to the Hall. For me. Please, can you come out where I can see you?"

The room was arctic, cold enough to match the landscape outside the windows. As Jackie watched, frost crept across the glass, lacing and interlacing into a delicate feather pattern. The chill in the air gathered until it somehow turned solid, becoming a white-haired, white-skinned woman with a white dress patterned in the same feathery swoops that the frost had drawn across the window.

The Snow Queen frowned at the sight of her daughter's anxious face. "Jacqueline?" she said, and her voice was the sound of the wind blowing over ageless glaciers. "What's wrong?"

Jackie took a deep breath. "I need to use the Hall of Mirrors," she said. "I need to talk to some alternate versions of a friend of mine, before I can talk to the version of the friend of mine who exists in this mirror."

The Snow Queen's frown deepened. "We've discussed your tendency to use your powers for frivolous reasons..."

"This isn't frivolous, Mom. I think Vel is going to die if I don't do something, but I don't think she'll listen to me if I don't have more information. I need to use the Hall of Mirrors to get that information. *Please.* Help me save my friend."

"Ah." The Snow Queen stood in perfect stillness for a moment, considering her daughter—her strange, hot-blooded daughter, whom she loved so much, and understood so little. There was nothing she could have done differently with Jackie. She knew that. But oh, sometimes she regretted the distance between them. "You realize that you risk your life along with hers if you do this."

Jackie squared her shoulders. "I can't let her die. *Winter* can't let her die."

"But she is your friend before she is a potential servant of the season."

"Yes," Jackie admitted. "I know it wasn't supposed to be like that. But yes."

"Then yes, you may use the Hall of Mirrors." The Snow Queen

swept her hand through the air and held it out toward Jackie. A glittering key made of ice rested on her palm. "Be careful, my daughter."

"I will, Mom." Jackie took the key. The cold of it bit her skin, but her body was not warm enough to start it melting. "Thank you."

"Do not thank me," said the Snow Queen. "I have done you no favors." Then she was gone, dissolving back into stillness and the cold, and Jackie was alone.

It was almost a relief when the floor collapsed underneath her a few seconds later. At least that was normal.

Jackie Frost materialized on the steps of the Hall of Mirrors in a swirl of snowflakes. They stuck to her blue and silver spangled costume as she walked toward the door, becoming indistinguishable from the crystals and sequins that were already there. There was no keyhole. Instead, she pressed the key her mother had given her against the icy surface of the door itself, and it swung smoothly inward, allowing her to make her way into the endless maze of mirrors.

It was harder to navigate this way; harder to look for a version of someone else, rather than a version of herself. Possibilities looked out at her from every mirror she passed, Jackie Frosts and Snow Queens and Frostbites, and even the rare, pink-skinned Jacqueline Claus, Santa's adopted daughter. Jackie knew them all already; she had walked in their skins, if only for a few hours, on her first trips through the looking glass. Some of them she feared becoming. Others she mourned never allowing herself to become. And still she walked, until she found just the right mirror, just the right reflection.

The Jackie Frost who looked back at her had longer hair, a softer expression, and carried an ice wand in one hand. Snow Princess, delicate protectress of the North Pole, who had never spent a second on the Naughty List. *Not* one of Jackie's favorite potential realities, if she was being completely honest–and the Hall of Mirrors was a place for honesty. She touched the mirror's frame, only wincing a little as the cold of it bit into her fingertips.

"Show me Roadkill," she said. The image blurred, Snow Princess disappearing, only to be replaced by a Mad Max remix of the Velveteen she knew, all leather and rabbit fur and safety pins holding the whole ensemble together. Roadkill was crouching in an alley, stroking something that the mirror's frame didn't quite allow Jackie to see.

"Here goes nothing," muttered Jackie, and stepped into the mirror.

* * *

It had been another shitty night in Seattle. Two of the crows had flown away and not come back, which either meant falcons—possible—or asshole "heroes" trying to clean up the city again. Roadkill's money was on the heroes. Fuckers never knew when to leave well enough alone. So here she was, in another stupid alley, trying to wake up a tired old dog that had finally staggered off into the dark to die.

"Get up," she said, running her hand along the dog's side. He was a big boy, all corded muscle and strong bone. Age was the only thing that could have taken him down, and age didn't matter anymore, not once she got involved. The dog's tail twitched once, thumping against the pavement. Roadkill straightened, the undead crow on her shoulder flapping its wings once as it fought to keep its balance.

"Come," she said, and the dog, awake and undead at last, lumbered to its feet and moved to stand beside her. She allowed herself a smile. One dog was worth two crows. With West Nile tearing up the coast, there would always be more crows. She turned, ready to head back to her lair and get ready for another evening of petty crime and annoying The Super Patriots, Inc.–

–and froze. There was a woman standing behind her, blue-skinned and glowing faintly in the dark alleyway. She had white hair and was wearing a costume that looked like something out of an adult production of *Disney On Ice*.

"Don't freak out, okay?" asked the blue woman.

Roadkill frowned slowly. "Snow Princess?"

"Not quite. I mean, yes, in this reality, and also no, because I'm not from this reality. I'm here because I need to talk to you. I need your help."

Roadkill scoffed. "Okay, now I know you're from the wrong reality. I'm not the kind of girl who goes around helping people. I'm sort of on the opposite side of that equation, if you get my drift. Fuck off."

"No." The blue woman who wasn't the Snow Princess shook her head. "I'm sorry, but no. Of all the versions of Roadkill, you're the one most likely to talk to me. That means you're *going* to talk to me."

"Are you deaf? I said fuck off." Roadkill put her hand on the head of her new dog, which was starting to grow, a deep, unpleasant sound. "There's nothing you could possibly threaten me with that I'm going to give a shit about."

"In my world, Yelena is alive."

The words were simple. Their effect on Roadkill was not. She froze, all her bravado dropping away, replaced by a longing as cruel as it was sincere. "What?" she whispered.

"In my world, Yelena is alive," repeated the blue woman. "She didn't kill herself. Marketing convinced her she could still be their little darling, if she'd just lie about who she was and what she wanted out of life. They drove my world's version of you away, because they knew the two of you were too much for them to handle when you were together."

Roadkill's lips thinned into a hard line. "You're lying." The memory of Yelena's body was always there, fresh and cruel and horrible, if not as horrible as the memory that followed immediately afterward. Yelena, getting up again. Yelena, opening her eyes, finding herself trapped in her own dead flesh, and starting to scream.

"Why would I lie? Your powers changed when you found your best friend lying in a pool of her own blood. In my world, that never happened. That version of you is still Velveteen. She's still a hero. And she needs your help."

"I told you, I don't help," said Roadkill, numbly.

The blue woman shrugged. "How do you know if you won't even let me tell you what I need?"

Yelena, staggering toward her, blood still dripping from her fingertips... "What the fuck do you want?" asked Roadkill, banishing the memory to the depths of her mind, where it belonged. Where it would be waiting for her when she least expected it.

"My Velveteen has a boyfriend, an animus like her. Tag. He was..." The blue woman hesitated, looking like she wanted almost anything more than she wanted to finish her sentence. Finally, she said, "Killed. He was killed in a fight recently, and Vel sort of...lost it."

"She brought him back, didn't she?" Roadkill shook her head, feeling suddenly tired, suddenly sorry for a version of herself that she would never know or have the chance to become. "She couldn't leave well enough alone, and she brought him back."

"She did. But there's a problem."

"Zombie boyfriend isn't enough of a problem? You people don't fuck around when you complicate things."

"She doesn't know she's animating him."

Roadkill's eyes widened. "What? How is that even possible?"

"She's more powerful than she thinks, and she's in denial about what happened that day. She's been animating him constantly for more than two months."

"What? No." Roadkill shook her head. "She has to stop. Animating small things, like crows or cats, that's easy, I can have an army of those going twenty-four hours a day, seven days a week. I never sleep without a guard. But humans? That's *hard.* The longest I've ever managed a human was three days." Yelena had begged her to stop, toward the end; begged her to let the animation go, and allow the other heroine to die.

Sometimes Roadkill wondered whether Yelena had known that she'd be blamed for murdering her best friend, kicked out of her home and branded a supervillain immediately. Sometimes she wondered if knowing would have changed her decision at all.

She didn't think so.

"What's going to happen if she doesn't stop?"

Roadkill looked at the blue woman without flinching. "She's going to die," she said. "And there's not a damn thing anyone else can do about it. It's her, or it's no one."

"That's what I was afraid you'd say." The blue woman who wasn't the Snow Princess sighed, starting to turn away. "Thank you for your time."

"Wait!" It was probably a toss-up between them as to who was more surprised by Roadkill's exclamation. The blue woman turned back to her, curiosity writ large across her face. Roadkill swallowed hard, and asked, "Except for the whole undead boyfriend thing…is your version of me happy? Are things better for her?"

The blue woman hesitated. Then she nodded. "She has a home," she said. "She has friends, good ones, who care a lot about her. She has Yelena to fight by her side. Yeah. She's happy."

"Then you do whatever it takes to save her stupid life," said Roadkill. "Because my life? Is pretty fucked up. So somewhere, somehow, one of me has to be happy."

The blue woman nodded. "That's what I'm planning to do," she said, and stepped into the air, leaving a gentle snow falling in her wake.

Roadkill dropped to her knees, buried her face in her hands, and wept.

Jacqueline Claus sat at her dining room table, nursing a mug of cocoa and wishing that she dared to spike it with something stronger than marshmallows. Anything else would have interfered with the morphine, and so she restricted herself to sugar, but oh, she *yearned.* The sound of snow falling behind her was a welcome distraction.

"You can come out now," she said, and turned to see a blue-skinned, white-haired woman with her face stepping out of the shadows. Jacqueline blinked, raising an eyebrow. "What parallel are you from?"

"Not this one," replied the woman. "I need to talk to you."

"First tell me your code name." Jacqueline wasn't sure she had it in her to fight a version of herself who'd grown up to be Frostbite; not today, not when the cold was wrapped so tightly through her bones. She could take a Snow Princess, but this girl didn't look like a Snow Princess. That left…

"Jackie Frost. I figured there was no point in a code name when everyone would know who I was either way."

"It's a pleasure to meet you, Jackie Frost. I'm Jacqueline Claus." The understanding of their shared and divergent histories stretched out between them like tinsel draped around a tree. One of them, raised by parents who barely understood the needs of the flesh, but whose love, such as it was, had informed her substance; the other, given to Santa to be raised as his daughter, who loved her just as dearly as her birth parents would have, in a world where they were just a little braver. "What can I do for you?"

Jackie took a deep breath. "My world's version of Velma is still Velveteen. But I'm afraid that's starting to change. Her boyfriend died. She's animating him right now, and she doesn't realize that she's doing it. You know…"

"I know Marionette very, very well, and you want to know if there's any way the change can be a good thing," said Jacqueline. She stood stiffly, the muscles in her back complaining with every move she made. "You've been through the Hall of Mirrors."

"Yes."

"That's how you know that Marionette is my partner."

"Yes," said Jackie again, looking faintly abashed. "I don't understand how it works between you, but I know that you're always together…"

"Did you ever wonder how Velveteen's powers worked? How she was able to give life where there wasn't any?" Jacqueline shook her head. "She gave them *her* life. She shared her own energy with the things she animated."

"But Marionette isn't alive." And that was the crux of the matter: in the worlds where she was Marionette, Velma Martinez was already dead.

"I know. So does she, fortunately; it makes things easier on us. As a dead woman, she has no life to share. As an animus, she understands what the energy of life looks like, feels like, and how to call it to herself. She stays standing because she's animating her own body, and she's doing it with the life force of the creatures around her." Jacqueline offered Jackie a wan smile. "Most versions of Marionette are evil. They have to be, to keep doing what they have to do to survive."

"Yours isn't," said Jackie.

"No, I'm not," said a voice behind her, and she turned to see Velma—almost Velma, but not quite—standing behind her, wearing a black and white version of her original Velveteen costume. She was very pale. "I'm not evil because I don't have to steal the energy I need. Jacqueline gives it to me freely. It's killing her, even though she tries to pretend it's not."

"So why don't you stop?" The words were out before Jackie could call them back. She winced.

Marionette didn't seem to mind. She walked past Jackie to Jacqueline, and said, "I became Marionette when The Super Patriots attacked Portland. They killed the Princess. They killed Action Dude. They killed me. Only I got back up and kept fighting. Jacqueline has agreed to keep feeding me energy long enough for us to destroy The Super Patriots for what they did to me. And then I can rest." The exhaustion in her eyes was unbearable.

"The way you live now…"

"I'm not alive. Don't be fooled by appearances." Marionette shook her head. "I heard you say that your world's version of me was animating her dead boyfriend, and didn't realize it. You have to make her stop. If she kills herself, the power will snap back on her, and you'll have another Marionette on your hands. I wouldn't wish this existence on my worst enemies. I *can't* wish it on a girl I never got to be. Make her stop."

"I'll try." Jackie looked to Jacqueline. "What about you?"

"I'm fine." Jacqueline smiled bravely. "I'm Santa's daughter. I have a lot in me to give."

They had nothing left to say to each other, after that. Jackie disappeared in a swirl of snowflakes. Jacqueline turned to Marionette, opening her arms.

"Come on, dear. You need to eat before you go hunting."

Marionette fell on her like a starving wolf, and the morphine helped…for a while.

* * *

Jackie Frost materialized on the steps of the Hall of Mirrors in a swirl of snowflakes, fell to her hands and knees, and was messily sick. When she was sure her stomach had nothing left to lose she grabbed a handful of untainted snow, using it to rinse her mouth as she staggered back to her feet. She felt a little bad about leaving the mess for the elves to clean up, but that was what elves were *for*, and she had places to be. Even if they were places she'd be happier avoiding.

Two hours, a change of clothes, a magic mirror transport, and a taxi later, she was standing outside Tad's apartment door, trying to find the strength to knock. She had almost decided to go away and come back later when the issue was resolved for her: the door opened, and a confused-looking Tad blinked at her from inside the living room.

"Jackie?" His eyes widened. "Oh, crap, Jackie, you can't be here. I still have a secret identity to worry about." He grabbed her arm, looking quickly up and down the hall to see if anyone had noticed her. Then he hauled her inside.

Normally, Jackie would have slapped any man who dared to grab her like that. Under the circumstances, she allowed it to happen. "I need to talk to you," she said, as soon as the door was closed behind her.

"Phones work."

"This isn't a phone conversation." She took a deep breath, studying Tad's face. Vel was her friend, sure, but she was also a project; woo her to the Winter, one step, one crusade, one girl's-night-out at a time. Tad was just her friend. They'd known each other for years, and when she introduced him to Velma, she'd been expecting both of them to have a little fun, maybe fuck a little bit of their tension away. She hadn't been expecting it to get him killed.

Tad blinked, annoyance fading into concern. "Jackie? Is everything okay?"

She laughed unsteadily. "No, everything really isn't. Tad, do you remember the fight against the robots?"

"The ones that dentist built? Yeah." He rubbed the back of his neck with one hand. "That fight scared the life out of me."

Jackie winced. "Bad choice of words. Tad, look. Maybe you better sit down."

Tad paled. Tad sat. Jackie sat beside him on the couch and began to talk.

Somewhere in the middle of her explanation, he took her hands.

Sometime after that, she began to cry. Through it all, Tad looked stunned and maybe, just a little bit, relieved. It was an answer, after all; it explained everything that had happened since he saw that metal foot come down, since the world went away, only to come back in full color when he heard Vel calling his name. Yes, it all made perfect sense.

That didn't make it any easier to hear. Before she was done, he was crying too, and they clung to each other, and they wept.

Victoria answered the door. She was Victoria because she was out of uniform, although the only real difference between her street clothes and her superhero attire was in the number and size of the guns that she was carrying. "She's asleep," she said, when she saw Jackie and Tad standing on the porch. "Go away."

"Wasn't the Victorian Era supposed to be all about the manners and stuff?" asked Jackie, pushing her way past Torrey and into the living room. Tad followed.

"The world has moved on," said Torrey crossly, closing the door behind them. "She needs her rest."

"I know." Jackie took a deep breath. It seemed like she was doing that a lot lately. "Look. You want her to get some rest because you need her to recover from whatever's been draining her energy if we're going to get Yelena back, right?"

Torrey froze. "You called her by name," she said. Her gaze swung around to Tad. "Why are you here with her, and out of uniform? Aren't you still maintaining an alter ego?"

"You always said you were smart," said Tad, with a wan smile.

"Oh, sweet Epona." Torrey made a complicated gesture that might, in a world where a horse-goddess was the superior deity, have been the equivalent of a Christian girl crossing herself. "I'll get her for you." Then she fled the room, vanishing down the hall.

"Here we go," said Jackie. She looked to Tad. "I'm so sorry."

"Me, too."

Victoria returned a few minutes later, a groggy Velma behind her. Vel was wearing her bathrobe, and looked like she'd just been running a marathon, not taking a nap. She rubbed her eyes as she frowned at the pair.

"What's wrong?" she asked. "Why are you here in the middle of the day?"

"We have to talk to you," said Jackie gravely.

Velma looked from her to Tad, panic beginning to build in her expression. "What's wrong?" she repeated. "Did someone die? Oh, God—is Yelena okay?"

This time, it was Tad who said, "Maybe you'd better sit down," and took her hands, and led her to the couch.

"Velma, Tad didn't survive the fight against the robots," said Jackie. She stayed standing. "He died. You brought him back."

"What? No. I'd know."

"You do know. You just...aren't admitting it to yourself, because you don't want to lose him. But that's why you're so tired all the time, honey. Because you're licking your candy cane at both ends, and it's wearing down way too fast. If you don't let him go, it's going to kill you."

Velma shook her head. "No. No. You're wrong. You're—"

"Vel, we both know there's something wrong with me." Tad didn't let go of her hands. "I'm not one of those guys who starts pledging eternal love after the second date, but that doesn't mean I'm selfish enough to kill you for a few more days of life. You have to stop animating me. You have to let me go."

"No!"

"I've seen what happens if you don't," said Jackie. "It kills you, and then you bring yourself back as a sort of...energy vampire. You steal the life force you don't have from the people around you. I spoke to the only heroic version of Marionette in the multiverse. She begged me to stop you before it was too late. She's a version of you who's already paid this price, Vel, and it's too high. It's too high for everyone."

"Let me go," said Tad. "Please."

"But I love you," whispered Vel. "I can't do this alone."

"If you think that the loss of a lover renders you alone, you are a sadder, less observant person than I had ever dreamt," said Torrey. "You are not alone. You will be lonely, yes, but you will never be alone."

"I can't." Velma shook her head, tightening her grip on Tad's fingers. "I've lost Yelena. I can't lose anyone else. I just can't. Don't ask me to do this."

"The risks—"

"They're mine! I'm the one taking them, not you, so don't ask me to let you go because you think that's how you protect me! That's not how you protect me! You protect me by staying with me. You protect me by being here."

Jackie bit her lip before saying, reluctantly, "I may have another option." She didn't want to say this, sweet Claus, she didn't want to say this, but if Vel wasn't willing to listen to reason… "Can I use your mirror?"

Entering the Crystal Glitter Unicorn Cloud Castle was like walking into an explosion of fairy tale clichés, each one more sparkly and encrusted with gemstones than the last. Singing flowers dropped down from the ceiling to serenade their little procession, which was only slightly less bizarre than the fact that the footman was a kangaroo in a pink and purple tabard. He even had a mushroom cap with a pink ostrich feather in it.

Tad, who had never been to visit the Princess at home before, said in a horrified tone, "I don't know whether I should laugh or buy her a thousand shots of tequila as a form of apology for the collective subconscious."

"I go with a combination of the two," said Jackie. She turned to look at Velma, moving a bit more slowly than usual, due to the elaborate ball gown that had replaced her clothes when she passed through the mirror. At least it was blue. Velma's gown was burgundy with hints of pink, while Victoria was dressed in rust-red with copper accents. Of the three of them, Victoria looked the most comfortable. "You okay, honey?"

"Let's get this over with," said Vel. She sounded almost like she was drugged. "I just…"

"I know," said Tad, squeezing her hand. His clothes had been transformed into a theme park fantasy of Prince Charming's daily wear…but they were entirely in black. Maybe that was fitting, given the circumstances.

They kept moving.

The kangaroo led them through the twisting, largely pink palace until they reached a pair of uncharacteristically un-blinged oak doors. Then he turned and hopped away, apparently expecting them to know what to do from here. Jackie looked at the others, shrugged, and touched the nearest door with one faintly glowing hand, sending frost spiraling out across the wood. The doors swung open, revealing a gray stone cathedral with stained glass windows letting in the only light. There was a jarring lack of pink. Even the Princess, who was standing at the head of the room next to a long glass box, was wearing a dark gray gown, not a jewel or neon accent in sight.

"Y'all can come on in now," she said. "I'm ready for you."

They walked across the room to the Princess in a ragged formation, Velma still clinging to Tad's hand. He was crying. None of them commented on it. It seemed inappropriate to even admit that they could see his tears.

The Princess stepped off the dais and walked calmly over to the pair. She reached for their joined hands, and somehow, through the clever movement of her fingers, separated them, even though they would have sworn that wasn't possible. Taking both of Velma's hands in her own, she looked the other heroine in the eyes, and asked, "Can you let go?"

"I don't want to," whispered Vel.

"That's not the question."

Velma sniffled and looked at Tad, who smiled wanly. She looked back to the Princess and nodded. She didn't say it aloud. She didn't have the words.

"Good." The Princess released her, turning to take Tad's hands in the same fashion. "Now you, my boy…I'm so sorry this happened. We all know there are dangers to this job, and that doesn't make it any easier."

"Thank you," said Tad.

"I have to ask you: are you sure? This doesn't let you move on. Whatever Heaven you believe in, you're not going to get there."

Tad nodded firmly. "I'm sure. I may have known the job was dangerous when I took it, but that doesn't mean I'm ready to go."

"Good. Come with me." The Princess released one of his hands, keeping hold of the other as she turned and led him toward the dais. Tad glanced back at Velma, who was sobbing into Jackie's shoulder, and allowed himself to be led.

As they moved closer to the glass box, it became more obvious that it was, in fact, a glass coffin. A bowl of apples rested on a pedestal next to it, alongside a spindle. "Pick your poison, sugar," said the Princess. "I mean that literally. Either one will do you in, and then it's just a matter of waiting."

"Can I have a second?" asked Tad.

"Sure, honey. Take all the time you need. Just, once you choose, you gotta be ready to lay down, all right? The coffin has to close. That's what protects you."

Tad nodded.

The Princess stepped down from the dais, motioning for Jackie and Victoria to go with her. Together, they left the room, leaving Tad and Velma alone.

"Hey." Tad hopped down from the dais, feeling a little guilty about the energy he was using as he walked to his girlfriend, taking hold of her wrists. He tried to pull her hands down from her face. "Vel, sweetie, look at me."

She dropped her hands and raised her face, sniffling. Her eyes were red, and her nose was slightly swollen. He smiled.

"You are not one of nature's more photogenic weepers," he said. "Marketing must have hated it when you got upset."

Vel laughed a little, despite herself. "I think they died a little bit inside every time I skinned my knee and cried where the cameras could catch it."

"Good." Tad switched his grip so that they were holding hands again. "I love you, Velma. And even if you didn't know you were doing it, I want to say…thank you. For keeping me alive. For caring enough not to let me go. But now you have to care enough to stop. Everyone's counting on you. Yelena needs you. And I need to know that I'm not killing you. So can you do it? Can you let go?"

"I think so," she whispered. "We were supposed to have so much time. What happened to all our time?"

"We spent some of it. Now we get to put the rest of it in the bank. Come on." Tad pulled her with him as he walked back to the dais. The glass coffin was waiting, all silent invitation and cold inevitability.

Velma couldn't look at it. "The Princess says that we can wake you up with true love's kiss, and you'll be alive again. Is there anything you need to tell me?"

"Honey, if anyone's going to wake me up, it's going to be you." Tad dropped her hands, put his arms around her waist, and kissed her. After a moment's stunned hesitation, Velma looped her arms around his shoulders and kissed him back. They held each other for as long as they could, trading frantic kisses and bitter tears, until finally, Tad pulled away.

"I love you," Velma said.

"I know," he said, and smiled, holding up the apple he had taken from the bowl. "I'll see you soon."

The sound of his teeth tearing through the fruit was like the sound of a robot's foot crashing down on a city street. He chewed, swallowed, and fell. Velma darted in, barely catching him before his head could hit the floor. Carefully, she maneuvered him into the coffin and closed the lid–

–and fainted, as the band of energy that had been stretched between them for months finally snapped, and she was whole again. It was like a heavy rain falling on a dry lake: even though there was room for all the water, it was too much to bear.

There was no one there to catch her.

Velma awoke in the middle of a giant daisy that had been drafted into service as a bed. She was still wearing the ball gown. She sat up, sneezed, and accepted the tissue that was offered to her. "Thank you," she said, blowing her nose. Then she paused, blinked, and turned to see the Princess sitting next to the flower-bed.

"Morning, sunshine," she said. "You've been asleep for about twelve hours. How are you feeling?"

"…a little ashamed of how good I feel," said Velma. "It's like I was sick for a long time, and didn't know it."

"That's not too bad a comparison. Come on." The Princess stood, offering Velma her hands. "Up you get. You need to eat, and then we need to figure out what happens next."

"What do you mean, what happens next? I kiss Tad. He wakes up. We crush The Super Patriots."

"Oh, honey." The Princess looked at her sadly. "You only get one try. If you kiss him and he doesn't wake up, you can't try again."

Velma frowned. "So?"

"So unless you settle things with Aaron, I'm not sure you can call what you feel for the boy true love." The Princess shook her head. "You have to make things right before you can make them better."

For a long time, Velma just stared at her. The Princess sighed, and folded her into an embrace, and neither of them said anything at all.

Tired all the way down to her frozen bones, Jackie Frost stumbled through the mirror and into the warm snow of the North Pole. She staggered past the pond and the forest, and no snow fell; she would have needed strength to make it snow. As she approached the door to Santa's Workshop, it opened, and the big man himself stepped out, his red coat like a flame against the never-ending winter wonderland.

"You did well, my dear," he said, and wrapped her in a hug that smelled like cocoa and candy canes, and held her as she cried.

VELVETEEN vs. Jolly Roger

C ELIA MORGAN, GOVERNOR OF OREGON, shook her head. "No," she said.

"What?" Velveteen stared at her. In all the possible scenarios she'd considered for this day, the governor simply refusing her resignation hadn't even cracked the top twenty. "What do you mean, no? I'm quitting. You can't tell me not to quit."

"Perhaps not, but I can refuse to accept your resignation, which has essentially the same result." Governor Morgan pushed the paper back toward Velveteen. "You're still the official superheroine of Portland, with all the powers and responsibilities that the position conveys."

"But–" protested Velveteen.

Governor Morgan continued speaking as if she hadn't been interrupted. "At the same time, the state of Oregon recognizes that this is a difficult time for you. Because another superheroine is willing to take on your duties on a temporary basis, I have approved a six-week bereavement leave. I realize this is irregular, since the two of you were not registered as married, but I believe that teammates should be afforded the same rights under the law as domestic partners. Go. Grieve. Get your head together. Jory will keep the state safe while you're away."

Velveteen blinked, too stunned to speak. After a moment of silence, Governor Morgan took pity on her.

"We both know that whatever cosmic strings you pulled to get my sister returned to me, you pulled them for a reason," said Celia. "At the time, I suspected it was because you were getting ready to make a frontal assault on The Super Patriots, and didn't want any repercussions to find Oregon undefended. I should have been angry at you, playing on my emotions like that, but I wasn't angry then, and I'm not angry now. You gave me the most valuable thing in the world. Now it's my turn to give you the only thing I have that could mean half as much."

"What's that?" Velveteen asked.

"Time." Governor Celia Morgan, who had lost her only sister to The Super Patriots, and regained her from a bunny-eared, second-string heroine, leaned back in her chair and smiled. "Get those bastards, Velveteen. Make them pay for everything they've ever done, to anyone."

Velveteen nodded. Then, without another word, she stood and left the office. Governor Morgan watched her go, unable to shake the feeling that she'd never see the superheroine again.

"I did all I could," she whispered, and wished she could believe herself.

Velveteen stepped out of the office to find three women waiting for her in the reception area. Only three: the fourth, the receptionist, had fled at some point, doubtless fearing that a massive superhero battle was about to take place. She wasn't too far wrong.

"I know you weren't *really* thinking of leaving without us," said Jackie, folding her arms. She was wearing what passed as a uniform for her, a silver and blue ice skater's delight with so many sequins and semi-precious stones stitched into the fabric that it probably qualified as armor. "That would be silly, and if there's one thing a woman who brings toys to life and uses them to fight crime would never be, it's silly."

"She was doubtless just informing the Governor that there would be rather fewer superhumans in town for the next few days," said Victory Anna, whose attire was much more suited to an H.G. Wells fan convention. She even had a backpack-powered ray gun. All the rage with the modern gaslight costume set.

"She was leaving," said the Princess. It was a blunt statement, made all the blunter because it was coming from a pretty blonde Southern girl who looked like she was going to break into song at any moment. "She doesn't want any of the rest of us getting hurt, ain't that right, bunny-girl?"

"Yes," said Velveteen firmly. "This isn't your fight."

"Tag was my friend before you knew him," said Jackie.

"They have my girlfriend," said Victory Anna.

"I'm not even going to dignify that statement," said the Princess. "Bless your heart, I know it's in the right place, but if you want to leave without us, you're going to need to fight us first, and you're going to need to fight us like you really mean it. Can you do that, sweetie? Are you prepared for the consequences? Because I honestly don't think you are. I think you need your friends with you. And I'd like to think you're smart enough to know that."

Velveteen looked from face to face. Then, finally, she sighed. "All right," she said. "You can come with me. I guess having a flying carpet will come in handy, anyway."

"See? You're getting smarter already." The Princess linked her arm with Velveteen's, and the four heroines walked out in a line. They looked mismatched and shabby, nothing that could possibly challenge an empire. They didn't look back.

Three hours later, Victory Anna was sitting primly in the middle of the Princess's flying carpet, watching as Velveteen was noisily sick over the side. "If you can, try and hit a seagull," she suggested. "They're essentially rats with wings, so it isn't impolite, and at least if you can aim your vomit, we can pretend that it's an asset."

"Someone kill her," moaned Velveteen, before going into another series of dry-heaves.

"She doesn't fly well, does she?" Jackie was avoiding the whole "flying carpet" issue by skating alongside, using moisture pulled down from low-hanging clouds to form her ice bridges. The seawater was too salty to really work, unless she wanted to risk the ice dissolving under her skates and sending her plunging into the Pacific.

"Her powers don't require her to." The Princess was standing like the figurehead at the front of a ship, her toes actually skirting out into the open air. Her hair and dress both whipped out behind her in a way that was just so, so perfect that it would have broken the hearts of a thousand animators. This was her element. This was where she belonged.

"Neither do mine, and I appear to be doing quite well, thank you very much," said Victory Anna, as she powered up her ray gun. A seagull flew by. She blasted it out of the air and smiled. "I find this invigorating."

"You were a supervillain when we met," moaned Velveteen, before she went back to vomiting over the side.

"Victory Anna, stop shooting at the seagulls, they've never done you any harm," said the Princess, eyes still fixed on the horizon. "We're flying by a chart here, and I'd rather not lose my focus because I'm too busy yelling at y'all to behave like human beings."

"My human being status is provisional and has not been independently verified via scientific review," said Jackie.

The Princess shot her a glare, but didn't budge from her position at the head of the carpet. "Second star to the right," she said. "Straight on until morning. Hold your places, girls, it's going to be a long night."

Velveteen groaned.

The charts provided by Dame Fortuna had been long on symbolism, low on actual directions. According to the Princess, this was par for the course when trying to track down a magical hero who had chosen to go to ground. "You try drawing a map to the Crystal Glitter Unicorn Cloud Castle," she'd said. "It can't be done. It's all 'wish on a star' and 'believe in your heart.' Well, this is about as specific. I can get us there. No wishes required." That simple statement had somehow resulted in them flying for hours over the Pacific Ocean, startling yachts, ocean liners, and the occasional jumbo jet as they maintained their steady bearing.

Velveteen (who had long since run out of any cookies to toss, and was now reduced to tossing the memory of cookies that had been eaten years before) was on the verge of suggesting they turn around when one of the Princess's songbirds came flying out of a cloud bank, wings beating frantically as it tried to stay aloft. It looked exhausted. Velveteen understood the feeling.

"There you are." The Princess held up one delicate hand. The songbird collapsed gratefully into it, beginning to chirp and warble. "Really?" More chirping. "Are you sure?" A long, drawn-out note, that ended in the avian equivalent of coughing. "Oh, you poor dear. Of course." The Princess tucked the bedraggled little pile of feathers into the bodice of her gown before turning to the others, a smile on her face.

"We've got a sighting, ladies. Check your masks and ready your powers, because the *Phantom Doll* is moored just ahead."

"You mean we actually found him?" Velveteen stood up, forgetting to be airsick. "We actually found Jolly Roger?"

"We found Jolly Roger's ship," said the Princess. "Whether that comes with the man himself is yet to be seen—but yes, we actually found him."

"Let's see if he makes us walk the plank," said Jackie, with far more good cheer than the statement really deserved. She did a spin on her ice bridge, then skated down on the wide swoop that had suddenly appeared, causing her to resemble nothing so much as a glittery pinball rocketing toward certain doom.

"That girl's gonna die ugly one day," said the Princess fondly. She made a complicated gesture with her hand and, before Velveteen could take a breath, the flying carpet dropped straight down. Velveteen clung to the fringe, screaming. Victory Anna clung to the fabric, looking faintly put-out. And the Princess stayed exactly where she was, looking as serene as if she were not riding a piece of home decor down into the mists above the sea.

Jolly Roger's ship, the *Phantom Doll*, was almost as famous as the eponymous pirate, once upon a time. Despite Jolly Roger having left the team before The Super Patriots, Inc. could become the power that they would develop into, no fewer than five *Phantom Doll* play sets had been developed, and all of them had retained their value well on the secondary market. Consequentially, everyone knew what the *Phantom Doll* looked like.

But no plastic play set could encompass the reality of a great, barnacle-encrusted ship, its sails limp in the absence of a breeze, or its mahogany mermaid figurehead. It was the figurehead who greeted them as they approached, the Princess now steering her carpet low and tight above the surface of the water, Jackie skating carefully on an ice bridge that was mostly foam.

"Who goes there?" asked the figurehead. Her voice was much sweeter than anyone would have expected from a piece of wood.

"Um. Hello." Velveteen stood, feeling considerably better now that she didn't have as far to fall. "My name is Velveteen, and—"

"That name is more honest than it should be, but it's not enough. Not here." The mermaid turned her head, regarding them with blank wooden eyes. "What name were you born with, girl?"

"Velma Martinez," said Velveteen, who couldn't quite see the point in lying to a statue. It could be hers if she wanted it, if she was willing to fight for it, and because it had eyes, the whole *Phantom Doll* could be hers as well. There was something comforting in that knowledge. "Most people just call me Vel."

"A good compromise. Who are your friends?"

"Victoria Cogsworth, at your service," said Victory Anna.

"Jacqueline Snow-Frost," said Jackie.

"My name is Carrabelle Miller," said the Princess. "If you want to know what my parents called me, then you're looking for Scott Miller. But that's never been my name."

The mermaid nodded, seeming to accept this without question. "Why are you here?"

"We need to talk to Jolly Roger," said Velveteen. "I'm getting ready to go up against The Super Patriots—I mean, *we're* getting ready to go up against The Super Patriots—and I want to know if he can help us."

"Jolly Roger is retired," said the mermaid. "You have come for nothing."

"I don't think you understand," said Velveteen. "I was a trainee, and they nearly broke me. They did break my best friend, only she put herself back together and managed to run away. Now they have her, and I need to get her back. He has to help us."

"Jolly Roger is retired," repeated the mermaid. Her pretty wooden lips parted, revealing teeth that would have been better suited to an anglerfish. "Leave."

"No," said Velveteen flatly.

"Uh…" said Jackie.

Victory Anna's only response was a feral smile, and the sound of her ray gun powering up.

Velveteen held up a hand, indicating that the others should be still. Then, narrowing her eyes, she reached out with her mind and seized the *Phantom Doll*.

It wasn't like animating a doll or a statue, something that had no will of its own; the ship was awake, aware, and if it had been a true intelligence, she wouldn't have been able to take it at all. But the *Phantom Doll* was just an extension of Jolly Roger's power. The mermaid was just wood, animated by a magical hero who wanted to be left alone. Velveteen wanted the ship more in that moment than he did, and so she made it hers.

"Welcome aboard," said the mermaid, sounding dazed.

The Princess gave Velveteen a concerned look as the carpet rose up to the level of the rail, sailed gently over it, and touched down on the deck. Victory Anna bounded past her to the wood, seemingly unaware of the significance of the moment. As she passed, she said blithely, "Changing your name was a good idea, really. 'Scott' is a terrible name for a little girl."

Jackie skated to the deck, blinking after Victory Anna. "Uh, Princess, I don't think—"

"Leave it." The Princess smiled. "She's right. Scott was a terrible name for my parents to slap on their only daughter. Not their fault they were confused." Then she stepped off the carpet, which promptly lost the last of the tension that had been holding it rigid. "Vel, honey, you coming?"

"I am." Velveteen stepped off the carpet, eyes still narrowed in the way that meant she was working hard to use her powers. "He should realize I've taken his ship by now. He'll be here in five, four—"

The door to the captain's cabin banged open and a man in full pirate regalia burst onto the deck, a sword in either hand. "Stand, ye lily-livered villains!" he bellowed.

"You're a little off today," said Jackie, and then Jolly Roger charged, and the fight was on.

At the height of his power and popularity, Jolly Roger was potentially one of the greatest magical heroes the world would ever see. He could control the weather surrounding his ship, command the ocean, and with his trustworthy crew keeping the *Phantom Doll* shipshape, it seemed like nothing would ever defeat him. But that was before he left the crew stranded in Tijuana and parked himself in the middle of nowhere, using his powers only to keep himself fed, stave off scurvy, and cloak his location in a shroud of unyielding fog. He was out of practice. He was out of shape. And he was up against four superheroines in their prime, who felt that they had nothing left to lose.

He could have taken any one of them if they'd been fighting alone. He could potentially have taken any two of them, as long as those two weren't Velveteen and the Princess, since having his ship refuse to obey his commands while the rats from the hold swarmed him in a living wave was disconcerting, to say the least. But four of them? It was no contest. It was just a short, more than slightly painful trouncing.

When the fight was over, and Jolly Roger was tied to a chair with rope from his own deck, the four heroines assembled nervously in front of him. Velveteen and the Princess, at least, appreciated the enormity of what they'd just done. Victory Anna had grown up in a world where Jolly Roger didn't help to define the childhoods of a generation, and Jackie was, well, Jackie. Velveteen sometimes wondered if there was *anything* that could actually impress her.

"Ye've shivered me timbers but good," snarled Jolly Roger. Then he coughed, and continued, in a perfectly normal Middle American accent, "So I suppose you'll be plundering my ship and heading on your way, then. Could you give her back to me before you go? I know that her personality is technically just a side effect of my presence, but we've been together for a long, long time, and I don't know what I'd do without her."

"Your powers would generate a new ship in short order," said the Princess.

"Ah, but that ship wouldn't be my *Phantom Doll*, now, would she? I have a lot of good memories on this deck, although it's hard to bring them to mind when I'm being tied up by a bunch of children."

"A lady never reveals her age, but I assure you, we're not children," said Victory Anna. She powered down her ray gun, pointing the muzzle at the sky, where nervous seagulls rerouted their flight patterns around her. "Why are we bothering with this prat, Velveteen? It's clear that he can't help us."

"No, it's clear that he doesn't want to. Yet. That's going to change." Velveteen stepped forward. The others stopped talking, moving back slightly to make it clear that she was in charge; that she was the one he needed to worry about dealing with. "Hello, Jolly Roger."

"Hello, bunny-eared girl who's taken over my ship." He squinted. "You're an animus, aren't you? A damned powerful one, if my measure's not off. And the way you fight—you were trained by The Super Patriots. Have you come to collect the bounty on my head?"

"I've come because Dame Fortuna told me how to find you, and we need your help." Velveteen crossed her arms. "The Super Patriots are corrupt, and I think Marketing is evil, and they have my best friend, and we want her back. Not just her. We want all the heroes they have in their control to be able to choose their own lives, without being bound by illegal contracts."

Jolly Roger blinked, several times, before turning to the Princess. "Is she for real?"

"She is," said the Princess, sounding smug. "She would have been happy stayin' out of the way for her entire life, but The Super Patriots forgot the first rule of rabbits."

"Carrots?"

"Don't follow them into their dens. They're meaner than they look."

"Princess, untie him," said Velveteen. Eyes still on Jolly Roger, she continued, "You were the first one to get out; you were the first broken heart they couldn't bury. They've killed so many people since then, and no one's willing to stand against them. Please. Help us."

"You can't just punch a corporation into submission, girl," said Jolly Roger. Rats ran up his legs, heading for the ropes; he didn't flinch. "They have lawyers. Rules. Legal protections."

"Oh, but see, they were in charge of setting a lot of those legal protections, and they wanted to be able to stage messy coups for team leadership every once in a while. For the sales, you know." Jackie smiled, white teeth bright against blue skin. "So we sort of *can* punch a corporation into submission, as long as it's this one."

"Girl…"

"You quit." Jolly Roger's attention snapped back to Velveteen. She was staring at him pleadingly, hands now clasped in front of her chest. "After the fight, after Majesty and Supermodel and the trainees died, you walked away. You knew that it was turning bad."

"Oh, girl." Jolly Roger stood, rat-chewed ropes falling away. "It had been bad for a long time when we reached that point. The fight was…it was the last that was good in a lot of us, trying to do what we all devoted our lives to. Trying to make us into heroes, one last time. Supermodel was already too far gone. She'd been fighting against her own inner darkness longer than any of the rest of us had known that the danger was there. Maybe if she'd told us sooner…"

"Santa tried," said Jackie. "He put her on the Naughty List, year after year, hoping you'd get the clue."

"Ah, lass, we didn't put that much stock in Santa. Trick and Treat were only trainees then, and we still half-believed they were lying about their origins. You come from a holiday. You've always believed they were real places. For us, that's a pretty new sea to sail." He shook his head. "We didn't know. We couldn't save her."

Velveteen bit her lip. "Please–"

"We couldn't save *any* of them!" Jolly Roger wheeled on her, and for a moment–just a moment, but that was long enough–she could see the hero he'd been when he was in his prime. The man who'd helped to found The Super Patriots. The one who'd known how to bring the heroes of the world together. "Do you understand me? We had *eleven* trainees. Four of them were assessed as level five heroes. Only five of them survived, and if what news has reached me here is true, not all of them truly recovered."

Deadbolt had a drinking problem. Second Chance took risks that no one should take. Trick and Treat were, well, Trick and Treat. Only Imagineer seemed even halfway normal, and she'd always been a little odd. "What, you think those were the last casualties?" Velveteen demanded. "The Super Patriots *bought me* from my parents. Me, and all my friends, and they broke us just like your trainees got broken, only they didn't have the decency to do it in a battle, where other people would be willing to acknowledge we'd been hurt. They did it with focus groups, and with surveys and with rule after rule after rule, until most of us were too shattered to get away." Velveteen dropped her hands, looking at him. "You were the first one broken. Help me. Help us. This has to stop."

"I'm just an old, retired pirate, girl. There's nothing I can do." Jolly Roger tipped his hat to the group. "Thank you kindly for your visit, and for the rumble. You can show yourselves out." Then he turned, and walked back into his cabin, and shut the door.

"We can do this without him," said Jackie. Her words sounded thin even to her own ears. "He said it himself. He's just an old dude who got out of the game. The four of us mopped the floor with him. He wouldn't be any use."

"We only beat him because he's removed himself from the public eye," said the Princess. "Magical heroes, we need to be seen once in a while if we want to keep our powers charged. If he sailed back to shore, he'd be unstoppable."

"He's an icon," said Velveteen, reaching up to straighten her bunny-eared headband. "A figurehead, like that mermaid of his. We don't need him because he's awesome. We need him because he's Jolly Roger, the one who got away, and having him with us will mean that we're serious." It would bring all the undecided and half-decided heroes out of the shadows, the minor powers, the malcontents, the ones who would make up their army.

"Well, he shan't come, so you had best come up with another plan," said Victory Anna. "I could cobble something together in a surface-to-air missile array…"

"No." Velveteen dropped her hand. "He's coming. You three wait here." This said, she stormed toward the captain's cabin, her furious pose only slightly spoiled by the twitching of her costume's plush rabbit tail. She didn't knock. She just went inside. The door slammed behind her.

Jackie and the Princess exchanged a look.

"This is either going to end really well, or really poorly," said Jackie.

"How about we all just stand on the carpet for right now?" suggested the Princess, whose mother had not, after all, raised any fools. "Just in case."

The three remaining heroines moved, and waited.

Jolly Roger was sitting at the captain's table, morosely staring into his mug of rum, when he heard the cabin door slam. He didn't look up until Velveteen's palms impacted with the surface of the table, and she snarled, "You are *going* to help us, whether you want to or not. So stop fucking around and get your things."

"This is part of the narrative, you know." He looked up, and for the first time, Velveteen realized how tired he looked. "The wicked pirate captain, lured out of retirement by the needy young maiden who came from so far away. I couldn't have said yes to you the first time if I'd wanted to."

"Did you want to?"

"No." He took a swig of rum. "Lass, this is a bad idea. Whatever they've taken from you, count yourself lucky that they left you with your life, and let it go. Walk away."

"I can't do that."

"I think you'll find you can; you just don't want to, and that's something very different indeed. You're alive. You're free. If the presence of your day-glow friend means anything, you're being scouted to serve the Winter. Go with her, make a new life there, and never think about The Super Patriots again."

"They took my best friend." *They took my childhood, they took my first love but they did it so badly that I can't even be sure of saving my second love; they took so much, and they gave so little...*

"They took my true love." *You're not the only one who's lost something.*

"So help us stop them from doing this to anyone else."

Jolly Roger sighed. "The Super Patriots aren't the source of all the evil in the world. If you take them down, there will still be villains. There will still be great, world-shattering events. Things will still go wrong. There just won't be a single central face to put on your problems."

"When you were there, when you were a part of the team, did you mind-control the trainees?"

"What?" Jolly Roger blinked before shaking his head. "No. Supermodel was making their worst impulses stronger, but none of us knew about that. They were all with us willingly. I'd swear to that."

"Well, that's changed. We know, for a fact, that the trainee heroes are being mind-controlled. They're literally creating the people they want us to be. And there's a lot of data to support that, beyond my experiences. According to the power registry, one in every fifteen heroes is psychic. Telepathy, or empathy, or some other power that affects the brain. So how come we have all these teams made up of bruisers and teleporters and energy manipulators—even the occasional animus or fairy tale princess—but almost no one has a telepath? Where are they all *going*?"

"I—"

"They're manufacturing supervillains now, did you realize that? They said *I* was a supervillain, when all I ever did was walk away from them. I didn't want to be controlled, and so they said I was evil. I was never evil. My only crime was wanting to be left alone."

"Funny thing that," muttered Jolly Roger, and raised his mug of rum.

Velveteen stared at him for a moment. Finally, she shook her head. "You were my hero, you know," she said. "Even before I left, you were the one I looked up to, because you were the one who was brave enough to leave when you needed to. And now you're not even willing to stand up for people who have no power to stand up for themselves. You'd just leave them, and all the children who are going to come after them. You're no brave pirate captain. You're a coward."

"At last, you're starting to understand the situation." Jolly Roger shook his head. "I'm sorry, lass. Whatever it is you came here hoping for, it's not going to happen."

"If you won't come with us, will you at least tell us if there are any weak spots? I've never seen the CEO. No one has. It's just the heroes, and the staff from Marketing and Legal—"

"Don't be silly. The CEO is a man named Michael Wellman. He was Majesty's sidekick for a while, until he lost his powers."

Velveteen blinked. "No, it's not."

"What?" Now it was Jolly Roger's turn to blink. "What do you mean?"

"Michael Wellman died in the fight that killed Majesty. Right before you left. How do you not know that? There's a statue of him in the foyer of the Marketing wing."

"But..."

"The CEO who took over for him was never named in public, to avoid possible assassination attempts."

"I..." Jolly Roger stopped, straightening, a new coolness coming into his eyes. "Lass, what is the current lineup of The Super Patriots?"

"Uh. West Coast Division is Action Dude, Sparkle Bright, Uncertainty, Imagineer, Mechamation, and Jack O'Lope. They brought in Firecracker from the Midwest Division as a stand-in for Sparkle Bright while she was unavailable, but I'm not sure if she's still affiliated with the team. Midwest Division is Trick, Treat, Cosmo-not, Dotty Gale, and Firecracker, usually. East Coast Division is the American Dream, Flash Flood, Deadbolt, Second Chance, Firefly, and I think Leading Lady? I'm not sure who's in South these days."

"Are any of them psychic in any way? Not telepaths—just straight up psychics."

"Yes, sort of. The Nanny from the West Coast junior team is some sort of empath, although she's pretty much limited to knowing whether someone has been naughty. And I think she has to be in the room with them for that to work." Velveteen shook her head. "Everyone else has physical powers, or manipulates energy. Oh, and Imagineer is a technopath. So she's psychic, but only when she's dealing with machines."

"I see." Jolly Roger took a deep breath. Then he downed the last of his rum in a single gulp, stood, and slammed the mug into the table. "Tell your friends I'll have cabins made up for them. We set sail with the tide."

"I–what?"

"You wanted a pirate, lass. Well, you've got one, and we're going to pillage The Super Patriots before our fight is through."

"But you said–"

"You asked for my help. I'm giving it to you. Don't question, or you might make me change my mind, and you wouldn't want to do that, now, would you?"

"No, sir," said Velveteen. "I'll tell the others." She turned to flee the cabin.

"And give back my ship!" he shouted after her. The door slammed. He sighed, shoulders sagging.

He should have seen it. He should have guessed. There were so many clues, so many signs, but ah, he'd been so tired, and the fight had been so hard; he hadn't wanted to complicate things. Slowly, he turned to the closed cabinet that hung on the back wall, watching over everything he did. He couldn't see her portrait, but he didn't need to. Some things were too beautiful to be contained by something as simple as a sheet of polished oak.

"Oh, love," he said, resting his fingers against the cabinet door. "What have you done? What have I allowed you to do?"

Safely shut away, the painted face of his beloved did not answer.

The four heroines found themselves sharing a cabin, which was less ideal than it could have been, given Jackie's tendency to slowly drop the temperature of a room while she slept, and the way that all the ship's rats really wanted to snuggle with the Princess. Still, they had individual hammocks and plenty of blankets, and Victory Anna was able to cobble a space heater from a bunch of pieces she'd found in the hold. (None of them asked. Where Victory Anna's inventions were concerned, not asking was the only safe course of action, or at least the only course of action that allowed them to avoid headaches.)

"So you got your man," said Jackie, leaning out of her hammock to peer down at Velveteen. "I gotta say, I didn't think you'd pull it off."

"Neither did I," said Velveteen. "I'm still not quite sure how I swung it."

"What comes next?" asked the Princess.

"We go out and find our army." Velveteen folded her hands behind her head, staring up at the ceiling, or at least, staring up at Jackie in her hammock. "We gather every superhuman with a grudge, and we sail right through their gates. They should have left us alone. They should have left *me* alone."

"Ah," said Jackie. "So what you're saying is that things are finally going to get fun around here."

"Here's hoping," said Velveteen. "Good night, all."

The four girls slept as the *Phantom Doll* sailed proudly through the clouds with Jolly Roger at the helm, the world's last great hero, heading home at last.

VELVETEEN vs. Everyone

THE APPEARANCE OF THE *Phantom Doll* in the evening sky caught the world's attention in an instant. Jolly Roger's disappearance had never quite faded from the public consciousness: he was the first and greatest mystery of the superheroic age, the hero in whose wake all others followed. He was the one who did not die and rise again, or die and stay dead—a rarer but still possible occurrence. He was the one who simply vanished, leaving everything behind.

Children raced to their windows, only to be shoved aside by parents who had been children themselves when the *Phantom Doll* last sailed the skies. Blurry photos cropped up on every social media network, while the rare clear shots of the high-masted ship silhouetted against the rising moon were jealously watermarked by the lucky photographers who had taken them.

And on a rooftop in San Diego, a woman stood, her hooded face turned toward the sky, and waited. She had been waiting for a very long time.

"Let me get this straight," said Jackie. She crossed her arms, frowning at the woman in the bunny-eared headband. "You seriously have no plan beyond 'let's go and hit them until the candy comes out.' Because not all of them contain candy. Candy is not a default filling."

"Then we hit them until the kidneys come out," said Velveteen grimly. She looked around the circle of costumed heroes. "This is our only shot. Don't you get that? We need to do this now, before Sparkle Bright tells Marketing everything she knows about us."

"If she hasn't already," added the Princess. Both Velveteen and Victory Anna turned to glare at her. She blinked. "What? You know it's something we have to consider. They've had her long enough that she could have spilled every bean she's got."

"She hasn't," said Velveteen. "She never told them she was spending time as Blacklight; that means she's got some resistance to their mind games. Not much, maybe, but enough that she can keep her secrets for at least a little while. They'd be coming after us by now if she'd talked. She knows about my trip to Vegas, and that means she knows I was planning to look for Jolly Roger."

"And if The Super Patriots knew that, they'd have stopped us by now," said the Princess slowly. "All right. I like your logic. Still don't like your plan, though."

"What do you want us to do?" asked Jackie.

"It's like I said before," said Velveteen. "Now we get our army."

David Mickelstein—better known as "the Claw," especially now that he was committed to the supervillainous lifestyle—was preparing for a full frontal assault on Captain John's Steak and Seafood when a hand tapped him on the shoulder. He turned, raising his claws defensively, and stopped as he saw the woman standing behind him, her bunny-eared headband in her hands. She was back in uniform, a domino mask covering her face, and she was beautiful.

"Aaron never knew how lucky he was," he said.

Velveteen blinked. "What?"

"Nothing! Er. What are you doing here? Are you here to thwart me? Because I don't think this is your territory."

"David…" Velveteen smiled. "Don't you miss being a hero? Don't you want the opportunity to right a real injustice?"

He wanted to say that the lobsters even now being boiled to death inside that building were his brethren, and that their deaths were a real injustice. He wanted to ask where she was when he was being sidelined more and more as "difficult to market." He wanted to know what gave her the right to ask him a question like that.

"Yes," he said. "Why?"

"Because I'm finally going to take on The Super Patriots, and I need your help."

The Claw snorted. "Oh, yeah? You and what army?"

To his surprise, Velveteen smiled. "Look up," she said.

He looked up. He blinked. And he said, in an awed tone, "I'm in."

* * *

Dead Ringer drew her bell as she crept up on the mugger she'd been stalking. In a moment, he would understand why most sensible villains stayed far from her territory—which, if she was being honest with herself, was why she was reduced to chasing muggers, rather than sinking her teeth into a juicy supervillain of her very own. Still, anything was better than nothing, which was why she was so put out when a beam of what looked like solid neon gas lanced out of the shadows and hit the mugger in the chest, flinging him into a pile of garbage cans.

"What the—?"

"You may, of course, manage your vocabulary as you see fit, but I would prefer you not swear in my immediate vicinity," said a prim female voice. A short, curvy redheaded woman in a tight corset and impractical-looking boots stepped out of the shadows. There was a tiny top hat perched at a jaunty angle atop her head. Dead Ringer couldn't take her eyes off of it. "I believe you are the sonic heroine known as 'Dead Ringer' in this reality, is that correct?"

"Yes..." Dead Ringer eyed her warily. "Who are you?"

"My code name is Victory Anna. I, and my compatriots, have been shabbily treated by The Super Patriots, and have amassed sufficient proof to show that they are not acting in a heroic manner, and that we are thus not behaving villainously if we choose to go against them. We wished to extend an invitation for you to join us in this campaign."

Dead Ringer paused for a long moment, puzzling through that, before she asked, "Are you saying you have proof that The Super Patriots have been fucking us all over for years?"

"Not in such crass terms, but yes," said Victory Anna, a flicker of irritation crossing her face. "Will you stand with us?"

"I've been waiting for this moment since the day I left the fold." Dead Ringer returned her bell to its place by her side, a slow smile splitting her face. "Just tell me who I get to hit."

"That's the spirit," said Victory Anna. "Now, if you would simply come with me..."

The doorbell rang, interrupting what was otherwise promising to be an excellent argument about the virtues of hockey played on an indoor rink vs. hockey played on a naturally frozen surface. "I'll get it," said Misty, hopping to her feet. Gordon and Ethan watched her go for a moment, admiring the process of her walking away, and then went back to the argument at hand. Misty shook her head. Boys would be boys. She was smiling when she reached and opened the front door.

Her smile died.

"No," she said, and tried to slam the door in the face of the woman standing on the porch.

Jackie was too fast for her. Quick as a wink, her fingers were wrapped around the edge of the door, sending frost racing across the wood. "Misty, please," she said. "Is that any way to greet an old friend?"

"A friend? You're a friend now? You come here, you tell Tad you need him in Portland, that there's a girl he 'simply must meet,' she's perfect for him, and by the way, you'll owe him if he'll at least give it a try. The next thing we know here, we're getting the notice of his death. And not even a funeral!" Misty glared at Jackie like she was willing the other woman's flesh to melt from ice into water. "You have a lot of nerve showing your face here, Jacqueline Frost."

"Misty? Is there a problem?" Ethan loomed up behind her in the doorway. Even in his human form, he resembled nothing so much as a grizzly on the verge of losing its temper. His eyes narrowed as he looked at Jackie. "You shouldn't be here."

"Tad made his own choices," Jackie said. "A lot of us haven't been given that luxury. Is Gordon here? Because I came to talk to all three of you, and I'm *going* to talk to all three of you. The only question is whether I do it standing on the porch, where all your neighbors can see, or whether I do it inside, where you have the home team advantage."

"Our neighbors know what we do for a living," said Misty dismissively.

"Sure they do. That means they'll be happy to come outside and get a show." Jackie pulled herself closer to the open door. "Let me in. For Tad's sake, let me in."

Misty and Ethan exchanged a look. Then, finally, they stepped out of the way, and Jackie Frost was allowed to enter the home of the famous Canadian heroes, Poutine, the Grizzly, and Gastown.

The bar where the Fairy Tale Girls spent their off-hours was located in a part of Fairyland that the Princess generally tried to avoid. It's not that it was rough, although it was; being friends with Jackie Frost had forced her to relax a great deal about going into places people thought of as "rough." It's that it was a mixed up maelstrom of fairy tales ideas and concepts, some so old that they'd been virtually forgotten outside of Fairyland, and going there tended to upset her stomach.

Not that she had a choice. They were gathering an army, and if she wanted this to work, she had to do her part. The Princess took a breath to steady herself, brushed the bluebird off her shoulder, and stepped inside.

A rousing cheer greeted her from the table nearest the door, as the Fairy Tale Girls raised their various brightly colored beverages in a merry hello. "Princess!" cried the closest of them, a willowy blonde whose hair extended well past her feet, forming a shaggy heap the size of a Saint Bernard next to her chair. "What are you doing here? We haven't seen you in forever!"

"I'm here because I have a job for you, ladies," said the Princess, stepping closer, looking around the table. Six of them were there. That was more than she'd been hoping for; she would have settled for three. "My friends and I, we're going up against The Super Patriots. We need your help."

"The Super Patriots? Why would we want to attract their attention?" The question was asked by a girl with skin as white as snow, and hair as black as her blasted heart. "They leave us alone. We return the favor."

"That may be, for now, but what happens when they decide that y'all are worth going after?" The Princess crossed her arms. "You know that day is coming. They've convened focus groups. They've done *studies*. One day, they'll figure out how to sell you, and when that happens, you're going to be at their mercy. Unless you come with me, today, and help me take them down. Now please. Help us."

The Fairy Tale Girls were a curious bunch. Magical heroes all, although none of them had the flexibility or raw power of the Princess herself–which was a good thing, since out of the six who were sitting in front of her, there were only two she'd have trusted with more than negligible authority. They looked more like a themed roller derby team than a group of heroes. But they could fight, and she'd trusted them with her life more than once. She needed them.

Snow Wight and Rose Dead, the phantom sisters of the Enchanted Forest. Rampion, whose hair could strangle the life from a man. Beauty, whose lover's lycanthropy had proven to be unexpectedly contagious. Brittle Red, with her basket of limitless tricks. And of course, their leader, Cinder, without whose word none of the others would move.

Slowly, the white-haired girl in the glass slippers inclined her head. "All right," she said, in a voice that grated like bottles breaking on stone. "We'll join your fight. Why the hell not? It sounds like a good time."

One by one, the Fairy Tale girls stood, leaving money on the table to pay for their drinks. They followed the Princess out of the bar, and as they walked, she only hoped that she knew what she was doing. If not, well…things were about to get interesting.

Jolly Roger stood on the top floor of the casino that bore his name, wishing he felt less uncomfortable; wishing he really knew what he was doing there. Dame Fortuna shared none of his discomfort. She crossed her arms, eyeing him like he was something she had scraped off the bottom of her shoe.

"You've got a lot of nerve coming here after what you did, after what you *didn't* do," she said. "I thought you were a running man nowadays."

"You're the one who told them where to find me."

Dame Fortuna shrugged. "That was just business. The little animus came here asking for information, and she was willing to pay the price I put in front of it. If you'd stayed in touch, you could have made a counter-offer. Maybe you would have topped her offer. I guess we'll never know, now, will we?"

"Toony…"

"Don't call me that. It's Dame Fortuna to you." Dame Fortuna's green eyes blazed as she stepped closer to Jolly Roger, a scowl distorting her perfect features. "You left us. You ran out, and you left us. How do you like the mess they've made of the world in your absence, hmm? You handed them the keys to our destruction." There was no need to specify who she meant by "them." There had only ever been one "them" where Dame Fortuna was concerned.

"I'm back now," said Jolly Roger. "I'm going to help set things right. But I need help to do that, Toony. The girl's trying to build an army. We're going to need luck on our side."

"I won't leave Vegas."

"Won't, or can't?"

For the first time, sorrow seemed to break through Dame Fortuna's rage. "Both," she admitted. "The web of chance and circumstance that keeps us safe here depends on me to maintain it. If I leave, and your army loses…I can't take that risk."

"But we can." Lady Luck stepped forward, Fortunate Son at her side and Showgirl close behind them. "We'll help you, Mr. Roger. For the sake of what you were to my mama."

I was more than you know, thought Jolly Roger, and said nothing.

Dame Fortuna said it for him. "No. Absolutely not. I won't have you risking yourself like this."

"I don't think you get to make that choice for me," said Lady Luck. "You raised me to be a hero. It's time that you finally let me do that." She met her mother's green-eyed gaze without flinching, and waited.

In the end, Dame Fortuna looked away first. "Damn you all," she muttered. "You bring my babies back, Jolly Roger, do you hear me? I won't forgive you if you don't bring my babies back."

"I will do everything in my power to see them safely home," said Jolly Roger. He removed his hat, bowing low to Lady Luck and the others. "My ship, and glorious battle, awaits."

As the *Phantom Doll* sailed away across the Vegas sky, only Showgirl looked back to see the shadow of Dame Fortuna standing on the casino roof. She was crying, and her tears became dice as they fell, tumbling down by her feet. Showgirl looked away, feeling vaguely as if she shouldn't have seen, and the ship sailed on.

Garden Show had turned her down. It wasn't really a surprise; her only power was plant control, and she wasn't particularly strong, which was why The Super Patriots had never tried to recruit her into active duty. Still, a pair of hands was a pair of hands, and Velveteen had been hoping they could at least coax the minor heroine into a supporting role in the battle to come. Instead, she had shaken her head and said, "I have things to take care of here at home, and that's never been my world. But my little girl…she's twice the elementalist I am. They'll come for her one day. Kick their asses."

Then she had closed the door, leaving Velveteen standing alone on the front porch.

Velveteen sighed, turning to head back to the magic mirror checkpoint that Jackie had created for this recruitment pass. She could head back to the *Phantom Doll*, find out whether the Princess had been successful in recruiting the Fairy Tale Girls, and maybe then…

A group of people in brightly colored costumes were standing on the sidewalk, preventing her from making it back to the alley where she'd hidden the magic mirror. Velveteen stopped, tensing. She hadn't come expecting a fight. She had no backup, and nowhere near enough toys.

"Can I help you?" she asked.

"I hope so," said one of the women. Her costume was a dozen shades of blue, and there were green streaks in her curly brown hair. "We heard tell you were assembling an army."

Velveteen blinked. "Mississippi Queen?"

"In the flesh, my dear." The Claw's old mentor smiled, her teeth very white against her dark skin. "We want to join you."

"But…" Velveteen took another look around the small cluster of heroes. She couldn't have named them all. The ones she did recognize were all employed by The Super Patriots. "Your contracts…"

"Allow us to fight against management if we have reason to believe they may have been compromised by a supervillain," said a woman Velveteen didn't recognize. Her costume was also blue, but it wasn't the stylized blue of cloth; it was the muddy blue of living water, and it flowed around her body like the tide. Catching Velveteen's look, she said, "Lake Pontchartrain. Water control."

"With Lakey along, my limitations don't matter," said Mississippi Queen. "She generates more than enough water to share a little with me."

"Rue Royal," said a man. "I freeze time."

"Epiphany," said a woman. "Photon manipulation."

"Ash," said a man. "Fire control."

Mississippi Queen smiled again. There was a dangerous edge to the expression. "So, you going to let us march in your little Mardi Gras parade? I promise you, everyone here knows how to party."

"They're not going to take this lying down," cautioned Velveteen.

"Honey, we wouldn't be here if we thought they were. You wouldn't need us, and we'd be able to be good little corporate soldiers, keep our doors closed, and only come out when a better form of management was in place." Mississippi Queen shook her head. "You need us."

This time, Velveteen smiled. "You're right," she said. "We do. Follow me."

Together, the six superhumans walked into the alley. There was a bright flash of light, and the smell of snow, and they were gone.

"I have to go."

"No."

"This isn't up for debate."

"Then you're doing something wrong." Celia Morgan stood, turning her back on her sister as she looked resolutely out the window. "Let them fight The Super Patriots. If we're lucky, they'll win, and things will be better. But you're not going."

Jennifer—better known as "Jory" when she was in her green and brown uniform—actually laughed. "Did you forget who was the older sister here? You can't forbid me to go."

"I've been alive in this reality longer than you have. I think you can't claim to be older than I am. Not anymore." Celia whirled. "I lost you once. I will not lose you again, do you understand me? Once was one time too many. I can't survive it a second time."

"Cee..." Jennifer walked to her sister, placing her hand against Celia's cheek. "You aren't going to lose me, I swear. The current team doesn't have an earth manipulator of my strength. They can't take me out unless they can *hit* me, and that's not going to happen. But they can hurt Velveteen and her friends, and without her, I wouldn't be here to have this argument with you. Now come on. Stop fighting with me, and let me go."

"I can't lose you," whispered Celia.

"You won't. I will always find a way to come home to you. You're my baby sister, and I love you." Jennifer kissed Celia's forehead. "But right now, the world needs me to be a hero, and since that's the only thing I went to school for, I figure I should go ahead and be one."

"Come home?"

"I always will."

Then Jennifer was gone again, and Celia Morgan, the woman who had become Governor of Oregon to avenge her sister, put her hands over her face and cried alone.

The deck of the *Phantom Doll* was packed with bodies. Some of them floated in the rigging, or hung suspended from ropes; Snow Wight was phased halfway through one of the masts, and no one quite dared to tell her that she was standing in the middle of a giant piece of wood. Feeling sick to her stomach, Velveteen allowed Jackie and the Princess to help her up onto a wooden crate. They stepped into position to either side of her. Victory Anna was nearby, assembling another of her ray guns.

Velveteen took a deep breath. *Only for you, Yelena,* she thought, and clapped her hands. "Hi, everybody. Can I have your attention, please? Everyone, can I have your attention?"

The crowd kept talking.

"SHUT THE HELL UP!" shouted Jackie.

The crowd stopped talking.

"Uh, hi," said Velveteen. "Thank you all for coming. I'm, um. I'm Velveteen, and I guess I'm leading this little corporate takeover. Everyone who's here is here because you have a reason to hate The Super Patriots. Maybe not the idea of them, but the thing that they've become. They destroy us. They chew us up and spit us out, and they do it pretending it's about justice when it's really all about the bottom line. They take away our identities, even our minds, and it's time for that to stop. All of it."

A few people in the crowd shouted encouragement.

Velveteen took another deep breath. "You've been divided into squads, and we have a plan of attack, at least in the beginning, but we all know that no plan survives its first contact with the enemy. So here's the real plan for today: win. Don't die. Try not to kill anyone. And take those bastards down."

"What about the mind control?" asked the Claw. "We know they're controlling half the heroes they'll send up against us, and we don't have any psychics."

"Leave that to me, boy," said Jolly Roger.

"So do we know what we're doing?" asked Velveteen.

This time, the cheer was all-consuming. This time, the fight was really on.

There was nothing subtle about a pirate ship sailing through a clear sky; the advantage of surprise was never going to be on their side, save perhaps in the sense that The Super Patriots had been given a very long time in which to become complacent. On some level, the people who ran the corporation believed that nothing would ever challenge their right to control the superhumans of the world. Still, the paparazzi were piled four-deep around the gates at headquarters when the *Phantom Doll* sailed by overhead, circled once, and came in for a landing on the perfectly manicured lawn.

"Aim for the rosebushes," said Victory Anna, with undisguised spite. "Let's damage their landscaping like they've damaged my heart."

"You are a very unique lassie," said Jolly Roger, and tweaked the wheel to the right, sending the ship's prow tearing through the heart of the ornamental rose garden. Victory Anna squealed with glee.

Somewhere in the building, an accountant who was watching the scene outside on a monitor moaned in financial agony.

"You don't know the half of it," drawled the Princess. She was wearing a new ball gown, this one six shades of pink encrusted with sparkling pink crystals that matched her tiara. If only she'd been followed by songbirds instead of ravens, she might have looked positively sweet. "We ready?"

"No," said Velveteen. "But we're going."

The heroes swarmed from the boat. Some launched themselves into the air: Whippoorwill, with her wings spread proud against the sky, Epiphany, riding a beam of glittering light in Mardi Gras colors, even the Princess, standing once more on her trusty flying carpet. Others ran. In at least one case, the ground itself reached up to form a bridge, allowing Jory to sail into her place in the lineup.

They didn't attack. They couldn't attack. There were ways these things were meant to be handled, appropriate forms that distinguished the heroes from the villains. In the aftermath—and there would be aftermath, no matter who won—they would need all the footage taken during the fight to show that they had been in the right. From beginning to end, they had to be heroes.

Velveteen walked to the front of the formation, a stream of dolls, plush toys, and action figures marching along behind her. Victory Anna and Jackie stood to her left; Jolly Roger and the Claw stood to her right. For just a moment, it seemed like everyone was holding their breath, waiting to see what would happen next.

"You can stop pretending you don't know we're here," said Velveteen. She scanned the grounds as she spoke. There were topiaries shaped like animals. She could use those. *You never believed I'd move against you,* she thought, and said, more loudly, "If we're going to do this, let's do this. Or are you scared of a bunch of second-stringers who don't have focus groups to tell them what to wear?"

The mighty doors of the headquarters of The Super Patriots, Inc. began to slowly swing open. The gathered heroes tensed, waiting to see what would come next. And out marched, and flew, the assembled forces of the West Coast, the West Coast Junior Division, and so many, many more. On and on they came, full heroes and trainees alike, their fists clenched and their faces dark with grim determination.

"Oh, God, they're sending the kids," whimpered Jory, who had talked to Celia more than enough to know what had happened to this dimension's original version of her. "They can't really expect us to fight kids, can they?"

"No," said Epiphany, who was hovering next to her, a sad expression on her pointed pixie face. "They expect us to turn around and run away rather than be the people who came here and raised arms against an army of children."

"Vel…" said Jackie, uncertainly.

"Try not to hurt them," said Velveteen, and while she never raised her voice, everyone on her side heard her. That was Cinder's doing. Glass can cut, but it can also transmit sounds, when it's bent the right way, when it's held in the right hands. "The kids are innocent, or as innocent as any of us were when we were their age."

"So about as innocent as a kegger," muttered Jackie. "Got it."

"If it's you or them, choose you," continued Velveteen. "I'm sorry. But choose you."

"You're trespassing!" shouted Sparkle Bright, striking a perfect pose in the air. The Super Patriots had more fliers, noted Velveteen, almost dispassionately; they would have the air advantage. Fine. That just meant they had to be grounded. "Remove yourselves immediately!"

"I invoke the hostile takeovers clause of the corporate governing contract," Velveteen shouted back. "A supervillainous force has seized this building. We fight for justice!"

"No!" Sparkle Bright's face contorted in camera-unfriendly rage. "You don't fight for justice! *We* fight for justice!"

Velveteen's smile was slow, intended to provoke a violent response. "Oh yeah?" she asked. "Prove it."

Sparkle Bright shrieked, a whip of solid red light lashing from her hands to hit the spot where Velveteen had been standing only a second before.

The fight was joined.

At first, The Super Patriots took the superior position. They had more fliers, after all, and high ground is important in any sort of battle. What they didn't bank on was the sheer number of elementalists fighting on Velveteen's side. Swallowtail was grounded by a carefully timed strike from Lake Pontchartrain, who was in the process of flooding the south side of the lawn. Mississippi Queen was riding a raft around the newly created water, and from there, she sent twisters and aggressive waves after the fighting heroes. Action Dude tried to shout for someone to take out the water manipulators, and received a face full of lake water for his troubles.

Handheld screamed when he saw Swallowtail fall. He tried to run to her, and was hit by a blast from Victory Anna's ray gun, mere seconds before a blast from Imagineer's hand-held phaser sent the Victorian gadgeteer sprawling. Victory Anna cried out in pain when she hit the ground.

Sparkle Bright, who had been blasting away at Epiphany, whipped around in the air, the light surrounding her hands going from white to blue to solid black in less than a second. Her cheeks took on a greenish cast as she frantically scanned the fray. "…Torrey?" she said, loud enough to be overheard.

Epiphany held her fire.

"Don't worry about it," called Imagineer, adjusting the settings on her phaser as she stalked toward the fallen Victory Anna. "I've got the stupid little steampunk girl. You kill the firework before it starts infringing on your copyrights."

"GET THE HELL AWAY FROM HER, YOU BITCH!" Sparkle Bright dropped out of the sky like a meteor bent on revenge, blasts of black light lancing from her fingers as she fell toward Imagineer. Imagineer yelped and turned to fire at her team leader, only to go down in a heap as a lion-shaped hedge punched her upside the head.

Victory Anna didn't move.

Sparkle Bright—Yelena—hit the ground, stumbled, and ran to gather the fallen gadgeteer into her arms, ignoring the fight that was blazing on around her. Miraculously, the fight returned the favor. Or maybe not so miraculously; everyone on Velveteen's side had been warned that this might happen, and everyone who was fighting for The Super Patriots was used to thinking of Sparkle Bright as an ally.

"Torrey? Come on, Torrey, open your eyes." She shook the bruised gadgeteer. She only dimly understood what she was doing here; she remembered being grabbed in Portland, and being locked in the back of a van, but things went blurry after that. Judging by her white uniform, she'd gone back to The Super Patriots. She'd have to kill them all, once she knew Victory Anna was okay. "This is a really lousy thing to do when we've only had one proper date. Come on."

Victory Anna didn't move.

"Dammit, Torrey, this sucks. You spin this amazing love story for me, all dimensional crossings and destinies and versions of me who did it better, and now you're just going to go and die on me? You can't do that. I won't let you." Yelena bent and pressed her lips against Victoria's, only dimly aware that the people around her had stopped fighting to stare. She didn't care anymore.

Victory Anna squirmed. Victory Anna opened her eyes. And then, with surprising strength and unsurprising enthusiasm, Victory Anna began kissing her back.

On the other side of the battlefield, the Princess used a croquet mallet she'd produced from somewhere to hit Jack O'Lope's arrow back at him. Rose Dead, who was standing nearby with her hand sunk up to the elbow in Dotty Gale's chest, gave her a chiding look.

"You did that, didn't you?"

"Sweetie, I'm a living fairy tale," said the Princess, gearing up for another swing. "If I say a kiss makes everything better, then a kiss makes everything better."

The battle raged on. Heroes fell on both sides. Poutine was able to stretch out of the way of most attacks, but the Grizzly was bound by the limitations of his bear form, and was taken captive. One of the Candy sisters, frozen by an ice blast, shattered when she tipped over and hit the ground. Jackie blanched. Then she paused, and skated closer to the candy-coated mess.

"She wasn't real," she said, relief beating back her anger. "She was just a candy golem!"

"You didn't know that when you hit her," snarled a voice from behind her, and she turned to find Trick and Treat bearing down on her position. She yelped and raised her shield, barely blocking their shadow blasts before they could strike home.

"You tried to kill our daughter!" shouted Treat, sending another blast in Jackie's direction.

"She was trying to kill me, too!" shouted Jackie, as she desperately reinforced her shield. "Guys, a little help?" Trick and Treat were full holiday guardians, and Jackie, for all her power, was only a trainee. She hadn't accepted the burden and the strength of Winter.

"Get back!" Dead Ringer leapt between Jackie and the Halloween heroes, her bell out and ringing madly. Trick fell back, stunned. Treat…didn't.

The sound of Dead Ringer's lifeless body hitting the turf somehow managed to be very loud, despite the noise on all sides.

The fall of Dead Ringer was initially unremarked. She hit the ground hard, and she didn't get back up, but lots of heroes had hit the ground hard; lots of heroes had failed to get back up immediately. Then one of Velveteen's model horses, doing a sweep of the damage, reached her body. The tiny plastic stallion tapped her nose with a hoof. The fallen heroine didn't react. The horse turned and bolted back toward Velveteen, ducking and weaving across the battlefield.

Meanwhile, Velveteen had problems of her own. "We know they have Midwest here with them," she snarled to the Princess, throwing a sharp-clawed teddy bear at the face of an unsuspecting member of The Super Patriots. "Now I'm getting word that Leading Lady's been seen near the building. Did they call in East? Because if they called in East, we're screwed."

"No more than we were a few minutes ago, when we thought we were just going up against two of the four teams," said the Princess. "Most of South is here with us, and they're having trouble hitting their own associates. The Super Patriots are having trouble, I mean. The Southerners are kicking ass and having a lovely time." Maybe *too* good of a time, when you got right down to it; Lake Pontchartrain now covered half the lawn, where Mississippi Queen and the Claw were taking on any attackers who got too close to the water. Jackie Frost kept freezing the surface of the water just enough to fool non-aquatic heroes into thinking it was safe to walk there, and then laughing hysterically as they fell into the frigid waters below.

"I don't care; we didn't give them this much warning." Velveteen shook her head. "Something's wrong."

The plastic horse, which had fought its way through dangers no plastic horse should ever have been forced to face, reached her ankle. It reared up on its hind legs, whinnying to get her attention.

Velveteen bent and picked it up. "Hey, little guy. What news do you have?"

The horse whinnied again.

"I'll never understand how you can talk to toy animals when you can't talk to real ones," said the Princess. "Sometimes, sweetie, your power set just doesn't make that much sense." She stopped talking as she realized that Velveteen wasn't smiling; wasn't reacting to her; wasn't, in fact, doing anything but standing and staring, pale-faced, at the horse in her hands.

"She's dead," she whispered.

"Honey?"

"Dead Ringer. Trick and Treat hit her—I knew that, Jackie saw it coming, and then she drew them off so that Dead Ringer would have a chance to recover—but she's not going to recover, because she's dead. They killed her." Velveteen shook her head slowly. "They actually killed her."

"My," said the Princess. "That…changes things a bit, doesn't it?"

Velveteen nodded grimly. Most superhuman fights weren't intended to be deadly; everyone pulled punches, everyone held back, just a little bit, to keep from crossing that line. Once the line was crossed, there was no going back. You had heroes, and you had villains, and the heroes were never the ones who drew first blood.

"Princess?"

"Yes, dear?"

"Do you think you can get Cinder to do that trick with my voice again? I have something this whole fight needs to hear."

The Princess nodded, stepping back onto her carpet. "Wait right there, sugar, and don't get caught. I'll be back in a jiffy." Then she was gone, zooming off into the fray.

Battles, large and small, raged all over the property. One on one, two on one, even five on one, there was no end to the combinations the heroes had divided themselves into. But all of them froze when Velveteen's voice rang out across the battlefield, tired and cold and angry.

"Dead Ringer is dead," she said. "Trick and Treat killed her with a blast intended for Jackie Frost. We have lost a comrade. We have lost a friend. And The Super Patriots have lost the high ground. If you are fighting for freedom, if you are fighting for the right to make your own decisions, if you are fighting for *me*, this is your moment." There was a very small pause before she added, "Light 'em up."

Brilliant flares of light marked four positions on the battlefield as Sparkle Bright, Epiphany, Gastown, and Showgirl unleashed their powers. Cinder placed herself in the path of Epiphany's blast, becoming a living disco ball as she shattered the single deadly laser beam into a hundred, all of which somehow seemed to avoid her allies as they lanced into the crowd. The newly-freed Grizzly ran past on all fours, Brittle Red astride his back with a machine gun in her hands, whooping enthusiastically as she fired into the crowd. Her bullets were less discerning than Cinder's refractions, and Poutine and Rue Royal had to dodge quickly to avoid being shot.

The Nanny, longtime member of The Junior Super Patriots, West Coast Division, hung back at the edges of the fight. "This isn't right," she muttered, looking from one cluster of furiously swinging superhumans to the next. "This isn't right at all."

"What's wrong?" demanded Handheld.

"They're not naughty." She turned on her team leader, her umbrella already out and in her hand. "I swear to you, I don't know how I know, but I know. These people? They're not naughty. They're here for the right reasons."

Handheld, whose psychic powers were limited to communication with machines, had nonetheless learned to respect the Nanny's appraisals of others. "They shot Swallowtail out of the sky," he said.

"But they didn't kill her, and they could have. We didn't afford them the same favor."

Swallowtail was still out cold. Handheld looked to her, and then back to the Nanny. "Can you get to Velveteen? Can you tell her…tell her that we surrender, but only if she'll help us get Swallowtail to cover?"

The Nanny blinked. "What about the others?"

"Apex and Super-Cool won't surrender, even if it's that or die. Bedbug will follow Swallowtail. I don't know about the Candy sisters." To be honest, he'd never known about the Candy sisters.

The Nanny nodded. "I'll be back," she said, and opened her umbrella, soaring away into the cold blue sky.

Lady Luck and Fortunate Son fought back to back, spinning the probabilities around them to fell their enemies and help their allies hit their marks. Neither of them seemed to be doing much to the naked eye, but the sea of bodies and bloodstains around them testified to how effective their methods really were.

"I can't say as I've ever loved you more," panted Fortunate Son, yanking the luck out from under Firefly and sending her sprawling into the turf. "Your momma's going to be proud of you."

"I'm already proud of you," said Lady Luck, hitting Poutine with a burst of good fortune that helped her twist out of the way of Jack O'Lope's latest volley of bullets. "This is a good day."

"Yes," agreed Fortunate Son. "It is."

They were both so focused on their work that they'd forgotten they weren't the only probability manipulators on the field. Second Chance, who had been a trainee when Majesty died; Second Chance, whose powers allowed him to try again if he failed something the first time. He fired his blaster at Fortunate Son and missed, the shot deflected by their swirling shell of probabilities. Time rewound, and he fired again.

This time, he didn't miss.

Fortunate Son was born lucky: he was the sort of man who would trip and fall on the sidewalk rather than walking in the path of an oncoming bus. And so, when Second Chance fired, Fortunate Son's powers moved him just a hairsbreadth to the side. Still close enough for the shot to hit home…and at the same time, far enough that it didn't hit its intended target.

Lady Luck screamed as she fell, a blistered wound covering half her chest. Fortunate Son shouted in dismay, and flung a ball of bad fortune at Second Chance before diving after his fallen wife. He didn't see Firecracker slam into Second Chance; he didn't see the two of them engulfed by the unforgiving waters of Lake Pontchartrain. He had no eyes left for anything but Lady Luck, who was gasping and glassy-eyed with pain.

"Come on, baby girl, don't you do this," he said, gathering her up into his arms. "Don't you leave me. Shit, you think I know what to do without you? I'm a mess when you're not running my world."

"Let me," said a voice behind him.

He turned, and there was Showgirl, glittering like a sequined dream. "Showgirl, this ain't the time–"

"This is the perfect time," she said, and leaned forward, pressing her hand against Lady Luck's chest. The fallen heroine gasped, eyes going wide. "You've never respected me much, have you? I can't say I blame you. I never tried to force the issue. But you could have asked what my secondary power set was."

"What are you–"

"Sonny?"

He turned back to his wife, who was wide eyed and blinking at him. He helped her sit up, hands shaking. "It's all right, baby girl. You're all right."

"The show must go on," said Showgirl, and jumped back into the fray.

While this, all this and more, was going on, Velveteen fought her way steadily toward the doors. She was backed by Jolly Roger, Jackie Frost, and the Claw. Maybe not the most predictable of teams, but it turned out to be an effective one. Heroes fell all around them, and they pressed on.

Halfway there, a teenage girl in an old-fashioned nanny's uniform, clutching an umbrella in one hand, descended from the sky. She put her hands up as soon as she landed. "Please don't hurt me," she said. "I come in peace."

Jolly Roger stared at her. "We're in the middle of a battlefield, girl," he said. As if to illustrate his point, Whippoorwill went flying by overhead, blown backward by a blast from Jack O'Lope. "If you're here to surrender, go get on the boat. We'll deal with you later."

"I'm not, quite. I just…" She turned to Velveteen. "You're not naughty. You've never been naughty. How is that possible?"

Jackie snorted. "I could've told you that."

"I just wanted to be left alone," said Velveteen. "You're the Nanny, right? Is the rest of your team okay?"

"I don't know about all of them. One of the Candy sisters got busted like a pinata, but I've always suspected that they weren't all real. Please." The Nanny seized Velveteen's hand. "You're not naughty, and some of the people we've been working for *are*. Please, can we switch sides?"

There was a deeper question there, because it implied that Velveteen had a side to switch *to*: that this was more than just a temporary thing. She took a deep breath, sighed, and nodded. "Yes. Any of you who want to change allegiances, just go to the *Phantom Doll* and wait for us there. We'll be back soon."

"Thank you," said the Nanny fervently. She reopened her umbrella and soared away into the sky. Velveteen and the others watched her go.

"You sure that was wise, girl?" asked Jolly Roger.

"No," said Velveteen. "But it's a chance I wish I'd been offered. Come on." They resumed moving toward the doors. Jackie blasted anything that got past Velveteen's marching array of toys, and Jolly Roger and the Claw handled those who managed somehow to come in close. It bought them ground, yard by yard, until they were standing right outside the entry hall.

Apex, American Dream, Super-Cool, and Action Dude barred their way. All four heroes hovered a few feet off the ground, their expressions ranging from heroic determination to quiet desperation.

"Please don't make me do this, Vel," said Action Dude.

"Fucked up times five billion," muttered Velveteen. Then she raised her voice, and said, "You messed up, Action Dude. I thought you were smarter than this."

"What do you mean?"

"I mean I can see inside, asshole." She closed her eyes and raised her hands, and the statues that lined the hall stepped off their pedestals and grabbed the last line of defense keeping her outside. The heroes struggled. The statues tightened their hands, and kept tightening until the struggling stopped.

"Did you…did you kill them?" asked the Claw, in a hushed voice.

"No," said Velveteen coldly. "Come on."

And she stepped inside.

The fight was losing momentum. Velveteen and her allies were outnumbered to start, but for every one of them who fell, they were taking out two or more of the corporate heroes. Their minds were clearer. Their tactics were harsher. They had, in the end, one hell of a lot more to lose. Rampion watched impassively as her hair choked Flash Flood into unconsciousness. Nearby, Victory Anna was tying up Mechamation, while Imagineer studied her thoughtfully.

"We would have given you much better toys, you know," she said.

"I'm a grown woman," she replied. "I have no time for toys. Now be silent, or I'll shoot your fingers off."

Sparkle Bright and Firefly were in the air above the artificial lake, blasting each other with glittering bolts. Sparkle Bright seemed to be wavering, and dipped lower in the air…allowing Mississippi Queen to lasso Firefly with a watery rope and yank her into the water, where Lake Pontchartrain made short work of her.

The former trainees of The Junior Super Patriots, West Coast Division, watched from the deck of the *Phantom Doll*. Only four of them had chosen safety: the Nanny, Handheld, Swallowtail, and the Bedbug. All of them were now absolutely sure they'd done the right thing.

The sound of the doors slamming shut was enough to catch their attention, even over the noise of the fight. "What do you think's happening in there?" whispered Swallowtail, her hand groping for Handheld's.

"Nothing good," he said, and took her hand, and held it, glad to be out of the fight at last.

The elevators were operational, but being slightly smarter than moss, the four heroes had chosen to take the stairs. Better a little panting than a lot of plummeting. Velveteen walked in the lead, a carpet of dolls and plush toys scampering ahead of her, while the others followed.

"She's going into the holidays after this, aye?" asked Jolly Roger of Jackie, pitching his voice softly so as not to be overheard. He barely needed to worry; Velveteen was off in her own little world, splitting her concentration in a hundred directions as she controlled her tiny army.

"For a year," said Jackie. "I don't think she's going to choose any of us, but she promised us a year."

"Well, for our sake, lass, I hope you're right. We need more like her."

"I don't like this," said the Claw. "Does anyone else feel like this is too easy? We should be fighting more, and instead, we're just walking."

"They never thought we'd make it this far," said Jackie.

"Aye," said Jolly Roger. He sounded almost regretful. "That could be the explanation."

"Do you have a better one?" demanded Jackie.

"Maybe we were supposed to make it this far," said Velveteen, causing them both to jump and turn guiltily toward her. She kept climbing stairs. "Doesn't this all feel a little scripted? Like we were supposed to do the things we've done since we arrived?"

"Dead Ringer *died*," said the Claw.

"I know. That makes it worse." There was a door at the top of the stairs. Velveteen focused on it, using the need to know what was on the other side to keep herself moving. "But someone's been doing all these things, all along. Some of the corporate decisions we've seen…they're just not good business. Someone had another motive."

"Lass…"

"I wondered if you'd know who it was." Velveteen reached for the doorknob, and pushed open the last door.

It opened on the back of a palatial office, one that was large enough to take up an entire floor. It had its own elevator bay, and its own stairway opening. The desk was the size of a luxury sedan. There was a single chair behind it, turned so that whoever sat there could watch the fight happening on the lawn outside. The four heroes entered, surrounded by toys, and formed a ragged line across the expensive carpet. The person in the chair said nothing.

Finally, when the silence began to take on physical weight,

Velveteen asked, "So who are you? The head of Marketing? The final boss?"

"No, dear." The voice was female, sweet as lead sugar and ten times as poisonous. It seemed to leave a sticky residue on their ears, like even hearing it was enough to require a hot shower and a thorough scrubbing. "I'm nothing so petty as the head of Marketing. I'm the CEO. This is my country, and in it, I am Queen."

"Ah, lass," sighed Jolly Roger. "I was afraid it might be you."

"Roger." The woman in the chair actually sounded pleased. "So this is what it takes to make you come back and take up your responsibilities again. You just needed an impossible crusade. If I'd realized that, I would have allowed an animus onto the junior team years ago."

"Uh, pardon the ignorant blue girl, but who the fuck are you?" Jackie sounded annoyed. It was beginning to snow around her, large, fluffy flakes that stuck to the carpet at her feet. "You're the CEO? Great. You're fired."

"What do you mean, allowed an animus?" asked the Claw, suspiciously. "They're rare. You didn't have an animus before Vel because there wasn't one available."

"Who tells us how rare certain power sets are?" asked Velveteen. Her eyes remained fixed on the chair. "Most of the reports are published by The Super Patriots, Inc. If they wanted to change the frequency of a power set's manifestations, all they'd have to do is change a number on a computer somewhere…"

"There have been more than you could ever know in your general family tree," said the woman in the chair, her voice taking on a light sing-song quality. "Animators and reanimators and resurrectionists and speakers to the dead. Oh, there are many kinds of animus, little toy box girl with your tin soldier army. I let them have you because you seemed harmless, and because I was curious. I wanted to know if you were any threat to me, if you would become a threat to me. And you know what?"

"What?" asked Velveteen, her hands balling into fists.

"You were never a threat. You never became a threat. You were a toy, just like the things you played with, and I proved it when I had you broken and thrown away." The chair finally turned, revealing the woman who was sitting there.

She was beautiful, almost indescribably so. Her skin was like cream, and her wavy, naturally golden hair made every blonde any of them had ever seen look like the victim of a bad dye job. That hair fell to cover half of her face, but perhaps that was for the best, because the half that was still visible was lovely enough to eclipse every other wonderful thing in the world. Her one visible eye was cerulean blue, heavy-lidded and filled with promises, and her lips teased the possibility of the sweetest kisses anyone had ever known.

"Supermodel?" said Jackie, snow beginning to fall harder in response to her surprise. "But you're dead."

"So the papers said," said Supermodel. She directed a half-smile at Jolly Roger. "Hello, darling. Welcome home."

"Oh, I'm not coming home," he said. "This place stopped being home a long time ago."

Supermodel stood as fluidly as a dream, long legs falling into a perfect runway strut as she walked toward them. "Oh, honey. You still don't understand. What's mine is mine, and stays that way, forever. I don't give up on my pretty things."

"You're a horrible person," said Velveteen. She sounded almost surprised. "I mean, I've heard about the big fight, the one where Majesty died—where you supposedly died—and they all said that it wasn't your fault, that your powers messed with your head. But they didn't, did they? You were like this all along. This is who you really are."

Supermodel stopped and blinked at her, an expression flickering through her single visible eye that could have been taken for fear. "I don't know what you're talking about."

"Vel, maybe you shouldn't antagonize the evil blonde Jessica Rabbit," said Jackie, the snow starting to fall faster around her.

"Can't you see the strings? She's trying to wrap them around everyone in this room." Velveteen froze. "No. You can't see them, because you're not...you aren't..."

"They don't have your power set," said Jolly Roger grimly. He drew his sword. "Only an animus can truly sense another animus."

"But we can't have the same power set," protested Velveteen. "We don't do the same things at all!"

"An illusionist and a photon manipulator both work with light," said the Claw. "Things take many forms."

Like Lake Pontchartrain and Mississippi Queen, or Epiphany and Sparkle Bright. Velveteen nodded slowly. "So you're the first animus," she said, to Supermodel. "I can't say I'm particularly impressed."

"Says the girl dressed like a reject from the Playboy Bunnies," sneered Supermodel. "You're worthless. You're beneath me."

For a moment, Velveteen almost believed it. Supermodel was so beautiful, so perfect, and she…well, she wasn't either of those things, not really. Surely Supermodel knew what she was talking about.

"Fucked up times infinity," muttered Velveteen.

"What was that?" asked Supermodel.

"I said, you're wrong." Velveteen raised her head, fixing her eyes on the other animus. "You screwed up, Supermodel. You built yourself this awesome empire, you suppressed the powers that could hurt you, you did everything that you could to make sure you'd never be challenged. But you made one major mistake."

"What the hell are you talking about?"

The air was full of strings no one else could see, all of them leading from Supermodel to someone else. Velveteen reached out with both hands, letting her toy army fall, forgotten, as she grabbed the nearest strings and *yanked*. Supermodel screamed. In the second before the office erupted into chaos, Velveteen said, through gritted teeth, "You taught me how to handle rejection. Now let's fucking dance, you bitch."

The fight was on.

Most superpowers come down to energy manipulation, of one sort or another. Maybe it's light, or heat, or cold. Maybe it's love. Or, as in the case of the rare superhumans categorized as "animus," maybe it's life. Velveteen grabbed the strings of life connecting Supermodel to her subordinates, pulling as hard as she could as she tried to free them from the grasping superhero-turned-supervillain. Supermodel pulled back with equal strength, spinning out new threads all the time.

"You can't beat me," hissed Supermodel. "I am better than you will ever be. Surrender now, and maybe I'll allow you to live."

"I'm sorry," said Velveteen. "I couldn't hear you above the sound of how outdated you are." The two of them seemed to be standing in a bubble of absolute calm. If she really focused, she could almost make out the shapes of her friends through the candy-colored shell that had closed off the rest of the world. In a way, she was glad that they were so fuzzy, so distant and removed. *It's best if you don't have to see me fall,* she thought, and kept yanking on those strings. On those endless, endless strings.

"You are an ugly, worthless little worm," said Supermodel. Strings lanced out from her body, wrapping themselves around Velveteen's wrists and ankles, like the strings on a puppet. "Any fame you accomplished, you got because my Marketing department found a way to sell you to a public that didn't even know you were worth wanting. Any fans you have, you owe to me. Pay me tribute. Bow down before me. Love me like you were designed to love me."

"I'm thinking no," said Velveteen—and then the strings drew tight and she screamed, feeling the essence of what made her *her* being ripped out of her body, only to be replaced by crushing emptiness and a void that could only be filled by love. Love, and admiration, and adoration, those were the boulders that would bridge the opening chasm, and there would never be enough. There *could* never be enough, because the gap was so deep, and the darkness at the bottom was so hungry. She screamed again, and even that was swallowed by the darkness. Not even sound could escape the black hole of her worthlessness.

Supermodel slunk closer, gathering in the slackened strings until they were tight and sustaining once more. "See? You can't compare yourself to me. You never could. I'm so sorry all those people misled you, making you think you were worthy, that you were worthwhile. People never seem to understand how building up the self-esteem of social outcasts actually hurts them in the long run. We never gave you the opportunity to find your place, because we kept making you think that you could somehow march in here and steal mine. You poor deluded thing. You were always going to lose. The only question was how much it was going to hurt."

The hunger on her half-visible face was raw and undisguised as she reached for Velveteen, fingers spread. Velveteen didn't pull away. Supermodel took Velveteen's head in her hands, cupping it, and pulled the other heroine closer, until their lips were virtually touching.

"I'll try to keep this from hurting you too badly," she whispered, mouth curling into a brittle, terrible smile. "But we both know that I'm going to fail."

"Yeah," said Velveteen, eyes suddenly focusing as the vacant look that she had been feigning for Supermodel's benefit fled. She reached up and grabbed Supermodel's wrists, yanking her closer, yanking her so close that the strings bound them both like a spider's web. "You are."

Supermodel screamed, and everything went white.

Meanwhile in the office, the Claw, Jackie, and Jolly Roger were busy trying to deal with a world that had come to sudden, violent life.

Everything was moving, from the walls to the stapler on Supermodel's desk, and it was all dead-set on murdering the three of them. Velveteen and Supermodel were locked together in the middle of the room, and neither of them seemed to realize that they weren't alone. None of the animated objects got too close to the two heroines, which probably helped them to remain oblivious. Jackie wasn't sure what they were doing, exactly, but she was willing to bet that it wasn't the sort of thing that was aided by an attack from a murderous rubber tree plant.

"What the twisted candy fuck is going on in here?" she demanded, blasting Supermodel's chair with a solid bolt of ice that blew a huge hole in the upholstery. The chair didn't seem to approve; it shrieked, although it didn't have a mouth, so it probably shouldn't have been able to do that, and dove for her, casters spinning madly.

"There's too much life for the room!" Jolly Roger shouted, parrying an attack of paperwork with his sword. "Both of them, they're spending it like pocket change in attacking each other, and it's spilling out into everything else!"

"Well, *make them stop*!"

"Lass, if I knew how to make an animus stop doing anything, we wouldn't be standing here today," snarled Jolly Roger, slashing again at the paperwork. "My Nicole and I would have left this life behind, and spent the last decades on the high seas, where there was nothing to infect her with the need for more love than one man could give."

"Uh, guys? Not to distract you or anything, but should we be helping Vel not die?" The Claw clipped a rampaging rubber tree in two with one snip of his mighty claws. "And how can Supermodel be an animus? She's in all the books as a psychic of undefined focus and scope."

"Who wrote the history books?" Jackie blasted the fax machine before it could sink its teeth into the Claw's leg. "If she didn't want anyone to know…"

"She was always proud," said Jolly Roger. "But it was fame that killed her soul." He hacked at the papers one last time, reducing them to confetti. Regretfully, he turned toward Supermodel and Velveteen. "I know what needs doing."

Everyone was exhausted. No, more than exhausted; everyone was defeated, even the ones who were technically winning by any objective measurement. Powers were failing. Inertia was setting in. Half The Super Patriots were tied up or sealed in the hold of the *Phantom*

Doll. The rest were still fighting, or trying to, anyway…save for those who would never be fighting again. Lake Pontchartrain was sitting on her own bank, crying steadily into her hands. Fortunate Son looked shell-shocked as he bent the luck again and again, trying less to guarantee victory for his side—victory already seemed assured—and more to keep anyone else from being killed.

No one was walking away from this fight unscathed. Not the winners, not the losers, no one. Every side had lost people. Every hero had been forced to face the fact that sometimes, their powers ended lives. It had been years since there was a super-battle of this scale, and all of them were coming to realize that peace was the better option. Peace didn't force you to look at someone you knew as they bled out on the cold ground. Peace didn't make you choose who lived and who died.

Some of them had stopped fighting altogether, and simply stood staring up at the top level of the headquarters, where strange sounds and lights had started a few minutes before. They all knew, on some level, that the battle was decided down in the mud, but the war was being decided up in that room, amidst a chaos that none of them was brave enough to approach.

The only real question, at this point, was whether there was any way a victory for The Super Patriots would be a victory for the world. Down in the mud, even those who fought for the corporation were coming to wonder whether losing might be the best outcome for everyone.

Everyone except the dead.

Velveteen had all the strings in her hands now, and she was pulling; pulling so hard that she could feel parts of Supermodel starting to come loose as fractures formed deep inside the other animus. She wanted to let go. She wanted to stop this, and find another way. And she knew that letting go would be a fast way to a faster death. Supermodel wasn't fighting fairly. She had no interest in letting her opponents live.

"What happened?" Velveteen whispered, still pulling, still yanking strings from their moorings. "How did you get like this?"

"I needed more," snarled Supermodel, trying to pull away. "I just…needed…more."

"Get a puppy! Do something! Don't enslave generations of superhumans to give you more fodder for your ego!" The strings were cutting into Velveteen's hands, but that was all right; that was how it was supposed to be. The pain centered her, and kept her from forgetting she was hurting a real person. Her actions would have consequences, and those consequences…

Those consequences were going to change everything.

Supermodel pulled away again, so suddenly that Velveteen almost lost her grip. The motion caused her hair to sway away from her face, and for a moment, Velveteen saw what was beneath. She frowned, puzzled. She'd been expecting a ruined face, a huge scar, and what she saw was the other half of the most beautiful woman in the world. Then, like a glass breaking, she realized that the hidden half of Supermodel's face *was* scarred. A tiny, tiny scar, right above her lip. And for that, she had shut herself away in a tower and become a villain. Because if she wasn't beautiful, what was she?

"You were the best of us," said Velveteen. "That's what you were."

Supermodel screamed.

The strings began to snap in Velveteen's hands, and as they broke, the candy shell that had appeared around the two heroines thinned, becoming a veil, and finally, clearing away entirely, revealing Jolly Roger. He was standing behind Supermodel, a look of profound regret on his heartbroken face. Velveteen looked down.

The sword protruding from Supermodel's stomach was only visible for an inch or so before it entered Velveteen's. The pain followed the sight, and she released the dissolving strings entirely, taking a step backward. The sword's bloody tip emerged from her body.

"Ack," said Supermodel. Then, with no more fanfare than that, she fell. The sound of her body hitting the floor was followed by the sound of Jolly Roger's sword landing beside her. Then the old pirate dropped to his knees, gathering her into his arms as he sobbed.

Velveteen wobbled. Velveteen asked, "Is it over?" And finally, Velveteen followed the older animus to the floor.

The last thing she saw before everything went black was Jackie, snow falling around her. "We won," said Jackie. "You did it."

Velveteen smiled, and the rest was silence.

VELVETEEN vs. The Epilogue

THE CATHEDRAL ROOM OF THE Crystal Glitter Unicorn Cloud Castle was quiet. A single figure sat next to the closed glass coffin. She had put her bloodstained uniform back on, complete with the bunny-eared headband on her head and a thick roll of bandages wrapped around her midsection. She had removed her domino mask and was holding it in her hands, turning it thoughtfully over and over, like she expected it to somehow start giving her the answers that she needed.

"I thought I should come tell you what happened," she said. Her voice was soft, and the room rendered it even softer, pulling it up into the vaulted ceiling, silencing her echoes. This conversation was for the two of them alone: for the girl in the rabbit ears and the boy who slept in the coffin made of glass. "There were just so many moving pieces, and I never quite realized how much this was going to change things…for everyone…"

Velveteen staggered out of the headquarters on her own two feet, although even a fool could have seen that the Claw and Jackie were bearing most of her weight. As for Jolly Roger, he had a burden of his own to bear: the body of Supermodel, draped across his arms like a bride being carried to her bridal bed. Her hair was her veil, hiding her face forever from the world.

"You're alive," said Sparkle Bright, a smile spreading across her face. Fireworks accompanied her expression, exploding in bright sprays all around her. She ran forward, stopping herself just short of sweeping Velveteen into a hug. "I was so sure—Vel, are you okay? Is it over?"

"That depends," said Velveteen. "Are you on our side again?"

"The power of love, and Epona's own grace, has returned her to us," said Victory Anna, walking forward to stand beside the willowy blonde. The smile on the redhead's face was almost as bright as Yelena's fireworks.

"And I'm changing my name," said Sparkle Bright. "I like Polychrome much better."

"The focus groups will hate it," said Velveteen, with a pained smile. "I'm so glad to see you both."

"We're glad to see you two, sugar," said the Princess, gliding in on her magic carpet. "Looked like you were having a little trouble up there."

"Yeah, well." Velveteen glanced back at Supermodel's body. "Things have costs. We need to remember that, so that we never have to do this again. This should never have happened in the first place."

"Vel?" The voice was horribly familiar, and so was the tone: apologetic, hopeful, sad. Filled with years of history, and even more years of isolation. Almost against her will, Velveteen turned and watched as Action Dude settled lightly to the battle-scarred lawn. His blue and orange uniform had somehow, against all odds, remained virtually pristine. Looking at him was like looking at her own alternate future, one where this became her home. She could stay here, rebuild The Super Patriots as a force for good, and he'd be there with her every step of the way. "Are you okay?"

"I'm bleeding on the lawn, your CEO is dead, and I'm going to pass out again soon," said Velveteen, more harshly than she meant to. Maybe a little harshness was justified. "No. I'm not okay. I don't think any of us are okay, and that's probably a good thing, because we'd have to be sociopaths if we were okay right now."

Action Dude winced. "I didn't mean it like that."

"I know." Velveteen closed her eyes, sagging against the Claw. "I'm just tired. Princess?"

"Yes, sweetie?"

"How bad is it?"

The Princess, who had been present for the entire fight, took a deep breath before she said, "Well, honey. It ain't good."

"Both sides lost people." Velveteen looked down at her domino mask, turning it over and over between her fingers. Tad, asleep in the coffin, said nothing. "I always knew there would be deaths, just like I knew toys would be broken every time I went out on patrol, but knowing something and seeing it are different, you know? People died because of a fight I said we should have. I know a lot more people died because of what Supermodel and The Super Patriots, Inc. did, but that doesn't really matter. Not when I close my eyes and try to sleep."

She sighed, and it was the lost, hollow sound of a woman who had never been allowed to be a child, and whose adulthood had been scarred by weapons she had no way to defend herself against. "Lake Pontchartrain had the highest body count. She drowned at least three people, and she's actually being a lake right now, here on the castle grounds. The Princess said she'd been wanting a water feature, and told Lake Pontchartrain she could stay for as long as she needed to get her head back together. I feel really bad for her. But the Claw is with her—you remember the Claw, my old teammate? He was good, and then he went bad, and now he's good again, because I asked him to be. He only ever needed permission to be a hero."

Velveteen closed her eyes, leaning sideways until her cheek was pressed against the glass. "I really wish you were here right now. I really wish that I could talk to you. Because it's not over yet, and what comes next is going to be hard."

Velveteen insisted that Action Dude, Dotty Gale, and the American Dream accompany her as she limped her slow way around the battlefield. Jackie Frost and the Claw walked with them, still holding her up, and glared at anyone who seemed to question their presence. A larger group formed behind their small one as every standing hero fell into step, all of them waiting to see what would happen next. Only Jolly Roger walked away, carrying Supermodel's body with him as he retreated back into the familiar safety of his beloved *Phantom Doll.*

"This is on you as much as it's on me," said Velveteen, indicating the damage around them. "You were being mind-controlled, and that sucks, but there were ways of breaking out of that. Polychrome proves it. So did Tag, and so do I. So you don't get to say 'oh, people died, but it wasn't my fault, a bad woman was controlling me.' Do you understand? You have to own what you helped to build, and what you helped to destroy."

"That's a lot to put on us," protested Dotty Gale. There were bloodstains on her silver slippers.

Velveteen looked at her dully, and asked, "Does that mean it wasn't a lot to put on me?"

Dotty Gale looked away.

"Vel, you need to get off your feet," said Jackie. "You're still bleeding. I'm honestly not sure how you're still standing."

"That's okay. Neither am I. But I'm not dead. I know what that feels like now, and I'm not there yet." Velveteen stopped walking, letting go of the Claw in order to turn herself around and face the others. "We can't dismantle The Super Patriots, Inc. It matters too much. The world needs to be protected from us, and the only way to do that is if it's protected *by* us. But this company, this structure, it needs to change."

"Are you going to help with that?" Action Dude's question was earnest, accompanied by an all-too-familiar look of pleading hopefulness. It made Velveteen's heart ache to look at it.

But she didn't look away. Instead, she shook her head, and said, "No. I have other commitments, and they're going to take me off this plane of existence for a while. Besides, I left when I was eighteen. I don't know how you people do things. This is all on you, and you'd better get it right, because I'm coming back, and when I do, I'm going to check up on you."

The American Dream frowned. "Was that a threat?"

"I don't know." Velveteen looked slowly around, taking in the destruction her forces had wrought. Finally, she looked back to the American Dream, cocked her head, and asked, "What do you think?"

"They're going to keep training children, because kids with superpowers are accidents waiting to happen, but they're not going to buy them the way The Super Patriots used to," said Velveteen, cheek still pressed against the coffin. "Kids will be able to see their parents, and once they've learned to control their powers, they can leave if they want to. No focus groups, no forcing pre-teens into combat. Just school for people who can fly, or bench press trucks, or talk to animals. They'll have the training we should have had, and maybe they'll live longer."

She sighed. "Of course, there will still be kids like me, and like Yelena, ones whose parents can't wait to be rid of us, and they'll still get the old fosterage contracts, but instead of living in dorms, they'll live with heroes who'll serve as foster parents. They'll have people around who can understand them, and things will be better. That's all we can really hope for, right? That things will be better, and we'll have fewer funerals to attend after I make it home…"

"Jolly Roger?" Velveteen knocked on the door to the captain's cabin before pushing it open. "Are you here?"

"I am, lass." The old pirate was sitting at his table. This time, his cup of rum was filled to overflowing, and spills on the table made it clear that this wasn't his first. "I wondered when you'd get around to me."

"I'm not going to be getting around too much after this," said Velveteen, touching her heavily bandaged side. "We only have one healer operational, and she's looking after people who are a lot more messed up than I am."

Guilt twisted Jolly Roger's face. "I didn't mean to—"

"It's okay. We both did what we had to do if we wanted to survive. I can forgive you if you can forgive me." Velveteen leaned back against the wall. "Where's her body, Jolly Roger?"

"There." He waved a hand, indicating his bunk. There was a figure there, swaddled in blankets, face hidden. "I'll be taking her away with me, if it's all the same to you. She and I, we have a history between us."

"Is she going to wake up? Because I know there are dimensions where I've died and gotten back up again. I'm pretty dangerous in those worlds."

Jolly Roger sighed. "I wish the answer was 'yes,' and damn the danger, but no. She's gone. I'm going to take her to the sea, where she always should have been, and I'm going to bury her somewhere that will never be found. I want my girl to rest in peace. That means taking her away from all of this nonsense, and leaving her alone."

"I'm sorry."

"Don't be." He took a swig of rum. "She made her choices. We all did. But oh, you should have seen us when we were younger, when we all believed in doing good, not doing for ourselves. She was the most beautiful woman in the world. She still is, to me."

"Your mermaid looks a lot like her, you know."

"Funny thing, that." Jolly Roger smiled. "You did well, lass, and I'm glad that I helped you, no matter how much it cost us both. You never get anything good in this world without paying for it. Remember that, no matter what you decide to do with yourself when the cleanup's done and the bodies have been buried. We pay for everything that's ours, and if the cost is dear, it's because the prize is even dearer."

"I'll remember," said Velveteen. "After you take Supermodel away…will you be coming back this time? The world still loves pirates, you know. There's always a place for you here."

"I think this was Jolly Roger's last hurrah, lass," he said, and stood, walking over to wrap her in a hug that smelled like rum and saltwater and adventure. "I'll hang up my sword, and leave the piracy to the younger generation. You would have made a fine pirate, my dear."

Velveteen, hugging him back with her eyes full of tears, laughed.

Jackie Frost helped them get the fallen home for their funerals, opening mirror portals between the battlefield and their home states. Since some superhumans couldn't be autopsied, and cause of death was generally clear, only cursory medical examination was needed before the bodies could be released for burial. Velveteen and her "team"– Jackie, the Princess, Polychrome, Victory Anna, and oddly enough, the Claw–attended every funeral, regardless of who the dead had been fighting for. They were all superhumans together. That was enough.

At Dead Ringer's funeral–her civilian name, it turned out, was Maryanne Bellman–her mother asked Velveteen to provide a remembrance. There was no way to politely refuse, and so Velveteen, in her black costume with the matching domino mask, took the podium, and said, "Dead Ringer and I entered training around the same time, although we were with different teams. There was a photo shoot with the two of us, back when she was Liberty Belle, and I remember she had the most amazing laugh. It was like listening to sunlight. She did…she did a lot of good. Maybe that's silly now, because she's not going to do any more good for anyone, and I'm so, so sorry, but while she was with us, she did a lot of good. She saved a lot of lives. And I guess that's all that any hero can ask."

She was crying as she walked back to her seat, where the Princess was waiting. Velveteen put her face down against the Princess's shoulder and sobbed silently, letting the funeral run on all around them. The Princess stroked her back with one black-gloved hand. "Shh, darling, shh," she whispered. "Happy ever after isn't easy. If it were, we wouldn't fight so hard to have it."

When they got back to the somewhat battered headquarters of The Super Patriots, Inc., Jolly Roger and the *Phantom Doll* were gone. They'd been expecting that, but still, it made Velveteen's heart ache a little to look at the torn-up earth where the ship had been. The roses were squashed, just like Victory Anna had requested.

"Hey Jackie," said Velveteen suddenly. "Think you can manage another magic mirror?"

"Sure. I'm feeling pretty solid. What do you need?"

"Can you go find Garden Show, and let her know that we have a landscaping emergency that could really use her skill set?"

Jackie Frost blinked. And then, sounding delighted, she laughed. "You got it."

"There were parts I couldn't be there for, of course," said Velveteen. The glass was beginning to warm beneath her cheek. "People told me about them, or I guessed. No one can be everywhere at once, right? I mean, except for maybe Uncertainty. And there was so much to do…"

Trick and Treat stood before the twisted, blackened doorway, their daughter—their only daughter; the other two had always been candy golems, created to draw fire and provide their precious girl with the chance to escape if the need ever arose—standing between them, terrified and trembling. Trick put a hand on her shoulder, trying to be reassuring. Treat just stepped forward, took a deep breath, and knocked.

The hinges didn't just creak as the door swung open; they *howled*, damned things protesting their enslavement to the sky. Beyond the door was darkness. Then lightning flashed, revealing a teenage girl with pale blonde hair streaked in bands of green and orange. She was wearing a patchwork witch's costume in purple and orange and green, and pumpkin-shaped earrings dangled from her earlobes. There was no mercy in her face. She might look like a sixteen year old girl, but she scowled like a wicked queen.

"What do you want?" she asked, eyes going from Trick to Treat before settling on the girl who stood between them. Her scowl faded somewhat as she studied her. "And who are you?"

"This is Mischief," said Trick, voice unsteady. "Our daughter."

"Huh." Hailey kept studying the girl, who had hair that started white at the crown of her head and darkened to orange before fading to yellow at the tips. "What do you do, Mischief?"

"Um." Mischief looked to her parents for approval before turning back to Hailey and saying, "I'm a matter manipulator, but everything I manipulate sort of turns into candy."

"Uh-huh. What are your limitations? How much can you handle?"

"She's been running two candy golems at all times since she was four years old," interjected Treat. "She's good."

"Is she, now?" Hailey turned her flat-eyed gaze on the two former guardians of her season. "Why are you here, Trick, Treat? Why have you brought your daughter to meet me? What are you hoping to achieve? And don't lie to me. You may be powerful, but I *am* Halloween, and I'll know if you try to lie."

"We want to come home," said Trick. "This world is…"

"It has too many themes," said Treat. "They can never make up their minds whether it's a comedy or a tragedy or a farce, and nothing makes sense, and we're tired. It was fun being heroes for a little while. We're done. We just want to come home and be guardians again."

"You abandoned your duties once," said Hailey. "Why should I trust that you won't do it again?"

"We're parents now," said Trick. "We understand responsibility. And Mischief…this world isn't where she belongs. She should be in eternal autumn, where the bonfires light the night, and trick-or-treat is the first question anyone will ever ask you. We should never have come here. We should never have forced her to grow up here. We want to come home."

"And what about you, little girl?" Hailey turned to Mischief, who managed, barely, not to flinch away. There was nothing young in Hailey's eyes. She looked older than the season, and nowhere near so kind. "What do you want?"

"I want to know what home is," said Mischief.

That seemed to be the right answer. Hailey stepped to one side, beckoning the small family forward. "Well, then. Welcome back."

When the door closed behind them, it disappeared, and it was as if they had never been there at all.

"You're breaking a lot of rules right now," said Jacqueline Claus, sitting at her table with her hands wrapped tight around her cocoa mug, trying to pull the warmth of it into her bones. That was getting harder and harder these days. "If your mother catches you…"

"She'll give me hell and a half, but I've been on the Naughty List before." Jackie Frost sat at the other side of her parallel self's table, watching the pink-skinned girl with obvious concern. "I came to you because I needed help, and I'm not blind. I knew that you needed help as much as I did. I just couldn't give it to you."

"And now you can?"

Jackie nodded. "My Velveteen stopped animating her boyfriend. He's asleep now, with the Princess, waiting until Vel can wake him up. We went up against The Super Patriots not long after that. They didn't give us any choice."

"What happened?" asked a voice from behind her—almost familiar, but not quite. Velveteen had never sounded so…thin, like a paper doll that had somehow learned to speak. Jackie managed not to jump. It was a near thing.

"We won." Jackie forced herself to keep looking straight ahead. She didn't want to see Marionette again if she could help it. "We took them on, and we won."

Jacqueline's eyes widened. "How?"

"The head of the corporation, in my world at least? It's Supermodel. She didn't die, or maybe she did die, and then managed to get back up again. She's an animus, like Velma. She's still sucking the good out of the world. That, and her pet psychics…it's enough to keep her in power, even when she does things that no one should be able to forgive."

"An animus," breathed Marionette. "That makes so much sense. Yes. I can see it. I can raise an army against it. Everyone is afraid of me. If I tell them this will not just end me, but end a greater threat…"

Jackie couldn't miss the sudden exhaustion that washed across Jacqueline's face. "You'll need to get your strength up, then," said the girl who had willingly slaved herself to an undead horror, because when that horror had been alive, they had been friends. She gave so much.

She had so little left to give.

"I'll do it," said Jackie.

You could have heard a snowflake fall in the silence that followed. Jacqueline finally broke it, saying, "You don't understand what you're offering."

Jackie Frost, who had never really had a reputation for generosity—and had never sought one out, to be completely fair; she was happy being the selfish spirit of Christmas, the child with outstretched hands and no thought for whether anyone else had any gifts beneath the tree—shook her head. "I do understand, and I know that it will hurt. But if you can survive it this long, I can survive it once, and she's going to need you with her on the battlefield. I get to go home after this. You have to stay here. So let me do this one thing for the both of you, because you helped me once, and because it's the right thing to do."

Jacqueline smiled slowly, sadly. "We really are the same person, aren't we?"

"No," said Jackie. "But sometimes I like to think I could have been you, if I'd been a little more willing to share."

"Just close your eyes," said Marionette behind her, voice whisper-soft and hungry. Cold fingers slid around the back of Jackie's neck. "It'll all be over soon."

In the end, of course, she couldn't keep herself from screaming. No one who heard thought any less of her. How could they have? When your very essence is being eaten, it's only natural to scream. And eventually, the screaming stopped.

Eventually.

The Princess didn't necessarily enjoy drinking with the Fairy Tale Girls. They were too rowdy for her tastes, and their humor tended to be crass and inappropriate. It had taken her nearly a decade to make Brittle Red understand that racial slurs and transphobia weren't funny, and while the weapon-toting heroine tried to censor herself, she still slipped sometimes. Beauty was quick to defend her, saying that she didn't mean anything by it, and no amount of explanation seemed to get the point across. Still, even flawed people can be good people, and when the Princess called, they had come. That seemed to be worth a round or two of drinks.

Cinder had retreated to her usual silence. One of her arms had been smashed during the fight, and she was still piecing it back together; light could shine right through the gaps in her body, which was disconcerting enough to make the Princess glad that it was drinks, not dinner.

"That was a lot of fun," said Rampion. "We should overthrow things more often."

"Just remember that unless they're evil, that's a sort of supervillain thing to do," said the Princess. "It's better to be heroes. Keeps you out of trouble."

"We're always trouble," said Snow Wight.

"That's true enough, but there's a big difference between 'oh, that's Snow and Rose, they're trouble' and 'oh, that's Snow and Rose, call for an exorcist.'" The Princess shook her head. "Stay in the first column. It's better for your health."

"What will happen now?" asked Rose Dead.

"New management, new rules, and we wait to see how things settle out. That's the trouble with living in the real world. Nothing ends easy. You don't just get a pretty scroll that reads 'happy ever after' and takes your troubles away."

The Fairy Tale Girls were briefly quiet, thinking about this. The stories that they drew their power from might be twisted, but they were still, at heart, hopeful; innocence fueled even the most monstrous of interpretations. Easy endings were all they really knew.

Finally, Brittle Red asked, "You wanna hear a joke?"

"No, I don't believe I do," said the Princess. "But the next round's on me."

The Fairy Tale Girls cheered.

"Jackie's fine," said Velveteen. "It took her a few days to get her strength back to the point where she could take a mirror home, but she said that dimension's Santa was very nice to her, especially considering what she'd done for his daughter. She's at the North Pole now, recovering. I'll see her soon. She said to tell you that they're going to take really good care of me while I'm there, and that you shouldn't worry, okay? There's nothing for you to worry about at all." A tear ran down her cheek, landing on the glass, where it glittered like a diamond.

Velveteen looked at it for a moment before she took a deep breath and said, "So there's something else I need to tell you, before I go..."

It wasn't a surprise when Aaron showed up at the Crystal Glitter Unicorn Cloud Castle two days after the battle. It *was* sort of a surprise when the Princess let him in. Velveteen (she never took the ears off anymore; she hadn't thought of herself by her civilian name since she stepped into Supermodel's office, and she was direly afraid she'd finally allowed that part of herself to die, sacrificed to the black chasm Supermodel tried to rip into her soul) was sitting in the library when she heard the sound of footsteps, and a throat being cleared. She looked up, and blanched at the sight of the Princess, in blue jeans and tank top, standing in front of a shamefaced Aaron. He was wearing tan slacks, a black T-shirt, and a hangdog expression, and he'd never been more handsome.

"You've got company," said the Princess. "I'll just leave the two of you alone, and remember, I can have an army of SWAT-trained raccoons in here in under a minute, so no throwing things, animating the furniture, or sex on the ceiling." Then she was gone, moving with surprising speed for someone in heels that high.

"What are you doing here?" Maybe not the friendliest opening a conversation had ever had, but even as she spoke, Velveteen realized that it was the right question.

"I wanted to see you," said Aaron, stuffing his hands awkwardly into his pockets. "I checked for you in Portland, and Yelena's new girlfriend told me to go fuck myself. She, um, was pretty firm about that, actually."

Velveteen snorted. "Let me guess: she threatened to shoot you with a gun that she physically shouldn't have been able to lift, right?"

"Yeah. Also, who's Epona, and why do I need to be worried about her wrath?"

"She's a horse goddess. In Torrey's original dimension, her worship was sort of the dominant religion. I think. Talking to her is hard sometimes."

Aaron smiled a little. "Yeah."

He didn't say anything after that. For several minutes, neither did Velveteen. Instead, they both looked anywhere but at each other, the awkwardness in the room slowly growing. Finally, grumpily, she stood and demanded, "Aaron, why are you *here*?"

"I wanted to see you," said Aaron again. "I wanted to tell you I'm sorry. Marketing said…they said that if I didn't go along with them, they'd have to transfer you to the Midwest Division, because what we'd been doing wasn't appropriate. They never out-and-out said it, but they made a lot of comments about how 'support heroes' don't last long in the Midwest. I thought they were going to kill you if I didn't let them make me a couple with Yelena. I'm so sorry. I thought it was the right thing to do."

Velveteen stared at him. Aaron had been the first of them to figure out how to play Marketing, how to twist what they wanted until it turned into what *he* wanted. But the flip side of that was that he had always put more faith in Marketing and in their power than Velveteen had. If they'd told him that she'd be killed if they didn't break up…

"They lied to you," she said.

Aaron shook his head. "I don't think so. I think that out of the three of us, I was the only one they told the truth. They wanted us to be more marketable. You needed one lie. Yelena needed a different one. I just had to go along with it."

Velveteen sighed, looking down at her feet. "Why are you here, Aaron?" she asked, for the third time.

"I wanted to see you."

"You keep saying that."

"I just feel like…things with us shouldn't have ended the way they did. They shouldn't have ended at all. You were the love of my life, Vel, and you still are. I think you always will be. I wanted to see you, because I wanted to ask if there was any way that we could have a second chance."

"A second chance." Velveteen raised her head, looking at him. He looked back, hope and fear written baldly on his face. "You let me go because you thought they'd kill me. You stayed with them because …what, you thought they'd kill us both? You couldn't desert Yelena? Where were you when they turned David into a supervillain, Aaron? Where were you when I couldn't make the rent, when they sent the junior team to take me out, when they were wearing Yelena down to nothing? Where were you then?"

"Vel–"

"No. I am willing to believe you broke up with me to save me. It's the sort of noble, shitty, self-centered thing you're good at. But everything after that? Everything after that is on you. You were supposed to be a hero, Aaron. You were supposed to be *my* hero. I love you. I'm going to love you until I die, and that makes me furious, because you don't deserve my love. You deserve the life you let Marketing design for you." Velveteen was unsurprised to realize that she was crying. "Get out of here. I don't want you, and you can't have me, so go."

Aaron looked at her for a moment. Then, finally, he nodded. "All right, Vel," he said. "It was good to see you." He turned and walked away, leaving her alone in the library.

She managed to stay on her feet until she heard the door slam in the distance. Then her knees went weak, and she collapsed back into her chair, sobbing.

More tears had joined the first one on the side of the glass coffin; Velveteen felt vaguely as if she should be wiping them away. But they were so pretty where they were, and selfish as it was, she wanted to leave *something* behind her when she left.

"I don't know what he expected," she said. "I don't know if he thought that he could just walk back into my life and be welcomed with open arms or what, but I sent him away. I loved him more than anything once, and I sent him away. I just thought you should know that."

She sighed. The sound seemed very loud to her own ears.

"So I guess you know what happens next. I promised the holidays a year, and I have to give it to them. You don't break your word. Not to people like that. Not to anyone, if you can help it. You don't need to worry about anything while I'm gone, okay? The Princess will be here, so you won't be alone. Jackie will be with me, at least while I'm in Winter, and she'll make sure everything's fair. Yelena and Torrey are going to be the official heroes of Portland until I come home. They're even living at the house, so that it won't be standing empty."

They were so happy together, Polychrome and Victory Anna, Yelena Batzdorf and Victoria Cogsworth, together the way they were always intended to be. And all it took was destroying two worlds and overthrowing the CEO of a multinational corporation to get them there. Privately, Velveteen didn't think she'd ever be going back to that house on a permanent basis, even if she got to go back to Portland. After a year, it would be theirs, and they'd both waited long enough to be happy. She didn't want to get in the way.

"I love you, Tad," she said, and stood, bending to kiss the plane of glass above his face. It was still cool, unlike the warm spot where she'd been resting her head. "I'll be back as soon as I can, okay? And maybe by then, I can wake you up. So just wait for me."

Her footsteps echoed as she walked across the silent room to the door, and opened it, letting herself out into the hall. The Princess was waiting there for her.

"All done?" she asked.

"I've done everything I can do."

"All right." The Princess started down the hall. Velveteen fell into step beside her. "You feeling okay?"

"Yes. No. I don't know." Velveteen laughed, a little unsteadily. "I just can't believe it's over. The Super Patriots are under new management, Yelena's happy, things are finally starting to look like they might work out…and I have to go. I don't want to go."

"I know. But sometimes we have to do things we don't want to." The Princess stopped in front of another door, offering Velveteen her hands. "You know we'll be here when you get back. Take as much time as you need, all right?"

"I will." Velveteen took the Princess's offered hands. "I love you a lot."

"Oh, sugar. We love you, too. Now go on. Go do what you need to do."

Velveteen nodded and pulled her hands away as she turned to open the door. On the other side was a small green garden. At the center of the garden was a doorway made of braided candy canes and silver tinsel. She smelled snow. No one was waiting for her, but she didn't really need anyone; this was a journey she knew how to make.

Head high, Velveteen stepped through the doorway, and was gone.

The Princess stayed where she was for a few minutes, looking at the empty space where the gate to Winter had been, where her friend had disappeared. Then, without saying another word, she closed the door and walked away. The story was finished, after all. There was nothing left to say.

McGUIRE BEGINS
by Paul Cornell

I VASTLY ADMIRE SEANAN MCGUIRE. (Hmm, that sounds like the first line of a Monty Python lyric. The rest of the song should express the singer's enjoyment of various authors in a variety of assonant ways.) She writes from the heart, and this is obvious, and this, simply this, has gained her an enormous following of people who read her work and feel that she is like them and that her prose speaks both of them and for them. This, ladies and gentlemen, is what it's all about, what this game all we novelists play is meant to come down to. It's really simple, and almost impossible.

The book you've just read is an example of how Seanan stands for...well, I was about to say things, but really she stands for people, and they're more complicated. Velveteen is 'what if there was super hero prose that represented super heroes as if they were in the real world, but not the old real world, the new, more real real world, with knowledge of genre tropes and with people like us in it?' (And I hope I've just then approximated what it's like to be on the receiving end of one of Seanan's information-heavy gasped speeches.) This represents a companion to similarly stacked sentences about zombies and cryptozoology. All of these books are an attempt to grab existing genres and renovate them, often knocking a few walls down in the process.

I think my favourite Seanan moment was when she was a contestant in Just A Minute, an onstage game show I was running at Worldcon. She stopped the game to call up her mother to witness to the fact that she had not actually lied about a trivial fact, and thus conceded a point in the game. This call hugely entertained the audience, got Seanan caught up on how things were going at home...and won her the point. She does many things at once. And if she doesn't like this game she'll play her own instead.

I think, in a few decades, when she's done everything and won everything, Seanan will make a fine old lady. There's something of classic Americana about her. She's clearly a product of American virtues. She's simply decided that in her case they'll be alt virtues. When she's sitting on her cabin porch with a shotgun, chuckling about all the young people she's wiser than, she'll be redefining, just by sitting there, who you might expect to find in that cabin with her, why she might want a shotgun, and, what the hell, probably concepts like chuckling and porches too.

Right now, she's already redefined everything around her. And I think she's just getting started.

APPENDIX A:
VELVETEEN AND ALLIES

VELMA "VELVETEEN" MARTINEZ
Assessed power level 4

Age: Twenty-four.

Age at time of power discovery: Unclear; presumed twelve.

Appearance: Velveteen is a Hispanic female of average height and weight, with shoulder-length dark brown hair, brown eyes, and pleasant features. She does not display any visible deviation from the human norm.

Power set: Semi-autonomous animation of totemic representations of persons and animals, most specifically cloth figures, including minor transformation to grant access to species-appropriate weaponry. Capable of short-term resurrection, although this will eventually prove fatal to both Velveteen and the resurrected if it continues too long.

Profile: Velveteen was acquired as a corporate asset by The Super Patriots, Inc. at the age of twelve, and was one of two animus recruited despite the standard injunction on individuals within that family of powers. She remained with the company for six years, departing on her eighteenth birthday after a conflict with her teammate, Sparkle Bright. This conflict was orchestrated by the Marketing Department, under the orders of the CEO.

Following her departure from The Super Patriots, Inc., Velveteen spent several years living paycheck to paycheck in the California Bay Area before moving to Portland, Oregon to pursue a possible employment opportunity. She was accosted at the Oregon border by The Junior Super Patriots, West Coast Division, but managed to enter Oregon before she could be apprehended. She was granted a superhero license by the governor, and became the official hero of Portland.

Since then, Velveteen has demonstrated the ability to adapt her powers to a wide variety of situations, and seems to have finally accepted that she is more than just a support hero. Do not approach without good cause.

Default costume: Brown/burgundy leotard, brown tights, burgundy boots and gloves. Brown bunny ears on a headband. Assorted toys and dolls for animation.

Known alternate versions: Roadkill, supervillain, Earth C-5; Marionette, supervillain, Earth B-1; Marionette, anti-hero, Earth B-2.

YELENA "SPARKLE BRIGHT/POLYCHROME" BATZDORF
Assessed power level 3

Age: Twenty-four.
Age at time of power discovery: Eleven.
Appearance: Polychrome is a Caucasian female, approximately 5'9", with blue eyes and short blonde hair. As Sparkle Bright, she wore her hair long and was rarely seen without makeup.

Power set: Photon manipulation, including self-powered flight, and basic construction of light-based illusions. She has shown the potential to create much more advanced illusions than she has demonstrated thus far in the field.

Profile: Sparkle Bright/Polychrome was acquired as a corporate asset shortly before her twelfth birthday, and proved to be an excellent subject. With the proper grooming and coaching techniques, she was trained to become a team leader, and filled this position with all apparent willingness until she came into contact with her former teammate, Velveteen, who had at one time been her closest friend.

It is unclear what gave Sparkle Bright/Polychrome the strength to resist her conditioning, but she began violating rules, carefully at first, and then with increasing boldness, until she left her position to join Velveteen in Oregon. Approach only with caution. She appears to hold a grudge against the corporation as a whole.

Default costume: Black body suit with rainbow sash.

JACKIE FROST
Assessed power level 3

Age: Unknown.
Age at time of power discovery: Unknown.
Appearance: Jackie Frost is a blue-skinned humanoid with white hair, blue eyes, and a tendency to glow softly in low light. She is approximately 5'10." Her ears are pointed, as fits her general "Christmas" theme.

Power set: Elemental control and creation of ice. Immunity to cold. Travel through "magic mirrors," a designation which does not yet have a firm definition.

Profile: Jackie Frost is the daughter of Jack Frost and the Snow Queen, current guardians of the Winter. Efforts to convince her parents that she would benefit from membership in The Junior Super Patriots have resulted in all of Marketing receiving large amounts of coal on Christmas for the past several years (see *Profile: Santa Claus* for more information). She has thus been allowed to grow up without the tempering influence of other superhumans to balance out her naturally abrasive personality.

Jackie is impulsive, unpredictable, and a close friend of Velveteen's. Recent events have indicated that she is being groomed to eventually become one of the protectors of the Winter Country. It is unclear whether this is something Jackie is actually interested in doing.

Default costume: Varies from appearance to appearance, but is always essentially a blue and white ice skating uniform. Jackie does not wear a mask.

Known alternate versions: Snow Princess, superhero, Earth C-5; Frostbite, supervillain, Earth B-1; Jacqueline Claus, superhero, Earth B-2.

CARRABELLE "THE PRINCESS" MILLER
Assessed power level 4

Age: Twenty-three.
Age at time of power discovery: Eleven.
Appearance: The Princess is a woman of average height, with blonde hair, blue eyes, and abnormally clear skin. She is generally regarded as being very attractive, although this may be a function of her powers.

Power set: The Princess possesses a variable power pool of all abilities assigned by the little girls of the world to their ideal fairy tale princess. She has reliably demonstrated the ability to talk to woodland creatures, command birds, animate vegetables, talk to furniture, shrug off supposedly mortal wounds, sing enemies to sleep, break glass with high notes, find her way out of supposedly infinite mazes, and never smear her makeup.

Profile: The Princess's powers activated during a visit to a popular theme park, triggering a musical number which swelled to involve 90% of the park guests and employees before reaching a crescendo. Birds flocked to her side, and the park's management offered her an immediate contract. She currently resides in the Crystal Glitter Unicorn Cloud Castle, an impenetrable fortress constructed outside the boundaries of reality as we know it.

The Princess is polite to a fault, something which most people attribute to her Southern upbringing, combined with her position as conduit of the world's children. Her attachment to Velveteen and Jackie Frost is really the only questionable thing about her.

Default costume: The Princess frequently goes into combat wearing impractical ball gowns which do not seem to impede her movement in the slightest. She is one of the only known heroines who actually *prefers* to fight in heels.

Known alternate versions: Vamprincess, superhero, Earth E-9.

TAD "TAG" SINCLAIR
Assessed power level 3/informed power level 2

Age: Twenty-five

Age at time of power discovery: Eight

Appearance: Tag is a Caucasian male of average height and weight, with brown hair and blue eyes. He does not display any visible deviation from the human norm.

Power set: Semi-autonomous animation of graphic representations of persons and animals, including minor transformation to grant access to species-appropriate weaponry. No known secondary powers.

Profile: Originally "Graffiti Boy," Tag was acquired as a corporate asset following discovery by his second grade art teacher that he could bring chalk drawings to "life." Early examination showed his power levels to be limited only by the resources available to him, although he has difficulty maintaining multiple manifestations for long periods of time. Because of this, Tag is the only known animus to be officially classed as a level three hero. He is listed in all publicity material as a level two support hero, maintaining the corporate policy regarding animus.

Tag integrated well with The Junior Super Patriots, Midwest Division, but was dismissed due to abuse of his powers (see *Tag: Dismissal Report* for details). He worked temporarily under the name "Street Art" before settling on the name "Tag."

Default costume: Black body suit, utility belt, domino mask.

Current status: Missing, presumed dead.

VICTORIA "VICTORY ANNA" COGSWORTH
Power level pending assessment

Age: Unknown.
Age at time of power discovery: Unknown.
Appearance: Victory Anna is short, standing only 5'2", with red hair which is customarily worn in sausage curls, blue eyes, and freckled skin. She has never been seen in what would be considered "street clothes."

Power set: Victory Anna is a gadgeteer of currently unmeasured potential. Anything she can conceive, she can construct, and anything she constructs will probably begin trying to kill you in short order.

Profile: Originally from an alternate world where superpowers began appearing in the population during the Victorian era, Victory Anna was propelled into the multiverse following an unfortunate accident involving a broken time machine and a blackcurrant trifle. She became stranded in a transitory world for the next four years, where she established herself as an ally of the local supervillain community and entered a relationship with Polychrome, that world's version of Sparkle Bright. She would probably have stayed there indefinitely, had the world not ended, resulting in her being propelled into Earth A.

Victory Anna is currently sharing a home with Velveteen, and seems to be quite bitter about the entire situation, although she has emerged on the side of the heroes in this dimension. Only time will tell if this continues to be the case.

Default costume: Victory Anna seems to have a limitless supply of what she calls "adventuring clothes," and is never seen in the same outfit twice. She favors corsets, Victorian hunting jackets, impractical boots, and very small hats, to offset her very large guns.

APPENDIX B:
RELEVANT TEAM ROSTERS

The Super Patriots, Original Lineup:
Majesty: Flight, super-strength, invulnerability.
Jolly Roger: Magical hero, "pirate themed" powers.
Supermodel: Animus, control of others through manipulation of their life force.
Dame Fortuna: Probability manipulation, officially redacted from most records.

The Super Patriots, West Coast Division, Current Lineup:
Action Dude: Flight, super-strength, invulnerability.
Sparkle Bright: Flight, photon manipulation, photonic camouflage (ability untrained). DEPARTED
Uncertainty: Probability control.
Imagineer: Technopath.
Mechamation: Technopath.
Jack O'Lope: Spirit of the American West.

The Junior Super Patriots, West Coast Division, Current Lineup:
Handheld: Technopath, machine control, team leader.
Swallowtail: Flight, energy protection.
The Bedbug: Energy projection, insect communication.
Super-Cool: Limited invulnerability, super-strength, and flight. DECEASED
The Nanny: Weather control, limited flight.
Apex: Flight, super-speed. DECEASED
Mischief (formerly "the Candy Sisters"): Candy-themed matter manipulation. DEPARTED

The Fairy Tale Girls:
Snow Wight: Phasing through solid matter, nightmare generation, limited flight.
Rose Dead: Phasing through solid matter, possession, limited flight.
Rampion: Prehensile hair.
Beauty: Shapeshifting (dire wolf form).
Brittle Red: Matter generation, specific type: weaponry.
Cinder: Glass-themed matter manipulation and control.

VELVETEEN VS. THE MULTIVERSE

August 2013

Velveteen vs. The Multiverse by Seanan McGuire was published by ISFiC Press, 725 Citadel Ct., Des Plaines Illinois, 60016. One thousand copies have been printed by Thomson-Shore, Inc. The typeset is Berthold Baskerville, Comicraft Atomic Wedgie, Comicraft Atomic Wedgie Outline, and ITC Kabel Ultra printed on 60# Nature's Natural. The binding cloth is Arrestox B Blue. Design and typesetting by Garcia Publishing Services, Woodstock, Illinois.